Indecision's Flame

Book One

by JS Ririe

Indecision's Flame
By JS Ririe
Publisher: Jan Hill Books
Copyright 2018 by Jan Hill Books
Cover Image by: Evgeny Ustyuzhanin

Praise for: Indecision's Flame by JS Ririe

"This is a romance that has it all. Complex characters, and exotic location that captures the reader's imagination. Mesmerizing. Byrlee is a heroine for the 21st century. Keeps you awake until 2 am wondering if fate will reward her resourceful spirit." - Peggy O.

"I am totally hooked on this book and cannot wait for the rest of the story."
- Joan M. (Beta Reader)

"This is a well-written story that has a lot of twists and turns that keep you turning the pages as fast as you can read." - LCD (Verified Amazon Reviewer)

AUTHOR'S NOTE: Since the setting for this novel takes place in the Australian Outback, certain colloquial words like "bloody" instead of "very" have been used to set a more authentic flavor. These are deliberate changes. Please join my mailing list and stay updated with my latest releases and more. The link to join is: http://eepurl.com/dCPYVf.

Dedication:

To everyone who still believes in romance, even if it is found in the most unlikely places.

~JS Ririe

Chapter 1

"I'm going home! I'm going home!" The words pounded in my ears as each second in the sky brought me closer to the land and family I had not been a part of for over five years. I knew why I had to go. Scores had to be settled and hearts healed before I could move forward into the future I so much wanted, but I wasn't sure I could summon the inner courage or the strength to do it on my own. I had spent too much time running, hiding, hating, and avoiding anything that had to do with my past.

Forcing myself to go back to the place where I'd lost everything was harder than leaving, but anger and youth can be a deadly combination—even for a girl who had never been any place on her own before deciding to run away. Now, the past I had tried so hard to forget was coming back, and I wished I could find a way off the plane before it landed. I had thought of little but my reunion with my father and Uncle Ned for three months. Months I had prayed would pass rapidly, but whose passing made it even more evident that I could hide my secret no longer.

It wasn't some awful secret that would bring any shame, and it was what had prompted this trip in the first place. But

I still wasn't sure that my estranged family would ever forgive me for what I had done. If my mother were still alive, I could have talked to her about how drastically my life had changed. She would have understood why I had run away, and why I had ended up following my heart instead of my head. But she was dead, and with her passing, a part of me had died as well. I had stood over her grave and cursed God for taking away the only person who had ever understood the real me, I had kept so carefully hidden from others—the girl with unspoken dreams too big to capture, and a heart that desired truth more than anything else in the world.

"Oh, mother," I thought as I watched the white clouds mingle with the blue of the sky outside my airplane window and wishing I could be floating on one of them, leisurely and without purpose. "I understand now why you were taken away from me, and I'm not angry at God anymore. He's brought us back together in a most unusual way and someday . . ."

"Miss," the flight attendant was passing down the aisle. "Would you fasten your seatbelt? We'll be landing in Sydney in a few minutes."

I smiled as she hovered in the aisle to make sure I followed her instructions. She was pretty and confident, and I wondered if she always knew what to say and do. My own hard-earned confidence was rapidly draining now that I was so close to home.

Unexpected chills suddenly rippled down my arms and legs, even though it was warm enough in the plane. I watched the woman next to me try to stuff an inordinate amount of possessions into her handbag. She'd been knitting and talking the entire way. Fortunately, it had been to the person on the other side. I had kept my eyes on the plane's window, much too focused on self-preservation for idle conversation. I steeled myself against the 100-degree-plus temperatures and humidity that would hit the moment I stepped out of the terminal.

I hadn't told anyone I was coming home and wasn't the least bit sure if I would be welcomed with open arms and a home-cooked meal like the prodigal son in the Bible. I had walked away from my father and hadn't looked back. I hadn't even considered his pain when he came home and found me gone. I had just packed my suitcase and walked out the door while he was away from home, checking on his herds of sheep and cattle, along with the miles of fences that were supposed to keep them safe from their only natural predator —the wild dingo.

I knew what I had done was wrong, but my own pain had stripped all sense of humanity and compassion from me, and I had lashed out at the only person I knew I could hurt. I blamed my father for ruining my life and getting my mother killed so she would not be there to see me graduate from school, get married and raise a family. I'd left him a horrid note telling him how much I hated him and that I never wanted to see him again—emphasizing the fact that I hoped he would rot in that place designated for the most vile and reprehensible sinners.

After less than adequate thought, I had scraped together what money I could and bought a one-way plane ticket to Los Angeles, California. Visiting the land of promise with its glamorous movie stars and musicians was something I'd always thought of doing, but it wasn't a panacea to my problems. So before my limited amount of money ran out, I found a place to live and a job waiting tables. Eventually, I enrolled at UCLA, where I graduated with a degree in business management. My life had been busy, but I stayed mainly to myself, nursing each pain and betrayal until I met a family that changed everything.

I looked down at the ring on the third finger of my left hand and thought about Ben. He was the one who'd encouraged me to make peace with my past before we were married, and he had helped me understand the importance of family even when they'd hurt me beyond belief. I had fought him on the idea of going home for months, but finally realized that I could never be happy in a new life while the old one was still causing me so much pain. I had grown up, and I'd changed, but what if I hadn't changed enough to accept the people who had once meant everything to me?

And what would I say when I saw my father? "Hi, Dad, it's your daughter. The one who's been gone for five years and who didn't let you know where she was because she was too angry. And by the way, I've joined a church where you're not supposed to smoke or drink or cuss or commit adultery or do any of the things our family is so famous for. And I'm going to get married, but you can't be there because your standards are so far beneath the ones I have now adopted as my own."

That rendition of facts sounded both cold and cruel. Here I was, a member of a church that preached tolerance, understanding and love for all mankind, but I couldn't forgive my own father for the part he had played in my mother's death and the total destruction of the only life I had ever known.

"Ben, I can't do this," I thought as tears formed in my eyes and slid silently down my cheeks. I brushed them away with the back of my hand, hoping the lady who was still sitting next to me didn't notice, ask questions or offer sympathy. I was having enough trouble trying to decide what I was going to say to the man I'd deserted—the man who had helped give me life. How could I ask for his forgiveness when I had yet to forgive myself?

The plane was starting its descent. I looked out the small window at the gleaming skyscrapers of the business district that towered above the wharf's side buildings of an earlier era—and an era of growth and expansion before

Australia became a largely urban nation. I saw the world-famous opera house with its uniquely shaped roof, and the Harbour Bridge with hundreds of cars traveling its six-lane highways. It was hard to believe that less than two million people lived outside the cities of Perth, Adelaide, Brisbane, Canberra, Melbourne, Darwin, and the city of diverse populations I called home, Sydney.

It wasn't actually my hometown, although I had spent four years there while going to school. I didn't even live in a town. I lived on a homestead miles into the Australian Outback, where the endless horizon, dusty, red clay soil, rolling sand dunes, gibber plains and stunning nature were impossible to describe to anyone who had not seen them.

Ben had tried to understand how lonely and yet how fascinating the Outback was with its strange indigenous animals: kangaroos, koalas, wallabies, poisonous snakes and spiders, lizards, and even camels. Along with its scorching sun that dried up the rain, leaving little water available for any living creature, and its shimmering mirages at the edge of the horizon that had led thousands of men to their deaths as they went searching for diamonds, silver and gold. But that was understandable since he had spent almost his entire life in Southern California among millions of people, where every convenience imaginable was available. Life in an unforgiving, inhospitable part of God's creations was as foreign to him as being in a family that wanted to be together forever was to me.

Throughout the entire flight, I had tried to concentrate on the fact that since he had never seen Australia, I couldn't possibly expect him to comprehend the harshness of the kind of life I had lived until being sent to boarding school as a teenager. Still, I wished he had felt it important enough to come with me so he could see with his own eyes just how impossible my given task had become.

I was terrified even thinking about seeing my father again. I needed Ben's arm around me for strength as I reentered my past. I had come to rely on him so completely. He was my knight-in-shining armor, my voice of reason, and my permanent touch with the reality I had come to believe in. I missed him dreadfully and didn't know how I would garner the courage to step off the plane. I just wanted to go home to the life he promised. Confrontations were abhorrent to me, and the next few days would be filled with them.

Without giving it much thought, I closed my eyes in silent prayer as the plane touched down, and was soon feeling the pull of the brakes press against my body with such force I had to grab onto the armrest for support. I was home and had no idea what my reception would be. Even mentally reversing roles with my father hadn't helped. I had never really known him. He was a hard-working, hard-drinking man of few words, and my mother had always served as a buffer between us.

The plane taxied to a stop, and I was suddenly hit with a thought that had not been considered before. What if something had happened to my father or to Uncle Ned and his family? If they were not where I had left them, they might never know why I had run away, or that I had finally come home to make amends. I wanted my family of origin to have a happy ending, but that hardly seemed possible now.

The ranch was over 300 miles from Sydney. By air, it took little more than an hour to get to the closest town that had been given the name of Edna by some of the earliest settlers. Traveling by vehicle would take 6 or 7 hours, depending on traffic and the condition of the roads. The last 40 miles—once I was back on Hawkins' property—was little more than a dirt-packed trail, unless major construction had taken place during my absence.

I had brought very little with me since there was no way of knowing exactly how long I would be staying. My return flight was scheduled for two weeks from today, but if no one in my family was glad to see me after the way I had left... I chewed down on my bottom lip. I had come too far to turn back now, and just being here had to count for something. Regardless of what might happen, I had promised Ben that I would try to repair our broken relationship so the two of us could move forward with our wedding. Making peace with my past had seemed like a reasonable request when given, but Ben had no idea how totally dysfunctional my family was.

At first, I had been angry with him for sending me into the unknown by myself, but during the long hours I had spent in the air, I'd finally accepted that he had been right. My past wasn't his problem. It was mine to resolve. If things worked out, he would join me. If not, I would go back to him alone.

It was as hot and sultry as anticipated when I left the air terminal, and I had to inhale deeply to force the moist air further into my lungs, where it would make breathing easier. I had forgotten how heavy the air in Sydney was. Maybe I should have waited until winter to come, but that would have meant postponing our wedding for another six months. I didn't want that. I loved Ben and wanted to be his wife.

I set my watch to ten in the morning before walking to the rental lot where the jeep I had reserved before leaving America was supposed to be waiting for me. My dark hair was matted to my forehead, sweat was glistening on my neck, and the knot that had been in my stomach during the flight from Hawaii had now settled in my throat. I wanted to turn around and rush back to Ben, but I was half a world away and in a few hours, I would be too far into the outback to get cell phone reception.

I signed the paperwork before driving the Jeep Cherokee off the lot, and then heading towards the outskirts of the city. I was grateful that while streets might change direction or disappear completely, famous landmarks rarely would. I rolled down the windows and drove along the beach. There were hundreds of people sunbathing near the water's edge with the usual cans of light beer in their hands. It was the country's national drink, and I remembered holidays with my own friends on these same beaches with our Styrofoam containers holding enough beer for everyone to feel a buzz. Nothing had seemed wrong about drinking neck oil and staying out all night back then. I had become quite worldly until learning the truth, and that truth had led me to Ben.

Before getting on the freeway and heading north, I pulled into a McDonald's and ordered a chicken sandwich, fries and a soda. Breakfast had been served on the plane two time zones earlier, and I was hungry. While waiting for my order to be delivered by a cute girl on roller skates, I placed an overseas call.

"Hi, sweetheart," I said when Ben answered. The tears were forming again, and I bit my lower lip to keep it from trembling. "I can't believe how much I miss you, and it hasn't even been a full day since I left."

"I miss you too, but this isn't forever," he said. "How was your flight?"

"Uneventful!"

"But that's good, isn't it?"

"I guess so. I just wish you were here. You make me feel like I can do anything."

"You give me too much credit, Bry. You are the strongest woman I've ever met, and you know why this has to be done alone. If we were together, you wouldn't be able to sit down for any heart-to-hearts. We would be off sightseeing and having fun. This is the time for you to reconnect with your family in a positive way."

"I hope you're right," I replied as the waitress brought my order. "Can you hold on a minute? My food's here."

I thanked her and then picked up my cell again. "I'm sorry for sounding so childish, Ben, but I'm scared. It's not like I'm coming home after a brief absence. What I did and the things I wrote were unconscionable."

"You were a child who had just lost her mother in a tragic accident with no explanations as to how it happened. Regardless of the way you left, your father will be thrilled to see you again. That's just the way it is with parents."

"Maybe with your parents," I responded, trying to swallow a sip of my soda. "What if he isn't there? Something could easily have happened to him during my absence. The outback isn't exactly a safe place to live. And even if he is there, he always drank too much, and we never had a real discussion about anything. What if I just make everything worse?"

"He can't hurt you again unless you allow him to, Brylee. Quit borrowing trouble! He'll be there, and everything will be fine."

"I wish I could be sure of that, but there are no guarantees in this life, except for the proverbial death and taxes."

"At least you haven't lost your sense of humor," he replied, and I could hear the edge of laughter in a voice I had grown to truly cherish. "As for the rest of your concerns, you have taken care of your mistakes. Your father's not going to hold anything against you. He's only going to be grateful that you finally came home."

Suddenly, he yawned.

"I woke you up, didn't I?" I asked.

"Only a little. I was waiting for your call. I couldn't exactly sleep until I knew you had safely arrived."

With those few words, he instantly seemed more than a million miles away, even though our connection was clear. I was invading the time when he should be sleeping. What could we possibly talk about now that hadn't already been discussed a hundred times? This was my mess to resolve, and I didn't want to belabor the issue until I had something new to report. That would only happen after I had seen my father.

"I'm sorry," I said. "Go back to sleep. I'll call you again on Sunday when I'm back to civilization. And don't worry about me. I've just had a little too much time to think during my flight. I'm sure everything will turn out okay."

"It will," he said with another yawn. "And in two weeks, you'll be home so we can start planning our wedding. Did I tell you that Becky is already making a list of people to invite to your shower?"

"It will be a very short list," I responded. "I didn't exactly make a lot of friends going to college, and no one from here will be able to attend, even if they do forgive me."

"None of that matters right now. The future has yet to be written. Besides, I have twenty-six first cousins, and the number of relatives explodes exponentially from there."

"You know the thought of meeting all that family terrifies me," I responded. "I still get tongue-tied around your grandmother."

"Gram doesn't mean to make you nervous. She's just a little old-fashioned when it comes to relationships. You are the perfect girl for me, and I've made sure everyone knows it."

"I love you," I told him.

"I love you too," he replied. "Be safe, and I'll talk to you soon."

I closed the flip screen on my cell phone and put it on the passenger seat of the jeep. I really was on my own now. There would be no Ben to talk to when I needed encouragement or someone to lean on. But if I didn't waver, my new beliefs would give me the strength to confront my past, make restitution where possible, and learn how to live with everything else.

It wasn't exactly an optimistic outlook, but it was enough for now. My eyes closed as I thanked God for my safe trip, my new life with Ben and the food I was about to eat. Then I took another sip of the soda before trying my sandwich. It was going to be an uncomfortable few days.

Chapter 2

It wasn't long until the busy streets turned into the long winding road that would lead me across miles and miles of lonely highway back to the home of my birth in the Australian Outback. A land where the wind, the heat, the relentless sun, the occasional rain, the flash floods and the constant threat of fires were but a few of a rancher's biggest concerns.

My mind drifted back to the past as the tires on the jeep rolled past one mile marker after another. I had lived a sheltered life on the ranch with my parents, or so it had appeared at the time. I'd never seen them argue or fight. Perhaps there had been too much silence, but I had never known anything different, so it did not seem unusual to me. I played with my dolls, read my books, and otherwise occupied myself so I would not disturb anyone.

Other than my mother, Keida had been my best friend. She was the aborigine woman who worked in the house and took care of the family's needs. She made sure meals were on the table, the laundry done, and the house clean. I had seen her at my mother's funeral, but couldn't remember if we even talked. She was not given to lengthy conversations, but she had always let me know that she cared in less obvious ways.

I was seventeen and a senior in high school on that fateful day that destroyed my life, but not just any high school where I could go home at night to be with my family. Like all the girls from the outback—whose parents had been able to scrounge together enough money—I had been sent to boarding school in Sydney at the appropriate age and only saw my parents on holidays.

It wasn't so bad as long as I stayed out of the headmistress's way, but I had cried the first year anyway. I didn't like the noise of the city or having to room with other girls when I had never been around them before. The only young people I'd known growing up were my twin cousins, NJ and Molly. They were four years younger than I, and our families rarely saw each other. There was always too much work to be done on the ranch, and playing with other children was a seldom indulged luxury.

Nonetheless, Betsy Montgomery, Torrie Ames and I had eventually become friends at boarding school. They were far more gregarious than me, but finally talked me into sneaking out with them at night during my senior year. We would go to the beach and meet up with guys from one of the neighboring boarding schools. It was on one of those escapades where I had my first real taste of alcohol—not just the wine we were required to drink at Mass—but the hard stuff that was nasty and burnt my throat going down. I pretended it was good and drank it occasionally to fit in, but I never liked the taste or the way it made me feel. Cigarettes, cigars, chewing tobacco and weed were also prevalent, but I didn't like the smell or the spitting. I had seen enough of that growing up with my father, Uncle Ned and the ranch hands they employed.

Good old Uncle Ned had given me my first cigarette when I was ten. I had tried smoking it like he instructed, but all it did was bring tears to my eyes and make me throw up.

I promptly told him smoking was disgusting. He immediately replied that I was a "prissy" little girl, but admitted that sometimes even he wished he didn't have the habit. It was a costly and hard one to break.

Trying drugs, even weed, like most of my schoolmates did, scared me. I was afraid of their ability to make me do stupid things like sleep with a guy I didn't like or say something I didn't mean. Several of the girls in my school has ended up pregnant that way. While I had done my share of hugging and kissing, for some reason I instinctively knew that chastity wasn't old-fashioned or outdated. I wanted my first time to be with the man I married.

"Wow!" I thought as I squinted in the harsh sunlight that even the visor on the window couldn't soften. "What happened to that timid girl who wanted everything   but never found a single goal worth pursuing until she met Becky and Ben?"

My hand slammed down hard on the steering wheel. "My father happened, that's what," I told myself, looking for the exit that would keep me going in the right direction. "He killed my mother as surely as if he had shot her with one of the guns he kept in the den to kill dingoes and anything else that threatened his cattle and sheep."

All the violent emotions I thought I had worked through were now coming back with such intensity that becoming physically ill was a real possibility. Australia had a way of doing that. Men and women worked hard and loved hard in the outback. That passion for living was what kept them alive when the sun, the wind, the rain, the fire and the floods threatened to destroy all they had worked for, including their own lives.

Two hundred and twenty miles inland, I stopped in the little township of Edna to put more gas in the tank, get a large bottle of water, and take a few moments to stretch my legs. It was the last parcel of civilization until I reached home, and that was eighty miles away over roads that had been bad when I was growing up. I wasn't ready for the desolation or disagreeable conversation that lay ahead, but I couldn't disappoint Ben.

Edna was like most of the other small towns in the outback. There were dozens of bungalows with corrugated iron roofs that had turned a copper color from the sun, with cast iron balconies and wood-shuttered windows. There were a few locally-owned stores, several churches of different denominations, a bank, a post office, a local library, a k-6 school, a one-screen movie theater, a small airport, a 20-bed hospital with two doctors, several nightclubs, a pub on every street corner and two motels with swimming pools.

Australians loved getting away from the city and from their jobs, and the government had made that easy for them. Most people had 4 to 5 weeks of paid vacation each year, along with numerous government holidays and "sickie" days that most people used up regularly. Eventually, even a town like Edna would become a sanctuary for them.

But for now, the town and the main road ran parallel to the railroad tracks that spanned the southeastern corner of the continent from Sydney to Adelaide. Ranchers from all over the area loaded their sheep and cattle into two or three trailer road trains (semi-trucks as they were called in the U.S.) to transport them to the railhead in Edna for shipping to the cities or slaughterhouses. Quite often, the animals would die in transit. When they did, the drivers unloaded their carcasses into vast pits situated along the roadway where they would be burned. One sick animal could contaminate an entire load and wipe out a rancher's income for years.

Despite new cattle and sheep strains and feeds, most of the animals still grazed in areas of intense heat where calves and lambs born between dawn and late afternoon struggled to survive their first day. And when drought reduced the amount of natural fodder and the carrying capacity of the land, there was always a race to round up the herds and get them to market before they died of starvation or became too thin to bring a reasonable profit.

My father was one of the few ranchers who had combined cattle and sheep in the same operation. Despite my intense anger over my mother's death, I still hoped life had been good to him.

The jeep I was driving had been shiny black when leaving Sydney, but by the time I drove onto Hawkins' land the dust had turned it into a dull tan that resembled everything around it. The trees were the same dull gray-green and the dry grass brittle and unbending unless crushed. Little broke the monotony of the outback except the shrill of colorful birds that swooped through the sky on their way to their nests and the few wildflowers that managed to survive without water.

To foreigners, the outback was often deceiving in its simple outward appearance. But it was teaming with seldom-seen life if one knew where to look. Unfortunately, I had never been one for adventure. My mother, with her gentle and fearful nature, had mostly kept me confined to the house with her.

Anxiety mounted as the tires on the jeep rolled onward. Nothing on the ranch appeared to have changed; even the ruts in the road leading to the house were bringing back memories. It still smelled and looked like home. The ground lay cracked in unusual patterns as the moisture was pulled from the soil by the ever-present sun. The same sun that beat down mercilessly while drying up the riverbeds and causing ranchers to drive shafts deep into the earth in hopes of finding the subterranean rivers that would help maintain their way of life.

I tried to still my rising emotions, but the closer I got to the small oasis where my ancestors had homesteaded, the more apprehensive and uncertain I became. It would be a bittersweet homecoming, and what would I do when I got there? Did I walk up to the sun-beaten door and knock? I couldn't exactly push it open and make myself at home, even though I knew my father's doors were never locked. He believed that if people needed or wanted to get inside a bolt of any kind would not stop them.

It would be easier to go to Uncle Ned's first and let him act as my shield when it came to dealing with my father. I liked him and his wife (well, his common-law wife). To my knowledge, they had never married, but they had two children and always seemed to get along. NJ and Molly would be out of high school by now.

But going there first would be the coward's way out, and I knew Ben expected me to face my past and my fears head-on. He said that was the only way I would be able to resolve anything and come out feeling like a victor.

"Dang it all," I thought as the jeep made a turn to the west. "Why couldn't you be here with me, Ben? We promised to support each other in everything, and I have never needed your help and encouragement more."

Those thoughts had barely slipped from my mind when the house I had not seen for five, emotion-packed years suddenly appeared. It stood just as I remembered it. The variegated earth tones in the weathered siding matched the hard, dry earth it had been constructed on, and the long front porch with the swing where I had spent many happy hours as a child still hung suspended from the open rafters. The screen door had not been latched securely, and I could almost hear the squeaking sound it made whenever the wind blew.

Much to my surprise, a few flowers hung in pots along the top of the veranda, but nothing else looked even slightly alive or inviting. As soon as the tires on the jeep quit rotating, and I had taken time to steady my nerves, I found myself standing in the insufferable heat surrounded by an unexplainable nostalgia that made my heart race.

It was so quiet I could hear the birds shrilling in the distant trees. It was an eerie kind of sound that sharpened my senses almost to the point of fight or flight. But since walking up to the front door and knocking seemed intrusive, I decided to check the outbuildings while my nerves settled. If anyone had been home, they would have heard the jeep coming from miles away and made their way to the front gate to welcome any visitor. I wasn't so sure that would include me.

So I walked away from the house as an emptiness I could not explain seemed to fill my soul. Things might look the way I remembered them, but the air felt different. I couldn't put what I was feeling into words. Perhaps my fear of the past and the present colliding had finally caught up with me.

I had always loved the shed where the tools were stored. If there was one thing a resident of the outback could count on, besides the caustic weather, it was all the repairs left behind after one of Mother Nature's tantrums. That was one of the reasons I had never gotten to know my father. There was never time for anything besides the manual labor he always seemed to take great satisfaction in completing, unlike nurturing his relationship with his wife and his daughter.

My foot stopped almost in midair. I hadn't come home to dredge up the past. I had come to make peace and all the negativity I felt inside, without even seeing my father's face, had to be put aside until our initial reunion was over. I would try to recall more practical matters until then. Like the fact that during my childhood, there had been a bunkhouse filled with ranch hands to help with the outside chores and Keida to do the cleaning and cooking inside. Now it looked like no one lived on the premises. Where were all the people who should have been milling around? And what was I going to do if no one returned to the ranch?

I found a hammer and a bucket of nails and headed towards the fence that lined the southern edge of the long driveway. The top boards on one section had fallen to the ground, and I hoped the physical exertion of repairing it would help lessen the anxiety that was threatening to choke me. I had never done much physical labor as a child, but I helped Ben's family build a cabin by the lake and knew how to drive a nail into a board.

The boards for that project had been straight and new, but the first one I lifted into place was weathered and worn like everything else on the ranch, polished to a gray hue by the constant sun and wind. The same elements were drying my skin even now. It would take a truckload of moisturizer to restore the damage even a few days in the outback brought.

But I couldn't worry about that now. I had to keep myself busy or waiting around to see what happened next would drive me insane. I wasn't sure I could handle such a long and heavy board on my own, but after resting one end of it on the section of fence underneath, I managed to get the tip of the nail into the wood. The rest came easy. Striking a nail so hard and accurately that it entered the wood without flipping back or dropping to the ground was the emotional release I needed. It no longer mattered that I was not a Daughter of the Outback. I was a college graduate. I knew my individual worth, and soon I would be married to the man who had made all my dreams come true.

Chapter 3

I must have been working for over an hour before hearing the sound of horses' hoofs in the distance. All the dread I had been trying to control by beating my fears into submission hit in an instant. Had there been time to get to the jeep and drive away I would have done it, but there was no choice left except to face whatever was coming.

After taking a deep breath, I looked over my shoulder and saw four riders on horseback. I knew by the way he sat on his horse that one of them was my father. I had watched him ride since childhood. The hammer dropped to the ground as I rose to my feet, and the rapid beating of my heart almost gave way to lightheadedness. But I was not prone to fainting, so I stood my ground and waited for their arrival.

It took less than a minute for the first rider to reach me. He drew back sharply on the reins, and the huge brown horse—whose back stood nearly as tall as me—came to a stop in a cloud of dust.

I brushed at the swirling mass of earth in front of my face and then coughed as the residue hit my lungs.

"Who are you?" a deep voice demanded through the lingering haze. "And what are you doing on Hawkins' land?"

I looked up into the harsh, darkly tanned face of a man I had never seen before. As if to get a better look at me, he took off his copper-tinted sunglasses and tucked one of the handles down the front of his khaki-coloured, collared shirt that was open at the neck. He was wearing tightly fitted jeans and cowboy boots. His eyes were dark as charcoal as he squinted against the dying sun and pushed his broad-brimmed hat further back on his head.

His hair was black and hung down past his eyebrows, and his shoulders were strong and hard as were his sunburned hands and forearms. He had two small silver hoops in his left ear. I could see the beginning of geometric tattoos where his rolled-up sleeves exposed more of his arms. But it was his cold, cruel lips that held my attention. They were curled into a sardonic smile. He appeared to be a man who had no qualms about inflicting pain. He coughed occasionally as if he needed to clear his throat. I had heard that sound often while growing up.

I hated him instantly and not just because he was the exact opposite of Ben with his blue eyes, warm smile, light brown hair, and skin just kissed by the California sun. Ben was my surfer hero, and I loved him with all my heart. I wanted desperately to be back in his arms, where I was safe from the ordeal that was unraveling all my resolves.

"I asked you a question," he repeated with added emphasis on each word. "Who the bloody hell are you and what are you doing here?"

I wanted to say something, anything that would explain my presence, but it was as if I had lost my ability to speak. All I could do was continue to stare at his uncompromising face.

This man looked like the land he seemed to belong to, the Australian Outback with all its hardness and sudden death. I was surprised that I could study his face so easily from behind my own sunglasses, but he intrigued me. I wondered how many hearts he had broken over the years. Ben could never be like that. He was open and honest and when he looked at me, I felt all warm and toasty inside. If that wasn't true love, I had no idea what was.

"Don't just stand there like a shag on a rock," he mocked. "I asked you two very simple questions, unless you're a mute and unable to speak. Who are you and what are you doing here?"

I was still too shaken to answer, and that seemed to amuse him even more.

"Well, no matter. I suppose we'll find out soon enough, but you do look grossly out of place in those fancy duds. And just because I'm a curious bloke who has no use for intruders, I would like to add another question to the ones I have already asked. How did you know where the hammer and nails were kept? No one enters the outbuildings without permission."

By that time, the world had quit reeling enough for me to find my voice again, albeit with far more timidity than I wanted. "I was fixing fallen boards. The fence needs repairing. I see no harm in that."

He laughed, long and low. "You appear to know how to hold a hammer, but what do you know about fixing fences? And once again, who are you and why the hell are you here?"

His constant demands were making me angry, and I knew how to do mad. I'd had plenty of practice the past five years.

"Enough," I spat out, purposefully letting my own eyes show utter disdain for his arrogance and ungentlemanly behavior. It hardly mattered that he could not see them through my dark glasses. "And why should you be questioning me? You don't own this ranch."

I breathed deeply, hoping I was right. Anything could have happened while I was gone. What if my father had sold out to this horrid man? But no, he would never do that. Besides, I could see the man who had helped give me life clearly now. He was on his horse, Thunder, and coming our way. He would give me a logical explanation for this unpleasant encounter, even if he told me to get lost in his next breath.

The man only laughed again. "You're a haughty one. I'll give you that, and you've got more balls than most of the blokes I know. But I was the one asking the questions—which you have yet to answer."

"My presence here is none of your business," I retorted. "I'm here to speak to Mr. Hawkins."

"And mending fences while you're waiting. That's a new one. I'm sure he'll be impressed.

"You're a horrid man," I said. "And you have no tact."

"I'll take that as a compliment," he replied, giving me another sadistic smile that made my anger and dislike even greater. "And you've got a bit of viper in you. I like that in a woman."

"I don't care what you like," I said, turning my back on him and bending down to retrieve the hammer I'd let fall to the ground before he began verbally accosting me. My knees were beginning to shake, but I was determined not to give my identity away to anyone but my father.

Then suddenly I heard the voice of the man I had come such a long distance to see. It came through the dust and the darkness of mind that had haunted me for more years than I wanted to recall.

"What's up, Jake?" my father asked. "And who's our little visitor. We don't get many of them way out here."

I wanted to turn and face him, to throw my arms around his neck and tell him how sorry I was for everything I had done. But I stood rooted to the spot; my back to him and my face to the ground even after the other riders had stopped on the dirt road beside him. Their horses were snorting after a long, hot ride.

"Is everything okay, Jack?" a female voice asked.

"That's just what I'm about to find out. Are you lost, miss?" my father asked.

Standing upright with the hammer in my hand, I forced myself to look up at him. If sorrow for sin that had not yet been brought to proper restitution was the first step towards utter and complete repentance, I was certainly feeling that now. My father's dark hair was speckled with gray, and he looked as if he had shrunk several inches in height during the time I'd been gone.

"I don't know," I said, removing my sunglasses.

"Holy Dooley!" he exclaimed as his hand flew to his mouth. "I can't be . . . ."

In the next moment, he was jumping down from his horse and gathering me into his arms. "Is it really you, Brylee, my girl?" he asked as he stroked my hair and looked deep into my eyes.

"Yes, it's me," I said as I felt the strength of his embrace. "I've missed you so much, father, but I was afraid to come home after what I had done."

"Let's not talk about that," he said as tears slid down his leathery cheeks. "You're here now, and that's all that matters. Look," he continued, addressing the others. "This is my daughter, Brylee. Come home to us after all these years."

I looked up at the remaining riders. There was a woman in her early forties with blonde hair and green eyes, and a young boy, not more than seven, who was riding my old horse, Rupert.

The man I had already confronted was still looking at me as if I were a fly that could be killed with a single swat. I knew I would never like him if first impressions proved correct. I wasn't so sure about the others.

"My God," my father said, unaware that the way he was using Heavenly Father's name made me both uncomfortable and sad. "I can't believe you're here."

"This is a pleasant surprise," the woman said. "Your father has told me a lot about you over the years. You're a very beautiful young woman."

"Thank you," I muttered, wondering how this woman I had never seen before could tell anything about me I was so covered in dust and sweat.

My father must have noticed my unease. "This is a little awkward," he admitted, frowning in the way I remembered so clearly. "I forgot that you've never met LeAnn, and this young, strapping lad is our son, Trevor, your half-brother."

I felt my world slipping again as I made some mental calculation. Trevor's existence meant that my father had been seeing this woman before my mother's death. This revelation brought back all the anger that had momentarily lifted when I had been in his arms. How could I ever forgive someone who had betrayed both my mother and me?

"Hi, Brylee," Trevor said, looking down at me with a smile as if my being there was something ordinary and natural. "Father didn't tell me you were coming, but I'm ever so glad you did."

"Me, too," I replied, forcing an unfelt smile. This boy didn't deserve my rudeness. He was a victim of unfortunate circumstances just as I was. "How do you like riding Rupert?"

"He's a fine horse. Father said you trained him when you were a little girl, and I was to keep him in good shape for when you came back."

"He did," I said, wishing with all my heart that I had never come home. I wanted to be understanding and kind, but mostly I wanted to be back in Los Angeles with Ben. He would know what to do to keep my world from crumbling again.

"Do you want to ride him back to the house? He was your horse first, and I don't mind walking," Trevor continued.

"No," I replied a little too abruptly, and then watched the offer of friendship slip from his face. He was too young to understand the revelation I had just been forced to accept, so I tried to soften my next words. "I have a hammer and some nails to return to the tool shed, and I haven't been on a horse in ages."

"Then I'll walk with you," my father interjected. "Your sister and I need a few minutes to get reacquainted. Jake, would you take my horse and see that he's fed and rubbed down?"

"Sure, boss," the man with the cold, hard eyes said. He clicked his tongue and led the black horse my father had been riding away.

"I'll see you at the house in a little while, love," my father told the woman.

"And I'll see that the guest room is ready by the time you get there. Come along, Trevor, let's give your father and Brylee a chance to talk."

They rode off after the man named Jake, and I was left alone to deal with the fallout of my father's latest betrayal—a lover and half-brother I had known nothing about. Could this trip get any worse?

"Why didn't you tell me you were coming? I would have driven into Sydney to get you," he said as he picked up the can of nails, and we began walking towards the tack room in the barn where all the tools were kept. He didn't try to hug me again, and I kept my distance from him.

Still, I glanced at his profile without turning my head. "I didn't want to put you out. After what I did, I wasn't sure you would ever want to see me again."

"How can you say that?" he asked, stopping abruptly and tilting my chin upwards so it was impossible not to look at him. He smelled of body sweat, horse and tobacco. "You're my little girl, and no matter what happened in the past, I love you and always will."

"But the way I left..." I stammered, not having the faintest idea how I was supposed to deal with what I had just been told, let alone anything else he may decide to mention.

"I knew why you felt you had to get away. Your mother's death was a terrible tragedy, and I didn't handle it the right way. I kept thinking that we would have time to talk once everything settled down, but by then, you had already disappeared. No one knew where you had gone, not even your friends at school. I needed to know that you were safe."

My emotions were doing summersaults. I wanted to continue hating him just as much as I wanted to feel his forgiveness and love.

"What I did was despicable, Brylee," he said before I could formulate an appropriate response. "I should have been honest with both you and your mother."

"Then why weren't you?" I asked, trying to keep the contempt from my voice but not entirely sure if I really cared.

This man I had hoped to make amends with had just delivered a blow that made my guilt over not having had enough insight as a teenager to make a good decision seem like an innocent oversight. But as I took a deep breath, I told myself that nothing would be accomplished by this visit if I let what I was feeling rule either my heart or my head.

"I didn't tell you because I was a coward and didn't want anything to change."

His admission was both stark and chilling and made me look down at the dust that covered my shoes. While I appreciated his honesty, it did little to offset his revelations. I had just learned that he'd been lying to both my mother and me, and a little boy, who knew all about me, was now involved.

"We can't always have everything we want," I managed to blurt out.

"I know that, but I didn't want anyone to get hurt."

"My mother died, and I ran away. There was plenty of pain involved!"

"I didn't plan any of this, Brylee. You have to believe that."

"What I believe or don't believe doesn't change the facts. An innocent woman is dead because you were drinking and drove anyway. You had an ongoing affair, and I have a little half-brother who was born before I even left home. How am I supposed to deal with any of that?"

"You're right," he said, lifting his shoulders and shaking his head. "You need time to get used to the idea of having a new family."

I stopped abruptly and looked over at him.

"Can you tell me one thing, father? Did you ever really love my mother?"

"Bloody right, I did," he responded without hesitation. "But we were so young. Your mother was still in high school when we met. Her parents wanted her to go to the university, find some rich, suitable bloke and marry him. She was the most beautiful, fragile thing I had ever met, and her father treated her atrociously. She was nothing to him but a pawn—something to be used to further his professional goals and bring more money into the family coffers. We fell in love and wanted to be together. I had no skills, except helping my parents run this ranch, but that didn't stop me from wanting to protect and keep her safe."

I had never heard him speak of my mother in this way, not even at her funeral and wake, but if he had loved her so much, why had he turned to someone else?

"You've never talked about my mother before. It must have been hard," I said, wanting to be supportive, but still wanting to rant and rave like a spoiled child.

"It was more than hard, Brylee. The ranch wasn't doing well and my parents weren't any more excited about our union than her family. They all felt it was a poor match because of our different backgrounds, but when you're young and in love, passions sort of sweep you along. We really thought we could make things work, but then my parents both died within a few months of each other. Your mother was a city girl who never adjusted to life in the outback. We simply grew apart and started needing other things."

"You mean you started needing another woman?"

"It didn't happen like that."

We were standing in front of the barn, and my father leaned against the short fence that was still used as a hitching post for horses.

"I can only tell you that she didn't want me near her in a husbandly way after you were born. You have no idea how hard that was for a virile man who was used to having women around."

I wanted to believe him, but the misunderstood husband was the oldest excuse in the world for being unfaithful.

"Maybe she just felt guilty for not being able to give you a son," I said without thinking. "That's what most men want, isn't it, someone to carry on the family name? But you have a son now, don't you, father?"

It wasn't my intention to be cruel, but there had been too many shocks during the past few minutes. All I knew was that my father had cheated on my mother. The reason behind it didn't really matter that much.

"You have every right to hate me, Brylee," he said, pulling a pack of cigarettes from his shirt pocket. "But I hope that some day you will be able to forgive me for hurting both you and your mother. And yes, I have a son now, but he's no more important to me than you are."

I wiped at the tears that were forming in my eyes while my father lit a cigarette and blew a smoke ring into the air.

"I do understand that men have needs," I said, turning my head away from the smoke that now irritated my eyes and made me cough. I had been away from it for so long. "But how could you be unfaithful to my mother?"

"Because I was a weak man, and I thought it was okay with her since she seemed happier once I quit trying to get close. Her life always revolved around you."

"Not always."

I thought about being sent away from home when I didn't want to go. My mother could have helped me earn my GED, but she had sided with him. If things had been so bad between them, why had I never noticed?

"I never quit loving your mother, but I'm not sorry I met LeAnn. I wish you could accept the fact that I'm not the man I was back then. Just as I'm sure you're not the same girl who ran away from home."

His words stopped my next outburst. I had changed since meeting Ben and his family. Perfect people didn't need the atonement for the sins and mistakes they would inevitably make. Although my needs for repentance were different from his, my father deserved the chance to explain.

"Point taken," I said, not wanting to make our reunion more difficult than it already was. "I've made a new life for myself in the United States."

"So, that's where you've been all these years. What have you been doing?"

Now wasn't the time to mention my new faith or my plan to marry Ben in a place where my father could not go. We were barely able to speak to each other without lashing out.

"I've been going to school," I told him. "I graduated from UCLA in Business Management and hope to own a company one day. But until then, I'll be looking for employment as soon as I get home."

"So this really is only a visit. I was hoping you had come back for good.

"You don't have to say that, Father. I'm sure your life is very complete with your wife and your son. My presence will only complicate things."

"That's not true," he said. "LeAnn knows how much I've wanted you to come home. She's a good woman in spite of the way things happened."

"I'm sure she is, or you wouldn't have married her," I replied as a knot of revulsion and dread tightened in my stomach. How was I supposed to be in the same room with the woman who had stolen my mother's place?

"We're not exactly married, Brylee. I've been through that once, and she understands that I have no desire to enter a union like that again. We're committed to each other, and you don't need a piece of paper for that."

"But what about Trevor?" I had to bite my tongue to keep from saying something even more unkind about the little boy who had so unashamedly accepted me as his sister.

"He was given my last name at the hospital. So in the eyes of the law, he is my son both biologically and legally."

"I see," I said, wishing the world would quit spinning so I could think again. This was too much for anyone to take in, especially a girl whose life had been rearranged in the last half hour.

"I guess I need to put these away," I said, picking up the hammer that was once again lying in the dirt along with the bucket of nails and heading towards the tack room.

"I'll take them," my father said. "You shouldn't be working on your first day back. Go on to the house and get acquainted with everyone. I'll call Ned and tell him you're home as soon as I come in."

"I'd rather stay with you," I said. "I know this visit wasn't planned. I could get a room in town if it would be more comfortable for everyone."

"Absolutely not!" he retorted. "This is your home, and I want to hear all about your adventures. You must have hated me a great deal to move so far away."

"My destination wasn't planned, but like you, I'm not sorry I went. I learned a great deal and made some incredible new friends."

He coughed. It was deep and made his face turn red. It lasted so long.

"Are you okay?" I asked him.

It took a moment or two before he was able to speak again. "You know how this land makes your mouth as dry as the bottom of a cochy's cage. It sort of gets into your lungs, but it's nothing that a good stiff drink won't cure. I'll have LeAnn get the good brandy out after dinner for you girls. Jake and I prefer whiskey."

He threw what remained of his cigarette on the ground, rubbed it out with the toe of his boot and took the hammer from my hand. The next few days were going to be rough. If only Ben were here, I might not feel like my life was sinking into a black hole of nothingness again.

Chapter 4

"Dinner's ready," **LeAnn** said with a smile when I walked through the back door of the ranch house and into the kitchen of my childhood. Nothing outwardly had changed—except for some new curtains at the windows—but it felt entirely different.

"Jake has already taken your suitcase to the guest room. I'm sorry I can't put you in your old bedroom, but that's been Trevor's room ever since we moved in."

"The guest room is fine," I told her. "You're being very kind."

"And why shouldn't I be? You're Jack's daughter. He loves you, and that's good enough for me. Now, why don't you wash up so we can eat while the stew is still hot? I've put everything you'll need in the upstairs bathroom."

I nodded my thanks and walked up the long staircase with pictures of dead ancestors staring down at me into the hallway leading to the bedrooms on the second floor. The master bedroom was on the ground level, next to the living room and office, with the kitchen being on the opposite side of the house. I used to sneak down the stairs at night when I got scared and crawl into bed with my parents. They had seemed genuinely happy then. But that was a long time ago, and now I was back in my own home as a guest. It couldn't get much stranger than that.

Fresh towels had been set out, and I washed what grime I could from my hands. It would take a long, hot shower to get rid of the dust in my hair, and the clothes I was wearing would have to be washed. Blisters were beginning to form on the fingers and palm of my right hand where I'd gripped the hammer much more tightly than necessary. I should have looked harder for a pair of gloves. Ben would laugh if he saw me now. He often called me 'a dainty little thing' even though he knew I had grown up in the middle of the Australian Outback.

"You're pretty," Trevor told me when I met him in the hallway a few minutes later. "You look just like the picture of that lady in the den, but then I guess that's because she's your mother."

"And you're bright for such a young kid for noticing that," I responded, quite taken aback that a portrait of my mother hadn't been relegated to the attic when his mother moved in to take her place.

"That's what father always says. He tells me that I'm just like you, but that's okay because you're my sister."

"Siblings do tend to have many of the same qualities," I told him. "It's too bad I didn't know about you sooner."

My words were meant to be reassuring, but I doubted that knowledge would have stopped me from running away. However, it might have kept me from coming back to a place filled with people and remembrances I wasn't sure I could navigate without falling completely apart and saying or doing things I would only regret.

"Do you want to go riding tomorrow?" he asked as he took my hand and led me down the stairs to the kitchen. I was surprised we weren't using the dining room. That's where we'd always eaten during my childhood. "You could ride Rupert, and I could ride one of the other horses. Father says I'm old enough and good enough, too."

"I'm sure you are," I replied, looking down at the top of his head. It was impossible not to like the little boy who was trying so hard to make me feel like part of a family I didn't feel capable of accepting.

"Know what else he said?"

"Not a clue," I told him.

"He said I'm almost as good a rider as you."

My brow furrowed. "That's nice. Everyone in the outback needs to know how to handle a horse."

He looked up at me with wide, innocent eyes that only heightened the shame I felt for not being more like him. Riding Rupert was one of the few outdoor activities my mother had allowed, but I had never ventured far from the house on my own. It wasn't safe, and there was never anyone around to go with me.

"Father said we should take the horses out as often as possible while you're here."

"I'd like that," I responded as I quickened my pace to keep up with him. We almost sprinted down the last few steps and into the spacious, overly warm kitchen where the table had been set for five.

"Who else is eating with us?" I asked as Trevor pulled me down into the chair next to him.

"I am," Jake said as he strolled into the room from somewhere in the front part of the house. He was big and tall and commanding, but I was determined not to let him get the upper hand again. "And that happens to be my chair you're sitting in."

"Quit teasing, Jake," LeAnn said. "There aren't any assigned chairs at my table."

"Spoken like a true big sister, who would like her younger brother to act like a gentleman for a change," he replied, giving her a kiss on the cheek.

"You know how much I hate it when you provoke just to get a reaction. He isn't always like this, Brylee. He's just trying to impress you. It isn't often we get pretty girls out this way."

"I think Miss Hawkins knows exactly where she stands with me."

He gave me a look that made the hair on the back of my neck bristle. It was apparent that he disliked me every bit as much as I loathed him. At least now I knew why he was hanging around the ranch.

"Let's quit all the talk and eat," my father said while placing a big pot of mutton stew in the middle of the table. He had never done that for my mother, but then we'd always had Keida around to serve our meals. "And I suppose in honor of the occasion, we should say grace. It isn't often that a lost member of the family comes home."

The sincerity of his words made me want to cry. How could I continue to dishonor someone who was trying to be nice when he had every right to treat me just as badly as I was still treating him?

He didn't close his eyes. He just took LeAnn's hand in his right one and Trevor's in his left. I had no choice but to take the small, tanned hand Trevor so willingly offered, but a feeling of trepidation encompassed me when Jake's fingers closed grudgingly over mine.

"Thank you for this food, God," my father said as he looked around the table at each one of us. "And thank you for bringing Brylee home. Now, let's eat. Amen."

"Amen," I reiterated as I briefly closed my eyes. Heavenly Father understood why they prayed as they did. They had yet to learn what I had.

I glanced briefly at the faces of the people who sat around the table. My father looked so much older and thinner than I remembered, but I could tell that LeAnn really cared about him. That should have made me feel better, but it didn't because I was an outsider, an interloper in my own home and that wasn't likely to change.

"Well, honey," my father addressed me as he broke off a piece of bread and dipped it into the stew to help soak up some of the juice. One had to eat mutton before it got cold or end up with a covering of tallow on the roof of the mouth that could be decidedly unpleasant. I no longer appreciated the taste, but would pretend to enjoy the meal just to be polite.

"How long will you be able to stay with us?" LeAnn asked.

"A few days."

I didn't want to commit to anything more just in case things became unbearable, and I felt the need to leave before my scheduled time was up. Despite the generous display of hospitality from some members of my new family, I wasn't sure how many more revelations or insults I could take.

My father gave me a searching smile. "We were hoping for longer. There's a lot of catching up to do."

"And we will," I promised before turning my attention to the woman sitting next to him. "The stew is good, LeAnn."

My emotions were flipping around like a chicken whose head had just been severed from its body. I might not want to accept what I had found by coming home, but the Saviour expected me to be kind.

"I'm glad," she said. "If I'd known you were coming, I would have fixed something a little fancier."

"Now, don't apologize, love," my father told her. "Brylee is used to eating like this. At least she was before leaving home."

"Where have you been?" Trevor asked as he bit down on a piece of meat.

"Don't talk with your mouth full," his mother chided. "It isn't polite."

"Sorry, mum," he said, swallowing without really chewing. "It's not every day I get to meet my sister."

"I live in Los Angeles," I told him, not really sure how familiar with geography he might be.

"Is that why you sound so funny?"

"I didn't know I sounded funny."

"Well, you don't sound like you live here."

"I suppose that's because I've been away for a long time and have lost some of my accent."

"What have you been doing?" LeAnn asked. She didn't seem the least bit uncomfortable having me back on the Hawkins' Ranch after such a long and unexplained absence, or the fact that she had assumed my mother's position in my childhood home while I was gone.

"I've been attending school. I graduated from UCLA in May with a degree in business."

"Now, isn't that just bloody great," Jake said as he looked at me with what could only be described as contempt. "The boss's daughter graduates from college with a business degree and suddenly finds herself back at the home she left just in time to claim her inheritance."

"It's not like that," I said. " I didn't come here to get anything."

"And you expect us to believe that. It's a little too convenient. What's it been, five, six years since you left?"

"Shut up," LeAnn told him. "We're all family here and should at least try to be civil."

"You're far more trusting than I am," Jake replied. "It wouldn't be the first time a long-lost family member returned to try to get something for nothing."

Tears of anger and pain were forming, but I would never let the arrogant man at the table see just how much his words hurt. I had no intention of claiming a legacy of any kind. My life was with Ben. I only wanted to straighten things out with my father. There had been no way of knowing he had another family who obviously meant a great deal to him.

"LeAnn's right, Jake," my father said. "We are family, and we need to stand united, regardless of how uncomfortable that might be for some of us. Besides, I'm very proud of Brylee. I know it's what her mother always wanted."

"Would you like some coffee?" LeAnn asked as she rose from her chair at the table, picked up the silver pot that had been used for generations and began refilling the cups on the table. "I should have asked when you first sat down."

Another moment of anxiety washed over me. Everything about my life had changed, and I would never fit in with anyone in the room, no matter how hard I tried. "Water's good. I had almost forgotten how hot it gets here."

"It has been a scorcher," my father said. "We haven't had rain since April."

I wanted to ask him about the ranch and why there weren't any men to help out living in the bunk house, but after Jake's accusations, I decided it would be best to keep my questions to myself.

We finished the meal in near silence. At its conclusion, LeAnn told Trevor it was time to put on his pajamas and do something quiet before going to bed. He protested, but was having trouble keeping his eyes open. I understood exactly how he felt. Days in the outback started before the sun was up, and I doubted he took a nap. As much as he appeared to love the life he was living, he wouldn't want to miss anything.

"He's a cute boy," I told LeAnn after he had gone upstairs and we were left in the kitchen to put everything back in its place. My father and Jake had disappeared after eating chocolate cake. "You must be very proud of him."

"I am," she said. "He's the best thing in my life, next to your father."

"I can see how fond you are of each other," I reluctantly admitted.

"We've had our rough patches over the years, but it's all been worth it. I hope you will be able to forgive my overly vocal brother for his rude behavior. He's not usually like that."

"I'd probably feel the same way if some uninvited guest appeared at my door."

"He's just being protective. It's in his nature."

I helped her clear the table and offered to wash or dry the dishes, but she refused by telling me that I needed time to relax and unpack. She was right. I was tired, and since small talk was nearly impossible, I decided to follow Trevor's lead and retire for the night. I might not be able to sleep, but at least I could lie in bed and think.

My father touched my arm as I put my hand on the railing. He had a glass of whiskey in one hand and a cigarette in the other.

"Why don't you join us in the den after you've unpacked. LeAnn's getting the good brandy, and we have a lot to talk about."

I looked past him into the room where he had always been sequestered alone in the evening when I was young. Jake was sitting on the leather sofa with a drink in one hand and a heavy haze of smoke swirling in the air around him. I didn't want to be in the same room with him again if it could possibly be avoided.

"I think I'll just turn in if it's okay with you," I said with what I hoped was a very weary smile. "It's been a long day—all the time zone changes."

"I forgot about jet lag," he said. "We'll have time to talk tomorrow."

I wanted to kiss him goodnight, but something held me back—something very unattractive—my pride.

"Thanks for the warm reception. I shouldn't have shown up without letting you know I was coming, but I was afraid I might back out."

"You don't have to explain. I'm just glad you're here."

"Me too," I said, "I'll see you in the morning."

Chapter 5

The light was streaming in through the open window by the time I woke up the next morning. I had fought for sleep to come and tossed and turned for several hours trying to calm my mind into making some sense of all that had changed at home during my absence. But I had never once considered the idea that my father might have a new family—one that had been formed while he was still married to my mother.

I put my hands behind my head and looked up at the ceiling of the guest room. The sun was making spirals of light that danced with each burst of hot air outside. I still hadn't decided what I was going to do. I had an amazing new life with Ben, and it bore little resemblance to the one I had left behind. My new faith had literally moved me away from decades of tradition into a life of simplicity and beauty that I did not want to change.

How could I stay here, where everything my old life represented was in direct opposition to what I now believed and tried to live? I loved my father. He was a good man by the world's standards. He was honest in his dealings with other people, worked hard, and apparently loved far more deeply than I had been aware of as a child. The vices he had embraced were expected, even applauded, within the ranks of the people he had always known.

Five years ago, I had felt much the way he did. I saw nothing wrong with drinking beer, wine, coffee, and tea, watching R-rated movies, or surfing, sunbathing, and going shopping on Sunday. They were personal choices, harmless activities. How wrong I had been about so much back then.

But I had nothing in common with my homeland now. I was definitely a stranger on a distant shore and wanted nothing more than to be magically transported back to the life I had chosen with Ben. But that wasn't going to happen today, maybe not even tomorrow. I couldn't go home until I had made peace with my past and my father, and I had no idea how I was ever going to make that happen. His choices had profoundly affected me, and a simple apology would not suffice. I needed to know why mother and I had not been enough for him, and I needed to understand why she had died.

I slipped out of the bed and onto my knees. I loved the fact that I now understood about Heavenly Father and his reason for sending each one of his children to earth. I had prayed occasionally growing up, but nothing like I did now. My mother had been raised Catholic. My father claimed to be an agnostic, and that combination made religion a tense subject in our home. Still, my mother had taught me what she knew about God. I was happy she was back home, where she could learn more about him and accept the fact that her past beliefs would not bring exaltation, only eternal life.

I'd had a fleeting moment when I first saw my father riding towards me on his horse, when I thought I might be able to help him understand, too, but that wasn't going to happen now. He lived with a woman he wasn't married to, and they shared a son—a son who had been conceived and born while my mother was still alive.

How could I ever explain my new religion to him, or the fact that I was getting married and he couldn't attend the ceremony? Maybe he wouldn't even want to be there after all that had happened between us. Given the way we had both chosen to live, if I told him anything about what I now believed, he would only scoff and think I had set myself up as his judge. Maybe that's how I really felt inside, although it wasn't the least bit Christlike. In my mind, the way he was living wasn't right, but he didn't know even a fraction of what I did. My own conversion had not taken place overnight.

Music was playing on the radio when I walked downstairs. It was nearly eleven in the morning. I had been so tired the night before that I hadn't even bothered to set an alarm, and my cell phone was useless since there weren't any towers close enough for a signal.

"Good morning, sleepy head!" LeAnn greeted me when I pushed the swinging door leading into the kitchen open. "Would you like some coffee? It was fresh a few hours ago, or there's iced tea if you prefer. It's going to be another bloody sweltering day."

"I'm really not thirsty, but thanks for asking," I told her, feeling even more out of place than I had the night before. She moved around the kitchen as if she had every right to be there, but I couldn't really blame her for that. She was in my mother's home at my father's invitation. I was the one who had severed my right to be there by running away. "Where is everyone?"

"Jake and your father took the plane up to check on the cattle on the north range. Things have been dry for a long time, and they wanted to make sure there was enough grass left for them to eat. We won't be rounding them up for a few more weeks."

"When did you get a plane?" I asked. Five years ago, my father was still herding both cattle and sheep on horseback.

"The plane came when Jake did, more than a year ago. It's just a two-seater, single-engine plane, but it's made things so much easier for your father and me. Jake was a bush pilot before we convinced him to come work with us."

"I'm surprised he would come way out here after living such an exciting life. But then he doesn't seem to like strangers much."

"Jake's a good bloke if you can get past his rough exterior. Like I said yesterday, he's rather protective when it comes to family. We've been through a lot."

She pulled a pack of cigarettes from her shirt pocket. "You don't mind if I smoke, do you? I couldn't help but notice that you haven't picked up that bad habit." She lit one and inhaled deeply, then blew out a cloud of smoke.

I was becoming increasingly uncomfortable and suddenly realized that the whole house reeked of stale tobacco—something it had not done when my mother was alive. She had insisted, quite vehemently, that my father smoke outside because the smell made her lungs hurt. It seemed odd to be remembering that now.

"Where's Trevor?" I asked to break the awkward silence.

"Most likely out in one of the sheds, taking care of his animals. Your father brings all the little ones who've lost their mothers back to the ranch. Trevor takes care of them, and he's earning money for college in the process. Your father and I both agree that he needs an education before deciding if he really wants to spend his life ranching with us. It can be a hard life, as you well know. I can't begin to tell you how proud he is of you. What made you decide on business when there are so many other fun things a young woman could be learning?"

"I'm not sure," I replied. My mind wasn't focused on her question. I was thinking about my little half-brother and how close he was to our father. I had never been encouraged to go to college, and I had most certainly never been given small animals to raise or been groomed to take over the ranch one day. "I guess it just seemed like a good choice at the time."

"Well, I'm sure it will be useful in whatever life you decide to pursue."

"Is there anything I can do to help?" I asked, hoping to stop the bitterness that was forming in my heart again. I didn't like what I was feeling. Jealousy is a harsh mistress, and I couldn't really blame my father for loving his own son. After all, I was the daughter who had run away and never looked back until now.

"Not at the moment. The guys won't be back until closer to one, and there's no way to contact them. I wish we had all the technology you're used to. I know how hard it is to be without a cell phone, but I'm afraid they haven't made it this far yet. However, we have installed satellite TV if there's something you would like to watch. Murdock Enterprises owns most all the media around here. They push Australian programs, but some of it isn't that bad."

"I'm not much into television," I told her. "I haven't had a lot of free time with school, work and friends."

"I used to think about going to the university in Sydney when I was young, but I had other responsibilities. And when I met your father, I knew I could never leave Edna."

She'd given me the perfect opportunity for finding out more about their relationship, but I wasn't sure additional knowledge would change how I felt. I hated what she had done to my mother almost more than I hated the part my father had played.

After all, if LeAnn hadn't been there, open and willing to embrace what he had to offer, he never would have betrayed my mother. But then, not many people believed what they had done was wrong. People changed and got tired of each other all the time. That's what divorce was for. As for living together outside of marriage, the world promoted it as being a more realistic lifestyle since it was less confining than marriage and made the ending of the relationship far easier to resolve.

"How long have you known each other?" I asked, hoping I wouldn't regret it.

"Well, let's see," she sighed, putting her cigarette in one of the numerous ashtrays scattered around the kitchen. "I guess I've known your father for about fourteen years. I was serving drinks at one of the local pubs in Edna when he and a group of his hired hands came in for a few pints. They'd been at the railhead loading cattle."

Fourteen years, I thought. That would have made me all of nine when they met. How could my father have deceived my mother and me for that amount of time without getting caught? Tears of anger and frustration began tickling my nose, so I looked away and bit down on my bottom lip. She didn't seem to notice.

"I guess you could say that we hit it right off."

"Even though you knew he was already married?" I was being judgmental and knew it, but in light of the way I had learned about their relationship, I felt I had the right. She appeared far too cool and composed to me.

"He was going through a rough time and needed someone to talk to."

"He had us."

"You were a child, and your mother . . . . Well, all I can say is that your father loved her, but sometimes that isn't enough, and men do have needs."

With every fiber of my being, I wanted to challenge what she was saying. She shouldn't have gone after my father when he belonged to someone else. And she shouldn't have had his child while my mother was still alive. It wasn't right, and it wasn't fair!

"I don't expect you to understand what happened between us, Brylee," she continued. "But you have to believe that our relationship, innocent as it was in the beginning, never altered his feelings for you. He always told me what a beautiful child you were, and I always wanted to meet you. Now that I have, I can see why he is so proud of you. You're a strong, confident, beautiful young woman who seems to have her life together, despite some of the things that took place in her past. Not many people can say that."

"I've learned a lot over the years," I replied.

"So what are you planning to do now that you've graduated from college?" she asked, ignoring my comment. It was probably for the best considering my fragile state of mind and how close I was to telling her how I really felt.

"I'm not sure."

I could have told her about Ben, our upcoming marriage, how we hoped to own our own business someday, and have a large family who would be sealed to us forever. But she wouldn't understand, and I didn't owe her any explanations. I had come to see my father, not all the new people who had become his life.

The screen door slammed, rescuing me from thoughts that were destroying the relative peace I had felt until arriving at the ranch.

"Hey, Mum," Trevor shouted. "I got them fed and watered. When will Father and Uncle Jake be back? I've got something important to tell them."

"Don't you dare step into my clean kitchen with those dirty boots on," she warned as he stuck one foot on the worn linoleum. "I just mopped the floor."

"Sorry, Mum, but I was just so excited," he said, obediently withdrawing. "Tabby's walking!"

"Who's Tabby?" I asked.

"She's my newest bum lamb. Father brought her in last week. Do you want to see her?"

"Sure," I told him with a shrug of my shoulders. Anything was better than standing in the kitchen talking about something that was becoming increasingly distasteful. Besides, Trevor really was a charming little boy, and I shouldn't blame him for what his parents had done.

"There are some extra rubber boots by the back door," LeAnn offered. "You don't want to ruin your good shoes in all the muck."

"Thanks," I told her as my stomach began to rumble. Fortunately, it wasn't loud enough to be heard.

The boots were black and ugly, but they served the purpose and could easily be hosed off.

"Mum told me I couldn't wake you this morning because you needed your rest," Trevor told me as he led me through some low-growing shrubs I didn't remember being there to one of the smaller outbuildings.

"I guess I was more tired than I thought. I don't usually sleep this late. How many animals do you have?"

"Six," he said with pride. "Father took three of them back to their herd yesterday. It's good they grow up, but I still miss them when they're gone."

"I'm sure you do. It must be lonely growing up way out here."

"Sometimes," he admitted, opening a gate so I could enter the building with him. "But it's been better since Uncle Jake got here. He takes me up in his plane sometimes, and that's fun."

"Don't you miss having kids your own age to play with? I know I did when I was your age."

"But you're a girl," he frowned, as if that was something I should have known. "Father says I have to learn how to be a real man and that takes a lot of hard work."

I suddenly felt sorry for him. Our father might be preparing him to take over the ranch when he was older, but he was being denied a real childhood, just as I had been. I had never learned how to play and have fun, or how to relate to people my own age. My mother had taught me what she could and then sent me to boarding school because it was what my father wanted. Being separated from her was awful. She had been my best friend—my only friend growing up—and our separation had nearly destroyed me.

"I'm sure it does," I said, forcing my thoughts away from the additional pain I was feeling. "Do you really like animals and working outdoors? I never did much of that when I was young."

"Father said you couldn't because your mother didn't want you to get dirty. What did you do all day?"

Another eruption of pain pierced my heart. Apparently, my father wasn't hesitant when it came to sharing what had happened during my formative years with his new family. "I kept busy. I had dolls and books, and I spent a lot of time with my mother."

He wriggled his nose, and I knew he wasn't really interested in what I was saying. I followed him into a room where a line of stalls had been built. The wood looked new, and the animals were cute. I gingerly rubbed the nose of the first lamb I saw.

"He won't bite," Trevor said. "He just wants to lick, but you'll get used to the slobber. It doesn't hurt. It just feels funny."

"That it does," I replied as the warm, slimy moisture slid between my fingers. I wished I could pull it away and go back to the house to wash up, but for some reason, I didn't want my little brother to think I was either afraid or disgusted by something he so obviously loved.

Watching Trevor interact with animals our father had given him made me realise that the man I had come home to see was virtually a stranger. Sure, I had loved him in my own way, but had always been afraid of him. He was gruff and overworked, and my mother acted as a buffer when he thought I wasn't behaving as I should. He wanted me to experience what it meant to live in the outback, and she wanted me to be raised like a lady. It had been a constant source of contention between them, but I had never heard them actually fighting.

I had accepted the idea of never being allowed to spend much time in the barn and sheds because she told me it wasn't fitting. I only learned to ride because my father considered it a necessity and because my mother enjoyed an occasional ride when the weather was cool enough.

As a rancher's daughter, I was a total disappointment. No wonder my father was working so hard with Trevor. He wanted someone who would love the life he had chosen as much as he did. Besides, he needed someone to carry on the family name, and luckily for him, he now had a son who could do that.

In my heart of hearts, where I mostly refused to go for any enlightenment, I wished things had been different when I was growing up. But there was no use crying over spilled milk as Uncle Ned always said. I couldn't change the past any more than I could predict the future, but at least I had met Becky and then Ben.

"Hey, sis," Trevor said, yanking on the bodice of the short-sleeved, white eyelet shirt I was wearing. "You're not listening to me."

"I'm sorry," I told him. "I was just thinking about what things were like when I was a kid."

"I can't imagine being in the house all the time like you were. It would drive both mum and me crazy. But if you didn't get to raise animals, how did you get money to go to school?"

"Just how old are you?" I asked.

"I'm seven, but mum and father always talk about me going to the university when I'm old enough."

I looked at him with surprise. I hadn't seriously considered higher education until I stood outside the gates leading onto the UCLA campus and finally came to the realization that learning everything I could wasn't such an impossible dream.

"You should go to school, Trevor," I finally said. "I worked very hard for a year after going to America, and then was able to obtain what is called a Grant for Displaced Students From Other Nations."

The look on his face told me he had no idea what I was talking about, but he had asked a question and my answer had been an honest one. "I also had a job the entire time I was getting my undergraduate degree."

"What did you do?" he questioned as he patted the head of a small lamb that was playfully bunting him with its nose.

"Mostly, I served food at a restaurant, but I also worked in a library on campus."

"I don't like to read, but mum makes me."

"That's good because you need to learn lots of things so you'll be prepared."

"But I am prepared," he challenged. "I'm going to take over the ranch someday just the way father did."

"Then you're set." I tried to smile, but feelings of jealousy were resurfacing. Why hadn't our father taken a real interest in me, and why hadn't he given me animals of my own to raise? But most importantly, why hadn't he loved me like he so obviously loved his son?

I looked down at Trevor as he nuzzled a little white lamb in his arms. I loved children and wanted to love this little boy who was trying so hard to include me in his world. He was my brother. We shared much of the same blood, and it shouldn't matter how he came into my life. Regardless of formalities or even legalities, he was family. They all were!

And I knew Heavenly Father expected me to love and accept them. I just didn't know if I had the faith, courage, or interest in doing so.

"Why didn't you come home sooner?" Trevor's question broke into my disturbing thoughts.

"It's complicated," I told him, brushing his soft, blonde hair with the back of my clean hand and looking at the small animals in the pen in front of us. "But maybe I would have come sooner if I'd known I had a little brother."

I heard the small, single-engine plane approaching before I saw it. Trevor took my hand and pulled me into the bright sunlight. It was too hot to even be sticky, and I could hardly wait to get back to the cool breeze that came straight inland from the ocean in California.

"Father and Uncle Jake are coming. Don't you want to see the plane? It's really cool."

I didn't protest. I simply ran with him to the dirt airfield behind the main barn. I was surprised I hadn't noticed it the day before, but then all of the ground was so brown and barren that it didn't look any different than the driveway or the other adjoining land. The only spots of green came from the small lawn, the trees and the low-growing shrubs directly around the ranch house. If it didn't rain soon, even those few things would wither and die just like everything else that surrounded them.

My father had sunk several wells on the property—that much I did know—but without rain, they would dry up when the underground rivers did. Water was the main worry of outback ranchers. The legacy left to my father had consisted of thousands of head of sheep that were better able to survive in the high, arid regions that made up a good portion of the 3000-acre ranch. But he had added cattle to the mix just to see what would happen. His enterprise was far from being one of the biggest ranches in Australia, especially since corporations had been buying up most of the smaller ones as rapidly as they could.

Men with massive amounts of money had approached my father many times about selling, even when I was young, but he had always refused. He wasn't about to give up what had been left to him by his ancestors, and it looked as if he was planning to leave everything he still had to my little half-brother.

"Hey, sport," our father said after the plane landed, and he had climbed out through the passenger door. Trevor broke away from me and ran straight into his welcoming arms. I couldn't remember ever doing that. "How are all your animals doing?"

"Great!" Trevor told him with pride. "Tabby's walking. You've got to come and see her."

"I'm coming," the man I really wanted to get to know said with a laugh as my little brother pulled on his hand. "But can't I say hello to your sister first?"

Trevor wriggled his nose. "I forgot she was company."

"Not to worry," he responded, looking in my direction. "Maybe we can change her mind."

I tried to smile, but my heart wasn't in it.

"How did you sleep?" he asked as Trevor stood obediently by his side, but not relinquishing his hand.

"Good," I replied. "I'd forgotten how quiet it is here."

"Not much like the big city, is it?" he said, turning abruptly away from me. It made my heart sink. "Hey, Jake . . . ."

The man with the dark, brooding eyes stepped in front of the plane where I could see him. He was wiping his hands on a rag and gave me a look of complete disdain. "What's up, Jack?"

"Why don't you refuel the plane and take Brylee up after lunch. She might enjoy seeing some of the changes we've made. We need to check on the feed situation on the south ridge anyway."

Jake's sudden laughter was disconcerting. "Wouldn't miss it, boss, provided she wants to go. My plane is far from the luxury airliner she's used to."

LeAnn's brother gave me another scathing look when Father glanced in my direction. It was obvious he would rather have a wild dingo in his plane than me. And unless something drastic happened to change his mind, he would never give me a chance because he already believed I was after something that now belonged to someone else.

"I would love to see what you've done, father, but I'm sure Jake has more important things to do than show an interloper around."

Going anywhere with a man I didn't trust made my stomach lurch. I just wanted to talk to my father alone, but it didn't look like that was going to happen any time soon.

"Nonsense," father said, putting his free arm around my shoulders. He seemed to have lost muscle tone in addition to height. "Jake knows you're family, and checking on the herds is what we spend most of our time doing. Uncle Ned said a pack of wild dingoes got into his herd last week and killed a dozen head of sheep. We can't afford to have that happening around here again. We'll lose enough animals if this drought doesn't let up soon."

"Has it been worse than usual this year?" I asked as we walked towards the shed where Trevor's small animals were housed, leaving Jake by his plane.

"No worse than any other," he told me. "But those vultures who want to buy up all the land are still circling. I won't be forced into selling what I have worked my whole life for."

"Have a lot of other ranchers done that?"

"Afraid so! Other than your Uncle Ned and me, there's only a handful of small places left in the whole area."

"But why would people sell out? Their ranches have been in their families for generations, just like this one."

"People get tired of all the hard work with so little to show for it most years. Besides, big corporations can run things more efficiently, and they aren't bankrupted by one or two bad years like the rest of us."

"But you're doing okay, aren't you?"

The moment the words slipped out, I knew I should have remained silent. Jake was hovering in the background, just waiting for me to betray my true intentions. He would never accept that my only concern was for my father.

"Everything's fine," he replied, glancing in Trevor's direction as my little brother prodded Tabby to her feet. "We Hawkins are strong people. Aren't we, son?"

I couldn't watch them interacting so amicably together again, so I looked away and allowed my brow to furrow. No matter what I did, I would never have the place in my father's heart that my little brother did.

LeAnn was waiting for us in the kitchen, where she had set out meat and cheese and other ingredients for sandwiches. There was homemade potato salad, dill pickles, canned peaches, and iced tea.

"Hi, love," she said to my father when he walked into the room and kissed her.

How different things were for my father now. I had never seen my parents show any affection towards each other. All their interactions had been formal and stiff, but that had never concerned me because it was all I had ever seen.

"Mr. Tucker called again," she continued." He said he would be in his office all afternoon."

"That vulture!" my father nearly shouted. "Doesn't he know by now that some of us just aren't interested in selling out?"

"Now, dear," she said, placing her hand tenderly on his arm. "They don't know the kind of men you and Ned are. That reminds me. Your brother called earlier to say they would be over for a barbecue tomorrow night. He was surprised, but overjoyed, to learn that Brylee was home again."

"He's not the only one who was surprised." I heard Jake mutter under his breath. He had his back to me, but I was certain he meant for me to hear. No matter how much he baited me, I would not buy into his mean-spirited behavior again.

"How is Uncle Ned?" I asked. "The twins must be grown up by now."

"Ned's as ornery as ever, and the twins have been giving him a run for his money since they turned twelve. That little gal of his does like the young blokes. They've been swarming around her for years. Ned's just grateful she made it through high school without getting knocked up. They're both studying at the University of Sydney. NJ wants to go into something foolish like Marine Biology, and no one seems to know what Molly is doing, except for chasing ner-do-wells who enjoy wasting her old man's money."

I gave my father a surprised look. "It's good they're both getting an education."

"I suppose," he countered. "I have to believe my brother knows what he's doing."

"Kids come with their own personalities," I said, and immediately regretted it. I knew very little about my younger cousins, except what they used to look like. Molly had dark red hair and big green eyes, and NJ was a younger version of his father—a big guy with a hearty laugh and a heart of gold.

"Now, Jack," LeAnn said. "No need to get worked up over your niece. Molly's a good girl for the most part, and there are lots of things worse than starting a family a little too early."

"Like what?" I wondered. Had I been gone so long I had forgotten how life in the outback worked? Or had my joining a church with beliefs most people would never accept made all the old customs and traditions I had been raised with seem wrong?

"I'm not getting worked up," he told her. "I'm just stating an opinion. That girl's too pretty for her own good, and she has no sense when it comes to men."

"She's a child," Jake said. "But that doesn't stop a bloke from looking at a female who knows what she's got and isn't ashamed to flaunt it."

"Jake, shut up before you say something that makes everyone mad," LeAnn commanded as her face reddened. "She's family."

I wanted to leave the room. Ben would never say those kinds of things about a girl, no matter what her reputation might be. He believed the best about people and was the most generous and wonderful man I had ever known. If I could just make it through this trip, I would be back home with him, preparing to become his wife. I just hoped he would never have to meet my new family. They would shock him with their language and vices, just as they were doing to me.

"Molly's nice," Trevor defended his cousin. "She always plays with me when they come to visit."

"I didn't mean to disrespect her," Jake relented, looking almost embarrassed for saying what he had in front of a child. "I know how much you like your cousin."

"I do like her," Trevor said.

"As you should," LeAnn told him. "Now get yourselves seated around the table. I don't want anything to spoil in all this heat."

I chose to wait until everyone else was sitting down. I didn't want Jake claiming I was sitting in his chair again.

"Have you been able to figure out what's wrong with the air-conditioning, Jack?" LeAnn asked as she handed my father the platter filled with cold cuts. It was obvious he was the head of this family. "I don't dare light the oven. It would make the entire house hot as Hades. Jake's the lucky one. He has that bunk house all to himself, and it's situated underneath a nice big tree."

"Like that helps," Jake scoffed. "But at least I can walk around in the buff if I want to."

"Mind your manners," she told him with another angry look. "There's no reason to talk like that at the dinner table, especially in front of impressionable children."

I knew she was including me, and I was glad because I felt like a child. I hadn't heard talk so bold and distasteful since leaving home. How could adults justify being so crude? But Trevor didn't seem to be ruffled by anything that had been said.

"I'm sure Brylee has done her share of skinny-dipping. I'm right, aren't I?" He gave me a challenging smile.

"No," I retorted. "I've never done that and never will."

"Either a liar or a prude," he leaned over and whispered in my ear since I had the bad fortune of sitting next to him again. "I guess I'll just have to wait and see for myself which one it turns out to be while you're here."

"You'll have a long wait," I whispered back. I was trying my best to be polite and not engage in any confrontations, but he was being intentionally insufferable and refused to leave me alone.

"I'll see what I can do about the air this afternoon," my father told LeAnn while I slipped a few pickles onto my plate. "Brylee is going up in the plane with Jake to check the cattle on the south range. More of the cows should have calved by now."

"I hope he'll behave himself," she said, frowning in her brother's direction. "We don't want Brylee thinking we're uncivilized."

"I'll be a perfect gentleman."

"Like you really expect me to believe that," she said with a snicker. "You've never been a gentleman in your life."

"I haven't had any complaints from the ladies. Most women want a take-charge kind of bloke, rather than some pretty-boy who only cares about his appearance."

"Is that the kind of man you want, Brylee?" she asked.

"Hardly," I responded. "I want a man who knows how to treat a woman with love, respect, honesty, kindness and tenderness."

"A real sissy man, if you ask me," Jake interrupted.

"Well, nobody asked you?" LeAnn shot back. "What's gotten into you anyway? You can be a real jerk, but you've never been this bad before."

"Haven't you seen a young rooster strutting his feathers in front of a beautiful girl before?" my father told her. "Besides, Brylee can take care of herself."

I silently thanked him. I had never met a man as overbearing as LeAnn's brother, but I wouldn't have to tolerate him much longer. In a few days, I would be on my way home to Ben and this nightmare would be over. I just had to find time to talk to my father alone. He was the one I had come to see, and I didn't really care what LeAnn and Jake thought of me. But I would miss Trevor. He was a child who could easily steal part of my heart.

Lunch was over all too rapidly, but I had eaten very little. The butterflies in my stomach refused to settle down because there was no recourse except to follow Jake back to the single-engine, white plane that was waiting for us on the short runway if I didn't want to cause another battle of wills. He refused to walk with me, but sauntered several feet ahead, letting me know that spending his afternoon in the air with me was as distasteful to him as it was to me.

"I hope you don't get airsick," he said as he climbed into the plane, leaving me to open my own door and get inside as best as I could.

"Never have before, but then this is my first time in a small plane," I told him as I looked around for the seatbelt that had fallen to the floor of the plane and barely escaped me slamming the door on it. "But they can't be that much worse than flying in a big one when there's a lot of turbulence outside."

"You're wrong about that," he replied as he turned the key on the instrument panel, and the blade on the nose of the plane began to rotate. "It's going to be one bloody, bumpy ride, so belt up and hang on."

I could hardly hear what he was saying; the sound of the propeller was so loud, but I had a sick feeling that he intended to make this trip as unbearable as possible.

"Can't we call a truce for the rest of the day?" I asked as we began to move forward. "I know you're a good pilot or my father would not let me go up with you. But I also know that being a good pilot means you could make this a very unpleasant afternoon if you want to. I don't have a strong stomach, and I don't think you want me making a mess in your cockpit any more than I want to make a fool of myself by doing it. I'm only going along with this for my father."

"Then we agree on one thing, at least," he replied without looking at me. "We're both doing this for your father."

I held my breath until we reached the end of the runway, then, fearing I might pass out from lack of oxygen, I took a deep gulp of air just as the wheels left the ground. The clanging and banging were nerve-jarring, but I figured I could survive anything as long as we didn't crash.

To say that I enjoyed the flight was stretching it, although I saw the ranch from an entirely different perspective. We weren't that high when compared to a commercial airliner, and the land was mostly flat near the homestead, so I could easily see the herds of cattle and sheep. I could also see where the natural fodder was running out and the small oasis where wells had been bored and water was still available.

It was when we got closer to the mountains that my real worries began. The trees became thicker, and I knew if we went down, we wouldn't be found for days. The tall, dry grass was plentiful, and there was no way of knowing what was hiding in the underbrush, especially poisonous snakes with their beady, black eyes and deadly bite. But instead of running with that unsettling thought, I quickly pushed it aside. We weren't going to crash, and Jake wouldn't keep me out any longer than necessary. He was no more enamored of our forced outing than I was.

So I tried to center my thoughts on ancestors who had settled the land more than two hundred years ago. How brave and courageous they must have been to strike out on their own in a land they knew nothing about. What had it been like to walk across the red, burning sand for the first time, not knowing what to expect? They had nothing but a few tools, their bare hands and a whole lot of grit with which to carve out a living. And had the women who were part of their lives come willingly with them? It only made sense that they would, but then I had never asked any questions about my forefathers, nor had I given more than a cursory glance to the thick, worn Bible in my father's den where most of their names had been recorded.

It was a harsh life and one that I would never voluntarily choose for myself, but my father loved it, and apparently so did Trevor, LeAnn and Jake. Well, they could have the hot, dusty outback, offensive language, bad habits and constant worry over water, marauding animals and copious buyouts. Their existence lacked everything I had come to value since meeting Ben, and I had no desire to step one foot off the path I had set for myself. I would make the best of the time I spent here, and then I would joyously board the plane for home, taking nothing with me but a few more memories.

"Wouldn't Ben laugh if he saw me now?" I thought about this as we flew through a low-hanging cloud. He truly thought I was fabricating my upbringing when I claimed to having been raised on a ranch in the Australian outback instead of a big city like Sydney, Melbourne or Adelaide because I wasn't at all what the movies depicted my country's men and women as being like.

I wasn't big-boned, overly-adventurous, sunburned, crusty-speaking or hard-drinking. To him, I was one of the most feminine and gentile girls he had ever met, even if I didn't know anything about the truths that made him who he was. I had my mother to thank for teaching me how to act like a lady, but even that had come at a price. I had never learned the first thing about life on the Hawkins' ranch, and I was afraid I might end up paying for that oversight before leaving Australia behind for a second time.

Still, I had to give Jake credit for one thing. He was a good pilot, and he was keeping his word about not doing something intentionally cruel that would make me lose the light lunch I had just consumed. If he didn't change his mind, the afternoon might rank just shy of being totally intolerable.

"There's one more place we need to check," he shouted at me, ending a near hour of silence, which I much preferred to having a conversation with him.

"Where's that?" I raised my voice in return.

"About a mile north of here. A few heifers are late calving. I need to make sure they're okay. If the calves are born during the heat of the day, they'll never survive."

"Why didn't they have their babies in the early spring like they were supposed to?" I stupidly asked.

He snorted. "It wasn't planned, I can assure you of that. Sometimes Mother Nature has a mind of her own, and sometimes the bull just isn't into the cow."

I wanted to say something snide in return, but he made a low swoop that would take the plane in the opposite direction. It was far too quick and abrupt and made my head spin, but since I was the one who had asked for a truce, I couldn't be the one to end it. So I closed my eyes and tried to keep breathing as the plane began its one hundred and ninety-degree rotation.

"You gonna be sick?" Jake asked with amusement as the plane hit an air pocket and plummeted several feet. "You'll never be any good at spotting danger or trouble if you can't keep your eyes open during a routine change of direction."

"I didn't know this was a job interview," I shot back, forcing my eyes open. It was sultry and hot in the plane since it lacked any moving air. It shouldn't be like that while flying, but this plane wasn't exactly new. I figured it must be at least thirty years old.

"It's not an interview for anything, Miss Hawkins, but I think you've been away a touch too long. You might not like riding in my plane, but it has certainly made life easier for everyone out here. Just ask your father if you don't believe me. He's getting too old to spend all of his days in a saddle."

His barb was a direct hit. He was saying, yet again, that I didn't belong in my own home. But even if Jake never believed it, I had not returned to Australia to cause any trouble or make any demands. From what I had observed, there wasn't much left to leave to anyone. I just needed some time alone with my father to explain why I had even bothered to come. Our short walk to the house the night before didn't exactly count as having a heart-to-heart.

"Looks like it's a good thing we came," Jake suddenly said, pointing to a large, black mound that was lying on its side, legs stretched out and flaying with pain. "That cow is trying to give birth. Stupid animal! There's shade a few hundred feet away, and she lies down in the blazing sun."

The shade he was referring to came from a few Wattle trees whose long roots were able to sink far enough into the ground to find water when every other variety simply dried up and died. There were dozens of varieties of Wattle trees in the outback, like the Clay, Sydney Golden, Old Silver and Twisted Desert. Each had its own shade of blossoms, mostly golden, that added bright splotches of colour to an otherwise mostly dry and dingy-coloured landscape.

"Where are you going to land?" I asked, looking around for a piece of flat ground large enough to put the plane on.

"Any place I feel like," he retorted, tipping the nose of the small plane downward. "You might want to hang on now. It's going to be a little bumpy."

I didn't need to be told twice. My knuckles were already white from gripping the leather strap above the door. From the corner of my eye, I could see just the slightest lift to his lips. He was laughing at me again.

It was hard to contain my relief when the plane bumped its way to a stop in an open clearing. The cow lay a short distance away in the hot, smoldering sun. I felt sorry for her and the calf she was carrying. I might have been away from the ranch for an extended period of time—nine years to be exact—but I still knew how easy it was for an animal to give up when there was no help at hand when it was needed. I also knew that Jake was right about his plane being one of God's tender mercies, even if no one on the ranch ever acknowledged it. If we hadn't come along, both mother and baby would die.

I purposely lagged behind when he went running across the clearing to assess the situation. I didn't want to watch an animal give birth, and I certainly didn't want to get blood or anything else on my clothes. They would be ruined, and I had brought very little with me.

"Can't you move any faster than that?" He hollered without looking at me. "The calf's coming feet first. Get the rope behind your seat and bring it to me pronto. I may have to pull it if I can't get my hands inside far enough to turn it around."

I shuddered at what he was suggesting, and certainly didn't want to obey his command, but he would not be the one hurt if I refused to help. The animals would most certainly die, and my father would be disappointed in my lack of action. So I scurried back the way I had come, but it took longer than anticipated to get inside the plane and find the rope. It wasn't behind the passenger seat. It was in the cargo hold, along with a whole lot of other items I could see no practical use for.

By the time I made it to him, carrying the rough hemp rope over my shoulder, his arm was inside the huge animal, and he was swearing and sweating profusely as he tried to turn the calf manually. I watched in a kind of disgusted fascination while trying to shut out the sound of his voice by humming, but it was impossible not to get caught up in the life-or-death struggle going on in front of me.

"Can I do anything to help?" I asked in a timid voice when he stopped to take a deep breath of depressingly hot air. It was a gut reaction, one I hoped he would refuse so I could go back to the plane and wait.

"You can talk her into not dying before I'm finished, if you have the stomach for that," he challenged. "If she gives up before the calf is turned, it's over for both of them."

"What am I supposed to say?" I asked as I walked up to the head of the beast that was lying on her side, her huge belly moving slowly up and down. There was sheer terror in her large, black eyes.

"Bloody hell," he snarled through clenched teeth. "Don't you know anything? It doesn't matter what you say. She's an animal, not your bloody best friend."

Jake's face was flushed, and the sweat was streaming down his forehead and neck as he continued to shove the calf's hoofs back inside its mother's womb so it could be turned around.

I didn't know what to say to either him or the cow lying in front of me in so much pain. Had it been any other situation, I might have thought it highly laughable, but there was no humor in what was happening. I tried to touch the massive head, but she whipped it around, spraying me with mucus from both her mouth and nose.

"Yuck!" I cried out, taking a step away from her.

"Quit being such a drongo," Jake shouted. "I've almost got the calf turned, but you've got to keep her from moving around."

I stepped back towards the cow's head. Her eyes were still large and glassy, and I wasn't sure she hadn't already given up the fight. It was scorchingly hot, and we had no idea how long she had been in this condition. I looked at the few Wattle trees in the distance. They were the only sign of life in this barren wasteland. The watering hole had to be miles away.

"Damn it all to hell," Jake suddenly yelled. "The bloody mother is a goner. We'll lose her, but maybe we can still save the calf if we get it cut out in time. There's a knife for that purpose underneath my seat on the plane. Get it!"

This time, I didn't question him, and I didn't protest, even in my mind. I didn't want to see the baby die even if we lost its mother. The knife was exactly where he said it would be, shoved down inside a heavy, leather pouch with a brass snap that kept it from getting tarnished.

When I got back to him, the mother had quit breathing. Jake took the knife and plunged it deep into her side. I almost lost what was left in my stomach in a series of short, dry heaves, but managed to turn my head away when the blood and water spewed forth.

"Come on, little one, " he coaxed. "Give me a bloody break."

He was straddling the cow now, and I marveled at his ability to work under such austere conditions. I would never have done it, but then I wasn't a rancher. Surprising myself after what I had already seen, I watched in complete absorption as he made the hole even larger before literally ripping the cow open and reaching inside for the calf. His arms were heavily muscled and tanned, and literally gleamed with moisture. He looked like the bodybuilders I had seen on television.

"Got it," he finally said as he pulled a small, lifeless animal out of its mother's body into the hot afternoon. He clawed at the mucus that covered its face. I watched in amazement as he opened the calf's mouth and blew great big gusts of air into it.

"Damn it," he swore again as he pounded on the little chest and forced air into the calf's mouth again.

"Is it dead?" I asked.

"Not if I can help it," he shouted back. "Take that knife and cut the umbilical cord as close to the mother's body as you can so we can tie it off."

My clothes were already ruined, but I didn't want to touch the blood and afterbirth. It was disgusting! And how could Jake put his lips on those of an animal? It wasn't right. No wonder my mother had never allowed me to go with my father when he was attending to the herds. She wanted to keep me safe and happy, not exposed to the reality of life and death in the outback.

"Don't just stand there like a Prima Donna," Jake yelled when I hesitated a moment too long. "Cut the damned cord, or I'll have to do it myself."

I leaned over the cow's lifeless body, took the blood-covered knife by the handle, and reached down to grab the cord that had kept the baby alive until now. I nearly wrenched again, but managed to complete his forceful request.

"Now, tie it off," he instructed.

I wasn't sure I had the physical strength or the mental reserves to do such an unaccustomed task, but since my clothing was already ruined, I looped the cord into a knot while fluid shot everywhere. When I was done, I threw the knife on the ground and took a step backwards, flaying my hands in the air as if the motion alone would rid them of the lingering slime and grim.

"Is the baby going to be okay?" I asked as he took a short break from administering a very repugnant type of CPR.

"I have a weak pulse, but we have to get it back to the ranch where Jack can look after it. He's the best vet in the outback, even if he hasn't had any formal training."

"Are you sure we have time? We're miles away."

"We will if you quit asking simple-minded questions. And pick up the knife. I don't want to lose it."

He had the calf in his arms—afterbirth, blood and all—and was running towards the plane.

"What about its mother? We can't just leave her here like this to be devoured by wild animals," I replied after I had the knife in my possession again and was running after him. It was no longer bright and shiny. I wondered how many animals' lives it had saved, but wasn't about to ask. Jake had something more important on his mind.

"We'll come back later and bury her if we get the chance," he said, eyeing me with less contempt than before. "Now get in the plane."

I did as instructed, and without standing on ceremony, he dropped the newborn, slimy calf in my lap. Despite its less-than-savory appearance, I knew I had just witnessed a miracle—the kind that happened often in the Outback, where ranchers had no one to rely on except themselves. As we soared into the air, I couldn't stop staring at the calf's long eyelashes and the shallow movements of its chest. The poor little thing was an orphan now.

Jake called my father on the radio and told him what had happened. The moment we landed, he took the calf from my arms and rushed into the nearest shed with Trevor right on his heels. I just looked down at my arms and my clothes and fought off the tears. I wanted to be back in the city with Ben, where my life was far more pleasant. Jake could have all the animals and any money that might come with it. I just wanted to go home.

Chapter 6

Had I been a good daughter of the land, I would have followed them into the barn to help care for the newborn calf, but all I wanted was a hot bath that would rid me of the dirt, the blood and the filth of a life I had never known before.

"You've had quite an afternoon," LeAnn said when I walked into the kitchen. "I do hope the poor little thing makes it. At least it has a chance now that your father can work on it. He really is amazing when it comes to taking care of animals."

"I hope so," I told her as I took off my dirty shoes and left them by the back door. "Is it okay if I shower and change?"

"Of course it is. You don't have to ask," she said as she continued to mix something in a big bowl that sat on the cupboard. "You can bring your clothes down when you're finished, and we'll wash them. But I'm afraid you'll never be able to wear that blouse again, unless you would like me to dye it another colour."

"That's not necessary. I have other things I can wear."

I wasn't trying to be abrupt or ungrateful. I just wanted to feel normal again.

But she didn't seem overly concerned about my discomfort. "It took me a while to get used to life out here, too. It's not a place I ever expected to live, but when you really love someone, you're willing to make a few concessions. And it's a great place for Trevor. He loves everything about it. He really is his father's son."

"True enough," I replied, walking through the kitchen and into the hallway that led to the stairs. The tears I had been trying to hold back after such a heart-wrenching ordeal now gushed forth as a new wave of anger and jealousy swept over me. How could I ever expect to belong here again? Their lives were complete without me, and it was quite apparent that at least part of them wanted me gone. Well, they would have their wish. I'd leave, just as soon as I had a chance to have a real conversation with my father.

"Wow!" Trevor said when I came down to the kitchen a short time later to see if any help was needed with the evening meal. "That's sure a fine new calf. I've named him Newton."

"Interesting name," I replied.

"Why? I just named him with the first thing that came to mind. He is new, and it took a ton of work to get him here. He's lucky, you know." He fixed me with his big brown eyes that looked so much like my own.

"How's that? His mother's dead. That doesn't sound very lucky to me."

"He's lucky because we're his family now, and we'll make sure he has everything he needs."

"Oh, for the wisdom of a child," I thought as I watched him remove his mucky boots and wash his hands at the sink by the back door. I had to quit thinking about my mother and the pain I still felt at not having her as part of my life. It was ruining even a simple conversation with a child.

Then, almost as an afterthought, I wondered if he might be including me as part of that family. I had often heard the old saying that when God closes a door, he opens a window. Was Trevor my window? I might not know him very well, and I might not like how he got here, but we shared some of my father's genes. Would it be possible for me to learn to really love him? He was certainly giving me every chance to be a part of his life, but was I smart enough and forgiving enough to reach out to him with the same love he was offering me?

"Hey, Trevor," I said. "Do you think you could take me out to the barn to see Newton after supper?"

"You bet," he replied with a bright, cheerful smile. "Newton's even luckier than I thought at first because he has a sister too."

Tears tickled my nose at his admission. The Lord was certainly giving me a far different experience than the one I had expected. But just because something was different didn't automatically mean that it was any worse or any better than what it might have been. If my inner confusion would just dissipate, even somewhat, I might be able to think a trifle more clearly. And even if I couldn't, at least I might be able to make my time with Trevor more meaningful. It wasn't so terribly awful finding out I had a little half-brother.

"Hey, there, young bloke," LeAnn said as Trevor walked into the kitchen. "Let's see those hands. You didn't spend near enough time getting all the dirt out from underneath your fingernails ...?"

"No, mum," he replied.

"Then back to the sink in the laundry for you. I'll not tolerate dirty hands at my table."

The tone of her voice made me automatically look down at my own hands. They were good because I had just gotten out of the shower. But my hair was still damp, and I hadn't bothered to apply any makeup. But what did it matter? There wasn't anyone around to impress anyway.

"You've had quite a day," my father said as he took his place at the head of the table. "Jake said you did a fair job helping him with the calf."

"Did he?" I did not dare to look at the man I had spent a most unpleasant afternoon with. I had certainly let him know by my actions that I no longer had the stomach or the desire to be a rancher's daughter. That meant he had no reason to continue hating me. I wasn't a threat to anyone, unless he truly believed I was just looking for easy money. "All I did was cut the cord. Jake did everything else."

I wanted to tell them how he had breathed life into a slimy calf's mouth, but decided it wouldn't advance my cause, and it definitely wasn't a conversation to have around the dinner table.

"I wish I'd been there," Trevor lamented. "I always miss out on the good stuff. I would have known exactly what to do, and I wouldn't have been scared either."

"I wasn't scared," I told him as I moved mashed potatoes back and forth across my plate. "I've just never had that experience before, and it caught me off guard."

His eyes suddenly looked as big as saucers. "You mean you never got to help birth animals when you were little? Father lets me do it all the time. He says I need to know how to do everything if I'm gonna take over the ranch someday."

His words cut into the tender part of my heart that still wanted to be part of my family of origin, but nothing was his fault, and I couldn't take my feelings of bitterness, frustration and betrayal out on him.

"I'm sure you'll do just fine," I told him. After all, I could hardly expect to be included in future events just because I had shown up unexpectedly to confront my father about a very painful past that had turned into an even more distasteful present. Even Jake had more of a right to be there than I did. He was actually helping my father. How tired and thin the patriarch of our family appeared when I really looked at him.

"Now, son," our father said, looking at Trevor with great tenderness. "Brylee was raised far differently than you've been. Her mother didn't think it was proper for a young lady to spend time in the sheds with the animals. She was supposed to find a rich young man and get married."

"Are you getting married?" Trevor asked me.

"Well, certainly," I said, looking down at my left hand. I had secured the engagement ring Ben had given me within the safety of my suitcase before working on the fence the day before. I hadn't wanted to damage either the band or the diamonds. "There is someone special back home."

"But that's wonderful," LeAnn said, not mentioning my slip in referring to Los Angeles as my home. "No one should have to go through life alone. I can't tell you how happy I am that I met your father. He's the best man I have ever known."

The ball was back in my court, and I wasn't sure what to say. My father was a good man, but he never should have cheated on my mother with someone he met at a bar.

"I'm glad you have each other," I said after a very elongated pause. Nothing would be resolved if I couldn't put my feelings of hurt and betrayal aside and really listen to their side of the story.

"Is that right?" Jake responded as his cold eyes bored into mine. "And here I've had the feeling that you don't much approve of any of us."

"Shut up, Jake," LeAnn told him. "Brylee's had a lot to take in since she got here. Give her some time to adjust to her new family."

"Your sister is right, Jake," my father interjected, much to my surprise since he hadn't done it before. "We're used to each other's banter, but Brylee wasn't raised like that. We don't want to drive her away before we have even had a chance to get acquainted."

"It's okay, Father," I said. "I didn't come here to make any waves. I just wanted to see you again and was hoping we would be able to spend a little time together, just the two of us."

"How about after dinner?" he suggested.

Trevor moved around on his chair. "Brylee wants to see Newton after we eat."

"I'm sure there will be plenty of time to do both," was our father's prompt reply. "Now, let's finish this meal before everything gets cold. It's just about the best one I've ever eaten. You've really outdone yourself tonight, love."

But things didn't turn out as either of us thought they would. When Trevor and I returned to the house after spending some time with the new calf, Uncle Ned was there, but I didn't see my aunt.

"As I live and breathe, there she is," his base voice boomed as I stepped onto the front veranda. "You've given all of us a lot of sleepless nights since you took off, young lady. The twins thought a wild animal might have gotten you, but I assured them that people don't pack suitcases for a date with death."

I smiled up at him without speaking. My actions had hurt more than just my father, but instead of censuring me any further, he simply gathered me into his arms and gave me a sound kiss on each cheek. "It's mighty good to see you again, Brylee. Jack tells me you've been in the United States of America and have graduated from college."

"I have," I told him, wishing the pounding in both my head and my heart would quit. "I meant to write but never seemed to get it done."

Along with my father, Uncle Ned was one of the last real ranchers in the area who had been born during the 1940s when most of the world was at war and automation had yet to be introduced into the wilds—or the "Back of Beyond" as many of the old timers still called the Australian outback. They lived life hard, and they always said exactly what was on their mind.

"You were mighty angry when you left," he continued as Trevor disappeared into the house. "I know how close you and your mum were, and I don't mean to sound harsh since you've just arrived, but you need to know that your actions hurt your father deeply. Damned near ruined his life, especially his health. He would never tell you that himself, so I decided to do it for him. Now that's out of the way, why don't you grab a grog, and we'll sit down and get reacquainted. I brought enough neck oil to give all of us a buzz."

His statement about my father's health, when coupled with the observations I had already made, only added to my distress, but I knew he wouldn't say anything more about it, even if I asked. Besides, I had a more pressing problem. If I refused to drink one of the beers he'd brought, I would have to tell him about some of the changes I had made in my own life, and that would only start a conversation I should be having with my father.

But when he turned and extended a cold tin can in my direction without even waiting for anyone else to leave the house, I knew my moment of truth had arrived. Changing my entire life hadn't been easy, but I had done it with some amazing support. The question was whether or not I could stay strong when facing my family. No one would know if I gave in just once, and it would certainly make my time here easier. But would I be able to face Ben when I got home if I did? He was my life now, and I wanted that eternal marriage and forever family we were planning.

"Thanks for the offer, Uncle Ned, but I don't drink."

He gave me a look of complete disbelief that made the heat rush to my face, and I felt myself leaning into the porch railing for support.

"Well, I'll be damned," he finally said with studied amusement. "So you've become a tea-toddler. Good on ya! Though I have no idea why any Aussie would ever do that. It just means more for the rest of us?"

I knew I had hurt his feelings—even if he would never admit it—from the amount of pressure he was exerting on the can. I could see the indentations his fingers were making and I was afraid it might explode.

"It's a little more complicated than that, Uncle Ned," I said. "I don't drink coffee or tea either."

"What's wrong with you, girl?" his booming voice continued. "Beer's the national beverage. Don't tell me you've gotten yourself mixed up with some strange cult that deprives you of all the niceties of life."

"No," I replied.

Few people in Australia had even heard of the Church of Jesus Christ of Latter-day Saints. I certainly hadn't, and I knew my family was no exception because they didn't even attend the church they claimed to believe in. But starting a conversation about religion when emotions were already heightened would only widen the gulf between us, and I couldn't afford to do that if I wanted to clear the air with my father before going home to Ben.

"I just decided that a little more clean living was more my style. I hope you can understand."

While he just stood there looking at me, my aunt stepped through the front door onto the veranda with an open can of beer in one hand.

"You won't believe what I just learned, Nora," Uncle Ned said to his common-law wife. "Jack's daughter has given up all the vices. She must be downright close to sainthood by now."

"Give the girl a break," Aunt Nora responded with the same startled look my uncle had just given me. "You've pestered that girl since the day she was born, but she's a grown woman now and can live her life however she wants."

"Thank you, Aunt Nora," I said. "It's good to see you again. How have you been?"

"Can't complain too loudly. I've got a few creaks in my bones that weren't there when you left, but I guess that comes from having two kids who are off to college."

I sighed, feeling a great amount of relief now that we were now talking about something other than my unexpected return and how much everything had changed during the interim. "It hardly seems possible that they're old enough for that. They were both still in braces when I last saw them."

"Well, they're out of braces now," she said. "I thought it would be easier having them out of the house, but all I seem to do is worry more. It's become very easy to understand why your mother was so lost once you had gone away to boarding school."

"You think my mother was lost without me!"

It was more of a vocalized statement than a question. I had always known that she missed me and was glad when I came home, but I had never thought about how much her life must have changed not having me around. Even with all the time we had spent together, she was never one for expressing how she felt inside.

"Land child, you were the light of her life."

She motioned for me to sit beside her on the double swing that hung from the veranda rafters. Uncle Ned had joined the other men who had followed her outside and were now standing in the driveway admiring his new truck. LeAnn was still inside with Trevor.

"It's hard for any mother to see her children leave home, even if it is for the right reason," she continued. "I'm just beginning to learn how much I took life for granted when my own kids were little."

"But children grow up, Aunt Nora. That's the way it's supposed to be."

She ran the back of her hand across her cheek, and I knew she was wiping away a tear or two. "I understand that intellectually, but my heart doesn't agree. I worry about NJ because he takes chances and drinks too much like his father, but I worry about Molly more. There's just something about my little girl the young blokes can't seem to resist, and I'm afraid she'll hook up with some drifter before she has the chance to meet the right guy."

I was surprised by my aunt's willingness to share her concerns, but it was rather comforting after my brief conversation with my uncle. "Molly has always been both strong-willed and beautiful, Aunt Nora, but I can't see her settling for anything less than what she really wants."

"She got her dogged determination from me, but it still isn't easy having her so far away from home. I was used to seeing her most every day and knowing where she was at night." She suddenly stopped speaking and pulled her bottom lip into her mouth. "I'm sorry if Ned was too blunt with you. I told him to give you a chance to settle in before speaking his mind, but he doesn't often listen to me when it comes to things like that."

My chest tightened with more remorse, but I couldn't change what I had done. I just hoped that someday my family would forgive me. "I wish I hadn't caused everyone so much pain, Aunt Nora. I don't have any excuses. I was just hurt and confused."

"And you blamed your father for what happened because he was the one driving."

"I didn't mean to," I told her.

"And he didn't mean to be the cause of an accident that took your sweet mother's life. He's been through his own hell these past years, and it's cost him a lot more than you will ever know."

Uncle Ned had said practically the same thing just moments before. I might be an absentee daughter who had caused a lot of heartache, but I still deserved to know what was going on.

"Is my father sick?" I asked her directly.

She took a drink from her can.

"It's not my place to divulge sensitive information, love. You need to sit down and talk to him. He'll answer any questions you ask, I'm sure."

"I've been trying to talk to him ever since I got here, but he's been so busy, and he does have a new family to think about."

"I was wondering when that was going to come up," she said, taking another drink of her light beer. "I'm sure you don't like having LeAnn in your mother's home, but she's been a God-send for your father."

I had just opened my mouth to reply when Uncle Ned walked back up the steps to the veranda.

"Why are you women sitting here gabbing when everyone else is going to the backyard for some light refreshments?"

"We're just having a little girl-talk, Ned," Aunt Nora told him, rising to her feet and crossing the wooden floor to his side.

I wished he hadn't interrupted our conversation so abruptly. There was so much I needed to learn, and Aunt Nora appeared to be in the mood for talking, but the closeness of the moment had been broken.

When we got to the back of the house, I saw Trevor throwing a horseshoe towards a peg that had been pounded into the ground. Uncle Ned's sheep dog, that always traveled with him in his pickup truck, was frolicking at his heels, wanting to be included in the activity. I watched them for a few minutes. Trevor might not understand how totally isolated he was right now, being away from kids his own age, but someday reality would hit him just as it had done me. I hoped he would be better prepared to face life away from the outback than I had been. The whole ordeal of leaving home for the first time had brought more heartache than joy for me.

LeAnn had prepared a big bowl of fresh fruit and an assortment of pastries, along with the inevitable coffee and beer. My father, Uncle Ned and Jake were laughing as they talked, each with a can in one hand and a cigarette in the other. Aunt Nora and LeAnn were standing side-by-side at the table, chatting like the best of friends. I hung back, wondering if I would always feel like an outsider. But if I hadn't left home, I would never have heard about the gospel or met Ben. I was glad now that he hadn't come with me. I couldn't worry about his reaction to my family with everything else that was going on.

"You didn't have to go to so much work," I finally told LeAnn as I noticed a vase of fresh wild flowers in the center of the lawn table.

"It was my pleasure, love," she replied, placing her hand reassuringly on my arm. "We all want you to feel welcome here. This is your home, after all."

I smiled my thanks, but it didn't feel like home to me. Even the familiar faces seemed like strangers we had been separated for so long.

"Father, would you have time to talk to me now?" I asked him after Uncle Ned and Aunt Nora left. We were alone in the kitchen. Trevor had gone up to bed, and Jake and LeAnn were finishing the last of their beers outside. "We didn't get a chance to talk earlier, and you are always so busy during the day."

He put his coffee cup down on the dining room table and looked over at me. "The ranch won't run by itself."

"I know that," I told him. "And I know my coming back has been a big shock to everyone. I just didn't know how to do it any other way. I didn't even know if you would want to see me again after the way I left."

He fixed me with a glance that reminded me so much of the gruff and distant man who had scared me so much as a child. "Your leaving was more than hard for many reasons, but I have never blamed you for doing what you felt you must."

"It was hard for me too," I said. "I was young and impulsive and didn't understand that my actions had consequences."

"I guess that's a lesson most of us learn the hard way. I know I wasn't an easy father to live with, Brylee, but it wasn't because I didn't love you. I was just raising you the way my father had raised me. You know how crotchety your grandfather could be."

"I really don't remember him. He died when I was three."

"That seems like an eternity ago. It's a bloody shame when parents and kids never get to know each other before it's too late to salvage a close relationship. I guess that's why I try so hard with Trevor. I don't want to lose him, too."

"You never lost me, Father. I lost myself."

"That's not how it seemed when you left. I didn't know if I would make it through those first few months, not knowing where you were or what had happened to you. I kept expecting you to come back or at least write."

"I always meant to, but I could never get past the pain long enough to do it. I wish I could live that part of my life over. I would do things much differently."

"We all think that! But the truth is, we would probably do the same thing, even knowing what we do after the fact. I never blamed you for being angry or even for hating me, Brylee. It's how I felt about myself after what happened with your mother. I took her away from you. The two of you were so close it sometimes seemed like you were her child alone, not mine."

"I was always your child, Father, and I loved you."

"But not as much as you loved your mother."

"I didn't know you like I did her."

"And most of that was my own fault. I loved your mother dearly and wanted to make her happy, but she didn't like it out here, and she didn't want you to become a ranch hand. She wanted you to grow up to be a lady. She would be very proud of how you turned out."

His honesty touched my heart, and I bit my thumbnail to keep from crying. "I'm sorry we weren't there for each other."

"The past is over and done with," he said, taking another cigarette out of the pack on the table and lighting it. "I guess some things just weren't meant to be."

He smoked in silence for a minute or two. I just stood there wishing I knew what to say to make things right again.

"I'm glad you have LeAnn and Trevor," I finally told him.

He looked up at me and smiled. "It means a lot to hear you say that. I know it was a shock finding them here."

"You had the right to move on with your life."

"It took me a while to figure that out. I thought I might actually drink myself to death the first couple of years because that's the only thing that would take the guilt and pain away. I had lost both my wife and my daughter."

I tried to keep the bitterness from returning to my voice as I made my reply. This was the first truly honest conversation we'd ever had. "But you still had a son."

"LeAnn and Trevor saved my life. They finally convinced me I still had something to live for. I even hired a private investigator who traced you as far as Los Angeles, but after that, it was like you simply vanished."

He took another drag on his cigarette. The smoke burned my eyes and my nostrils, but I tried not to let it show.

"I'm sorry you had to go through that. I was just so angry at life."

"You could have talked to me," he said, blowing out another small cloud of haze before snubbing out the cigarette. "I wanted to tell you that it was an accident when you came home for the funeral."

"But I wouldn't even look at you, let alone talk to you, would I?"

"You had your own loss to deal with. Had I known you were going to leave, I would have said something once the service was over. There really wasn't time before."

"I'm here now," I told him.

"Then perhaps it's time for me to come clean about everything, but I'll warn you up front that it is not a story I am proud of, and it's not one you are going to want to hear."

He cleared his throat, and I wondered if it was a stalling tactic while he decided just what he was going to say, or provide time for us to be interrupted again.

"We'd been to a small dinner party in town—something that hadn't happened for years—as you well know. I thought she'd had a good time, but we got into a heated argument on the way home."

"What were you arguing about?" I asked, as my chest tightened with fear.

"Don't worry, love," he said, patting my hand as it gripped the back of the nearest chair. "It wasn't about you. While your mother was never too happy about me practically forcing you to attend boarding school, she knew she had taught you everything she could. She also knew it was important for you to see that there was life away from the ranch."

"Then you must have been arguing about LeAnn?"

"Trevor too,' he admitted. "But I'm sure that comes as no surprise."

"Had she known about your affair for long?"

"Not until that night. It was pretty easy to keep it from her since she never left the ranch, but someone at the party must have mentioned seeing the three of us together."

"Maybe you should have thought about that possibility before you went."

"Oh, I did! I weighed my options for days, but she actually seemed excited about going, and I figured my secret would be safe enough since we wouldn't be dining with anyone LeAnn and I knew."

"Edna's not a big place."

"No, it's not," he responded, reaching for another cigarette. "But people tend to stay out of each other's business. It's in their own best interest since there are few people around here who don't have a number of skeletons in their closets they would like to keep hidden."

"And you didn't deny it."

He lit the cigarette before answering. "I may be a hypocrite, but I'm not a liar, Brylee. I think at some level your mum already knew. It's not like I stayed in town overnight that often, but my excuses for doing so seemed flimsy even to me."

I wasn't sure I wanted to hear more, but backing away from the first honest conversation we'd ever had wouldn't solve anything either. "Why didn't you just divorce if you were both so miserable? It's not like that many couples stay together anymore."

"We talked about it a few times, but it never seemed like the right thing to do. I married your mother because I loved her, and had committed to take care of her in both the good times and the bad. It's just unfortunate that our good times didn't last long."

"Why not?" I asked. "I understand that ranching is hard work, and she never seemed to be entirely well, but if you really cared about each other . . . ."

"I wish I could give you an uncomplicated version of what happened, Brylee, but there are never any easy answers to life's most perplexing problems. We were incredibly busy, and there was never enough money, but there were other reasons your mother preferred staying out here, even though she hated it."

"What possible reasons?"

"You do know that her family basically disowned her when she married me?"

"Yes, and I know she really missed them, even though she wouldn't talk about it."

"She had good reason not to, especially after you were born."

"Why, especially after I was born?"

"Because she took you to meet them. I begged her not to go, but she insisted that her family—meaning her tyrant of a father, mostly—would not reject a grandchild."

My nerves were starting to tingle, and my father was pausing in his narrative. No one had said much about my maternal grandparents before, especially my mother, and while I wanted to know about them, I was scared. Our family had been messed up from practically day one for a reason. "Please go on," I responded.

"She got as close as the front entry of the mansion, but when her bloody father saw her standing in the sunlight with a small child in her arms, he exploded. I think his exact words were, 'If you think I'm going to accept the seed of a common convict as a part of my family, you are sadly mistaken.' Then he slammed the door in her face, or rather, his butler did."

"But why? Everyone out here is related to convicts in one way or another, including my maternal grandfather.

Mother told me her great, great grandmother came from a dubious heritage, although I had little idea what she was talking about at the time."

"I guess some convicts just have more clout than others. Your mother's people weren't from around here, and the only thing folks in Edna saw was a wealthy man from a big city who could make or break their livelihoods because he controlled who got loans when they needed one and who didn't."

"He must have been a horrid man."

"He was probably the cruelest man I ever met, and he treated your mother abominably. It nearly broke my heart seeing what his final rejection did to her. All she had ever wanted was his love, but she was never good enough for him. By the time she made the drive home, she was a changed woman. She'd already had to accept the fact that she would never have another child, and now she would never be part of her family of origin again. It was too much for her."

"Another child!" That was the only part of his revelation that seemed to matter. My mother was gone, and I had never met anyone in her family. "Why didn't someone tell me? I always thought I was an only child by choice."

"It's something we never talked about to anyone. It was much too personal and painful."

"I get that, but wasn't there something the doctors could do?"

He took a drag on his cigarette and then set it in an ashtray. The smoke curled into the air in a white, hazy pattern. Ben and I had talked briefly about how heredity might affect our own health, but I had never given any thought to the idea that I might not be able to have children.

"This isn't easy to say, love, but your mother should never have gotten pregnant in the first place. She was never well, even as a child, and the delivery was incredibly hard on her."

"What was wrong with her?"

"She had what was called consumption by the doctors of the day, and it never went away."

I looked over at him and frowned. My mother had always seemed tired and easily winded, but I had never suspected her of being truly ill. "That's an archaic disease. Wasn't she treated for it?"

"I'm sure she was, but some conditions never go completely away, and it didn't help that she was never a happy child."

There was so much more I wanted to know, but I would find a way to retrieve her medical records later. I needed to use the time I had now for other things. "That must have been very difficult. No wonder she always seemed so sad and lonely."

"Your mother was the loneliest person I've ever known. She was also incredibly shy, and I guess it was just easier for her to give up every association than risk being hurt again."

"But none of that was her fault. Couldn't you have made her talk to someone about what she was going through?"

"She refused every offer of help and eventually quit talking to everyone, except you."

"I'm sorry," I almost whimpered. "I never knew."

"And I wish you didn't have to know now, but I hope it helps you understand why I turned to LeAnn. I never went looking for anyone, but I wouldn't be here now without both her and Trevor. They're the best thing that could have happened to me."

"Better than me?" I asked.

"No," he replied, reaching across the table and patting my hand. "You're my little girl, and I'll always love you. It's just that you and Trevor came into my life at very different times."

"You didn't love my mother the way you love LeAnn, did you?"

"It was a different kind of love. Your mum and I were very young when we got married. She was barely out of boarding school, and such a pretty little thing. She was all soft and fragile and had the most beautiful blue eyes. It was exciting sneaking around to be together because her father didn't approve of me. He thought I was a no-good bloke from the wrong side of the tracks, and he was probably right about that. I had nothing to offer his daughter, except escape. I was nothing but a glorified hired hand to your grandfather."

"I always thought you were his heir."

"He had to die before that could happen. I was at his mercy until then."

"That must have been hard for both of you."

"It certainly wasn't an ideal situation, but you were on the way, and Annie was terrified of her father. So we eloped, and I brought her out here to live. When her father found out, he disowned her, and what had looked like such an adventure to both of us soon became a nightmare neither of us was prepared to live."

Even though I had always assumed I was conceived out of wedlock, this was the first confirmation of the fact, and it hurt. In that way, I was no different than Trevor.

"I'm sorry," I told him. "I didn't know I was an accident."

"Oh, love," he said. "I never considered your birth anything but a blessing, despite the fact that we should have used something to prevent it until we were better prepared to be parents."

"But if I hadn't been on the way, you might never have married my mother."

The pain in my chest was excruciating. Why had I ever come back? I didn't want to know any of the things I had learned over the past thirty hours. Those disclosures were destroying every ounce of positivity I had left about my past.

"I can't answer that, but I have never regretted being your father. You might not have been planned, but you brought great joy into both our lives."

"I don't know how you can say that," I replied, shaking my head while the light from the ceiling danced around in front of my eyes. Despite my every unwanted emotion, I appreciated his honesty. "You were very unhappy in your marriage, and then I ran away when you needed me most."

"You were a child who was supposed to feel nothing except unconditional love and acceptance. If anyone failed, it was me. I'm just a hopeless, old bloke who has never known anything except how to manage a ranch, and I'm afraid I've been doing a piss-poor job of that these past years."

Suddenly, I rose to my feet and encircled his neck with my arms. Maybe his life with my mother hadn't been good. Maybe he had felt unloved and needed physical contact just to know he was still alive. I could understand that. There had been times after my mother's death when I had felt that joining her in the ground was preferable to being alone in an unfamiliar country with a heavy accent and no friends.

Meeting Ben had been my salvation in more ways than one. Not only had he introduced me to the gospel of Jesus Christ, but he had also shown me how to love others without judgment or expectations. The question right now was whether I could extend the same consideration to my father and the people he had brought so unexpectedly into my life.

Chapter 7

It was almost dark when I made my way to the family burial plot later that evening. It wasn't the wisest thing to do since the dark brought out many nocturnal and unsavory animals, reptiles and insects, but I needed to be alone, and I was carrying a flashlight I found in a kitchen drawer to help me find the way. My heart was heavy and there was a great deal on my mind. Despite my resolve to live a more Christlike life, too many revelations and exposed secrets were making me question whether any part of my childhood had been as I remembered it, and I couldn't shake the thought that my parents might never have married if I hadn't been part of the equation. Their relationship could have easily turned into just another youthful fling.

My father had done the honorable thing by marrying her; I had to give him credit for that. But how long had it really taken for him to start resenting the wife and child who had not only complicated his life but made it downright unbearable at times? He was the most human man I had ever known and apparently a very passionate one as well.

There was so much to tell Ben when I went into town on Sunday and was able to call him, but I was most certainly starting to question how much I could say before his feelings for me started to change. His family had been members of the church for generations, and they lived what they believed. Mine was as messed up as any group of people could possibly be. And just spending what little time I had with them, I was beginning to understand that all the progress I had made in turning my own life around to a more hopeful and positive way of thinking and living could easily be undone.

I wasn't immune to their influence—at least not in the way I thought. I could stand up for the outward differences I had embraced without giving in. I had proven that by telling Uncle Ned I didn't drink, but what about all the old insecurities and self-doubt I had never outgrown? Just a simple look or harsh word could still cause my heart to crumble and make me forget that I was a literal daughter of my Heavenly Father, who had given me talents and abilities beyond my wildest imaginings.

Ben made me feel that way every time he even glanced in my direction, but I hadn't felt that way since coming home. All the darkness of my previous existence—the one my family was still immersed in—seemed to be closing in on me, and without someone to help me stay focused on the light, I feared I would not be the same person when I left the ranch.

But I wasn't going to let that happen, I told myself as I got closer to the cemetery. My childhood had been empty, even abnormal in most ways, since my mother had been my only real friend until I was sent away to boarding school. She had done her best—I understood that now—but it didn't remove the lack of understanding and personal scars that would most likely take a lifetime for me to fully understand. I had tried to immerse myself in a new life in Sydney, but I was the perpetual outcast who didn't know how to relate to anyone my age—especially when I felt a normal attraction to a boy.

No one had ever talked to me about relationships—how to begin and cultivate them, and how to know if they were good or bad. The only preparation I had received before being driven to Sydney and dropped off with the nuns was being taken to see the doctor in Edna to make sure I had the proper information about contraceptives and had been put on the pill, but I had been too naïve and frightened to even question why. I'd had some rude and disturbing awakenings living in a dormitory with girls who not only knew about life but who were determined to experience every part of it.

I had been away from home for four years when, without any warning, my mother was gone. I was called to the headmistress's office in the middle of geometry class and informed that she had been killed. No explanations had been given, just a compulsory word of condolence by a stern woman in an austere black habit with a white collar. I had taken the bus to Edna, where Uncle Ned picked me up and drove me back to the ranch. My father had planned for the funeral and wake to take place the day I got there, and I never saw my mother's face again.

Sometimes I believed I was as angry with him for the way he treated me after my mother's death as I was with him for causing it in the first place. If he had been sober, he would have seen the pack of dingoes before hitting one of them and causing the jeep to overturn. My mother would never have been thrown out, and I would not have been left to live the rest of my life without her.

I only knew that much about the supposed accident that had taken her from me because Uncle Ned felt it his duty to fill in as many blanks as possible, without overstepping any boundaries, before we got to the ranch and I was forced to deal with a closed casket, a funeral service, a wake, and a bunch of strangers. Maybe if my father had even acknowledged my presence, I would not have felt like I had to run away, but he hadn't even held my hand as the last rites for my mother were being spoken.

Now, at least I understood why he had been so completely distant and self-absorbed. Guilt was a relentless master that hardened the heart and made good decisions impossible to make.

I would never quit missing my mother, but I was glad I no longer blamed God for not providing a miracle that would have allowed her to remain with me. Being forced to leave my homeland, even for all the wrong reasons, had given me the strength to overcome many challenges and the wisdom to accept the gospel of Jesus Christ when it was presented to me. I could not imagine my life without it now, so I would fight through whatever was required while I visited with my family. But the moment the day of my departure arrived, I would be on that plane and back to the life I had chosen. Satan would not have his way with me.

While the walk through dry and dusty underbrush on my way to the family burial plot was short, most of my steps were tentative. I had forgotten the sounds of the outback at night. The cry of birds I didn't recognize, the fear of stepping on something revolting, and the howl of an occasional wild animal made me almost turn around and run back to the house. But this might be the only chance I have to talk to my mother in the last setting where we had been together.

Eight generations of Hawkins were buried in the small cemetery that stood behind the outbuildings and next to a wood and stone tool shed. The eldest patriarch of the Hawkins' clan—that I had been made aware of—had been part of the penal system. According to family lore, he had been arrested in England for stealing bread, been branded a thief, and put on a prison boat bound for Australia, which at the time was a British colony.

He finished out his seven-year sentence, but instead of returning home, he married a local girl—the daughter of a friend he met during his incarceration—and together they homesteaded in the Outback, where land was plentiful, and they shared the same background as most of their neighbors. Three children were born to their union, but two of them died during childhood—a girl from measles and a boy who became lost in the brush. His body was never discovered, but that was to be expected. Wild animals would have made sure no remains were left. The only surviving son had both a son and a daughter. The boy stayed on the ranch, and the girl married a newspaperman in Perth.

No other stories had been handed down, although they should have been because my own Grandfather Hawkins had lived with us until his death. I couldn't remember much about him when it came to physical characteristics, but I could recall his presence. His voice was gruff and his shoulders hunched, and when he looked at me, I felt instant fear.

My mother said he was basically a generous, accepting man—much more so than his wife, who had died two days before I entered the world—but he had lost most of his hearing in a youthful accident and found it very difficult to be around other people. I wondered why I was thinking about him now.

I also wondered what other thoughts would emerge when I stepped onto hallowed ground. I had never been one to believe in ghosts, magic or superstition, but I did have a healthy respect for things I could not see or understand.

The moon was full, and its bright, orange glow made everything seem surreal as I pushed my way through overgrown bushes and almost fell when my foot got caught in a vine running along the dry path I was trying to follow. It looked as if no one had been anywhere near the cemetery since my mother's body had been laid to rest. The small picket gate creaked on rusty hinges when I forced it open, and then I was inside the small enclosure with the remains of numerous dead ancestors.

My throat tightened as I walked past headstones to the corner of the plot of ground where a huge Gum tree had stood for what must have been well over a century. My mother had been buried beneath its protective branches. I had always wanted to believe that it was the precise spot she would have chosen had she been alive to make that decision. But instead of the newly turned earth I remembered from her funeral, a tall, granite headstone with an angel on top had been set to mark her final resting place. Tears dimmed my vision even more than the darkness of the night as I shone the light closer to the words that had been engraved. "Annie Hawkins, Beloved Wife and Mother, Born April 24, 1968 - Died September 7, 2007."

Cold chills ran down my arms even though the night was warm as I sat down in front of the monument. I had prepared myself for an onslaught of emotions that would leave me lying prostrate on the earth with regret and sorrow, but that didn't happen. I simply sat erect, staring at it for the longest time without moving as a calmness washed over my soul, leaving me with the complete assurance that what had happened was simply part of God's plan, and I was exactly where I needed to be.

If my mother had lived, I would never have felt it necessary to walk away from everything I had ever known into an uncertain future where my very survival could not be guaranteed. But I had endured, and in the end, even thrived as Becky and then Ben brought the truth of the gospel of Jesus Christ into my life.

What a blessed miracle that had been! I now understand that life does not end with death, and I will see my mother again. What a glorious reunion that would be because I fully believed that she had both learned about and accepted the gospel just as I had. That confirmation had been invaluable to my healing process. Once I made my own covenants with God in his holy temple, I would do the same for her vicariously. Then I would start digging into family history. I had no doubt that she was spreading the good news beyond the veil to family members who had been denied access to that great blessing during mortality. Perhaps she had even made peace with her father, like I hoped to do with mine.

But working in the mortal sphere to set things right wasn't going to be easy. My family was steeped in mortal vices and incorrect traditions, and from what I had experienced during the short time I'd been home that wasn't likely to change. But maybe if I could put away all the anger and bitterness that still existed in my heart, I could help them see that change—hard as it might be—was worth the effort it took if it moved a person even one step closer to becoming the kind of person he or she really wanted to be.

And if the promise was true that each person who lived on the earth would have the chance to hear the true message of the Savior, then I had every reason to believe that my family would someday be reunited. If not in this life, then most certainly in the next. I couldn't bring myself to include Jake as part of that unit. He was the bane of my existence, but that would change the moment I was no longer on Hawkins' land. He would become just another unpleasant, distant memory I might even be able to laugh about once I was reunited with Ben.

Judging anyone simply because they did not see life the way I did was wrong. If Becky and Ben had done that with me, I would never have learned truths that gave me the strength to overcome my own bad habits and behaviors so I could be baptised. My family deserved the same chance I'd had. Perhaps part of my reason for coming home was to introduce them to what I had found. When I thought about life through the light of gospel principles, my mother's death had not been in vain. It had simply opened the door to a more fulfilling way of living.

"Oh, mother," I sighed as I sank back and pulled my knees up so I could rest my chin on them. "I love you so much, and life would be so much easier if you were here, but I'm not angry with God anymore because you had to leave. I've learned so much since then and hope it has made me a better person, even though I don't feel any too charitable right now."

I looked up into the sky. The moon was almost hidden by the gray, twisted branches of the Gum tree. I had been so frightened of the grotesque shapes it formed, even in the daylight, that I had cried when forced to go there on special days to leave flowers as a child. How silly that seemed now. The very tree I had so feared had outlived generations of Hawkins, its bark so hard and thick that it had even survived the fire that had burned the original homestead to the ground. Looking at those branches now, I was certain it would still be standing long after everyone I would ever know on earth was gone. That thought brought a measure of comfort. Even when I was no longer around, the mighty Gum tree would protect my mother through any storm.

My vision returned to the stone monument with the angel on top. Why did so many people believe angels had wings when they were really only people who had gone before, people just like my mother and me?

I switched the flashlight to the off position and tried to relax. I wanted to talk to her the way I would if we were standing face to face. While she might not be able to respond, I knew she could feel my pain and my desire to reconnect with her.

"When you first died," I began, looking around to make sure I was still alone. "I thought I would never get over the resentment and bitterness. I didn't know the real God then, so I cursed the vague and vengeful one you taught me about because I didn't understand that he was really loving and kind, and that whatever happened was all part of his plan.

You were my best friend, my only friend as a child, and the most beautiful, gracious woman in the world. I wanted to be just like you with your soft hands, gentle smile and the beautiful way you played the piano. It never dawned on me that I would lose you before I even grew up myself. I always thought I would come home after boarding school, marry some guy from a neighboring ranch and life would continue the way it always had.

"I can't begin to tell you how scared I was when I ran away from home, but I knew I couldn't stay here with father. He didn't want me around. He wouldn't even speak to me. He stayed locked up in his den with his bottle of whiskey and only came out for the funeral and wake. He had everything planned before Uncle Ned even brought me home.

"Most everyone who even talked to me at your service called it a real tragedy and claimed it was best that I had not been involved in the planning of your funeral and wake, but they were wrong. I should have been allowed to pick out your dress and decide what flowers you liked best, but I didn't even get to say goodbye. Father had already decided that your casket would be closed, and I didn't have the courage to fight him on it. How could he have done that to me? It wasn't fair, and it wasn't right."

I was so lost in remembered pain and injustice that I nearly screamed when an owl in the Gum tree above me hooted. I shone my light in its face and watched as its dark eyes gave me what could only be interpreted as a menacing, yet knowing, look. That moment of connection with one of God's creatures made me realise, yet again, how interconnected everything in the world really was.

But before speaking aloud again, I took the time necessary to quiet my racing heart and refocus on what needed to be said since this could well be the last time I set foot in the Hawkins' Family Cemetery.

"There is no justification for me running away, Mother. I just reacted without thinking. If my own father didn't want or need me, then I would simply go someplace where he would never have to bother with me again. It didn't much matter where I ended up as long as it wasn't here, so I bought a plane ticket and flew halfway around the world. It never dawned on me that something truly awful could happen to me because I had already gone through the worst nightmare imaginable by losing you.

"That first year was the hardest. After spending a few months feeling sorry for myself, I got a job waiting tables and found this awful apartment. I suppose I was mostly tired of sleeping in women's shelters at night and living like a person who had no self-respect during the day. But what really brought me around was knowing that existing as a homeless person was not the life you had envisioned for me, and it would only make you sad if you knew."

Suddenly, my lips closed in silence as I looked towards the stars that were twinkling in a cloudless sky. That life seemed so far away now that I was back in Australia, but talking to my mother where we had shared our life, was cathartic, so I continued my tale about life in the United States of America.

"One of the first girls I met at the Outback Restaurant where I worked was named Liza. She had received a full-ride scholarship to UCLA and told me I should apply for one too. I told her there was no way I could possibly go to school. I was having enough trouble just paying rent. But she didn't back down, and soon informed me that I was too smart to waste my life serving other people's food, and she would help me figure out a way to do it. I didn't see how that was possible since I wasn't a citizen and was still waiting for a work visa. My boss was paying me under the table and sending leftover food from the restaurant home with me so I wouldn't starve.

"But I truly believe you were watching over me because I was led to a program that allowed me to stay in the United States of America and get the education you always wanted for me. Words cannot express how grateful I am for that. I just wish you could have been there the day I graduated. I wore a bright yellow dress—just the color of the sunflowers you used to grow in the garden—and the locket you gave me when I went away to boarding school. You know the one I'm talking about with the pictures of you and me inside? I still wear it every day. It keeps the connection between us from becoming lost."

Without even thinking, I reached for my most valued keepsake and was surprised by the throbbing in my heart when I felt its cool, smooth surface. But the ache was immediately replaced with the sweet presence of my mother. I knew she was in the cemetery with me, and I could tell her everything that was in my heart—even the things I had not been able to share with Ben.

"I was always the good girl you wanted me to be, mother, but you never taught me about boys. You never told me the things I needed to watch out for, or that some of them should never be trusted."

I paused while the enormity of what I was about to vocalize washed over me. I had always been so careful around men, especially after listening to the stories my roommates at boarding school told about their nocturnal adventures with the guys they met on the beach. I had been sheltered at home, but it was even worse at school because the nuns were formidable, and I was afraid to break any of their rules. They were not opposed to corporeal punishment by withholding food or using a ruler across the fleshy part of my hands. And attending church services where the priest ranted on about hell, fire and damnation for those who did not attend confession and do as they were told filled me with such anxiety that I basically retreated into my studies, where I felt safe, if not a part of the human race.

"Once at the university," I began again. "I tried to live by those same guidelines, but I wasn't a kid any longer, and I wanted to be accepted and liked. So I started attending a few parties and drinking a few beers like everyone else was doing, and soon discovered that I wasn't the social misfit I had always thought myself to be. The guys seemed to like me when I paid attention to them. That was okay until the night a sort of boyfriend I had dated for a few weeks started to get more physical than I wanted. I was okay with hugging and kissing, but he suddenly grabbed me really tight and said he was tired of my games—that the innocent act had gone on long enough, and he wanted a return on his investment of time and money.

"I knew most of the girls at school were liberal when it came to sleeping with the guys they dated, but just the idea of casual sex made me nauseous. I wanted to be loved as a person, not used as an object for personal gratification. I thought he felt the same way because he had always been a gentleman, and his change in behavior frightened me. We were alone in his car, and he was much bigger and stronger than me. Still, I thought I could reason with him, so I told him that I didn't know what he was talking about and to let me go. That just made him laugh, and he started to rip my blouse open. I struggled so hard, but he put one hand over my mouth so I couldn't scream. I could barely breathe. The whole thing was over before I knew it, and then he just pushed me away."

My narrative ended so I could clear the lump that had formed in my throat. The residual effects of one man's need for power had destroyed a very sacred and tender part of me.

"I climbed out of the car, went up to my room and showered. I never told anybody what had happened for over two years. I was filled with shame for not being able to defend myself and knowing it would be his word against mine if I went to the authorities. It's not fair, but girls are always blamed when it comes to things like that. I got tested to make sure I was okay, but the horror of that night has never gone away. That scares me because I met Ben, and knew from the moment our eyes met that he was the man I wanted to marry . . . .

"I hope you can understand what I'm talking about from your vantage point in heaven because no one else knows about that part of my life but my bishop, not even Ben. I didn't want him looking at me with pity or giving him any reason to distrust me. Maybe that's wrong, but I love him with all my heart and want our wedding night to be wonderful. He thinks it will be the first time for both of us, but what if I can't respond the way I want to because of what happened? I can still recall the scent of my assailant's cologne."

I closed my eyes and let the stillness of the night wash over me. Now that I had shared my greatest burden with my mother, I felt a calmness that had not been there since her death. I wished I could stay where I was forever. But morning would come, and I still had a great deal more to discuss with my father.

"Oh, mother," I sighed, wishing I could forget about everything I had learned during the past few hours. But she needed to know how I felt about my father and the new family he had brought into her home. She could understand my reservations and anger because she had been part of it too.

"How I wish I had known the reason you died that awful night long before now. Father said he still feels tremendous guilt over what happened, but I suspect there was more to it than just a confrontation over his affair and the child it produced. I'm trying really hard to be open-minded, forgiving and kind because it's how I have been taught to live the past couple of years, but I can't seem to erase a lifetime of attitudes and beliefs. I know you weren't happy in your marriage, but I also know you would never have done what he did. Maybe someday I can learn to forgive how you died, but I'm not sure I can forgive him for bringing that woman into your home. She's sleeping in your bed, using all of your things, and I'm supposed to be okay with it. What makes it even worse is that he shows so openly how much he loves her. He holds her hand, kisses her and helps her around the house. He never did any of those things for you. And to add to my wrath, her horrible brother is living in the bunkhouse. He's done nothing but accuse me of terrible, hateful things."

Just thinking about Jake made my blood boil. He acted like he owned the ranch, and my father allowed him to say and do anything he desired. How could I be expected to forgive so many things? But when I left, I had to feel good about what had transpired while I was here, or I would never be able to marry Ben. He expected me to live what I now believed.

So, I took another deep breath, hoping my outrage over things I could not change would dissipate. It wasn't right that innocent people had to suffer for the actions of others, but no one had ever said life would be fair, only that it would be worth it one day.

"I'm not furious with Trevor," I continued. "None of this is his fault, and he accepted me as his sister from the moment we met. But I wish the rest of them would just leave and never come back. I know that's unreasonable because father loves them, and I won't be here much longer anyway, but it's how I feel. I wish you could tell me what to do. I've traveled too far and endured too much to leave things the way they are."

Quite suddenly, it seemed as if my mother was sitting beside me in the dark in one of the frilly dresses she liked to wear while playing old songs from her childhood on the piano. I would sit beside her, totally captivated by the soothing melody while her fingers danced over the ivory and black keys. But this time, she turned her head and rested her hand on my arm. Her eyes were clear and bright, and I could hear her voice in my head telling me to follow my heart and never forget that there were many people who loved me, not just on earth, but in the life I would one day advance to. The intensity of the experience made my heart burn; it was so vivid and soul-consuming.

"Mother, don't go," I cried out as the feeling of her presence vanished as quickly as it had come. "I'm getting married soon. Who's going to help me pick out my wedding dress or tell me how to take care of babies?"

But her essence was gone, and there was nothing I could do to bring it back. God had given me a moment of personal revelation so I could gather strength. Now, it was up to me to use what I had experienced to make my heart whole.

I smelled cigarette smoke before I saw or heard any movement. "Who's there?" I called out, wishing I had more than just a flashlight for protection.

"Just me," Jake said as he stepped out of the shadows. "You shouldn't be out this late, especially alone. You never know what might happen."

My chest filled with apprehension as I rose to my feet. How dare he invade my time with my mother?

"Is that a threat?" I asked as my eyes narrowed and my jaw clenched.

"Just an observation. It might be the 21st century, but there are still plenty of wild animals in the outback, among other things."

"I'm well aware of that. I lived here for many years," I retorted, wondering just how much of the conversation with my mother he'd overheard. "How long have you been standing there?"

"Long enough to know that you don't care much for my sister and me. I suppose that's to be expected after the way you came back and what you learned."

"You're insufferable, and I need to get back to the house."

"Then I'll go with you," he said, grabbing my arm as I took a step away from him. "Wouldn't want Jack to think you had disappeared again without an advanced warning."

"What do you mean by that?" I snapped, managing to free myself from his grasp. "You don't know anything about me, and you're certainly not my family."

I started to hurry away, although I was well aware that any carelessness on my part could land me face-down in the dirt. It was dark and the ground was uneven and covered with vines and other hidden objects, but he fell into step beside me.

"I don't mean to pick at you all the time," he said, flicking the ashes from his cigarette onto the ground.

I looked up at him in amazement, regardless of the fact that it was too dark for him to see my face. Didn't he know how dangerous it was to smoke when everything was so dry? A single spark could ignite a raging fire that couldn't be stopped.

"But you're wrong about what makes up a family, Miss Hawkins," he continued. "You don't have to be related to someone by blood or marriage. Jack's about the best bloke I know—honest, generous and hardworking. So if you are wondering why I'm protective, it's because I care about your father, and I will not stand by and let some bloody slip of a girl hurt him, even if she is his daughter."

His blatant honesty and rather accurate observation about my feelings annoyed as much as it humbled me. I had learned about body language and being able to read people in a class at UCLA. It had been a useful tool when I met new people, but I hated it when anyone used the strategy on me. So I clenched my teeth to keep from saying something else he could use against me, but he must have taken my silence for complaisance.

"I'm not stupid, Brylee, and it doesn't take a genius to know you have an ulterior motive for being here. No one suddenly shows up after a five-year absence if they don't want something. You can act all innocent if you like, but I will stick to you like a leech if necessary. My sister and nephew have a right to be here, and I will not let you destroy what they have. So if you plan on causing any trouble, you might as well pack your bag and leave because I won't tolerate any interference. Is that clear?"

"Perfectly," I told him. "But why I'm here is none of your business."

"It is if it involves the people I care about."

"I happen to love my father very much."

"Then you have a mighty unusual way of showing it. Most people who love each other want to be together."

"You don't understand," I said, stopping in the light that came from the lone bulb on the front porch of the house. "I had my reasons for leaving."

"Sure, you did!" he countered. "You had been both judge and jury in deciding that your father had to be punished because he was drinking the night your mother died."

"Well, he was!"

"Maybe, but you don't know the whole story. If you did, you wouldn't have run away from home like a spoiled brat, letting your father worry for years because he didn't know if you were dead or alive."

He turned around to leave, but I wasn't going to let him go without an explanation. If there was more I needed to know about that fateful night when my mother learned about my father's affair and having another child with the woman involved, Jake was going to tell me.

"What makes you think I don't know the whole story?" I demanded, grabbing the sleeve of his shirt. He tore it away with such rapidity and fury that it reminded me of the night I had been accosted. I couldn't say the word raped. It made me feel like a victim who needed to be protected, and I had chosen to be strong enough not to fall apart.

"Don't ever grab me like that again, or you'll wish you hadn't."

"Is that another threat?" I managed to ask even though my entire body was shaking.

"No. It's a bloody promise! Nobody grabs my arm in anger, especially a woman."

"Why? Because you're such a powerful man who knows everything?"

I hated him as much as I hated the man who had stolen my innocence. He was rude and arrogant and powerful and angry.

He made a fist with his hand, and I recoiled in sudden alarm.

"I'm not going to hit you," he mocked. "I'm just telling you that you have to be more careful around people you don't know all that much about. Another bloke might not have as much self-restraint as I do."

My chest was heaving with both fear and anger. I wanted to hit him hard. If he knew something about the night my mother died . . . .

"I'm not scared of you," I said, refusing to let him know how much his very demeanor frightened me. "And I will find out what you're not telling me. You see, I love my family too, and I won't allow anyone to take advantage of them either."

"You have passion," he said. "I like that in a woman, but I have nothing to gain or lose by giving you certain information. It might even make things worse for you."

"That should give you a great deal of pleasure since you would like to crush me like a poisonous spider anyway."

He took a step away from me, and I let out an audible sigh of relief.

"You intrigue me, that's all," he said with a snort of laughter. "If you want to know what happened that night, ask your father. He was there. I wasn't."

"He already told me what happened. They were on their way home from town. He'd been drinking, they got into a fight because my mother found out about his affair with your sister, and the fact that they had a child together. The rest is pretty self-explanatory. He lost control of the jeep, they crashed and my mother died. What else is there to know?"

He threw his cigarette butt on the ground and rubbed it out with the toe of his boot.

"Oh, there's more to it than that," he said. "The accident wasn't your father's fault. It was your mother's."

"You're lying," I shot back at him as my eyes flashed with fury. No one spoke about my mother like that. No one!

"I'm not lying. I said you wouldn't like it, but it's still true."

"It's not true! My mother was an innocent victim. You said it yourself. You weren't even there."

"And you think your father and I have never talked during the two years I've been working for him? We've spent a lot of time together and certain topics tend to come up."

"You expect me to believe that my father wasn't at fault simply because he told you he wasn't? How convenient for all of you!"

"Aren't you acting just a little self-righteous, Miss Hawkins?" he replied. "You're not the only person in the world who's suffered great loss. Your father has spent the last five years reliving that night in vivid detail. Just ask LeAnn if you don't believe me. She's spent plenty of time holding him in her arms after he's had one of his nightmares.

And to top that off, he's had the guilt of believing he drove his own daughter away. I think he's already paid a pretty big price for his sins. Don't you?"

I tried to ignore what he was saying. One had to feel remorse over the bad things they had done for the right reasons. Otherwise, true repentance and forgiveness weren't possible. Besides, I had no reason to believe anything he said. He wanted me gone, and I was certain he would do or say anything necessary to make sure it happened, and soon.

"You still haven't told me what you claim happened that night. I think that's rather cowardly since you're the one who brought it up."

"Don't you hear yourself?" he said, shaking his head. "It's all about you and the pain you've had to endure. To hell with how much everyone else is hurting."

"That's not fair," I shot back at him. "I was a child who had lost her mother."

"You were nearly eighteen. And please correct me if I'm wrong, but you had already been away at boarding school for four years. It's not like you were a bloody little girl who relied on her mum for everything."

"But she shouldn't have died because of someone else's mistake."

"I agree! It was an awful accident, and it never would have happened if she hadn't grabbed the steering wheel while they were driving so she could have his complete attention. Your mum had her own passionate streak. That's why they crashed. Drinking had very little to do with it. Your father can hold his liquor."

"No," I said, as uncontrollable tears racked my weary body. "She wouldn't do that."

"How do we know what anyone would do when they're hurt and angry? I have no reason not to believe your father. What would be his motivation for lying to me?"

"To make him feel better!" I countered. "To make all of you feel better for the part you played in such a great deception."

"You still don't get it, do you? Your father was an excellent driver even when he'd been drinking. He would never have run into that pack of dingoes if something hadn't distracted him. Your mother grabbing the steering wheel at the wrong moment makes perfect sense."

"If that was true, why didn't he tell me? He barely looked at me when I came home for her funeral."

"He was going through his own bloody hell and knew how much you adored your mum. He didn't want to take that image away by telling you what really happened that night. In spite of what you may think, your father loves you very much."

"But I would have understood."

"If you think that, you don't know your father, or yourself, very well. He's the one who cheated on his wife. Your mother was hurt, angry, slightly tipsy and wanted to talk things out on the way home from the party where she had overheard some very damning information. Your father wanted to wait until morning. I'm sure neither of them was thinking clearly, or they would have pulled to the side of the road to settle things. It was just miserable luck for things to happen the way they did. Your father tried to keep the vehicle from overturning, but it was impossible."

I felt lightheaded and might have slumped to the ground if Jake hadn't caught my arm and eased me onto the bottom step leading up to the veranda. The way Jake told it, my father had been preserving my mother's good name by taking the blame for the accident that ended her life. If that was true, I had wronged him terribly by running away. But since no one had bothered to tell me the truth, I couldn't be blamed for reacting badly so badly.

"You're not saying anything," Jake's voice broke into my unsettling thoughts.

I pressed my forehead into the palms of my hands. "I guess I have nothing left to say. If what you've told me is true, I have a whole lot of thinking to do."

"It's true, all right. But if it helps, your father took full blame because, despite his weaknesses, he's an honorable man who loves his daughter. I just thought you ought to know."

I didn't even try to stand for the longest time after he'd gone. I'm not sure my legs would have supported the weight of my body if I had. Why hadn't my father been honest with me instead of hiding his grief and guilt in a bottle? I might have hated him, but I would never have run away.

Chapter 8

Father, LeAnn, Trevor, and Jake were gone before I even awakened the next morning. It had been a rough night with little sleep, and the note taped to the refrigerator letting me know everyone had gone to check on a herd of sheep and wouldn't be back until late afternoon left me feeling both sad and alone. But it was the postscript telling me to enjoy the day that brought unwanted tears. They knew I had only come for a short visit, but instead of including me in their plans— even if it meant waking me up—I had been left to amuse myself in a house that no longer felt like home.

I sat down at the kitchen table and put my head in my hands as tears slipped from my eyes and landed with a small splash on the clean, shiny surface. What was I supposed to do for the next eight or more hours? I could only spend so much time talking to Trevor's animals, walking around the old homestead or even attempting to saddle and ride one of the horses. Besides, the weather was unbearably hot, and I didn't feel like taking a second shower. But there was even less to do inside. Entering rooms where the doors had been closed was an invasion of privacy, and the attic likely hadn't been cleaned for years. It was simply a place where useless things with sentimental value were stored.

I could always drive over to Uncle Ned's. But there were too many conflicting emotions bouncing around in my head to make that advisable. I was better off nursing my feelings alone and deciding how I was going to approach my father regarding the statements Jake had made the night before, blaming my mother for the accident that had taken her away from me. I could even take a nap if I got too anxious or bored. The outback simply wasn't a place for strangers, and that was all I would ever be now.

LeAnn had left a loaf of homemade bread on the counter, so I cut a couple of slices and put them in the toaster. If I were going to be staying longer, I might ask her to give me a few lessons on bread baking. Ben would love it, and it would make his grandmother happy because she valued homemaking skills above any other womanly pursuit.

But that was not part of my plan. In less than ten days, I would be on my way back to the States. This was merely a necessary interlude to make peace with my past so I could have the beautiful future Ben had promised.

I spent a good portion of the day talking to Newton and wondering if I should attempt to fix him a bottle of formula. He seemed incredibly hungry, and his tongue kept trying to latch onto my hand every time I attempted to pet his head without being covered with slobber. But I knew Trevor had already given him his morning feeding, and didn't want to upset his schedule. A day in the outback always started before dawn and ended by dusk, and every minute of daylight was accounted for. There were just too many dangers lurking in the dark.

That's why guns and ammo were scattered around the compound, and why my mother had rarely allowed me outside without supervision. Keida had been responsible for my safety when I wasn't sitting by my mother's side and being tutored in reading, writing, math, history or proper deportment for a cultured lady. Poor Keida must have been lost after my mother's passing, and I hadn't even bothered to ask where she was now. Father had engaged her services right after I was born, and she had been a permanent fixture for the next eighteen years. Had father dismissed her after my disappearance, or had she left on her own because she couldn't bear being in the house without my mother? That was something I might never know.

With nothing more productive to do since LeAnn had left meat and vegetables simmering in a crockpot for our evening meal, I made my way up two flights of stairs and entered the attic. It was likely the only place that hadn't been disrupted by my father's new family. I wished I could stop thinking about them like that, but I wouldn't be around long enough to feel like I belonged. Perhaps I could find some memento of my mother to take home with me. All I had to remember her by was the locket I wore around my neck. I had been to overcome with grief at her passing to even consider the fact that I might need something more than that to help lessen some of my grief.

Fortunately, the door with squeaky, rusted hinges had not been locked and gave way after a gentle push inward. I coughed as the intake of stale, dusty air hit my lungs. I shouldn't feel guilty about looking around, but I did. This room had never been off-limits to me as a child. I had been allowed to play there without supervision as often as time away from studies permitted. Sometimes my mother would join me and relate stories from her childhood. Most of them were sad, and I would snuggle down next to her on the old horsehair sofa to offer what comfort my childish presence could.

Nothing had changed about the room since my last visit, but I couldn't bear to open the trunk where I knew most of her older clothing had been stored. She had let me use them for dressing up as I played with the dolls and tea set I had received on my fourth Christmas. I remembered it as being a happy time, but then children seldom see what is going on around them. They are much to self-absorbed.

Still, I had once asked where the toys from her childhood were, but she had brushed my question aside by saying it didn't matter because she was an adult now and just wanted her little girl to be happy. After what father had told me the night before, she must have left everything behind when marrying him and had never been allowed to retrieve any of the things she may have loved as a child.

More tears slipped silently down my cheeks. How could a man be so insensitive and cruel as to turn away his own child and grandchild? I could not understand that depth of hatred, and yet I was harboring my own anger and it was eating away at my soul. But that's why I had come home. Tomorrow was Sunday, and I would drive into Edna to call Ben like promised. I might even attempt to find the building where a branch of the church held its meetings. It would be very small when compared to the ward in LA I was used to attending, but at least I could tell Ben that the closest town to my family's homestead wasn't as primitive as I remembered. That might help soften some of the other things I had to relate about my very unsettling visit.

I left the confines of the attic a few minutes later and returned to my room to read more of the book I had brought with me. I would come back when my mood was less melancholic. I needed an infusion of strength before my father returned and I was forced to be more accepting of the rest of his family. But they didn't come when expected. In fact, I had stirred the meal in the crock pot several times and finally turned the heat off so some of the moisture would still be there when it was eaten.

I even returned to the barn, fixed a bottle of the formula Trevor used as best I could and fed Newton. The measurement wasn't right, but I didn't want him getting sick. I cried again as he swallowed my offering with huge gulps that allowed much of the mixture to slide down his chin. He was more of an orphan than me, and his large, trusting eyes brought feelings of love and protection I had never felt before, along with another bout of resentment for never being allowed to experience such a tender moment until now.

The still and often oppressive darkness of the outback had settled in before I heard hoofbeats and the sound of voices outside. But instead of rushing out to greet them and inquire as to what had taken so long, I remained in the kitchen and made the final preparations so everyone could eat. I knew they would be ravishingly hungry after more than twelve hours on horseback, and hoped they had not run into any devastating problems.

But no one was in the mood to talk when they finally came inside, although Trevor thanked me for taking care of Newton and LeAnn apologized for leaving me alone for the entire day. Jake didn't look in my direction, and my father just kissed my cheek before retiring to the den for a stiff drink. His behavior brought an unwanted flashback to my childhood and how uninterested he had been in me then. Perhaps nothing had really changed, and he was tired of acting like he cared.

I hurried to my room after the table had been cleared and fell to my knees in prayer. If this was the way I was to be treated, perhaps I should do more than call Ben when I got to Edna.

But by morning, I knew I could not run away. I had yet to tell my father about Ben, our upcoming marriage, and the church I had joined. But before tackling those issues, I needed to hear my fiancé's voice and know that he still believed in us.

So I climbed out of bed and got myself ready in the only dress I had brought with me—a white sundress with navy embroidery on the bodice and skirt. I wore a short-sleeved navy t-shirt underneath. It was hard adjusting to the dress standards necessary for obtaining a temple recommend when I was used to wearing shorts and a tank top. And it was difficult giving away most of my wardrobe when there was little money to buy anything new, but it was worth any sacrifice because I was going to marry Ben.

My father and LeAnn were sitting at the table drinking their morning coffee when I walked into the kitchen. I hadn't had a chance to tell either of them what my plans were for the day and hoped they would not be too upset. But then Sunday had never been any different than the rest of the week, except for an occasional evening cookout with Uncle Ned's family.

"Good morning," I said, trying to keep my tone light.

LeAnn looked in my direction. "Don't you look nice."

"Thank you. I thought I would drive into Edna this morning, if it's okay with you."

"Why shouldn't it be?" my father asked as his eyes narrowed. "It's your vacation, but where are you going all dressed up?"

"I thought I might look around a little and attend a church service."

His snort of laughter didn't surprise me. "That would mean a lot to your mother. She didn't go often, but she still believed. I know Father Frederick would be thrilled to see you."

I swallowed back a fresh onslaught of fear. I couldn't avoid telling my father about joining the Church of Jesus Christ of Latter-day Saints forever, but perhaps I could avoid it until we were alone.

"How is he?" I asked.

"I haven't seen him myself since your mother's service, but I think LeAnn has. How is the padre doing, love?"

She looked over at my father and smiled, and then placed her hand over his.

"Your father likes everyone to think he's a non-believer, but I still have hope that one day we will get him to confession. It would be good for his soul."

"I didn't think it was my soul you were most interested in, love," he replied with a wicked glimmer in his eye.

I looked towards the window, not needing to be reminded that they were living in sin and obviously still enjoying it.

"You are a reprobate," she chided. "But do tell Father Frederick hello for us, Brylee. He will be happy to know that at least one member of the Hawkins' family hasn't forgotten about his blessed son."

"I will if I see him," I promised, sitting down at the table with them and clasping my hands together. Most outbackers might not be church-going folk, but they were definitely steeped in tradition.

"What's that supposed to mean?" Father asked. "Even I would have heard if the clergy had been changed."

I suddenly made the decision to go for broke. There was no better time than the present to begin my own story of hoped-for redemption. "I've joined a new faith, and it has made me very happy."

I heard LeAnn's intake of breath, but my father just stared at me.

"That's an announcement worthy of making the oldies roll over in their graves," he finally said. "While I've never had much use for religion as LeAnn just stated, every member of my family has been Catholic, and so has your mothers. But you're an adult, so I'm not going to make too much of it, as long as you haven't joined some cult with fanatical ideas that will only get you into trouble."

I suddenly felt sick inside. I knew how some people viewed what I believed. We were different. We believed in the sanctity of marriage and family and taking care of the physical body, but there was more to it than that. We believed in a living prophet, modern revelation, priesthood authority and conducting our lives as Christ had taught. I had been one of the skeptics myself until reading the Book of Mormon with an open mind and having everything fall into place.

"I've joined the Church of Jesus Christ of Latter-day Saints, Father, and it has made me incredibly happy. I've learned so much about living a good life and have made some amazing friends."

"Then I'm happy for you," he said. "Although I'm suspecting you should have been taken to mass more often when you were little."

"I learned all about Catholicism at boarding school. It couldn't answer any of the questions I had."

"And why not?" he asked as his eyes narrowed with what I knew was more regret than anger. "What the padre's teach comes directly from the Bible, and it's the oldest Christian religion on record. It dates back to the Apostle Peter, who actually walked with Christ himself. Maybe it's a good thing your mother isn't here to see this day. It would break her heart."

"But I haven't done anything wrong, Father," I told him through fresh tears that could easily cause my mascara to run. "And mother does understand, but if you would rather not have me around because I have broken away from centuries of religious conviction, I won't bother you any longer."

LeAnn put her hand on his arm. "Don't let this ruin your reunion, Jack. I'm sure if Brylee explains, you'll understand. You don't have that much time left."

"You're right," he said, patting her hand. "There's no reason to discuss religion since it's never held much weight in our lives before."

"Thank you, Father," I replied, unaware of the subtle change of tone in LeAnn's voice as she talked about the amount of time we had left.

"You should eat something before leaving the house," LeAnn said, rising for her place at the table. "It's a long drive to Edna, and it isn't healthy to skip breakfast. At least have some toast and coffee."

"Maybe some juice and toast," I responded, moving across the worn linoleum floor to the cupboard with her. How could I possibly tell them about the Word of Wisdom when they already thought I had lost my mind by not drinking alcohol and joining a church they knew nothing about?

She caught my arm as I reached for a glass. "Just get the juice. I'll butter some toast while you visit with your father."

I didn't argue, but he was still frowning when I returned to the table. "I hope my going to Edna isn't upsetting any of your plans, but I promised to call Ben and don't want him to worry."

"That must be the young man who gave you the huge chunk of rock on your finger. I should have asked about him earlier. This Ben must come from an influential family."

I knew he was thinking about what affluence had done to my mother, but things weren't like that between Ben and me. He didn't care that I came with no dowry. He loved me for who I was, not what money I could bring to our marriage. We would build that foundation of security together.

"Ben is the most wonderful man I have ever met, and his family treats me with both love and respect."

"Then why didn't you bring him with you? A father has a right to sit down with the bloke his daughter is going to marry and set a few ground rules."

His assumption made me smile. "It was a little too soon for that."

"I suppose," my father relented before taking another sip of his coffee. "I told Trevor we'd go riding before it gets too hot. That boy was a born horseman. You're more than welcome to change your mind and come with us."

"Thank you. Maybe tomorrow," I told him, while wondering why anyone would want to get back in the saddle after the long hours of yesterday.

But before I had time to finish my juice and toast, Trevor came running into the kitchen, the screen door slamming shut as he did so. "Father, let's go! Jake and I have the horses saddled. I wish you were coming with us, Brylee, but Father said to let you and Mum have the day to get to know each other better."

"I'll come another time," I replied as the heaviness inside sank to an even deeper level. Why was no one in this supposed family able to make plans without discussing them with all the people involved first? I had no desire to spend any time alone with the woman who was now in charge of my mother's home.

"I'm on my way," our father said with a short laugh as he got up from the table and took his coffee cup to the sink. "Give your mum a hand, son. We don't want to leave her with too much work. Remember, we share everything around here."

"Help is always appreciated," LeAnn said as Trevor carried a plate with a piece of half-eaten toast on it to the sink. "You're going to make some lucky woman a wonderful husband some day."

Trevor laughed as she tussled his hair. "You always say that, mum."

"I say it because it's true! Women like men who help out. Don't they, Brylee?"

I appreciated her resilience to an awkward change in plans and decided to be equally as gracious in my response. "Truer words were never spoken. Housework is no longer only women's work."

"Does that mean women have to work outside more?" Trevor asked.

"Only if they want to," our father responded. "But let's not bother your sister with nonsense. Brylee has a long drive to make.

Trevor looked at me with a furrowed brow that I now believed must be a Hawkins' trait. "Where are you going? I thought you were spending the day with mum."

"Your sister should see a few sights away from the ranch while she's here," LeAnn interjected before I could respond. "Now, get on your way. I've got lots to do and don't need men under my feet getting in the way."

"Be safe," Father told me, kissing the top of my head. It almost made me feel like his child again. "I guess we'll see you back here later on."

"I won't be late," I promised, and then watched as he picked up his hat and gloves and followed Trevor, making sure the screen door leading to the back of the house didn't slam shut.

"I'm sorry things got out of hand," LeAnn said when they were gone. "We're not used to having company."

"I don't have to go into town."

"That's not a problem," she replied with a wave of her hand. "We'll have plenty of time to visit, and you need to take care of what really brought you here."

Her words had a double-edged meaning, but I was too emotionally drained to realize it at the time. Perhaps she simply believed what her brother did. "Is there anything you need me to pick up while I'm there?"

"Not that I can think of. We're pretty self-sufficient and generally only shop once a month. It works better for us that way."

I left the house a few minutes later. My heart was tangled in knots of doubt and confusion, and all I wanted to do was cry. I hadn't handled anything right since my return. Jake hated me. LeAnn tolerated me. My father was disappointed in me. The only relationship I hadn't ruined yet was with my little half-brother, and he was much too young to understand the dynamics of what was going on.

As one mile followed another, I fought the desire to drive straight through to Sydney and change my flight home. I had everything I needed in my purse, and the few articles of clothing at the ranch didn't matter that much. If I left right now, I would be back in Ben's arms by tomorrow night, and we could start planning our wedding.

But could I really run away a second time and live with myself? Coming home hadn't solved anything except for letting my father know that I was still alive. It had done little to heal the rift between us, and after telling him that my beliefs had changed, he acted like I had killed a member of the family. Religion was supposed to bring people closer to each other and the Savior, not drive them further apart.

It was 9:45 when I pulled into the parking lot in front of a very small building that served as a Latter-day Saint chapel. It looked like a refurbished storefront, while Father Frederick's huge, ornate Catholic Church was on the corner of First and Main. There was even a Buddhist Temple. But when I walked through the doors into the air-conditioned foyer, I felt like I had come home.

A man in a white shirt and conservative tie was standing inside, waiting to greet those who entered.

"Good morning," he said, extending his right hand in my direction and firmly shaking mine. "I'm Brother

Downing, Branch President. I don't believe I've seen you here before."

"I'm Brylee Hawkins, and I have only come for a short visit with my family."

"Are any of them members of our small branch?" he asked. "I've heard the name before but never seen it on any of my records."

"Hardly! They live 80 miles outside of town and don't have much interest in religion."

He laughed. "We get a lot of that here. People in the Outback are pretty committed to the old ways. They all claim to be Catholic, but Father Frederick says his congregation has shrunk so much that it needs to be put on life support. His members show up for baptisms and weddings, but that's about it. I think most religions suffer these days, but that doesn't stop us from worshiping the way we know we should."

"No, it doesn't," I replied, thinking back to my recent conversation with my father. "Would you have some time to talk after church? I'm at a crossroads and don't exactly know what to do."

"I'm sure that can be arranged. My wife knows better than to expect me home before late afternoon on the Sabbath."

I smiled my thanks. "Where should we meet?"

"Right here in the foyer would be fine. We can find an empty space then. I'm afraid I don't have an office. We're a very small congregation worshiping in a rented building."

"It's not the building that matters, and I really do appreciate your willingness to make time for me since I'm not exactly your responsibility. I know how busy Sundays can be."

"It is busy around here, especially if someone with a calling doesn't show up. You don't happen to play the keyboard or lead music, do you? Those are two very hard callings to fill."

"No, and I'm afraid I wouldn't be much help as a speaker or teacher. I've only been a member for six months."

"A real newbie, but you're definitely not in the minority here. Our branch is less than a year old. Before that, we had to drive all the way into Sydney for our meetings."

"Wow!" I said as the front door opened and a couple with a young child walked in. He turned his attention to them.

I found the ladies' restroom and shook my hair out after removing the clip that had kept it from becoming tangled on the drive. Just as I was about to leave, the woman who had arrived after I did joined me with her crying child. She looked about my age, so I smiled at her.

"How old is your little boy?" I asked.

"Not old enough for the nursery yet, I'm sorry to say. He's usually so good at church. I don't know what's gotten into him today. I'm Margaret Mitchell, not to be confused with the writer of *Gone With the Wind*. I barely made it through English lit. I'm not much of a reader."

"Neither am I, unless it's a good novel, or more recently, an assigned book for a class," I admitted. "I'm Brylee Hawkins."

"Nice to meet you, Brylee. You haven't been here before, have you? This is a very small branch so we pretty much know everyone. My husband works at the Postie. We're transplants from Sydney. I never thought I would be living on the edge of the Outback. Everything is so brown, unless one can afford to water every day."

I liked this young woman with the pleasant, open personality, warm brown eyes and cute little boy. "How long have you lived here?" I asked.

"One year next month. I told Errol I wanted to stay in Sydney, where we both have family and friends, but this is where his job took us. I'm still adjusting. What brings you here?"

"I came to see my father, Jack Hawkins. He lives even further from civilization than you do."

"I don't recognize the name, but I'm sure Errol does. Is he a member too? The missionaries really struggle finding people to teach or just fellowship."

She finished changing her son while I remained silent. Sending anyone to talk to my father about religion would be futile. Our morning conversation had taught me that.

"Why don't you sit with us, if you don't mind a noisy child?" she offered, seemingly not offended by the unwillingness to answer her question. "My husband will be taking care of the Sacrament, and then he has to speak. We all do double-duty in our small branch. I'm pretty sure they will ask you to speak next week, if you're going to be here."

"I don't know what I'll be doing. It will be my last Sunday before I head home."

"Where's that?" she asked.

"Los Angeles, California."

"You have come a long way to visit. Whatever took you there?"

It was a question I had anticipated, and my prepared answer would keep me from sharing details unless I really wanted to. "I was going to school on a scholarship that was too good to refuse."

"I thought about going to the university once, but not to make light of education, I think I ended up with an even sweeter deal," she responded. "Marriage and family has given me everything I ever wanted."

"I'm sure it will be that way for me, too."

"Oh, my gosh," she suddenly said as she picked up her son from the changing table. "I'm sorry I didn't notice your ring sooner. It's beautiful."

I held my hand up to the light that caught each facet of the biggest diamond in the setting. "You're the first one to say something positive about it since I got here."

"You mean your father hasn't been giving you tons of marital advice?"

"I guess there hasn't been time," I told her. "We've been pretty busy just getting to know each other again."

There were only fifteen people in the congregation, but the spirit was intense. I found myself listening to each song, prayer, talk and lesson with far more intent than I had ever done while sitting next to Ben. His presence still made my heart flutter and his touch still sent shivers up and down my spine. It was hard to concentrate on anything else when we were together.

I met Brother Downing after the new two-hour block, and he escorted me back to the small room we had used for Relief Society.

"Well," he said, after greeting me with another handshake. "How did you like our little branch? I'm sure it's not at all what you're used to."

"It was wonderful, though quite different from the big ward I attend back home."

"Like I said earlier, we're small in numbers right now, but have great hopes of becoming a ward one day. We have some fantastic missionaries in the area, but they need the members' help in finding contacts. I don't suppose you could help us with that?"

"I wish I could. In fact, that's one of the reasons I wanted to talk to you. I've been away from Australia and my family for a long time. I left after my mother was killed in an auto accident."

"I'm sorry," he said with genuine concern.

"Me too! My father was driving, and he had been drinking … I guess they both had. I was so angry with him for taking her away from me that I left without telling him where I was going. There had been no contact until I came home a few days ago."

"That must have been a bittersweet homecoming. What made you decide to come back?"

"I joined the church, fell in love, and am now engaged to be married." I glanced down at the ring on my finger again. It gave me the assurance that the future would be much more pleasant than the present or the past. "My fiancé wanted me to make peace with my father before we made wedding plans."

"That makes sense, but I'm guessing it's not something you wanted to do."

"I didn't see what possible good could come from stirring up bad memories, but I wanted to make him happy."

"I take it he didn't come with you."

"He said it was something I needed to do on my own, and he was right. But neither of us had any idea what I would be walking into."

"So it wasn't what you expected?"

My lips pursed as I thought about LeAnn, Trevor and Jake. "I guess you could say that. He's replaced me with an entirely new family, and it hurts."

"I can only imagine, but still, he must have been delighted to see you again."

"I'm not sure that's the word to describe what he's feeling. We're both trying, but so much has changed."

"Why don't you tell me about it. Maybe, together, we can figure things out."

My recitation of finding LeAnn, Jake and my half-brother, Trevor, at the home of my youth was interrupted by giant sobs and tears. I was no less emotional when I told him about the suspicions Jake harbored about my reason for coming, and the confrontation I'd had with my father that morning about joining the church.

I explained how Trevor was being prepared to take over the ranch when he was old enough—something that had never been offered to me. I told him about my complicated childhood, being sent away to boarding school when I didn't want to go, and the accident that had taken my mother's life and forced my decision to run away.

He listened intently and made appropriate comments when necessary, but he mostly allowed me to talk until my tale of lost hopes and dreams had ended.

"Sounds to me like you've had a rough few days, but you mentioned being engaged. That has to bring you a great deal of joy."

That comment dried up the tears in a hurry. "I'm sorry, Brother Downing, I didn't mean to burden you with all my troubles. I do have a great deal in my life to be thankful for."

"I'm not worried about that, Brylee. I have very broad shoulders. How does your father feel about your engagement?"

"Hard to tell. He didn't even mention my ring until this morning, and then his only concern was with the size of the diamond and my fiancé coming from a rather affluent family."

"Is that a problem he should be concerned about?"

"Never," I said with a shake of my head. "Ben's love is genuine. He knows my past and accepts me as the person I am now, not the one I used to be. And his parents treat me like a daughter. Things couldn't get any better when it comes to our relationship. It's what's going on with my father and his new family that has me so upset."

He leaned back in his chair. "It is a rather complicated story."

"And I reacted with the immaturity of youth after my mother's death. But I'm a grownup now and should be able to handle things better."

"It's always easy to look back on our lives and see where we could have made better choices, but we can't change the past. All we can do is live in the present and try to think through each decision made so we can build a better future."

"I'm not sure I can do that. My only desire right now is to drive to Sydney and fly home to Ben where I can feel safe again. I want to forget the past few days ever happened. All I've done since I got here is make matters worse for everyone."

"Aren't you being a little hard on yourself and maybe even a little unfair to your father? You've had a lot of new information to process. That's hard to do under the best of circumstances, but perhaps you need to look at things from their point of view. Imagine having to admit what you have done to someone you've already hurt. I'm sure they are trying to do their best, just as you are."

"But they don't want me around! I'm not anything like them and every time I open my mouth I say something wrong."

"That's to be expected since you're basically strangers. It's been my experience that most things in life work out the way they were meant to. I'm sure you had your own struggles when the gospel was first introduced to you."

"Most certainly! I thought my roommate was nuts because she went to church every Sunday and didn't do any of the things the rest of us did."

"Still, you came around. Perhaps you could try to approach this situation in a similar light."

"I can try," I responded, thinking back to all the patience Becky had shown for nearly a year before I warmed up to her and what she represented. She had left encouraging notes, brought me ice cream, took me to the beach, and invited me to visit her family without ever mentioning religion. Perhaps I was pushing too hard. Life hadn't been particularly fair to me, but I wasn't giving anyone at the ranch much of a chance.

Brother Downing must have noticed that I had run out of things to say because he asked me another question.

"What made you change your mind about joining the church after the way you had been raised, Brylee?"

My brow wrinkled in thought. "I'm not sure I ever thought about that. I just woke up one morning and decided I was tired of being angry all the time, but I have to admit that meeting Ben was a definite incentive to making a few changes. He baptized me."

"Just so you didn't join the church for him."

"I'm sure that knowing he cared about me was part of it, but I couldn't deny what I felt after reading the Book of Mormon and attending church a few times. I felt like I had come home, and knew I would be reunited with my mother some day."

"So family is important to you?"

"More than anything, but you're talking about my father, aren't you? He isn't even married to the woman he's living with."

"That can be easily remedied. Maybe they just need a reason to make it legal. Besides, you have a little brother now. How's that going to affect you once you've gone home? He's the one real innocent in all of this?"

"You don't mince words, do you?" I responded.

"It's my job to ask difficult questions, but I'm afraid I don't have many of the answers."

"Trevor's a great kid and accepts me for who I am. It's just hard knowing that my father cheated on my mother. I can't imagine the pain she must have felt when she grabbed that steering wheel, hoping he would talk to her about it."

"She understands now," he said. "Life seldom happens the way we plan, but there are some great experiences we would miss if everything worked out the way we wanted it to."

"I know!" I responded, wishing my voice didn't still hold a note of resentment. "If my mother hadn't died, I would never have heard about the gospel or met Ben."

"It's not just that," he responded. "This life was meant to be a challenge, and we're expected to walk by faith. We are also expected to love everyone, regardless of how they choose to live. That doesn't mean we have to change what we do, but it does mean that we have no right to judge."

"I just wanted to spend a few days with my father, apologize for what I had done, and go back to the life I've chosen."

"You're not a little girl anymore, Brylee, as you just said. You are an adult who's had some wonderful things come into her life despite tragedy. And while other people might not understand why you've made the choices you have, they can't take away what you believe unless you let them. Do you really want to be part of your father's family now, even if it isn't perfect?"

"I don't know. Everything is just so much simpler when I'm with Ben."

"Don't use that relationship as a crutch. Use it as an example when dealing with your father and your new family. Ben didn't give up on you just because you were different than the other girls he dated when you first met. He introduced you to concepts and ideas and let you decide for yourself. That's the only way genuine growth takes place. Force and coercion were Satan's plan."

"I know," I responded. "But I still wish I could go back and have a do-over with most of my life."

My confusion was genuine, but perhaps I just wanted to hear that it was okay to run back to Ben. I definitely didn't want to return to the ranch and have another confrontation with my father over things that could not be changed.

"We all wish that, Brylee, but trying to escape our past or present doesn't solve anything either. At some point, we have to do the work of finding lasting peace so we can carry it into the future."

"But Ben would never feel comfortable around my family! They drink and smoke, and swear and tell crude jokes and live with the mother of their children without getting married. The only thing they know how to do is survive in the Outback. Ben hasn't even been on a farm. His father's a doctor and his mother's a lawyer. They're busy people, yet, they still find time to attend their church meetings and raise a family of five children who are all active. They're centered! They're grounded! They know what they have to do to get back to Heavenly Father, and they are willing to do it."

"They sound like an ideal family."

"They're perfect, and they have accepted me even though I wasn't raised the right way."

"And you seriously think they would not understand about your own family? Some of the characteristics that make you so special to them came from your ancestors, and not your current environment."

"How could they? Sometimes I wonder if they would even want me around if they knew even a portion of how I lived before coming into their lives. I've made so many mistakes."

"We humans do have a tendency to bugger things up a bit, but you can't blame yourself for what you did before you were baptised. That's all been taken care of. Personally, I think any man would be lucky to have you. You're a survivor and will make it through whatever challenges come next."

"I wish I had your confidence in me. I feel like such a coward."

"We're all cowards at times, but you're also a young woman of great depth and understanding. I think you already know what you have to do before you go home, at least for starters. The old adage that Rome wasn't built in a day applies to more situations than you might think."

I thanked him for his kindness and wisdom. I couldn't desert my family again right now, even for the man I loved. They might not be ready to hear about the gospel yet, but I could show them by example that I was a new person because of it. I would go back to the ranch and be the best daughter and sister possible while I had the chance, and I would accept LeAnn and Jake as part of my family because that's what Christ would do. He hated sin, but always loved the sinner. I asked Brother Downing for a blessing before I left.

He promised me understanding and the ability to face whatever tests might come. He told me of the Saviour's love for my family, and that the greatest desires of my heart would be realised when the time was right. He also told me not to worry about things I could not change, but to trust in the Lord because he knew the end from the beginning. He didn't say that anything would be easy, only that I would be given the strength to endure whatever came. It was exactly what I needed.

Chapter 9

After leaving the small building that had been dedicated to God's work, I stopped at McDonald's, or Macca's as it was known in Australia, for a burger, fries and a chocolate shake. Then I took it to one Edna's small parks that was across the street from the local hospital and sat on a bench in the shade while I ate and thought. It was hot, and the few trees surrounding me did little to help, but it was better than having the sun's hot rays beating down on my shoulders, and I couldn't bring myself to eat inside with people who were laughing and talking. I needed to be alone while I decided how I was going to accomplish what I intended to do.

When my meal was finished, I called Ben. It was the middle of the night in Los Angeles, but he was expecting to hear from me, and I certainly needed to know that he still loved me even though we were half a world apart. I wasn't sure how to tell him about my father, LeAnn and Jake, but I wanted him to know I had a little brother.

"Hi, sleepy head," I said when he answered. "I've missed you."

"I've missed you, too," he responded, and I could envision his dancing eyes. "How's your trip going? Was it good to see your father again?"

"He's changed a lot, and it hasn't exactly been easy, but I am glad I came."

"That's my girl," he said. "I knew you could do it."

"I have a brother, Ben." I was testing the water to see how much I dared tell him.

"Really! He must be pretty little."

"He's seven."

"But you've only been gone five years..."

"I know," I replied before he could continue. "Trevor was born two years before I left home. My mother found out about him and his mother the night of the accident."

"Wow! That must have come as a real shock. I wish I was there to help you through this."

"Me too! There's been a lot to think about, but Trevor's a great kid. My father is busy preparing him to take over the ranch someday."

"Another surprise," he said. "It isn't every day a girl finds out she has a little brother who is going to be her father's heir. That must mean your father has remarried. Do you like his new wife?"

"LeAnn's fine. She's tried to make me feel at home, but Ben, she's not his wife."

"Really! So she and your father are just living together."

"It's not a big deal to them. Everyone down here lives that way."

"I'm sure it's not that bad. There have to be a few others who believe in the sanctity of marriage. I thought Catholics were big on stuff like that."

"They are, but not many around here seem to have any trouble fudging with certain rules or laws. My Uncle Ned and Aunt Nora haven't married either, and they have two children who are in college."

For some reason, it seemed easier to tell him about my family from a distance. Maybe that was because I couldn't see the shock or concern in his eyes.

"But not all of your family believes that way anymore," he said. "I'm so proud of you, Bry. You've been incredibly strong considering the environment you came from."

My heart sank at his words. How could I ever tell him I wasn't as strong as he thought? How I hadn't even been able to talk to my family about him and our plans for being married, or the fact that I had been assaulted on a date and never reported it because I was afraid? If we were going to spend eternity together, I should be able to tell him everything.

"They're not bad people," I said. "Although I'm fairly certain my father thinks I have joined a cult."

Ben laughed. "I used to hear that on my mission. I still don't understand how people can justify putting labels on things they know nothing about. Is your father giving you a hard time about it?"

"I think he's trying to tolerate the new me. He doesn't understand why I no longer drink, but he says he wants me to stay, and we don't have to talk about religion."

"That's good! How does he feel about us getting married?"

"We haven't talked much about that," I admitted with painful hesitation.

"Why not? Are you ashamed of me? Or maybe you're just having second thoughts now that you're with your own family again?"

"You're wrong on both counts," I said as my heart began to pound. "You're the best thing that's ever happened to me. I love you forever and always and can't wait to be your wife."

"Then why can't you talk about us? I have been telling strangers on the street that I am the luckiest guy in the world because I'm going to marry an angel."

The stress of the day must have taken its toll because I suddenly laughed. "I'm not an angel, Ben. I have plenty of faults."

"But you're perfect for me, and that's all that really matters."

My nose began to tickle and my eyes filled with tears. "Maybe I'm just scared to talk about us because he might want to come to the wedding, and he can't be with us for the sealing."

"There are ways around that, even if they're not what we really want."

"But I don't want to change any of the plans we've made, Ben. My father will It think I'm purposely excluding him from my life again."

"But this is different. You're not running away. You are simply marrying the man you love. He should respect your decision, even if he doesn't understand it."

"I know," I responded. "I'm probably overreacting, but you haven't met these people. They aren't like your family at all."

"I've met plenty of people like them. If your father loves you, he will understand."

I pulled my bottom lip into my mouth with my teeth. Ben only knew a good kind of love, not the corrosive kind I had grown up with.

"I'll talk to him as soon as the time is right," I promised.

"What if there isn't a right time? And what if your father won't accept it when you do tell him what you're going to do? Does that mean you'll walk away from me?"

"Never!" I said. I would do anything to keep my life with Ben.

"That's good because you had me a little worried. I don't like the idea of you being so far away."

"Just a little more than a week, and I'll be on my way home again."

"It can't be fast enough for me. Sometimes I wish I had never encouraged you to go."

I watched some ants on the table carry off some crumbs that had fallen from my burger. Oh, how I wanted to believe that we would be together for eternity, but I also wanted my father in my life. I didn't hate him anymore or hold him responsible for what had happened to my mother. He wasn't perfect by any means, but he was the man who had given me life, and he had kissed the top of my head that morning.

"I'm not, Ben. I needed to come for some closure, but I have been feeling lonely and out of place ever since I got here. Knowing you love me makes all the difference in the world, and I can't wait to come home."

"That's just what I wanted to hear because I'll be waiting at the airport with balloons, flowers and open arms."

My voice was cracking with emotion when I spoke. "I love you so much, Ben."

"Ditto," he responded. It was something we had learned from the classic movie *Ghost*. "And you be careful. I don't want anything bad happening to my future wife."

His future wife! I loved how it sounded and how it made me feel.

"I'll be careful," I promised. "And I will call you again next Sunday. I hate that there is no cell phone service at the ranch, but it's too far out for that. I didn't tell you that a branch really exists in Edna? There were only fifteen people there, but the spirit was amazing."

"I prayed you would have a good day. Did you meet some nice people?"

"Every one of them, including a girl named Margaret Mitchell—not to be confused with the author—and her cute little boy. I even had the branch president give me a blessing."

"That's what I love about the church. It doesn't matter where you are in the world, the minute you walk through the door into a chapel you feel right at home. You'll have to send the missionaries to your father."

I laughed at his suggestion. *Once a missionary, always a missionary*, or so the adage went. "That thought did cross my mind, but I have to take baby steps. I don't ever want him to think that I see myself as being better than him. We are all equal in God's eyes."

"Absolutely, but we still have the responsibility to share what we know with others. I should have sent a few missionary tracts with you. They could have been conveniently left around the house."

"And thrown into the incinerator as soon as they were found," I countered.

"What's an incinerator?" he asked.

I smiled because I finally knew something he didn't. "It's a 55-gallon barrel where the trash is burned. I wasn't kidding when I said that I lived in the sticks."

We talked for a few minutes longer, and then I knew it was time to say goodbye. He needed his rest, and I had a long drive back to my family's homestead.

I had just put my trash into the nearest receptacle when I noticed a green Land Rover that looked suspiciously like the one my father owned coming down the street. I wouldn't have given it a second thought since most everyone in the outback drove utility vehicles that could withstand the elements of the outback, but this one was being driven at a very reckless speed. A blonde woman was driving, and a child sat in the passenger seat.

A sick feeling in the pit of my stomach caused me to raise my hand and shout, but no one acknowledged my presence. By the time I made it to the edge of the road, the vehicle had made a sharp turn into the emergency portico at the hospital.

I ran numbly across the hot pavement, forgetting that I had arrived in town in the rental jeep. The sweat was pooling on my brow before I even made it inside. LeAnn and Trevor were standing by the admittance desk.

"What happened?" I almost shouted as I ran across the nearly vacant room to join them.

LeAnn turned to face me. There were tears in her eyes. "It's your father. He couldn't breathe. Jake flew him here two hours ago. There wasn't enough room in the plane for Trevor and me. We had to drive. The nurse went to check on him for us."

My little half-brother looked more than scared, so I put my arm around his shoulders. "It's going to be okay," I told him. "Father's strong, and he has good doctors, I'm sure."

I knew I couldn't realistically guarantee him either of those things. It was just what one said in emergency situations. Father didn't look strong, not like he had when I was growing up, but that might just be age. He was five years older, and while he was still tanned and active, he might have developed some health issues I wasn't aware of.

My greatest desire was to ply LeAnn with rapid-fire questions. She obviously knew a great deal more than I did, but I understood that she might not want Trevor to hear everything that might be said.

So, I opened my purse and produced a bill of currency. "Why don't you find all of us something to drink? It's hot outside and not much better in here." I ran the back of my hand across my forehead to help prove the point.

Trevor took the money with a listlessness I had not seen in him before. "What do you want?" he asked.

"Some Sprite or 7-Up," I told him. I had given up caffeinated soda when I joined the church.

"You know what I want," his mother responded.

Trevor obediently went in search of a soda machine. If I wanted to find out what was really going on I would have to talk fast. LeAnn was fidgeting and looked like she was about ready to burst into tears.

"What's wrong with my father? He hasn't looked well since I got here."

"I promised him I wouldn't say anything," she replied without looking at me. "He wanted your visit to be a pleasant one."

I didn't care about my visit now. It hadn't gone according to what I had envisioned anyway.

"Then he is sick! I may not have been a very good daughter the past few years, but he is my father, and I love him dearly despite our conflicts."

"He knows that, but you have been through enough. He doesn't want to burden you with anything more."

Just then, the double doors leading to the trauma center opened and a nurse joined us. "Are you Mrs. Hawkins?" she asked LeAnn.

"Not technically, but we've been together for fourteen years," LeAnn told her. "Please tell me what's going on."

LeAnn was so lost in the moment that she appeared to have forgotten my presence. But I was his daughter and could ask questions and get answers too.

"Mr. Hawkins is stable. He's on oxygen and is resting more comfortably than when he arrived."

"Can I see him?" LeAnn asked.

"I'm sure that can be arranged. Actually, he's been asking for you."

"Brylee," LeAnn turned to face me. "Will you watch Trevor? Just tell him his father is going to be fine."

She didn't give me time to protest. She was following the nurse before she finished speaking.

I walked to a window and looked out at a cloudless blue sky. Secrets! I hated them! After what I had learned about my mother's death, and what had led up to it, how could my father keep more of them from me? The tears came without warning. Why couldn't people just be honest with each other? But then, I had secrets too.

"I got them," Trevor said, interrupting my thoughts. "Where did mum go? I got her a Coke like she asked."

"She went in to be with Father."

He rolled the sodas onto the nearest sofa and handed me a fistful of change. "Is he okay? I was really scared."

"The nurse said he's resting comfortably."

"I hope so! I hate it when this happens."

"You mean this has happened before?" It appeared that even my little brother knew more about my father's condition than I did.

"Twice. Father starts coughing really hard and then he can't breathe. It's really scary."

"I'm sure it is," I told him, wishing he were old enough to tell me what I really needed to know. But I couldn't pry him with questions when he was already traumatized. "Why don't we sit down and get to know each other better? I would like to know all about my little brother."

Trevor chose a chair, opened a can of soda, and then frowned up at me. "Why didn't you come home before? Don't you like us?"

"I like you very much," I told him as the shock of his words hit home, but how could he think any differently when I had made no effort to contact anyone before now? "If I had known I had a little brother, I would have come a lot sooner. Now tell me, what do you like to do the most?"

"That's easy," he said with a smile that seemed to light up the room. "I like to be with Father and Uncle Jake on the ranch. But I especially like to go riding with them. You should have come with us today. It was so much fun until father couldn't breathe. I don't want him to die!"

"He's not going to die," I told the frightened little boy sitting in the chair next to me. "He's going to be just fine. He's a fighter, and he wants to be around to watch you grow up."

Trevor took a long drink of his soda and frowned again. I was soon to learn that children truly were without guile. They spoke exactly what was on their minds.

"Why didn't you visit with mum or come riding with us today?"

There it was, an honest question I didn't know how to answer. I had felt a twinge of guilt leaving the ranch to attend church that morning, but I had done it anyway because I didn't want to face any more accusations or conflicts. Now, I just felt horrid because something had happened to our father, and I might have been able to help. What if I never had another chance to talk to him, or to be part of the family he had offered me?

"I needed to go somewhere else today," I told him.

"Where?"

"I would like to hear the answer to that question myself," Jake said as he crossed the waiting room to join us in our chairs by the window.

"I didn't see you," I told him, wishing my hands had not begun to shake the moment I heard his voice. "How long have you been standing there listening?"

"I'm not in the habit of eavesdropping on other people's conversations, if that's what you're getting at," he said, giving me a sharp look. "But I know it would have meant a lot to your father if you had spent the day with your family. Sometimes you don't get a second chance."

My heart went cold with fear. "Has something happened I should know about?"

"Your father will be okay, this time. I was just making an observation." He turned his attention immediately away from me and to my little brother. "Hey, sport, how about handing me one of those sodas? It's been a long, dry day."

"Sure," Trevor said, giving him my Sprite.

Jake hesitated momentarily before accepting it. "You're certain it's okay with your sister. I don't want to take anything that belongs to someone else."

It was another dig at my reason for coming home, but I had the good sense to keep my thoughts to myself this time. It wouldn't hurt to drink a Coke one more time, if it came to that. What I didn't want was to get into another unpleasant confrontation with LeAnn's brother.

"No, help yourself," I told him. "We're almost family."

So there we sat. Three unlikely people forced to spend some time together with absolutely nothing to say. I couldn't ask Jake any of the questions that were flooding my mind with Trevor around, and he probably wouldn't answer them anyway. And how could I ask Trevor more about what he liked to do when it would only widen the gulf that already separated us, since I hadn't been around to find out for myself.

The sun was starting to set, Trevor was fighting to keep from falling asleep, and LeAnn had yet to emerge from behind the doors where my father had been taken. It had been a long day for all of us, and I had a feeling far more time would pass before I found out what was really going on with my father. Jake had gone outside to smoke his second cigarette. It was a filthy habit, and I was glad laws had been passed that banned smoking in public places like hospitals, stores and restaurants. Boozers, or pubs, were the exception, and there was one of those establishments on nearly every street corner in Edna. If there was anything Aussies loved more than having fun, it was smoking cigarettes and drinking their favorite grog. I was so glad I was no longer a part of that life.

"We really should get Trevor something to eat and home to bed," I told Jake when he had put his cigarette out and come back inside. It was useless asking him to be civil.

He had already made it perfectly clear that he detested me and wasn't going to extend any curtsies unless he was forced to.

I just wished LeAnn would come back. Something had to be seriously wrong, or she would not have left her son in a hospital waiting room for nearly two hours. I was trying not to jump to any fanciful conclusions, but it was becoming harder the longer I was forced to wait.

"I'll take him home in the plane," Jake unexpectedly volunteered. "I know you'll want to stay here until you can see your father. Do you want me to get you something to eat before we head out? I can feed Trevor when we get home."

His thoughtfulness almost made me forget that we were still adversaries. Maybe there was more to him than I had originally thought, or maybe he was just being kind because he already knew what was wrong with my father.

"I'll be fine," I told him, not wanting to be beholding to him in any way. "Trevor said there was a vending machine with sandwiches and stuff by the Coke machine."

"Suit yourself! Anything that has been sitting around for days in some cooler can't be worth the trouble it takes to eat it."

I knew I had offended him, but he was an enigma I didn't exactly want to understand. Most of the time, he was nothing short of boorish.

"Thank you for your thoughtfulness, Jake, but I'm not really hungry. I had a big lunch just a few hours ago. I'll grab something when I get back to the ranch if I need it."

I had wanted to say "home" like he had done when mentioning that he would feed Trevor, but it didn't feel like home anymore, at least not to me.

"Whatever floats your boat," he said, dismissing me with a shake of his head. "Well, sport, let's head out. I'm not sure what your mum has in the house to eat, but we bachelors can do just fine without womenfolk ear-bashing us all the time. Isn't that right?"

"I wish Brylee was coming with us," Trevor surprised me by saying.

I thanked him in my heart. It was nice to know that at least one person didn't hate the fact that I had come back unexpectedly and disrupted their lives.

"There's only room for two in the plane," Jake told him. "Your sister's a big girl and can take care of herself. Besides, she has a rental. She doesn't need us to get her where she needs to go."

I hated his barbs but decided not to engage in front of my little brother. I was much too worried about our father anyway.

Then Trevor did a very unusual thing for an Aussie. He ran up to me and gave me a hug and a kiss. "I'm glad you're here, Brylee. Will you come and see me before I fall asleep?"

I smiled through the tears of fear and uncertainty that were beginning to cover my eyes, but I wasn't going to let anyone see me cry.

"I promise to check in with you when I get back," I told him as I returned his hug. "But don't wait up if you want to sleep. It could be quite late by the time I get there."

Chapter 10

They had been gone less than ten minutes when LeAnn came back into the waiting room. Her red and swollen eyes told me that she hadn't quit crying. My father must be far worse than I had imagined, and I steeled myself for the worst.

"Where are Trevor and Jake?" she asked.

"Jake flew him home. He wanted to fix something for them to eat and get Trevor to bed. He was having trouble staying awake."

"I'm glad! Trevor shouldn't have to deal with all this grown-up stuff. He's just a little boy who deserves to be a child a little longer."

I put my hand on her arm. She was almost as thin as my father. "Trevor's resilient, and he knows how much his family loves him."

"But it's still not fair! A father should be able to see his son grow up."

I felt all the blood rush to my head and my vision started to blur. I had considered many things, but nothing final like what had happened with my mother.

"Are you telling me my father's dead?" I fiercely whispered. Life simply couldn't be that unfair. I had just returned home, and nothing had been settled.

"Not yet, but he doesn't have much time left."

"What's wrong with him?" I asked in little more than a breathy whisper as the room started to spin. I was tired of being left in the dark, but the woman standing in front of me was distraught. If I had ever doubted her love for my father, I didn't any longer. "I think I have a right to know. After all, I am his daughter."

"You misunderstand, Brylee," she said, fixing me with a look that was more than disconcerting. "We're not intentionally trying to keep things from you. We're glad you're here, but it's put us in an impossible situation. So many things have happened since you left, and we had no idea if you would ever return. We had to put you out of our lives. It was the only way your father could go on living. The guilt was destroying him."

"Are you saying it's my fault he's dying?"

"Most certainly not!" she responded. "It was going to happen eventually anyway, but I think he might have been well a few years longer if he hadn't blamed himself for everything that happened to both you and your mother."

"What's wrong with him? Heart? Cancer? Stroke?"

"He wants to tell you himself. I'll be waiting here when you've finished talking. He's in room 134, straight down the hall on the left."

"Thank you," I said, grabbing my purse from the end table. I didn't know what I was thanking her for, but apparently, she was the one in control right now, and I was grateful to be seeing my father alone.

I said a short prayer before pushing the door to his room open. It was now dark outside, and with the dusk came the terror of the unknown I had felt as a child in a land as old as time. My father was wearing a white hospital gown with tiny blue flowers on it. I wondered how they had been able to convince him to put it on. He was one of the most masculine men I had ever known. They had him lying in a white metal bed, and he was hooked up to oxygen, a heart monitor and an IV.

"Father," I whispered so I wouldn't wake him if he happened to be sleeping.

He opened his eyes and forced a tired smile. He looked so frail and spent all I wanted to do was cry, but I bit my bottom lip and crossed the room to his side.

"Brylee!" he said. "I'm sorry your homecoming hasn't been more pleasant. I didn't plan for this to happen."

I sat down on the chair near his bed. "You don't have to talk, Father."

He tried to force himself upright, but the effort was too great, so I leaned forward until I was holding his hand.

"Don't try to move. I just want to sit with you."

Tears were forming in my eyes, and the lump in my throat was threatening to choke me. I didn't know what he was going to tell me, but he needed to know how much I loved him and how sorry I was for pushing him out of my life. I would never forgive myself for that, and for what it was costing both of us now.

"You've turned into a lovely young woman, and I'm sorry I was so hard on you this morning."

"It's forgotten," I told him. "All that matters is for you to get well."

"That's not going to happen!"

"You don't know that!" I said. "We can bring in specialists from Sydney. These small-town doctors don't know everything."

"I've been to specialists in Sydney, and they all say the same thing. I am in the final stages of lung cancer, and I'm not going to get better."

"Cancer!" Just the sound of the word made gooseflesh of my arms and legs. Cancer was a death sentence unless it was treated early. Heavenly Father simply had to make him well. I could deal with LeAnn and everyone else as long as I still had him in my life. But without him, I wasn't sure I had the strength or the courage to even return to the ranch. "But you could quit smoking, and your lungs start repairing as soon as you do. I've read studies on it."

"So have I, but I waited too long. I knew something was wrong three years ago when the symptoms started, but I guess old habits really do die hard. It seemed rather silly to try to stop smoking when it was too late anyway."

"But maybe it would give you more time. I don't want to lose you! I just came back." I squeezed his hand—the one without the IV in the vein—as if by so doing I could transfer some of my strength to him.

"We have to face facts, Brylee. What happened today will keep happening until I'm gone. It's not a very pleasant way to go."

"You could stay here, where they can take care of you. I'll help out with things on the ranch. You won't have to worry about anything."

His voice became momentarily strong.

"I don't want to die in a hospital. I want to be home with my family, doing what I love, for as long as I possibly can. You need to understand that this is my decision to make. LeAnn has made peace with it. You will have to do the same for the short amount of time you're still with us."

I bit my bottom lip to keep from crying out. My father was dying, and he thought I was going to return home as originally planned. What kind of a daughter did he think I was? We had never been close, but we were trying to repair that. I had only run away because I was young, angry and frightened. He said he understood that. Maybe he felt I simply did not have the right to make any promises or demands.

"I wish I could change the past, but I know I can't," I sobbed out. "I just want to stay here with you for as long as possible? Am I being totally selfish for wanting that?"

It was his turn to put pressure on my hand. "I understand that this has been another shock, and it is one I had hoped to spare you after what happened with your mother. Losing the people you love is one of the biggest challenges of living, but it happens to everyone eventually. You can't be sorry for me. I have lived a full and rich life. The work I did brought great satisfaction, and the people I loved brought great joy. I've had experiences I never dreamed possible, and I got to see you again. I don't have any regrets, except for hurting your mother and you. Regardless of what happened with LeAnn, I did love Annie, and you will always be my little girl."

"That's all in the past," I assured him, as tears slid silently down my cheeks. "I understand so much more than I did when I came home, and I don't hate you anymore. I love you so much. I always did. I just didn't know how to be your daughter, or how to deal with Mother's death."

"And I didn't help anything by shielding you from the truth. You deserved to know exactly what happened that night and why. I really am glad Jake told you."

So Jake had been telling the truth. My mother had been at least partially responsible for what happened, but I could never be angry with her for reacting to what she had found out. Perhaps their marriage had not been the happiest, but she had the right to be honored and cherished for her role as a wife and a mother. Maybe it had been best learning the truth from Jake first. The initial shock of his revelation was wearing off, and I was able to think more clearly now.

"Me too!" I managed to say. "I just wish I had known before. I understand that you were only trying to protect me and didn't want me to think any less of my mother, but things might have turned out so much differently if I had known."

"Perhaps, but that is something we will never know. I think I was too ashamed of what I had done to admit it back then. I didn't want to see the disappointment and pain in your eyes. I saw enough of that when your mother found out."

"She had a right to be hurt."

"Yes, she did. And you had every right to leave. You think you didn't know how to be a daughter. Well, I didn't know how to be a father either."

"That's only because Mother and I were so close. We did everything together."

"And I never said anything to change it. I had no idea what to do with a little girl. It would have been so much easier if you had been a boy. I could have been tough with you because it was expected."

"That's why you and Trevor are so close. He is the son you always wanted."

"I won't pretend that I don't love my son. He's an amazing boy, but there's enough love in this old heart of mine for both of you, and always has been."

I leaned back in my chair. How could I be upset with him for loving the family he had now? They were everything my mother and me had never been. They gave him a reason for getting up in the morning, a reason to keep on fighting the cancer that was destined to take him away from all of us, and a reason to smile in spite of the fact that his daughter had run away.

"I'm glad you have LeAnn," I told him. "I can see how much you love her."

"How could I not love her? And we are incredibly happy most of the time. We can talk about anything, and she likes working with me on the ranch. But you have to understand that I didn't see her for nearly a year after your mother died."

"Why not?"

"Because in my own sick way, I blamed her for your mother's death and for you leaving. It wasn't very manly of me, but if we hadn't gotten involved, there would never have been a fight, your mother would still be here, and you wouldn't have had any reason to take off the way you did."

After my meeting with Brother Downing, I no longer looked at my running away as just insensitive and foolish. It seemed more like a right of passage. Everyone had to leave the nest eventually if they wanted to have a normal life. It was just too bad that I hadn't returned to the outback sooner. Not that my coming would have changed what was destined to happen, but it would have given me more time with my father. I was grateful to have learned the truth about life after death. Nothing was more important than seeing my parents again, especially now that I knew my father was dying.

"Did LeAnn understand why you stopped coming around?" I asked to stop my wandering thoughts.

"She tried to, but she was a young mother with very little money and no support. I'm afraid she thought I was the bloodiest jerk in the world. She went through a very rough spot after Trevor was born. I had never known her to be anything but strong, so I figured she could handle anything. What I did by deserting her nearly pushed her over the edge. If Jake hadn't been willing to take time away from his own life and come back and help, I'm not sure what would have happened to any of us. He's a good mate, and very likely the only reason we are together now."

I thought about the woman in the waiting room and the man who treated me so atrociously. The Parable of the *Mote and the Beam* from the Bible certainly applied to me at this point in time.

"I'm glad you were able to work things out."

"Except for the big 'C', I must be the luckiest bloke in the world. My kidneys should have given out long before my lungs did."

He tried to laugh, but it made him start coughing, and he had to draw more heavily on the oxygen that was pouring into his lungs through the tubes in his nostrils.

"I think things happened the way they were meant to," he said when he was able to speak again. "You've grown into a beautiful, confident young woman. That might not have happened if you had stayed here."

"Why not?" I asked. "I would still have grown up."

"But you might not have graduated from college or fallen in love with some bloke who has obviously made you very happy. I was abrupt when you told me about him this morning because I didn't want to think about sharing you with someone else."

His admission softened my heart even further. "I am happy, and I do want to tell you more about Ben."

"And I want to hear all about the bloke who has stolen my daughter's heart. Only love could cause a Hawkins to change as dramatically as you have. You were such a shy, scared little girl. That's why I forced your mother to send you away to boarding school. You needed to see that you could make it on your own. So what are you going to do now that you have a degree and plan to get married?"

It looked like we might finally have a chance to talk about more of the things that really matter to me, but it didn't happen that way. Just as I was about to answer him there was a knock on the door, and LeAnn poked her head into the room. "Am I intruding?" she asked.

I wanted to tell her that she was, but my father was motioning for her to join us. He loved her the way I loved Ben, and I was glad. That was the way love was supposed to be, but it made me feel incredible sorrow for my mother. She had missed out on most everything of real importance during her life.

"How are you feeling, love?" she asked, placing a tender kiss on his forehead.

"Not bad for an old guy who's dying," he replied. "Now, I want you girls to head home and get some rest."

"But I don't want to leave," I said. If I left him again, it might be for the last time. "Can't I just stay here with you?"

"There is nothing I would like more—if I planned on being awake, which I don't. The nurse gave me some pretty heavy drugs that should keep me asleep for hours. There's no reason for either of you to sit by my bed and watch me snore. I want my girls to get some real rest."

While I wanted to protest, LeAnn simply brought his hand to her lips and kissed it. "I'm not sure I can sleep in that big, old bed alone, but I am willing to give it a try if it's what you really want."

"It's what we all need right now. I promise not to go anywhere while you're gone. Now give me a kiss and scoot. You shouldn't be driving the roads of the outback this late at night. I imagine Jake has already left with Trevor."

"They've been gone for over an hour. He should be almost ready for bed."

"I don't know what we would have done these past two years without your brother," my father told her. "He's done everything I haven't been able to do myself. He really has been a God-send."

"That's quite an admittance," LeAnn responded with a sheepish grin. "Especially when you claim you haven't much use for God for most of the time."

"I've always known there is a higher being," he reluctantly admitted. "I just haven't had much time to figure out who or what he is. But I can tell you one thing, I don't like the idea of this life being all there is."

"There is more," LeAnn said through another burst of tears. "The God I know could never be so cruel as to keep two people who love each other as much as we do apart."

I wished I could talk to them about the God that was literally our Eternal Father, and the plan he had so carefully designed for each of his children, but now wasn't the time. They had too many earthly things on their mind.

"It's going to be okay, LeAnn. I'm just glad Jake will be around when it's over for me. He knows how to do most everything by now."

"Let's not talk about that tonight, Jack. You just need to concentrate on getting better."

"I wish that was the cure to my ailments, love, but we're both tired and might know more in the morning."

She put her head on his shoulder, sniffed back a few tears, and then turned to me. "Could I have a moment alone with your father? There's something I need to discuss with him."

"Sure," I said, but before leaving his room, I kissed his tanned, leathery cheek. "I love you, father. I will be waiting for you to come home."

There! I'd said it! The ranch was the only real home I had ever known. Being away at boarding school and living with roommates didn't count. Those were just places where I studied and slept while waiting for my real life to begin—the life I was going to build with Ben—but even that didn't seem like enough right now. Why couldn't I have Ben and my father, too?

"Spend some time with Trevor," he told me. "He's going to need his sister, especially the next few months. Regardless of all the unpleasantness, I know you came home when you were supposed to."

"I'll be here for as long as Trevor or anyone here needs me, Father. I'm not sorry I have a little brother."

I ran from the room as the tears rolled down my cheeks. My father was dying, and I was supposed to spend more time with the little brother I hardly knew. I wanted to be spending my time with him, but then everyone wanted that, and I was the least deserving. I couldn't expect to regain what I had lost, but I certainly hoped I would be given the time to build something new.

Le Ann joined me a few minutes later.

"Do you feel like driving?" she asked. "I'm afraid my nerves are pretty raw. All I want to do is close my eyes and think."

"Sure," I said. "I can even drive you back in the morning to get your car."

"That won't be necessary. I'll have Jake bring me back in the plane. It's much quicker than driving."

I might have suggested getting a motel room for the rest of the night, but I knew she would never agree. She would want to check on Trevor.

"How long will my father have to be here?" I asked, as we exited the building and walked the short distance across the street to where my rental jeep was parked. It seemed like forever since I had stopped to eat lunch and call Ben.

"I'm hoping only a day or two. His oncologist will see him first thing in the morning. He will want to make sure Jack's stable before we bring him home, and recheck his meds so there won't be as much pain."

"Is he in a lot of that?"

It was another one of those stupid queries people make to fill uncomfortable silences, but she didn't seem to notice.

"More than he will admit. Your father wants to protect us, but I know he's slipping away fast. Things have gotten so much worse."

"How long has he been sick?"

I hated bugging her when I knew she wanted to think, but she was really the only one I could turn to. Jake despised me, and it seemed unconscionable to ask my father about his condition when he was the one having to live through it.

"Things started getting really bad about a year ago. He was tired all the time, losing weight, and then his cough got so awful he started spitting up blood."

"Is that when you found out about the cancer?"

"Yes!" she said, tightening the seatbelt on the passenger side of my rental. "I wanted him to have surgery, but the doctor said it wouldn't buy him enough time to be worth the risk. The cancer had spread to his lymph nodes and there were spots on several other major organs. We were told then that it would only be a few months. I think he was holding on because he needed to see you one more time, and now he has been able to do that."

I turned the key in the ignition, hoping she couldn't detect how fast my heart was racing. My father had waited for me to come home. How could I ever have doubted his love?

"Does Trevor know how much time Father has left?" I asked her as we pulled onto the two-lane road that led into the outback.

"We haven't told him anything. He's just a little boy and doesn't need to be worried until the very end. It's what your father wants."

"But he knows Father is very sick. He needs to be prepared for the inevitable."

I heard LeAnn take a deep breath. I had definitely overstepped.

"Don't you think your father and I have discussed that, Brylee? When the time is right, he'll know. Until then, we'll all continue to shield Trevor from the awful truth. Is that understood?"

I wanted to contradict her assessment of the situation because I knew how hard it was to lose a parent unexpectedly, but she was right. It wasn't any of my business.

We drove in near silence. LeAnn had her eyes closed, and I was too emotionally drained to talk so the miles slipped silently by one after the other. I now understood why it had been so important for me to come home. My father had been waiting for me, but why hadn't that understanding come so much sooner? It was impossible to tell whether he had days or even weeks left.

This had certainly been a bittersweet reunion. A few hours ago, I had believed this could possibly turn into the happiest time of my life. I was in love and going to be married to the perfect man, and I had made the conscious decision to forgive my father for every real and perceived injustice he had ever inflicted. I had even decided to forgive the people he had brought into my mother's home. Now, he would never meet the man I had chosen to spend my life with, and he would never be there to see his grandchildren grow up either.

To stop feeling sorry for myself, I tried to concentrate on LeAnn and my little half-brother. I might want to hate her for the part she had played in the deception that had cost my mother her life, but as I looked at the woman resting in the passenger seat I could only feel compassion. She was going to lose the man she loved, and she had no idea that there was a way for them to be together again. It seemed odd that I would think about that now when all I had wanted since joining the church was to have my parents sealed to each other so we could be a forever family.

Life was both confusing and sad, but I was glad my Saviour and my Eternal Father were the ones who would be making the final decision on who belonged together. All mortals seemed to do was muddle everything up.

And then there was Trevor! How could I go back to Los Angeles and leave him behind? As long as he was in my life, I would never be entirely alone because he was part of my father, too. For the first time since I had met Ben, I wondered where I really belonged.

"We're here!" I said, touching LeAnn's shoulder after the long drive was over. She involuntarily jumped and then opened her eyes.

"I must have fallen asleep," she said. "I am so sorry! I should have kept you company. It's a long drive, and I know you're tired too."

"I'm fine," I told her. "Besides, I never sleep in a car."

She removed her seatbelt and climbed out into the warm night air. I had kept the air conditioning on during the drive back to the ranch so she wouldn't become overly uncomfortable. I followed her lead and found her stretching her back when my door slammed shut.

"I know it affected you deeply when your mother died," she said rather unexpectedly.

"I suppose it did," I replied. It was late, well after midnight, and I was exhausted. With all that had happened during the past eighteen hours, I felt like I was wandering through some deep abyss in a terrible nightmare. The trouble was, I knew I wasn't dreaming.

LeAnn walked slowly towards the house after our brief exchange, but stopped with her hand on the doorknob before entering.

"Before we go in," she said. "I would like to talk to you for a few minutes, if you don't mind. There are a few things I need to say, and if I don't do it now, I might not get the courage again."

I wanted to tell her that we'd had a rough day and needed some sleep, but something made me reconsider. "What do you want to talk about?"

She motioned for me to sit beside her on the hanging glider that I had shared so often with my mother. It was hard moving towards her. I was in no mood for more mind games or heavy discussions. I just wanted to throw myself down on my bed and think. As tired as I was, I doubted that sleep would come easily.

"I owe you more than an apology for the part I played in destroying your life," she began. "I never should have pursued your father when I knew he was married, but it really was love at first sight for me. He was warm and attentive, and he listened when I talked. I had been involved with more blokes than I care to remember before, but he was the only one who made me believe that I had more to offer a man than just my body. He taught me how to believe in myself as a woman and gave me a reason for not offering myself to every guy who wanted a part of me. I haven't looked at anyone else since the day we met. I don't know if you can understand that. Most people think I was crazy for falling in love with a married man who was old enough to be my father."

"I believe love like that can happen," I told her. Regardless of my personal beliefs or the pain I was going through, I couldn't condemn her. She had simply been following her heart.

"You're both forgiving and gracious," she said. "But it's okay if you're still angry with me. It's even okay if you hate me. I took something from you that can never be replaced. Finding me in your mother's house, sleeping in her bed and using her things had to be excruciatingly painful. I know a simple apology won't change anything, but I hope you will give me a chance—for your father's sake, if nothing more."

I looked sideways at the woman sitting next to me. "I am glad you have been there for him. I even told him that because I know he loves you very much."

Tears were tickling my nose again as I thought about how lonely and guilt-ridden my father must have been. It had never occurred to me until coming home that he had been suffering too. I had always believed that he simply didn't care because he had never spent much time with either me or my mother.

"Thank you for saying that," she replied, taking my hand. "Your father is the most wonderful man I have ever known. He may seem tough on the outside, but he's genuine, caring and loving inside, where it really matters. I don't know what I am going to do without him."

Sobs suddenly racked her thin body, and I put my arm protectively around her shoulders, surprised that I could even do so after all the revelations of the past few days. But there really were two sides to every story, and God was the judge, not me.

"Things will be okay, LeAnn," I told her, "You have Trevor and Jake, and you have me. We'll all be here to help you through this."

"You really do have your father's heart. I'm glad you've come home too, Brylee."

I watched as she crossed the wooden planks of the veranda to the front door. Her shoulders were squared and her head held high. She was a strong and proud woman. No wonder my father loved her. She was just about the most real person I had ever met.

"Don't stay up too late," she cautioned before stepping inside. "Tomorrow will be another long day."

"I won't," I assured her. "I just need a few minutes to unwind."

I sat in the still darkness of the night, rocking back and forth for some moments after she had gone. I was heartbroken over my father's diagnosis, but I was at peace, too. Learning the message of the gospel had taken away the sting of death. It no longer seemed sinister or haunting. It was just another step in eternal progression. The only sad thing about it was the loss felt by the people who had been left behind.

Chapter 11

"Did you mean it when you said you would be there for LeAnn?" A deep voice broke the quiet of the night. It startled me, but I was getting used to Jake's sudden appearances. It seemed like he was always lurking somewhere near.

"Where did you come from?" I asked.

He threw his cigarette butt on the ground and stepped up on the veranda with me.

"Around! I always like to check things out before going to bed."

"You keep some mighty long hours. Technically, it's already morning."

"I don't need much sleep. That comes in handy out here. But you haven't answered my question. Did you mean it when you said you would be there for LeAnn, or were you just being polite due to the circumstances?"

His sarcasm and skepticism were annoying after the day I had been through, but I wasn't going to let it throw me. "I'll be here for as long as anyone needs me."

"Interesting!" he replied, taking a step closer. I would have jumped from the swing in an attempt to make it into the house, but he would have no trouble overtaking me if he chose to do so. "I thought this was a short visit. Just long enough to check things out and make sure daddy wasn't mad at you for running away."

"Stop with the holier-than-thou attitude, Jake! I neither deserve nor need it. I may have come at an inopportune time, but I am trying to be both understanding and forgiving. You should try it sometime."

"Good on ya," he said, clapping his hands lightly together. "I like to see fire in a woman's eyes. Feisty women make passionate lovers."

"That's one thing you will never know about me from experience," I assured him. "A woman would have to be insane to get involved with you."

His laugh was disconcerting. "I have known my share of crazy women, but you might not want to dismiss me quite so lightly. I've been told I'm a pretty good lover. Besides, I think your father would like to see us together. That way we could keep the ranch in the family."

"My father would never want me to marry a man I detest."

"There's a fine line between love and hate, Miss Hawkins," he replied, as his hand closed around the rope that was holding the glider in the air. "Who knows, maybe we could learn to love each other. I admire your passion, even if it is negatively directed at me."

"It doesn't work like that," I assured him.

Jake was handsome in a rugged sort of way, with dark hair and chiseled features, but the coldness in his eyes still frightened me. I knew he could be incredibly cruel if he wanted to, but I had to give him credit for being loyal to his family. He was certainly doing his best to make sure I did nothing to hurt any of them. What he didn't seem to understand was that they were my family now, too.

"Why not?" he asked, interrupting my thoughts. "People can learn to love anyone if they're willing to try."

"Perhaps, but I already have a man I love, and we're going to be married as soon as I get home."

"There you have it!" he exclaimed, giving the swing a much harder push than it had been built for. "The truth always comes out in the end, doesn't it?"

"I don't know what you're talking about," I replied.

"Then let me enlighten you. Just a moment ago, you were assuring my sister that you intended to be here to help your little brother through the loss of your father, and now you say that you're going to marry some bloody bloke in California no one here has even met. Which one is it going to be?"

His accusations were ludicrous. I had just found out about my father's cancer. How was I supposed to know what I was going to do next?

"That's not fair," I challenged. "I just learned about my father's condition today, and didn't even know I had a little brother until I got here."

"And whose fault is that? You could have come home any time you wanted. Hell, a call or a letter would have been appreciated, but you were too busy nursing a wounded ego. To bloody hell with everyone else!"

I was trembling with anger, but this horrible man would not make me cry again today. "Why do you have to be so hateful? I know what I did was wrong. And yes, maybe some part of me wanted my father to suffer because I truly believed he was responsible for my mother's death. But you enlightened me on that, didn't you? And as long as I am at it, I will even admit that the main reason I came back was because Ben told me I needed to make peace with my past, or we would never have the right kind of future. Does that make you happy?"

My eyes were blazing, and I was shouting, but I didn't care. Jake deserved to get as good as he gave. The trouble was, he had forced me to face some of my own demons. I had never done that before, and didn't like how it felt.

"No," he said. "I don't like to see people unhappy, but you can't fix anything until you are willing to admit there's a problem. Perhaps you understand that now."

"Are you saying all the fault lies with me?"

"There's plenty of blame to go around. And whether you believe it or not, I do understand how you feel about my sister and your father. They made a mistake, but they're good people and don't deserve to be condemned because they fell in love. But what really gets me is your reaction to Trevor. He doesn't understand why you won't spend any time with him. He's a great kid and hasn't done anything wrong."

"Don't you think I know that? Maybe I'm scared of getting attached to people because I don't want to lose anyone else."

"You're getting married. That's attachment, isn't it?"

"In a much different way," I countered. Ben and I know each other, and we want to be together."

"And you don't want to be with your little brother? How selfish is that?"

"You're twisting my words."

"What's going on out here?" The screen door opened and LeAnn stuck her head out. She was wearing a nightgown. "All this shouting is going to wake Trevor up."

"Sorry, Lee. Brylee and I were just having a discussion."

"Well, it has to stop," she said, shaking her finger in our direction. "I don't care what your personal difficulties are. Jack is in the hospital fighting for his life. He won't be with us much longer, so can't you just pretend to be friends? I won't have his final days ruined by anyone. I don't care what you do to each other after that."

I hung my head like a rebuked child. She was right! Nothing mattered right now except my father's comfort and happiness. Everything else could wait, even my trip home to Ben if needed.

"It won't happen again," Jake assured her. "Brylee and I will be good, won't we?"

"We'll behave like proper adults," I responded, averting his steady, infuriating gaze.

"Then it's settled. Now go to bed, both of you. We all need some sleep."

She didn't leave room for us to say anything else. I followed her through the doorway into the house, and Jake disappeared into the night.

It was still dark outside when I heard LeAnn moving around in the kitchen below the guest bedroom. The only reason I knew I had been asleep at all was the remains of the nightmare I'd had. I could not recall the details, but it had left me with a feeling of anxiety and despair. I didn't want my father to die. I needed him, but fate was unforgiving. He was going to die, and I would never get to show him how much I cared unless I started this very day.

"Have you heard from father?" I asked LeAnn after showering and dressing for the day. I was scared, more scared than I had ever been. Even running away from home and starting over in a new country had not been as terrifying as the position I found myself in now.

"Not yet, but I wanted to get into town early. I know the doctor is usually there for rounds by seven."

I looked at the clock on the wall. It was four-thirty in the morning. I had only been in bed for a little over three hours.

"Are you going to have Jake fly you in?"

"No," she said, taking a sip of hot coffee. "I think it's important for your father to see you and me together. He needs to know there are no longer any hard feelings between us."

"I agree," I replied. "He needs to see us standing together in this."

"And we will," she promised. "I just hope you will be patient with me. I didn't mean to yell at Jake and you last night."

"We deserved it. Our voices were much louder than necessary."

"That is my brother's usual way of communicating, unless he is trying to impress someone."

"He needn't bother with me. He knows I'm engaged."

"I wish I could say that really mattered. I hope the bloke you're going to marry treats you well."

"He's wonderful and treats me like a queen."

"That is exactly how it has always been with your father. Even when we were having trouble, I knew that he loved me. That's why what is happening with him now is so hard. I have known about his condition for a long time, and always thought that when the end was near, I would be the one spending all my time with him. I'm having a little trouble adjusting to the fact that I am no longer the only woman in his life."

"You have nothing to fear from me, LeAnn," I told her. "I know how much my father loves you, and I would never do anything to undermine that."

"I understand that now. It's just that I can be unreasonable at times, especially when I'm scared. I have known this day was coming, but I'm not ready to lose him. We had so many plans. I guess that's what happens when you live in denial."

"There's nothing wrong with making plans. Sometimes hope is all we have."

"But what happens when hope runs out? I don't know if I'm strong enough to run a ranch and raise Trevor by myself."

"You won't be alone. Jake's here and so am I."

"That's fine for now, but you will want to get back to your own life. I know this was just a visit."

"Visits can be extended."

"But what about the young man you're going to marry? He is going to want you back home when you promised to be there."

"Ben will understand when I tell him what's happened."

"Then you are more than lucky to have him. Still, I wish your vacation hadn't been ruined. I know your father was hoping he would stay well until after you left."

"And not let me know he was sick until it was too late?" The very thought angered me. I might have run away, but I had been a confused and desperately hurt child. I was a woman now, and I certainly hoped I had learned a few things about responsibility and the need to be there for the people who really mattered.

She cupped her hands around her coffee mug and looked down into the steaming hot liquid. "I guess none of us is thinking too clearly right now. You have every right to be included in what happens with your father."

"I appreciate that," I assured her. "There have been far too many secrets already."

"You're right, of course," she reluctantly admitted. "We can't pretend the past didn't happen, just as we can't pretend this illness with your father isn't happening now."

"Illness?" I thought. This wasn't just an illness. His cancer was a death sentence because he had put off treatment too long.

"Did you get to talk to Trevor last night?" I asked to keep myself from saying something more that might be considered insensitive.

"He was asleep when we got home, and I didn't want to wake him up so early this morning. Jake is going to take him up in the plane later today to check out the sheep on the west range. They should be okay since there's still water, but you never know when a wild animal might get in. They can destroy an entire flock of ewes and their offspring in a matter of minutes."

I knew what she was talking about. Once, when I was very young, I went with my father on his horse to check on the sheep. It was supposed to be a fun day with a picnic lunch, but it hadn't turned out that way. When we got to the herd, several ewes were lying on the ground bleeding. Their stomachs had been torn open, and the ones that weren't already dead were bleating helplessly. My father had told me to shut my eyes and wait for him next to a big rock. But when he took his pistol out of the saddle bag, I forgot my promise and watched as he shot each bleeding ewe in the head. I screamed and screamed. That was the last time I had been allowed to accompany him anywhere on the ranch.

"Trevor and Jake get along well, don't they?" I asked, trying to stop the images that were forming in my mind.

"They should! Jake's been a part of Trevor's life since he was born. I still don't understand why he's never married. He's dated plenty of interested women and would make a wonderful father."

"I'm sure he has his reasons."

"Perhaps. I know it isn't right to want to control his life, but I still worry. He's almost thirty-five and needs to settle down. You wouldn't happen to be interested, would you? I know you have a boyfriend back in the states, but you're good for my brother."

"Not true," I countered. "We fight all the time. You heard us last night."

"What I heard was a man and woman who are attracted to each other, but who are both too stubborn to admit it. You are the first woman that Jake has taken an interest in for years."

"But I'm in love with my fiancé, and we are going to be married when I get back."

I was going to say home, but it didn't seem quite right. Home was where the heart was, and while mine would always be with Ben, right now a large part of it was centered on my father.

"You're lucky," LeAnn said. "Your father and I never thought getting married was that important. We knew we loved each other, and we loved our son. That was always enough until now. Would you like some coffee?"

I shook my head. "I would prefer juice, if that's okay. I haven't eaten anything since lunch yesterday."

"Then let me fix you something." She was on her feet before I could protest. "I only have coffee in the morning. Jack says I should eat more, but my stomach disagrees. I can have ham and eggs on the table in a few minutes."

"Please don't," I said. "Sit down and enjoy your coffee. I can fix my own toast and juice."

I thought she might protest again, but apparently she was every bit as exhausted as I was because she simply resumed her place at the kitchen table and took another sip of her coffee. "In my present state of mind, I would probably just ruin anything I tried to fix. I really am glad you're here."

"So am I," I told her while putting two slices of bread in the toaster. "If I'd had any sense, I would have come home years ago... "

"We all do crazy things when we're young. We think we have all the answers and that the world revolves around our needs and desires. That couldn't be more untrue."

"I thought I smelled coffee," Jake said as the screen door leading into the kitchen banged shut. "You two are up early."

"We wanted to get to the hospital before the doctor comes," LeAnn told him. "I hope it's okay if Trevor spends the day with you."

"I like having the little bloke around," he said, pouring himself a cup of the fragrant liquid and joining his sister at the table. "When are you going to tell him about Jack?"

"We haven't decided. I'm just hoping we can bring him home today. This is where he wants to be. You know how much he hates hospitals."

"It's not going to be easy, Lee," Jake replied without acknowledging my presence. "Jack is a strong man, and I love him like a brother, but he's not going to beat the big 'C' this time. We have to prepare for that."

LeAnn looked as if she was going to cry. "I know that, but I need more time, Jake. Can't I just go on for a little while longer pretending that he is going to be here until we're both old and gray? Trevor doesn't know how really sick his father is, and there's always hope."

"You know I'll support whatever decision you make, Lee. But I don't like seeing you cling to hope when there isn't any."

"No one, but God, can be sure of that, Jake. Miracles do happen."

I could see the sadness and pain in her face, and the brotherly love and concern in his.

"I'm not saying they can't, but Jack waited too long, and you have to be prepared for whatever the doctor tells you. Are you sure you don't want me to go with you? I could gas up the plane, and it would take us less than thirty minutes to get there."

"Brylee needs to be there when we talk to the doctor. What happens today will affect her just as much as it will affect the rest of us. Besides, Trevor loves flying. It will keep his mind off things he shouldn't be worrying about yet."

"I think you're wrong about that," Jake challenged her. "Trevor was terribly upset last night when we flew home. He doesn't understand what's wrong with his father, and why no one will talk to him about it."

"Don't make me do that yet, Jake! Just talk to him about all the animals. He never gets tired of hearing about them."

"I'll shield him for as long as I can, but you have to tell him the truth. You don't have to go into details, but pretending that everything will be okay isn't fair. What if you can't bring Jack home today? What am I supposed to tell Trevor then?"

"You don't have to tell him anything."

"Trevor isn't dumb. He's seen Jack's coughing spells and what it's like when he can't get enough air. I'm telling you, Lee, he is going to hate you someday if you keep hiding things from him."

"Okay, okay," she said, carrying her cup to the sink and rinsing it out. "I get your point, and I will tell him. But not right now. It's too early in the day, and I still don't know anything. Just be a good little brother and keep him occupied until I get back. I promise I will talk to him tonight."

"Backing out would not be advisable," Jake quickly responded. "I can assure you he will not understand why Brylee went to town with you and he didn't."

"Just keep him happy today, Jake. With any luck, Jack will be on his way back to the ranch after he meets with the doctor."

"You're not really planning on driving him back, are you? That's a hell of a trip for a sick person."

He still didn't look at me, but I knew he was well aware of my presence. He had been all along. He had simply chosen to ignore me.

"My car's in town, and someone needs to drive it back. It's just too bad your plane doesn't hold more than one passenger."

"Don't knock my plane. It might not be big, but it's gotten us out of a hell of a lot of trouble the past few years."

"I'm not knocking anything, Jake. Just take care of things here until I get back. We shouldn't be late, God-willing." She made the sign of the cross. "Are you ready, Brylee?"

I was just taking a bite of toast, but put it back on the plate. "As soon as I brush my teeth and get my purse," I said, following her out of the kitchen. I didn't want to be alone with Jake. Life was hard enough without receiving another tongue-lashing from him. Our pretense at getting along was just that—pretending. He would welcome the chance to attack my character if we were alone again.

I drove while LeAnn fidgeted around in the passenger seat. It was going to be another scorcher, and I had the windows of the jeep rolled up and the AC on high, not only to keep us from getting too warm but to help keep us awake. LeAnn looked as if she had gotten even less sleep than I had.

The sky was clear and blue. What I wouldn't have given for a few dark clouds and a little rain, but that seldom happened here. It was all or nothing when it came to any change in the weather. By noon, the temperature could be well over 110 degrees. I was glad we were making the trip while it was still early. The trip home wouldn't be nearly as pleasant.

"I think I'm going through nicotine withdrawal," LeAnn said as we passed mile marker #23. "I haven't had a cigarette since last night."

"Do you need to stop?" I asked, quite surprised that she hadn't lit up when we first started our two-hour drive.

"No," she said. "You must think all the adults on the ranch are insane for smoking when we know it's killing your father."

"Addictions can be hard to break."

"Especially if they're as nasty and deadly as smoking. I hope Trevor never starts. How did you keep from acquiring the habit?"

"Uncle Ned gave me my first and only cigarette when I was little. I coughed, threw up and was never tempted to try it again."

"What about your mother? Did she smoke?"

"No," I replied, wondering why I had never really thought about that before. In many ways, my mother had always seemed more like an older sister. She was only seventeen when I was born, and she had Keida to do the cooking and cleaning.

"That's quite remarkable, considering where she lived," LeAnn responded.

"I suppose." It would be quite natural to talk about how much my mother still meant to me—if I were with anyone other than the woman who had betrayed both of us. Still, I wished I could assure LeAnn that things would work out the way she wanted them to, but example was always the best teacher. I had just been lucky, that's all.

"It will be okay," I finally told her as her fingers continued to move around almost spasmodically. "Trevor's a smart kid."

"He is, isn't he?" she returned. "I hated getting pregnant while your father was still married to your mother, but I'm not sorry we have him. I haven't been able to get pregnant since. Jack always wanted more children, and so did I. But I guess that's not going to happen now."

"You have a great son. Some people don't even have that much."

"I know I am luckier than most. I've had nearly 15 years with the most wonderful man on the planet, but I still don't want to lose him—not ever. He's the most important part of my life."

I knew exactly how she felt. Ben and I had known each other less than a year, but I couldn't imagine my life without him either. He grounded me and gave me a reason for being. I would be lost without him, too.

"Let's try not to worry about the future right now," I told her. "We haven't even talked to the doctor. Things may not be as grim as we suspect."

Father was lying in his bed, still hooked up to oxygen and a heart monitor, when we got to the hospital shortly before seven. He looked ten years older than he had the day before. I hung back when we walked into the room, but LeAnn didn't. She walked right up to him and kissed him on the forehead.

"How are you feeling this morning, love?" she asked.

He opened his eyes, coughed, and looked up at her. "Am I ever glad you're finally here. I missed holding you in my arms last night."

Tears filled the corners of my eyes as I stood to one side. I was so tired of crying over things that could not be changed.

"Brylee's here," she told him, motioning for me to come closer. He moved his head around so he could see me better. I knew it must hurt him deeply to have the daughter who had just returned home see him in such a helpless condition.

"Just rest," I said as I walked to the opposite side of his bed and took the hand he offered.

"Has the doctor been in yet?" LeAnn asked as she brushed a speck of something I couldn't see off his pillow. "We tried to get here early so we wouldn't miss him. I should have stayed with you last night."

"Honestly, love! There was nothing you could do, and the doctor has yet to make his rounds. I wish you had tried to sleep longer. You know how much I worry about you."

"I couldn't sleep without you next to me either," she responded, raising his hand to her lips and kissing it. Her eyes were misty, but I knew she was trying to be brave for him. I felt like an outsider and wished I could think of a good reason to leave them alone. I wondered how Ben and I would feel after we had been together for ten or twenty years.

"Brylee," my father said, looking at me with a tenderness I had never seen before. "I'm sorry you have to see your old man like this. It hasn't been a very pleasant homecoming."

I wriggled my nose like Trevor had done several days earlier. "How you look doesn't matter. It only matters that we are together now. Were you able to get any rest?"

"A hell of a lot more than the two of you combined by the looks of your faces. Why don't you try to get some rest in the waiting room? I can send one of the nurses to find you when the doctor gets here."

"I'm not leaving," LeAnn retorted. "And the only way I'll sleep again is if I'm in that bed with you."

"Maybe I should see if that can be arranged," he told her as the edges of his lips curled into a sad and heartbreaking smile.

"Stop kidding, Jack! This is serious."

"I know, but we can't let it destroy what time we have left, love. Why don't you tell me what's been happening at home? Have there been any more late arrivals?"

She brushed the hair from his face. "I didn't even ask Jake, but if there are, he will take care of them. He's taking Trevor up in the plane again today."

"That's good. The boy needs to learn everything he can."

The words had no more than been uttered when he started to cough. He couldn't seem to catch his breath, and I had to stand helplessly by as his entire body shook and his face became gray in color and contorted in pain. It was the first time I had witnessed such a frightening event, but it wasn't the first for LeAnn.

"None of this talk is necessary right now," she said, trying to calm him. "All I want to do is see the doctor and get you home."

He lay there for some moments as the sound of the machines assisting him returned to normal, and I felt my heart quit racing.

"There is nothing I would like more, love." His tone was nothing more than a breathy whisper. "I hate hospitals, and the ranch won't run by itself."

"Jake has everything under control. I know he might not do things exactly the way you would, but he can certainly run things for a few days while you're getting better."

My father looked at her with more than just compassion and love. He knew he was not going to get better, but he wanted to give her the time she needed to accept the inevitable.

I stayed with them until the doctor arrived, and then excused myself so they could talk in private. It didn't seem right for me to be hanging around when the final verdict was delivered. They were the ones who would have to see everything through to the end.

"Oh, Mother," I thought as I made my way to the waiting room, fighting back fresh tears with each step. "I don't think I can make it through another funeral."

I hadn't noticed before, but the building seemed so cold and barren with its pale green walls, black speckled floor tile, and antiseptic smell. There were a few potted plants, but many of the leaves had brown edges. The receptionist looked tired as she quickly scanned the room for new arrivals and then went back to her other duties.

I wanted to call Ben and fill him in on what was happening, but didn't know what to tell him about when I would be coming back. Even with a wedding to plan and a man I loved with every fiber of my being waiting for me, I knew I could never leave Australia as long as my father was still alive. As soon as I knew something more concrete, I would make that call. But there was nothing he could do from halfway around the world, and it would only make him worry.

Loving Ben had been easy from the beginning because he cared so much about others. We met when my roommate, Becky, took me home to meet her family and attend her brother's homecoming. He had been in South Africa for two years on what she called a mission for the Church of Jesus Christ of Latter-day Saints. That had seemed such a strange concept to me. Why would anyone devote two years of his life—even to a cause he believed in—when he was young and there was so much in life to enjoy?

I was soon to learn that he was extraordinary in every way, not just his religious convictions. I had never intended to get involved with another man, but Ben was just so cute and personable that I couldn't seem to help myself. It didn't even matter that he shared the same strange beliefs as his twin sister, Becky. I mean, how could any sane person accept the story she had been telling me about the boy, Joseph Smith, who saw angels and who found a book written in a strange language buried in a mountain? It sounded like the stuff movies were made about, but once I had been to church with them a few times, I began to accept the idea that God did know and love each one of his children, and that we had not been put on this earth by chance. We each had a specific reason for being here.

It wasn't long until I found myself liking the idea of having a purpose, of knowing that I had lived with my Heavenly Father before coming to earth. I even liked the idea of being tested to see just how much I would sacrifice to return back to him when I died. But the thing that made the most sense was the idea of eternal families. From all I had learned, my family didn't qualify as Celestial material, but if the promise was true about each person being given the chance to hear and accept the gospel, then we still had a chance. If nothing more, it made me realise that life did not stop with death, and I would get to see my mother again.

"You're deep in thought," LeAnn said, startling me out of my reveries.

I hadn't heard her approach, and I hadn't been gone long enough for any deep discussion about my father's condition to take place, but when I looked up at her, a huge knot froze inside my heart. Her eyes were glassy, and she looked as if she were in shock.

I rose to my feet on wobbly legs. "What did the doctor say?"

"Sit down for a minute so we can talk," she instructed.

I dropped back to the warm spot on the tan leather sofa in front of the large picture window that looked out at the park across the street where I had eaten lunch the day before and talked to Ben. The window had been tinted to keep some of the sun's hot rays out.

She sat still for a moment or two beside me, clenching and unclenching her hands. I wanted her to say something, but knew I couldn't rush what was coming.

"The doctor had a bunch of tests run last night after we left. The cancer has spread to his brain."

I sat in stunned silence, waiting for her to continue.

"Your father has no more than six weeks. The doctor wants him to stay here, where they can keep him comfortable with narcotics, but he doesn't want that. He wants to go home."

"Then that's what we'll do," I said, clinging to the idea that six weeks might actually mean six months or even more. I jumped to my feet.

"Not so fast," LeAnn said, putting a restraining hand on my arm. I sat beside her again. "I'm not sure you understand what that means. Your father is going to be in a great deal of pain and will be given morphine, but it means we'll have to take care of him or hire a nurse."

"We don't need a nurse," I told her as the heavy weight inside continued to constrict my breathing. "We can take care of him ourselves."

"What about your fiancé?"

"Ben will understand! There's no way I can leave now. This is where I want to be."

"I was hoping you would say that," she admitted, her bottom lip trembling. "Dr. Allred said we could take him home today if that's what is decided. Mind you, the doctor's not happy about it, but he wants to do what's right for Jack. He'll be on oxygen, and both of us will have to learn how to change a drip line and administer the right amount of morphine when he needs it. He could become agitated more easily, will begin to forget things and could even lose his ability to speak. His body will deteriorate as his mind does. They will arrange for a Hospice check on him every few days, but mostly we will be on our own. Are you sure you want to take on that kind of responsibility? It's not going to be easy, and he's going to become a little worse each day until it's over."

My head was blanketed in fog, but I said yes anyway. "I'll do anything you need me to do, LeAnn. I just want to be with him."

"Then it's settled. Dr. Allred said Jack could do whatever he felt up to, but he would have to carry an oxygen tank with him. His lungs are too damaged for him to breathe on his own any longer. That means no more trips into the outback to check on things. Jake and I can take care of that, but we'll need you to help out around the house and take care of both Trevor and your father while we're gone."

"I can do that," I said, knowing that God would give me the strength to make it through any challenges that arose. "What are you going to tell Trevor?"

She shrugged her slim shoulders. "I don't know. How do you tell a little boy that his father only has a few weeks to live? He's a smart little guy and has probably figured it out on his own already, but I hate confirming it. He's too young to have to deal with this."

"You'll know what to say when the time comes," I told her, suddenly understanding her hesitation about destroying her son's life. There would never be a right time or a right way to tell him, and even unfounded hope was better than no hope at all. I felt so sorry for my little brother. I had been much older when I lost my mother, but it was an experience I would never forget.

LeAnn and I returned to my father's hospital room, where a nurse instructed us on the basic nursing skills needed to make sure he was as comfortable as possible. She told us not to worry about the amount of information given because she would send detailed instructions in a booklet prepared for that purpose that included what to look for as each day brought him closer to the end of his time on earth. It was a lot to take in because I was uncomfortable enough just worrying about him getting the amount of oxygen he needed.

Father wanted to ride home with one of us, despite LeAnn's protests that the trip would be much easier and shorter in the plane with Jake. But I understood why he wanted to make the trip by car. He loved the Outback and the life he'd had there. And whether or not LeAnn or I had come to terms with his imminent death, I knew he had. He wanted one more chance to drink in the beauties of the land he had called home for over 55 years.

I wanted him to come with me, but didn't feel I had earned the right to ask for that concession. He and LeAnn had a great deal to talk about, and all I would do anyway was cry. I would take several tanks of oxygen with me and stop at the grocers to pick up the monthly allocation of supplies, so no further trips to town would be necessary.

I watched until LeAnn and my father had left the parking lot and then called Ben. It was late evening there, and I hoped he would be near enough to his phone to hear it ring and answer, but he didn't. So I left a message telling him about my father and that I didn't know when I would be coming home. I closed by expressing my love and saying that I would call again as soon as I could.

Then I pulled onto the street in search of the market LeAnn recommended. There was very little traffic for an early Monday morning, but then Edna could more adequately be called a hamlet than a town, and I wasn't sure that I really missed all the traffic. It took over an hour to find everything she wanted, and the amount of money needed to cover the bill seemed staggering. But she had given me her debit card and password, and the clerk at the checkout station didn't bat an eye when I used it. But then identity theft and scamming others weren't a big concern in the Outback yet.

My purchases secured in every corner of the jeep, I made my way back to the ranch. I hoped someone would be there to greet me. But the moment I stepped onto the hard-packed earth, an eerie kind of silence seemed to engulf me. The lives of all the people who lived there had been irrevocably changed. There would be no more happy laughter, long days spent on horseback or even a moment of feeling truly alive for my father. He had come home to die, and everyone who loved him knew it.

"Let me help you with all of that stuff," Jake said, coming up so silently behind me I hadn't heard a single footstep.

My first reaction was to tell him that I didn't need any help, but then I remembered the promise we had made to LeAnn the night before. I would keep things between us civil, regardless of the amount of hostility he threw my way.

"Thank you," I told him as I pulled the first grocery bag I could reach from the jeep. "How's Trevor taking all of this?"

His jaw moved before speaking, and I knew he was planning his words more carefully than he might have done if the situation were far less grim. "Better than either LeAnn or I suspected. He held his father's hand all the way up the stairs and into the house. Damn near broke my heart, but that little bloke's got more grit inside than any of the other adults around here."

"He's been raised well," I said, reaching for a second bag while Jake picked up two very large oxygen tanks. "Has it been a busy day?"

"Just the usual. No more calves born out in the open."

"That's good," I responded, falling into step beside him. "I really do appreciate all you're doing to help my father."

"You don't have to make with the small talk," he retorted. "That wasn't part of our agreement."

"I know, but I really mean it. I'm glad you've been here for everyone."

"Do I detect a thawing of the ice queen?"

His sarcasm made me bristle. Why couldn't he accept a simple thank you without turning it into a battle?

LeAnn opened the screen door for us. "Just put the tanks in the bedroom, Jake. And Brylee," she said, turning to me. "Could you visit with your father and brother while I put some supper on the table. I'm afraid Trevor will wear him out with his incessant chatter, and he really needs to rest. It's been a long couple of days."

"I'll do it as soon as I bring the rest of the supplies inside."

No more was said, but I feared what was coming, and prayed that I would be more of a help than a hindrance.

Chapter 12

I got up early each morning to make sure Trevor was dressed and fed. LeAnn and Jake were off before dawn in the plane or on motorcycles—another time-saving addition that had been added to the operation during the time I was gone —to make sure the animals were safe. Uncle Ned came over nearly every evening, and he and Father would sit in the den drinking beer.

Sometimes Jake and LeAnn joined them, but I felt out of place, especially since I had spent nearly the entire day with him while they were working. They didn't smoke their usual cigars or cigarettes, and they didn't talk about my father's approaching death. They talked about the cattle and sheep market and made plans to get the livestock into Edna a few weeks earlier than they had done in previous years.

While they were visiting, I took Trevor on a walk or to check on his orphaned animals that were growing stronger and bigger each day. Sometimes we would saddle two horses and ride to a secluded glade not far from the house. He told silly jokes, and I pretended to get them. He told me about being home-schooled, and I told him how I had done the same thing when I was his age.

We didn't talk about the future or what was going on with our father until three days after he had been released from the hospital. It was impossible for Trevor not to notice the Hospice nurse and how she hovered around our father when she came. We were sitting on a blanket in a clearing, drinking lemonade and listening to the crickets, when he suddenly became very quiet and serious.

"Is father going to die?" he asked.

I tried to organize my thoughts. Apparently, LeAnn had not yet told him about our father's impending death, but it wasn't my place to share that devastating information.

"We'll all die one day," I responded, watching two vultures soar into the sky overhead.

He dragged the tip of a stick through the sun-baked earth. "I know that, but he's really sick. He won't even take me for a ride like he did last week. I asked him again today, and he said maybe later. Why won't anyone talk to me? I hear all of you whispering. I'm a man! Father even said so."

I touched his sunburned arm and tried to smile. He had fair skin, just like Ben. I was starting to love my little half-brother.

"Father is very ill," I told him. "But only God can decide when someone is going to die."

"I don't like God if he wants to take my father away from me."

"He's not unkind, Trevor. He loves each one of us, but what would happen if no one ever died?"

"I would like that," he said. "I don't like death."

"Few people do, but think about all the animals and people who get sick. Do you want to see them suffer?"

"No, but God could make them well if he wanted to."

"He certainly could, but then everyone would live. Wouldn't the earth get rather crowded after a while?"

"I wouldn't care as long as father was here."

"That's not our decision to make, Trevor, but we get to spend lots of time with him now. That's a good thing, isn't it?"

Trevor stomped his foot on the ground. "But it isn't the same. He hasn't left the house since he got home."

"I know, but in some ways it's even better than it used to be. Instead of always working, he gets to be at home with us. Have you ever played checkers with him? We did that when I was little."

"A few times, but he's been awfully busy."

"He has time now. Why don't you ask him to play a few games with you when we get back to the house? I know he would like to, and you might even learn how to beat him. He's awfully good."

"I guess I could do that," Trevor relented, giving me an unexpected kiss on the cheek. "I really am glad you're home. Are you going to stay with us forever?"

His honesty and acceptance touched my heart with a mixture of love and sadness, and I reached over to give him a hug.

"Forever is a long time, but I don't plan on going any place right now."

He gave me a funny, yet accepting look. "Maybe we should go back now so I can ask Father about checkers. We've been gone for an awfully long time, and Uncle Ned should be going home by now."

"I think he would like that very much," was my instant reply.

Together, we gathered up the blanket and cups and put them back in my saddlebag. I had forgotten how much I loved the outback. It wasn't lush and green like California, but it was my home. It was also home to the red kangaroo, possums, spiders, scorpions, Koalas—who weren't really bears at all—water buffaloes, lizards, wild pigs, the ever-present red fire ants and many other animal species that were indigenous to the region. And one rarely went through an entire day without seeing sunbirds, starlings, blackbirds or Kookaburras.

Ben had been excited about the prospect of visiting Australia when we had been planning my trip, but he had been born and raised in Orange County and was used to the city, where there was always something to do and somewhere to go. And while he was close to the Mohave Desert, he seldom went there. It was too dry, too hot and had too many creepy crawlies.

The man I loved liked the excitement of being around lots of different people, and thoroughly enjoyed the beaches with their waves to surf in and the abundant Palm trees that swayed rhythmically in the cool evening breeze. I liked all those things too, but after being home for a little more than a week, I realized that I had never stopped loving the place where I had been born. I loved the strangeness of it, the uncertainty, and the unsung beauty of a land that had never been tamed.

On Friday evening, my father called me into the den to talk. Uncle Ned had just left. We had talked a lot the past few days, but somehow this meeting seemed different—more serious and unnerving.

"Brylee, love," he said as I closed the door behind me and went to sit on the leather sofa in front of the window that looked out on the front driveway. It was relatively new. The one I remembered was old and worn, with burn holes in the cushions and ribbing showing at the edges. I wondered if he and LeAnn had purchased it together, or if it had come from her previous home, not that it really mattered now.

"Uncle Ned stayed later than usual tonight," I said.

"We had a lot to discuss, and some of it concerns you."

"But I'm fine, Father. You don't have to worry about me anymore. Ben will always be there for me."

"This Ben you keep talking about, are you really serious about marrying him?"

"Of course I am. I love him very much."

"And he's good to you?"

"The best! I can't see myself with anyone else."

"And you don't think you would ever want to come back home to live, permanently?"

"I don't know what the future will bring. Why are you asking me all these questions about Ben?"

"Because I've never met the bloke, and it's time for me to rethink my last wishes now that you're back."

"You don't have to leave anything to me," I assured him. "I haven't been a very good daughter."

"And I wasn't a very good father. If I had been, these past five years would never have happened the way they did. You would have been here with me instead of halfway around the world with strangers I know nothing about."

"They're all good people, and you would really like them. Ben has three sisters and one brother, three living grandparents, and more aunts, uncles and cousins than I can begin to count. They get together whenever they can, and they have accepted me without hesitation. So you see, you have nothing to fear when it comes to my future. I will be well taken care of."

His countenance changed so rapidly I almost wished I hadn't made them sound so perfect. They had their faults, but their weaknesses did seem minimal when compared to ours, so I hurried on to give him an explanation.

"You have to know that I will never forget about my family here. These past few days have made me realise just how important they are. I won't make the mistake of running away again.

"I'm glad you feel that way," he said. "But it doesn't negate the fact that my bloody actions caused you to leave your home in the first place. That never should have happened."

"Maybe it was meant to. I know you don't give much credence to religion, but you have to acknowledge fate. I needed to learn how to take responsibility for my own actions. Being alone in a strange country gave me the opportunity to find out who I really am and what is most important to me."

He ran his hand through thinning hair. "You'll never know how much a child means until you have one of your own, but I would have given my life to make you happy."

I watched as he started to cough, and my hand immediately went out to touch his, but he only inhaled deeply from the oxygen tank that was there to help him. I waited until his breathing became less labored before speaking.

"I know that, Father, but as far as I'm concerned, we have already settled our differences and everything has been forgiven. I just want to spend time with you building new memories."

How I wished I could ease some of his suffering, and it wasn't just the physical pain. He was in spiritual torment, only he didn't know it, and there was nothing I could do to help with that except reassure him that he was loved and the past had been forgotten.

"It would have been awful leaving this life not knowing what had happened to you," he admitted. "I'm so glad you came back when you did. Otherwise, it might have been too late."

"Don't talk like that. They could always find a cure."

"Not for me! I abused my body for too many years by smoking, drinking too much and working in the desert. I should have been smarter because I always knew that tobacco was bad for me. I just wish LeAnn, Jake, Ned and Nora would all quit before the same thing happens to them."

"Have you talked to them about it?"

"We all talked, but denial was an easy out until last Sunday. I really thought I could beat the odds and have a few more years, but it doesn't happen like that when you have turned your lungs to hard, black granite."

"I wish there was something I could do. I feel so helpless."

"There is something you can do for me, but it's not really fair of me to ask it."

I felt a moment of apprehension, but he was my father and he was dying. Nothing would be harder than accepting the reality of that.

"You can ask me anything. I want to be a real part of your family."

"That goes without saying, but so much has changed over the years. I have another child to think about, and while LeAnn and I aren't married, I still consider her my wife, and I need to know that she will be taken care of when I'm gone."

"Father," I said, looking at him with a heart filled with compassion and tenderness. He was losing so much, but he wasn't ready for the truths I had learned about becoming forever families—even if I found the courage to try to explain. "You don't have to convince me of anything. I know how much you love LeAnn and Trevor."

"I love them dearly, but I feel the same way about you. I don't have much to leave anyone, just a lot of acres of barren ground that will support a few sheep and cattle in a good year, but it's been part of our family for generations. I don't want to see it fall into the hands of some big corporation where everything it stands for will be forgotten."

My nose and eyes were burning with emotion as I watched the man I had always looked up to as being invincible, almost crumble with the weight of the burdens he bore. It seemed he had aged even more during the four days he had been home from the hospital. But pretending there was hope was futile. He needed to know that the people he loved would be okay when he was no longer around to take care of them.

"I will make sure that happens," I promised, not having the slightest idea how to stop a takeover should it happen.

"That's exactly what I was hoping. I want to teach you the financial side of the ranch. LeAnn doesn't have a head for business, and quite frankly, I don't think it's fair to force that on her right now. But you were born for this, Brylee. You said you didn't know why you went into business, but what if this is the reason? I've asked Jake about doing it, but he likes being out with the animals and mending fences and couldn't stand being confined to the house, looking through ledgers he knows nothing about. So, what I am asking is that you stay here and run things until some other agreeable arrangement can be made. This could be a great test-run to see if owning your own business with Ben is what you really want to do with your life."

I looked at him without speaking. I had expected anything but this. How could I stay here when the man I loved—the man I was going to marry—was so far away? I hoped the enormity of what he was asking didn't show in my face.

"I know you have your own life, but I have thought about this all week. We need you here, Brylee. All of us! I just wish there was time to get to know Ben. I would like to see the two of you together, then I would know for sure if he is the right bloke for you."

"But he is, Father, and I am sure he will come so you can meet him. I'll call him the next time I go into Edna, or I could email him if you wouldn't mind letting me use your computer."

"Most certainly you can use my computer, but he might not want to meet me if he knows what I'm asking of you."

"Ben's not like that," I said, defending the man I was going to spend eternity with. "He's kind and compassionate. He will understand why I need to stay here."

"Then he's a better man than I am. I can't bear the thought of never seeing LeAnn or my children again."

I wanted to tell him that he didn't need to believe that any longer. He and LeAnn could be together again if it were what they both wanted badly enough. But that wasn't his greatest concern at the moment. He needed to know his earthly family would be provided for after he was gone, and he was asking me to be a key player. I just wished the choice had not come down to respecting my father's dying wishes or being with the man I loved.

"I'm not saying that you have to stay here forever, just long enough to make sure things are running smoothly, and the right person is found to take over. I wouldn't ask you to do this if there were any other options."

"What about Uncle Ned?" I inquired. "I'm sure he would do it. He's been running his own ranch for over 20 years."

"I talked to Ned, and of course, he said he would fill in if necessary. But he's got more than enough of his own work to do, and it doesn't seem quite right to saddle him with more. I even checked into finding a manager, but men with the qualifications I need are hard to find. It's not like it used to be. Most people don't want to live in the outback. City life is so much easier. Workdays aren't nearly as long, and weekends and vacations can be spent playing. There is never time for recreational activities out here. Besides, I don't want to leave my family's livelihood in the hands of a stranger."

"But father, I don't know anything about running a ranch."

"I could teach you all you need to know."

I looked at him skeptically. My degree had prepared me for work, but not for taking over something as important as my family's future. I was scared to even attempt it. What if my mismanagement caused them to lose the ranch? It would ruin everything for my little brother.

"I know you haven't been around the past few years, but this is your home. You might not want to live here forever, but I've watched you the past few days. You love this land. It shows in your face every time I look at you."

There was so much at stake, I felt chills running up and down my arms. "What if I can't do it?"

"You can do anything you set your mind to! That's how I have survived all these years. My father taught me how to keep books. It's nothing fancy like you learned in school, but it works for us. Jake and LeAnn can teach you everything else since it doesn't look like I will be able to do much more than wander around the house until it's over now."

I refused to talk about him dying after the great sacrifice he had just ask me to make. "Jake doesn't really want me here."

"You misjudge him. He's not a bad man and is very loyal to his family. He knows everything that goes on around here."

"That's just the problem! I'm not his family. He thinks I only came back to see what I could get from you financially."

"That's ridiculous," he said. "You've never asked me for anything."

"And I never will. This is your land, and you can do with it whatever you like."

"My dying wish was to see my family reunited. I never thought it would happen, but it did. I know my request seems rather harsh, but it's something I feel very strongly about. I love you, Brylee. I just wish there was more time to get to know you better, but Trevor is going to need you after I'm gone. I know it was a shock finding out about him the way you did, but I am beginning to believe there was more than my selfishness involved in his conception. I was able to give you a little brother. That might not seem like such a big deal right now, but it could be, if you would allow it."

I looked over at him as my heart did a whirly-gig. He was my father, and I loved him. Nothing else seemed to matter right now. Not my mother's death, his affair with LeAnn, the shock of meeting Trevor, Jake's hostility or my desire to be with Ben. I had a responsibility to the man who had helped give me life, and I would deal with everything else when I had to.

"Father," I said, leaning forward and kissing his thin, sallow cheek. "I'll do it. I will stay here and learn the family business, and I won't leave until there is someone else who can run it the right way. I want the ranch to stay in our family."

"Thank you," he said as tears poured from his eyes. He wiped at them with a hand that was trembling. "I've never been much for religion. You know that, but if there is a God—and if he brought you home to me—then I thank him with all my heart. I know that's why it has taken me so long to die. I needed to see my little girl just one more time."

"I'm sorry for all the pain I've caused," I said as giant gulps of sadness betrayed the sorrow and pain I felt over having denied both of us the chance of being together. How could I have been so stubborn and blind? We all make mistakes, and we all sin. Wasn't that why we had a Saviour? "I just wish I had learned sooner that holding grudges always comes at too great a cost."

"I'm the wrong bloke to give you any advice when it comes to forgiving grudges or making good decisions. My fate was sealed when I put that first cigarette to my lips. It didn't seem quite so menacing back then—just a single sheet of paper with a few mashed-up leaves inside. I'm just glad you didn't follow in my footsteps in that regard, and I do hope that young bloke of yours knows just how bloody lucky he is to have you in his life."

"I'm the lucky one," I told him. "Being with Ben makes me want to be a better person. I wouldn't be here now if it wasn't for him."

"Is that right?" he said, giving me an understanding smile. "Make sure you thank him for me. I would do it in person, but I really don't want him to see me like this. I've never been sick like this a day in my life before now, and it's damned depressing. I will not have my future son-in-law feeling sorry for me."

"Ben isn't the pitying kind."

"Well, he's young, and hopefully living a much cleaner lifestyle than those of us in the outback do."

"He's the one who helped me change."

"That's good," he said. "I want you to have someone to lean on, someone who will always be faithful to you. Sometimes I wished I believed there was life after death. I rather like the idea of seeing your mother again and making things right with her."

"You'll get that chance," I said, kneeling in front of him so I could see his face more clearly. Perhaps this was the moment I had been praying for to introduce the gospel. He seemed to be in a more receptive mood. "You will have all the time you need and more."

His laugh was punctuated by another bout of coughing. I gripped his hand tightly because there wasn't anything else I could do.

"I've never read the Bible, and I haven't been inside a church since you were baptized. I'm not sure God even knows who I am."

"Oh, father!" I exclaimed. "God knows everything about us because we are his children. He wants us to come home to him."

"Is that what your new church teaches?"

"Yes, and so much more. Why can't you believe that God is real, and that we are not here by chance? It's all so simple, really."

"Because I'm a dying, old bloke who never gave religion a chance, although I was baptized the same as you. Why did you feel it was necessary to leave the Catholic church? Your mother was such a devoted woman."

"Because I found the complete truth elsewhere."

"Truth!" he mocked. "I guess we will have to agree to disagree on that because I certainly don't want to spend my last hours on earth arguing about religion with my daughter. I don't see that it matters much anyway. No one knows for sure what is going to happen when we die. For all we know, our bodies will rot in the ground and that will be the end of it. But I do want you to promise me that I will get the last rites from Father Frederick. It's what your mother would have wanted."

"I promise, Father, but I know that while our bodies might return to the dust of the earth, our spirits will live forever." I took a deep breath. "And we can be together as a family again someday, if we want it badly enough."

"If your religion brings you comfort, then I am happy for you," he replied before the coughing began again. "But what I am really concerned about right now is making sure this ranch stays in our family. Now, I'm tired, and I think we should both go to bed. We have a lot of work to do, starting tomorrow."

I wanted to tell him more about what I knew to be true, but I couldn't force him to listen to or accept anything. He was worried about this life, not the one he would soon be entering. When he got there, there would be people to teach him all he needed to know. I hoped it would be my mother. But even if it wasn't, I had to leave his life in God's hands.

I kissed him goodnight and headed up the stairs to my room. It was dark and still. Not even the birds and insects were making their presence known. It was a weird kind of eerie, almost as if the world was waiting for another life to end.

I spent the next few days secluded in the den with my father. I loved that he believed in me, but it was hard watching his health fail a little more each day, and I prayed every night that he'd last long enough to teach me what I needed to learn so his legacy for his family could continue long after he was gone.

As the hours moved relentlessly onward, I began to suspect that he'd kept every receipt and business transaction he'd ever made, but none of this information had been transferred to the computer. He had boxes of receipts and dozens of envelopes containing bank statements. It was very discouraging, and I could easily see why no one would want to take over as ranch manager. It would take me weeks to scan documents and enter figures so I could get a baseline of what had been happening over the past few years. It appeared that all formal record-keeping had stopped at the time of my mother's death. Either she had been the one keeping the books, or he had been too devastated to continue once she and I were gone.

There were many times during the hours I spent locked away that I wanted to throw my hands in the air and scream, but how could I fault him for not keeping better records when I'd turned my back on him during his hour of greatest need? Even in an unschooled way, I might have been able to help him.

LeAnn stayed home with Trevor so I could work without interruptions. I believe she knew that there was more to do than could possibly be completed during the limited time my father had left to help me. She brought in my meals, helped scan documents, made phone calls, and kept Trevor occupied with jobs he was not in the habit of doing.

We worked from seven in the morning until after eleven at night. My father stayed with me as long as he could, and while he rested, I kept going. I felt like my eyes would never recover from the abuse they were taking from spending 18 hours a day looking at a computer screen, but I was more worried about my father. Each day I could visibly see him become weaker and his skin tone a little grayer. He coughed all the time, and even with oxygen, he wasn't getting enough air. The Hospice ladies made the two-hour trip from Edna every other day to make sure we were doing okay.

The night before I was supposed to fly home, I finally emailed Ben. It had been impossible to get into town to call him. I might have done it sooner had I not been so busy and so afraid of what his reaction would be when I told him I wouldn't be at the airport as expected. Half of me wanted to be with him, planning our wedding, and the other half wanted to be right where I was, trying to help my father. It was an impossible situation, and I had never been any good at confrontations. The plane I was supposed to be on would already be in the air by the time he was able to get back to me.

Chapter 13

As the days went by, I felt like I was making some headway getting the ranch's financial records in order, but I had no idea how to run the day-to-day operations. I was terrified of failing that part of my forced education. It was okay as long as my father was there to tutor me, but what would happen when he was gone? Jake still didn't trust me. I knew that because of the way he glared in my direction whenever our paths crossed.

On the flip side, LeAnn was generous with her praise, and I was grateful she had been with my father during the years I wasn't around. Their relationship was built on trust and an incredible amount of hard work. I watched their interactions closely, not just to see how different it was from what he had shared with my mother, but to see if I could garner any information on how to be a more loving and thoughtful wife when that time came. I had nothing personal to draw from and was willing to take direction where I could find it.

The realization that I no longer harbored any ill will towards the woman who had taken my mother's place came suddenly. Perhaps God, without my knowledge, had been tempering my feelings so I could be of more help to my new family during a very stressful and difficult time. With the added benefit of being better able to create the life I envisioned when Ben and I were married. It simply no longer mattered that we were not related by either blood or marriage, but even that was about to change.

One Tuesday morning, right after we had finished eating breakfast, my father called me into his den to give me some news I wasn't exactly prepared to hear. He was still trying to spend time with me when his condition allowed, but each day it became more of a struggle for him to even get out of bed.

"Could you close the door, love?" he asked after I walked into the room. I was more comfortable with that term of endearment now that it had become familiar again. Americans were much more cautious with words like love. I figured it had something to do with the fast-paced lives they lived, and not wanting to have anyone expect a commitment when none was intended. "There's something important I want to talk to you about."

"Sure," I said, knowing that he could never tell me anything more shattering than the fact that he was dying. I had already accepted the fact that he wanted to leave the ranch to Trevor when he was old enough to run it. And in an odd way, I was glad he trusted me enough to get things running smoothly before I returned to Ben.

What I didn't know was how long I would have to remain in Australia after he was gone to fulfill that promise. My stomach churned each time I thought about Ben and my father at the same time. Going home to the man I loved would mean that my father was gone, and I would no longer have a reason to return to the land of my birth, except for an occasional visit.

But what if I couldn't get things running smoothly before I left them in someone else's hands? And what if Ben got tired of waiting for me and found someone else? I tried not to dwell on matters that were now out of my control, but each day away from the man I loved made the life we'd had together seem more remote. I needed his strength, but the only time I could feel his arms protectively around me was during some blissful dream. The harsh reality of daylight made me wonder if I would ever feel completely happy again.

"I think you know how I feel about LeAnn," he said, interrupting my conflicted thoughts.

"Yes," I told him. "You love her."

"I love her very much, and I need to know that she will be taken care of after I'm gone."

"I've already promised to do that," I said.

"And I trust that you will, but the government doesn't always see things the way we do. Legally, she has no claim to any part of the ranch because we aren't married. So I . . . ." He paused and took a deep breath, coughing as he did so. "So, I've asked her to marry me. I would like to have the ceremony here at the ranch tomorrow, if possible."

I had to take a deep breath of my own before answering. It was the right thing to do, but knowing he would be married to someone other than my mother changed everything. I wanted to be part of a forever family. How was that supposed to happen when my parents were no longer together? My faith was being terribly shaken. What if I found that I could no longer leave everything in God's hands? I couldn't help wanting what I wanted.

"That's wonderful," I finally said. "What can I do to help?"

"Well," he said, leaning back in his chair as if he had used every ounce of strength he possessed just to make the announcement. "I've asked Jake to fly into Edna today to get some rings. I want LeAnn to have one that's special. I think he knows his sister well enough to pick out something she will like."

Another sharp intake of breath made my heart hurt. Why did everything have to happen so quickly? I would gladly have looked for a ring for LeAnn, but now was not the time to be petty. Jake knew his sister far better than I did.

"I'm sure he will," I responded.

"But I want you to go with him so you can visit the florist. We don't need a lot of flowers, just a few roses and daisies. LeAnn doesn't want anything fancy. I wanted her to pick out a new dress, but she refuses to leave the ranch for fear something might happen to me while she's gone."

"I get that. Maybe I could pick out something pretty for her to wear if I knew her size."

"That's what I was hoping you would say. LeAnn never asks for anything, especially for me to marry her at a time like this, but I want her to have one very special day to remember. I know there can't be a honeymoon, but perhaps some arrangements could be made so we can have the house to ourselves for the night. It's a lot to take in, I know, but LeAnn deserves this and so does Trevor."

"Then we'll make it happen," I said, as my eyes brimmed with tears. I didn't want to go into town with Jake, and I didn't want my father to marry someone else, but these were not my decisions to make. I could go along with everything and try to be happy, or I could make a scene and spoil the day for everyone. After all, I still had Ben. LeAnn was the one who would soon be losing the love of her life.

"I can't thank you enough for everything you've done," he said. "I know none of this has been easy for you. And my marrying LeAnn isn't going to make things any better, but I do love her and want us to be married—even if it is for a very short time."

I swallowed back all my misgivings and fears.

"We'll make it the most special wedding any woman could ask for. What about a license and ceremony?"

"Buck Henry is an ordained minister, as well as my personal barrister, and he has connections at the courthouse. He'll perform the ceremony and bring the necessary paperwork when he comes. I guess it pays to have friends in the right places. Would you be one of our witnesses?"

"It would be my honor," I told him as I walked up behind him, put my hands on his thin shoulders, and kissed the top of his head. He was so weak he didn't even try to protest.

"I hate asking you to do so much in one day, but there really isn't time to plan anything more elaborate."

"Not to worry," I told him. "There isn't anything in the world I would not do for you. I just wish I had come home sooner. I missed out on so much by running away."

"Stop with the regrets, love. We all have them. I just hope fate deals somewhat kindly with me, and I have a few more weeks with my family."

"You will," I told him. "Your family loves you very much."

He opened a drawer in the mahogany desk and pulled out a small key. "There's a strongbox in the cabinet underneath the bookcase. Could you get it for me?"

I found what he had asked for. It could more accurately be called a small, fireproof safe, and he put it on the desk in front of him.

"Would you like me to leave?" I asked, knowing that I didn't want to see anything that was private.

"I have nothing to hide," he said, placing the key in the lock and turning it. The gray box opened. Inside were a number of folded documents. "You need to know what's in here anyway because I have decided to make you my executor, as well as one of my heirs."

My hands flew over my mouth.

"But why?" I asked, more than just a little shocked by his decision. This would not go over well with Jake. Both he and LeAnn knew far more about the ranch than I did—even after my crash course in the financial end—and Jake still believed I had come home with ulterior motives. This would only make things worse between us.

"Because I trust you to make the right decisions."

"But shouldn't either LeAnn or Jake be left in charge? I don't want him thinking I forced you into doing it. He already believes I came here to get an inheritance."

"Jake is part of the family, but he doesn't make decisions for me. You have every right to an inheritance. You are my daughter."

"I don't want anything, Father. I just came home so I could see you again."

"The time for recriminations is over. This is what I want. I've already discussed it with Buck. He's bringing the papers for you to sign tomorrow when he comes for the wedding. Besides, I have seen how much you've done since you got here, and the sacrifices you've been willing to make. This land is a part of you, just as it is a part of me. That's something that cannot be overlooked."

I considered what my father had said as I returned to my room to dress for my trip to Edna with Jake. Did my father really know me better than I knew myself? Did I love Australia and the ranch in the outback enough to stay here permanently?

And what about my other home? The one that was thousands of miles away with the man I was going to marry. Ben had not responded to the email I'd sent him about my reasons for having to stay in Australia longer than anticipated, and I couldn't help but wonder why. I needed his support now more than ever. I would call him while I was in Edna to see what was going on.

My father had given me a thousand dollars to buy a dress for LeAnn and order a few flowers and a small wedding cake. Other than the five of us at the ranch, the only other people attending the ceremony would be Uncle Ned and his family, and of course, Buck Henry, the family lawyer and self-ordained minister. I hoped LeAnn would be happy with the arrangements. It wasn't the kind of wedding I was planning for myself, but I would make the day as special as possible anyway.

Jake was gracious and even held the plane door open so I could climb in. I was wearing cream colored Capris and a black top. It seemed pointless to dress up when I knew I would be hot and sweaty long before my errands were done. Besides, I had only brought one dress with me, and I needed to keep that clean and sweat-free for the wedding. I just wished it wasn't white. That was what the bride was supposed to wear, even if she wasn't a virgin when she got married.

"I hope you don't mind my coming with you today," I told him after we were in the air. "I could have driven into town, but father thought this would be more convenient."

"It is and much faster. Everything in Edna is within walking distance. I hope you don't mind, but I divided our jobs. I don't like being away from the ranch for long."

He reached into his shirt pocket and pulled out a crumpled piece of paper.

"You can rip the list in two. I tried to divide things so they would be more convenient. You know more about girl things than I do, and besides, I have some personal business to attend to while we're there."

I took the crumpled paper without making a comment. There was no reason to start an argument. His jobs included buying the rings, seeing Buck Henry and whatever his secret business was. I was to buy LeAnn's dress, go to the florist's for flowers and to the bakery for a small wedding cake. It seemed like a fair division of labor and was exactly what my father had suggested.

I looked out at the white clouds and blue sky and wondered why my world had to keep spinning so fast. All I had wanted was to come home and see my father before I married Ben. And now it was my father who was getting married, and my wedding had been put on hold.

"I forgot to ask father about LeAnn's favorite colours," I said, trying to stop the melancholia from settling in. "Could you help me with that?"

I looked at his chiseled features and his narrowed eyes. I hoped it was only from the sun and not because he was being forced to spend part of a day with me. We had both been very careful not to get into any disagreements after our promise to LeAnn. Father's final days needed to be as pleasant as humanly possible. Besides, after tomorrow, we would legally be family.

"Never really thought about it, but I guess blue is as good as any."

His statement was brief, but I knew better than to pry. Jake and his sister were both very private people. I could understand that. I didn't like people knowing everything about me either. So I just sat back and tried to enjoy the rest of the short flight. I would have to rely on my own observations to pick things she would hopefully like.

It was nearly noon by the time Jake set the plane down at Edna's small airport. The day was already blistering hot, and beads of perspiration formed on my forehead almost immediately when I put my feet on the ground. I watched Jake smile as we made our way into the terminal.

"It's good to see you again, Jake," the girl at the counter said. "I didn't know you were coming into town today."

I could hardly miss the fact that she was both surprised and happy to see him.

"It was an unexpected trip," he replied as he closed the short distance between them and put his elbows down on the counter. "How's life treating you, Janet?"

"Couldn't be better, now that I've seen you, that is. Will you be coming to the dance at Quincy's on Saturday night?"

"Not sure!" he said. "Things are rather unsettled out at the ranch right now."

"I heard about Jack. How's your sister holding up?"

"It's been hard, but LeAnn's strong."

"Is there anything I can do to help?"

"Not a thing," he said as he smiled again and tilted her face towards his. "A pretty girl like you shouldn't have to worry about anything."

She blushed, and it left me with a feeling of irritation. It was obvious that she didn't know the side of him I did.

"Oh," she said, suddenly noticing my presence. "I didn't see you come in."

"She's with me," Jake told her.

Her countenance immediately darkened.

"It's not like that, Janet. She's Jack's daughter—the one who's been gone for five years. Didn't even leave a forwarding address."

His comment hurt, but it wasn't worth the effort to make a scene. People would either like me or they wouldn't. Besides, I had no plans of being here long enough for it to really matter.

"I didn't know Jack had a daughter, but then I have only been here for a couple of years. Are you planning on staying?" she asked me.

"I'll be here for as long as I'm needed or wanted."

"Don't let that comment worry your pretty head, Janet," Jake interjected. "She's engaged to some bloke back in the States."

"Oh," she said, dismissing me as a potential threat. "I hope you have a nice stay. I really am sorry about your father."

"Thank you," I told her, wishing everyone in town didn't know more about my family than I did. But then what could I expect after such a long absence? I didn't want to address Jake again since he was so obviously into the flame-haired girl at the counter, but I needed to know how much time I had to complete the errands I had been given. It wasn't going to be easy shopping for someone I barely knew.

"Do you want me to meet you here after we've finished?" I asked.

His look of annoyance made me frown.

"It's as good a place as any, I suppose! How long is it going to take you? I can be through in a couple of hours."

"I'm not sure, but I will hurry as fast as I can. I don't want to be away from the ranch any longer than you do."

"At least we agree about that. Why don't we meet up at Emma's Diner instead of here. It's a little place next to the only bakery in town. It shouldn't be too hard for you to find. You can get everything else at the shopping center on 2nd and Banks."

"I know where Emma's Diner is," I told him. "When do you want me to be there?"

"How about three? That will give me some time to visit with my girl, Janet." He gave her a broad smile and turned his back on me.

She was elated! I was angry! How many times was he going to humiliate me? I had never done anything to him personally, and I had kept my word to LeAnn. I'd been pleasant whenever we saw each other, but maybe those promises only applied when we were on the ranch. I looked at the back of his head before walking away. In my opinion, he needed a haircut and a change of wardrobe. He was wearing a t-shirt with khaki shorts and work boots. I doubted he had anything better to wear to the wedding. He would ruin the entire thing.

As I walked along the sidewalk in the scorching heat, a car passed by. Janet was driving, and Jake was in the passenger seat. He must have planned our arrival to coincide with her lunch break, but there wasn't anything I could do about that or about his ungentlemanly behavior. I had a wedding to prepare for, and I would do my best to make sure it was one LeAnn would never forget.

I was learning to love my soon-to-be stepmother and my little half-brother, despite the circumstances that had brought them into my life. But I was so tired of tears—tears that would not go away, soon any time soon. But I couldn't think about that now either. I was glad my cell phone could serve as a camera. I might not be able to make any calls from the ranch, but I had brought the adapter that connected it to a computer from Los Angeles. The decision I'd made during our time in the air that morning had almost shocked me, it was so personal and time-consuming, but I would take lots of pictures at the wedding and put them in a memory book for LeAnn and Trevor. It would help them remember the day after....

Oh, why did I have to lose my father so soon after losing my mother? I didn't want to be an orphan. I wanted one of my parents around to watch my own family grow up, but that wasn't going to happen now.

I thought about my mother as I walked along the sidewalk in the heat of the early afternoon. People were hurrying into the pubs for their noon respites. A cold one with fish 'n chips was a favorite noon meal. I had never become that fond of seafood, although I had lived in Sydney for nearly four years, where some form of it was served in nearly every eatery. It was too crunchy or too stringy for my taste. Even lobster failed to entice me. The thought of dripping butter was most distasteful. Thank goodness Ben wasn't fond of it either. He was more a pasta and salad kind of guy, and that was okay with me.

In less than 15 minutes, I was at Edna's open-air mall that Jake had referred to as a shopping center. Only a few buildings surrounded the courtyard, but from the number of people milling around, it must have become a very welcome addition to the little town with its waterfall in the center and a food court at one end. There were fewer than ten stores, and as I walked from one establishment to another, I realised it might be more challenging than I anticipated finding something appropriate for LeAnn to wear to her wedding.

There were plenty of shorts and jeans to choose from, but very few skirts or dresses. People in the outback rarely dressed up. Even attending church was mostly a casual affair. If there had been more time, I would have proposed a trip to Sydney or to one of the closer, but larger towns, where there might be a better chance of finding what I was looking for.

LeAnn was very slender. Most people would call her figure athletic, but I doubted she had ever played sports. She kept in shape by working hard and eating like a bird. I wanted to find her a simple summer dress that she might enjoy wearing again, but it was a year of flashy colours and big prints even in the few summer dresses I found. I asked every clerk I met if they knew where I might find something a little less ostentatious, but they all told me the same thing. If I wanted something like that I needed to go shopping in the city. The establishments in Edna catered to the needs of the people who lived there and fancy was not one of the requirements.

I was just about to give up and buy the least flamboyant dress I had looked at when I happened upon a sale rack of last year's attire in the back of a very small woman's clothing shop. And there it was, the perfect dress in the perfect size. It was made of light blue, silky fabric with tiny, white flowers embroidered on the ruffled edge of a skirt that would fall just above her ankles. I hoped she had shoes to go with it.

Suddenly, I felt more excited about the prospect of being in charge of a wedding and wanted to do something really special for both LeAnn and my father. It might be the last real act of service I could offer him, and I knew how much he wanted to make the day perfect. So I bought the dress and a simple silver locket to go with it. I would take pictures of my father and Trevor when I got home, crop them to the right size, and then reproduce them on the printer that was connected to his computer. It would be something new every bride needed on her wedding day.

I would ask Aunt Nora if she had something LeAnn could borrow, and I would purchase a blue garter belt for her to wear. There had to be a place in town that sold things like that. People might be practical at the edge of the outback, but they still got married, and they still believed in tradition. I would ask my father if there wasn't something old that he could give her. I knew he had a few things that had been handed down from one generation to the next. He told me they would be mine one day, but I wanted LeAnn to have something that had belonged to one of the women in the Hawkins' family. After all, by tomorrow evening, she would be a Hawkins too.

The next stop was the florists. I wanted some simple white daisies and blue baby's breath with just a touch of greenery for LeAnn to carry. They would match her dress to perfection. Roses seemed too heavy and formal for the type of wedding I was planning in my head. I just hoped the floral shop had what I envisioned because there wasn't time to order anything special since this would be our only trip to town. Father hadn't mentioned a time for the wedding, but I knew it wouldn't be too late in the day since he was at his best first thing in the morning.

When I explained the situation to the pleasant-looking man behind the desk, he assured me that everything I wanted would be ready by five. He had all the flowers he needed in stock for three boutonnières, an arrangement of long-stemmed daisies that could be tied with the blue and white ribbon I wanted, and a small centerpiece for the table. He even said he would throw in a few extra flowers, at no cost, to weave through LeAnn's long, blond hair. His kindness and generosity moved me to tears, and I thanked him before moving on to the bakery.

The lady who was busy arranging fresh cookies in the display case was equally as gracious. She assured me that a three-layer wedding cake with blue frosting flowers would be ready by five as well. It appeared that there might be a small rivalry between the flower shop and the bakery because she offered to throw in some home-baked rolls for the wedding supper. I told her it wasn't necessary since I didn't even know if we would be having one, but she insisted, so I let her.

I felt a moment of uncertainty when I walked back out into the sunshine. Jake wasn't going to like the fact that I had made a decision concerning his time without consulting him. But two hours wasn't long, and he would just have to accept it—unless he wanted to come back in the morning to pick everything up. A delivery drive of over four hours by two separate companies seemed a little excessive when we could transport everything ourselves in a fraction of the time.

It was nearly three when I entered the air-conditioned diner where Jake was supposed to meet me. He wasn't there, so I hung the dress in its garment bag on the coat rack near the door, and selected a booth near the window where I could watch for his arrival. A waitress in her early twenties came over to greet me.

"How are you today, love?" she asked in a most pleasant voice. I had missed hearing the Aussie accent since moving to the United States and had tried my best to minimize the one I had taken with me. "What can I get you to drink? I just finished brewing a great new tea."

I ordered lemonade. I was hungry but didn't want to be eating a meal, or worse, waiting for one to arrive when Jake got there. I was glad I had waited because my drink had yet to be delivered when he walked in.

"Have you been waiting long?" he asked. "My errands took longer than anticipated."

From the way he was smiling, I knew what he was referring to without asking. He and Janet had not been sharing lunch, but I certainly didn't want to hear about any of his escapades.

"No," I replied, trying to keep my tone light. "I just got here and ordered some lemonade. Do you want something?"

"Now, that's a stupid question to ask a bloke whose mouth is as dry as the bottom of a cochy's cage," he retorted. "It's mid-afternoon, and I haven't had a bite of anything since breakfast."

To my great relief, the pretty, blonde waitress brought my lemonade. "Why, Jake Johnson," she said, batting her eyelashes at him. "I haven't seen you for ages. Do you want your usual?"

I wasn't sure what surprised me more—all the women in town flirting with him, or the fact that his last name was Johnson.

"You know me too well, Beth," he said, "And bring me the coldest grog you've got to wash it down. You look especially beautiful today."

She blushed as she pulled her order book from the front pocket of her pink and white uniform. "And you're still that silver-tongued, handsome devil that no girl in town can resist," she said as he casually ran his fingers down her arm. I wanted to leave the table. Could he be any more obvious in his intentions towards the opposite sex?

"This is Jack's daughter," he said without looking at me. "She came back quite unexpectedly."

He was doing it to me again, making me feel like I did not belong, but I wouldn't give him the satisfaction of seeing just how much his unkind words hurt me.

"I'll have a burger and fries," I told her. Then I averted my eyes to the window and what was going on outside. A few people passed by with a water bottle in one hand and a few parcels in the other. The sky was still clear and blue, and every so often, a soft breeze would ripple the cloth awning on the building across the street. I knew the town would come alive with people hurrying to the pubs again once the sun went down, and it wasn't quite as hot.

"What are you staring at?" Jake asked me a few minutes later. "You've had your nose glued to that window ever since Beth took our orders. Am I that bad of company?"

I turned my head and glanced at him. "I don't want to fight, Jake. I just want to make tomorrow the best day possible for my father and LeAnn."

"Well, so do I," he said, giving me a blank look that assured me he had no idea what I was talking about.

I didn't feel like addressing the real issue of his rude and demeaning attitude. If I had learned anything since coming home, it was to pick my battles carefully because some things really didn't matter. Jake could only make my life miserable if I let him, and I would never do that again. Besides, an idea had come to me quite suddenly when I left the bakery.

"That's good," I replied. "Now that we're on the same wavelength, at least for the moment, there's something I would like to discuss with you."

"This ought to be choice," he said, slumping against the back of the booth we were sitting in. "I can't wait to hear what your pea-sized brain has come up with now."

Once again, I wanted to say something equally as distasteful to him as his comment had been to me, but I chose to take the higher road.

"Father would like a special wedding night—a nice dinner, romantic music, and all of us gone so they can have the house to themselves."

"Won't be a problem for me," he said. "I live in the bunkhouse. Trevor can stay with me. It's you who will have to vacate."

"I'm not asking you to watch Trevor. I thought he could drive into Edna with me and see a movie. We could even stay overnight. It would give us a chance to get better acquainted and do something a little different."

"Sounds like you have it all planned out. So what do you need me for?"

"Nothing, I guess. I just thought you might like to help out since it is your sister's wedding too."

"Look, if you want to plan something special, that's fine, but count me out. I am not into cooking and decorating and all that woman's stuff. Give me a few cold grogs, a lightly seared steak, and I'll be perfectly content. I know Jack feels the same way."

"What about LeAnn? Don't you think she wants something a little more festive to remind her of her wedding day? She and my father have so little time left."

"You surprise me, Brylee. I had no idea you'd grown so fond of my sister."

"LeAnn has been nothing but kind to me."

"But she's an interloper into your otherwise idealized childhood."

"My childhood wasn't ideal!" I told him as the waitress, Beth, placed our orders on the table and asked if there was anything else we needed.

"Not unless you're part of the menu," Jake told her. "I haven't seen nearly enough of you lately. Do you still hang out at the clubs at night?"

"Every night," she said. "You know I only work here to irritate the oldies, and I never know when I might run into one of my mates."

"You can run into me anytime you like," he told her.

"That runs both ways," she replied before moving on to another table.

He watched her hips move seductively back and forth before turning his attention back to me. "What were the two of us talking about?" he asked.

"My childhood, but that's hardly any concern of yours."

"On the contrary. You were your father's firstborn, and now Trevor is going to steal your birthright. Seems to me there are a few stories like that in the Bible. The older sibling is losing out to the younger one."

"Is that how you feel about your relationship with LeAnn? You are her younger brother."

"My relationship with my sister has nothing to do with what we're talking about. There is no inheritance in the Johnson family. Our parents were day laborers who struggled to keep food on the table until the day they died."

"And you don't think my parents did that? It took my father a long time to build up what he has."

"Your father had the ranch given to him. All he had to do was keep it running."

"So you're condemning my father as well as me."

"I'm not condemning anyone," he said, his mouth filled with a huge bite of a double-decker cheeseburger. He dabbed at the juice that was coming out of the corners of his mouth. "I'm just saying that some people seem to get more than their fair amount of luck."

"And you think my father is lucky to be dying when he's still a young man with a little boy to raise?"

"You're putting words in my mouth."

"No more than the ones you keep putting in mine. Despite what you think, I am not here to claim anything. I have been on my own for the past five years and can take care of myself."

"Then why did you tell your father you would stay here and run the ranch? I thought you were anxious to get back to that saintly bloke you're supposed to be marrying."

"Leave Ben out of this! I'm staying because my father asked me to take care of the financial end of the operation until a suitable manager can be found. If memory serves me correctly, and I know it does, he asked you first, but you refused. I wasn't his first choice."

"Hell, I'm not some bloody bookkeeper! I would die if I had to stay cooped up inside all the time."

"Well, lucky for you, my decision means you won't have to. And don't worry, I have no plans to stay here indefinitely. My life is back in Los Angeles with the man I love, as you so aptly reminded me."

I had said far more than intended, but he needed to understand that I wasn't a threat to anyone. I had simply made a promise to my father—one I intended to keep.

We finished the meal in silence. I was too angry to speak to him anymore. He was rude, arrogant and unkind. How anyone expected me to get along with him was a mystery. He had no desire to see anyone else's point of view. He just wanted to be adored by every woman he met. Well, the other women could have him. I only wanted Ben.

I had sneaked a few glances at him while finishing my burger and fries. Why was he so angry? And what had caused him to think of me as the enemy? I had tried to stay out of his way, but he was always showing up unexpectedly and telling me what an awful person he thought I was.

Quite suddenly, I realized that I had not mentioned what had been finalized at the florists and bakery. He would want to leave the moment we finished eating. "If I could have your attention for just a minute."

He looked over at me and glared. "Are you speaking to me?"

"Yes! I forgot to tell you that both the cake and the flowers will be ready by five. It couldn't be done any sooner. Do you want to wait around so we can take them home with us, or would you rather come back in the morning?"

"Sonny at the bakery already called me. Why else would I be sitting here in the diner with you? It's not like we're on some bloody date. This is just as unpleasant for me as it is for you."

"I'm sorry you feel that way," I said, clenching my teeth so I wouldn't say anything more. "I suppose you know about the flowers too?"

"What's not to know," he said. "Edna's a very small town."

I wanted to throw the rest of my drink in his face. He was so smug and hateful. Why had he sent me on errands he could have taken care of with a couple of phone calls? Maybe he just wanted some alone time with his lady friends and wanted to make sure I was aware of their infatuation with him. Well, he could drop of the face of the earth for all I cared.

He drank the last swallow of beer in his glass. "I'm sure you can find something to do for the next hour," he said, eyeing Beth appreciatively.

"I'm sure I can," I replied, hating the fact that he could get to me at all. I would spend what little time I had left in town planning the perfect wedding night for LeAnn and my father.

There was plenty of food at the ranch and plenty of wine. Making a nice meal for after the ceremony would be easy, but I wanted the night to be extraordinary. It would be one of the last they had together.

I would find a negligee that made her feel sensual and beautiful, and buy crystal champagne glasses and strawberries dipped in chocolate. I would even find a CD with romantic music and put rose petals on their bed.

I left Jake sitting in the booth at the diner and picked up the garment bag holding the wedding dress on my way out. It was cumbersome to carry, but there was no way I would ask him to do anything else for me. I could find my own way back to the airport with the dress, the cake, the flowers and everything else I needed to set my plan in motion. Jake could be just as unpleasant as he chose to be. I would counter his attitude with cheerfulness and industry. Then maybe he'd see me as more than a useless slug.

I didn't have much time, so I went back to the bakery to ask where I might find the things I was looking for. Mrs. Mahoney, the owner, directed me to a little shop two streets over that catered to the more sensual side of living. Under normal circumstances, I would never have gone there, but I was desperate. I had less than an hour to get everything done.

Before leaving the bakery, I arranged to have the cake delivered to the airport. I did the same with the florist. Mrs. Mahoney suggested I leave the dress with her while I ran the rest of my errands. She even told me I could ride with her in the van, if I could be back to the shop by a quarter to five. The chocolate-covered strawberries I wanted were already sitting in her display case. Apparently, they were a very popular item.

Walking into *The Boudoir* was an experience I never contemplated having. But I wasn't planning my wedding to Ben where worldly customs would be left behind when we made our vows. The shop smelled of heavy perfumes and a hint of chocolate, but I closed my eyes to what I didn't want to see and concentrated on lovely sleepwear, cutlery, stemware and tasteful garter belts.

From observations made since coming home, LeAnn wasn't an ostentatious woman. She valued the simple things in life that included industry, never being the center of attention and making sure the people she cared about knew they were loved. I somehow felt she would appreciate the elegance that made her feel sensual but did not draw attention to itself as being created merely to induce lustful thoughts.

So, I selected a long, black satin negligee with a tasteful cut, and added a blue garter belt, two champagne glasses, a silver cake knife and a ring pillow to my purchase. Trevor needed be part of the ceremony. He was young now, and it wouldn't matter what part he played, but when he was older he would be glad that he had not been left out.

Knowing what my father or my little brother planned on wearing to the wedding was impossible since men seldom discussed clothing. But since I had been left in charge, I decided to get both of them new, white shirts. Ties were out of the question since no one in the outback ever wore them. I momentarily contemplated looking at suits, but that seemed insensitive in light of what the future held. My father would be wearing one of those for another kind of service soon enough. Tomorrow was for the living.

My idea for a memory book was growing. Instead of just including pictures of the wedding, I should look for pictures of the family and include some of them. There was no way of knowing how it would be received, but perhaps it would bring comfort in the days ahead. I had less than a handful of pictures of my mother. Looking at them always helped bridge the gap between what I had lost and what I hoped to have again one day. I quickly scanned the rows of supplies in a scrapbooking store since I was running out of time, and was lucky enough to find a wedding album with accompanying pages that would save me from having to design some of my own. Maybe if I worked really hard, I would have it ready so my father could see it before he left us.

That thought forced all the sorrowful emotions I had been trying to keep inside back to the surface. I was happy and sad, angry and sympathetic, determined and scared, but mostly I was filled with love and compassion for the people who had come into my life in such an unexpected way. I had a little brother who had accepted me without reservations, and I had a new friend in LeAnn. It would not be easy to leave them when my work on the ranch was done.

During the few weeks I'd been home, I had come to understand that life was not just a matter of milestones like school, marriage or career. It was a matter of moments spent with the people who were most important. I had lost so many moments with my father by running away, and that pained me deeply. But I would not do it again, even if it meant a real showdown with Jake.

I was back at the bakery by the appointed time. The muscles in my arms and legs were burning from carrying so many packages. The wedding cake was sitting on the counter waiting to be packed so we could get it to the ranch safely. Everyone had been so thoughtful, and I knew both the florist and Mrs. Mahoney had given me everything at a little more than cost. It was their way of saying both congratulations and goodbye.

"It's beautiful," I told Mrs. Mahoney.

"So glad you like it," she replied with a sigh of relief. "I took a chance by making a few changes to what you said you wanted because I know what LeAnn likes. It's chocolate because that's her favorite flavor, and the top layer can be frozen for later."

"It's perfect," I said, putting my packages on the floor so my hands would be free, and I could get a better look at the cake. It was three layers as promised, with a small bride and groom on the top and tiny yellow flowers, green leaves and blue frosting ribbons. What she had created was even better than I had imagined.

"The bottom layer is Styrofoam. I figured with such a small wedding party you wouldn't want all that cake left over. It dries out awfully fast in this heat."

"I'll make sure they stay away from the Styrofoam, and I'm sure LeAnn will want to freeze the top layer like you suggested."

I really didn't know what LeAnn would do with the cake or anything else left over from the wedding. Maybe she was the kind of person who didn't want a lot of sentimental reminders. But it was always better to err on the side of too much than too little, and I didn't feel like anything I had done could be construed as excessive.

I was glad Mrs. Mahoney was focused on the wedding. This marriage would not be long and carefree. But it was the only option LeAnn and my father had if they wanted to make sure she and Trevor would be taken care of both legally and financially once he was gone. But I couldn't think about that now, or I would dissolve into a fit of heartache and tears. There would be time for that later.

"I wanted to make all the daisies out of frosting, but there wasn't time for them to dry," Mrs. Mahoney was saying when I forced my thoughts back to the present. "I hope the few silk ones I added will be okay. I put them together in clumps so it would be easier to cut the cake."

"The cake is perfect," I told her again. "I love the lacy edging on each layer. It's so delicate."

"It's my trademark," she said with pride. "I couldn't find the type of decorating tips I wanted anywhere so I had them specially made."

"They're amazing."

I felt rather foolish since I had never decorated a cake, nor considered what tools might be needed to do it. But I appreciated a master baker when I saw one.

"What can I do to help?" I said to break the awkward silence that had suddenly arisen between us. "I really appreciate all the trouble you've gone to for us on such short notice."

"I love my work," she said. "I see some the happiest and saddest times in people's lives. I actually sold your father a small cake for his wedding to your mother about twenty-five years ago now. My how time flies. That awful accident! Your mother was such a sweet young girl. Not to speak ill of the dead since I know you must miss her dreadfully, but I am glad your father has finally been able to move on. Men are never any good being on their own."

"That's what I've been told," I mumbled, wondering just how many people in Edna knew what had happened to my family and how poorly I had responded. Not that it would have mattered much to anyone. People lived together all the time, and babies were born out of wedlock every bit as often as they were born to parents who were legally married. And what family didn't have at least one prodigal child?

Mrs. Mahoney led me through the shop's kitchen to the back alley where the delivery truck was parked. I put the dress and other parcels in the back while she boxed up the cake and put it on a rolling stand so it wouldn't be dropped.

"I added several skewers to hold the layers together," she said as she put the box carefully in the back with the things I had already placed there. "I usually don't have to worry if I'm delivering the cake myself, but a plane ride can be bumpy. I wouldn't want anything to happen to it. Just make sure it stays upright."

"I will," I told her as I climbed into the passenger seat of the van.

"My husband usually makes all the deliveries," she said, adjusting the rear-view mirror. "But he's home today with the gout. It's not much fun getting old, but then you young people have years before you have to think about what happens when your body decides to quit working the way it should."

Fortunately, she turned her attention to her driving once we left the back alley. My feelings of elation over everything I had planned were suddenly bothering me. Maybe I should not have been quite so bold. I doubted either my father or LeAnn would mention it if I had, but Jake certainly would.

He was waiting for us inside the small air terminal surrounded by flowers. I had ordered one small table arrangement, three boutonnières and a bridal bouquet. The two larger arrangements of white and yellow daisies with blue baby's breath and ribbons were a total surprise. I had already paid for my order, so there had to be a mistake. I would take care of it later. Right now, I was tired and just wanted to go home.

"And just where do you intend to put all this stuff," he demanded, pushing himself away from the counter where he had been talking to Janet as the cake was wheeled inside. I looked down at the dress that hung over my shoulder and the numerous packages I was carrying. I felt like a pack mule. He had nothing with him, except for two small boxes in a see-through bag.

"My plane is a two-seater, not some jumbo jet, and the cargo hold wasn't designed to carry all this bloody crap."

"Well, you're just going to have to figure something out, unless you want to come back tomorrow because the cake, the flowers, and the dress are going with us."

I should have told him that I didn't order the two extra floral arrangements, but I was too angry at his lack of sensitivity to even to bring it up.

He surprised me by backing off. "Sonny told me the two big floral arrangements were his gift to the bride and groom."

"Then why were you needling me about it?"

"Habit, I guess," he replied. "I figured you must have told him about Jack's condition, hoping he would take pity on us?"

"How can you even think that?" I asked, once again hurt that he so thought so little of me and my feelings for my father.

"I'm sorry," he said. "I guess I was wrong."

I shook my head in disbelief. "Listen, Jake, I don't know how your friend Sonny knew about father's condition, but I didn't tell him. Since Janet knew, it must be all over town by now. This isn't about us, any, or our aversion to each other! It's about my father and your sister. They want to get married, and I promised that I would make the day perfect. I can understand that you don't want to help, and I accept that, but with all they have to worry about, is it too much to ask that they be given a few hours reprieve?"

Tears were running down my cheeks, and I knew my hands were trembling, but I didn't even care. He was the most infuriating and hateful man I had ever met, and getting away from him permanently could not come fast enough.

"Maybe I was out of line," he said, putting a hand on my shoulder. "You're either an awfully good actress, or else you really do care about LeAnn and Trevor."

"Of course, I care," I said, feeling the weight of his hand almost burning my skin. "I have never hidden the fact that I was shocked and hurt when I found out about them, but that doesn't mean anything now. After tomorrow, we'll all be family, and nothing in the world is more important than that."

"Wow," he said with shocked surprise, abruptly removing his hand. "You still have some Aussie in you. I thought all of that had disappeared after you ran away to the land of plenty."

"I know I messed up by running away, Jake. I was young and devastated by my mother's death, but we all make mistakes. Some of them can be corrected, others can't. But life goes on, and we try to make the best of it."

"I'm sorry you had to come home to so many changes."

"Is that an apology?" I asked. Maybe there was a beating heart underneath all that contempt.

"I wouldn't go that far," he replied as he looked over at Janet, who was helping someone else. "I don't agree with taking the coward's way out like you did, but I am willing to give you a chance to prove that I'm wrong about you."

"How considerate," I responded, trying not to become angry again. I didn't want anything ruining the last days of my father's life, especially something as petty as the power struggle that seemed to be going on between Jake and me. It was stupid anyway, and I had almost forgotten how it had started.

The cake and the flowers were loaded into the small storage compartment in the back part of the plane, and there was still plenty of room for the dress. The other purchases I had made were packed between the floral arrangements so they wouldn't tip over during the flight to the ranch. Apparently, Jake had just wanted to ruffle my feathers again.

It was after six when we got back. Trevor was so excited about the upcoming festivities that he literally jumped around wanting to see and help carry everything into the house. I gave him the smaller parcels with the shirts I had purchased for him and our father, the box carrying the boutonnières, and even the small candles I had purchased for the wedding night.

LeAnn was overcome with emotion when she saw the cake and flowers, but when I showed her the light summer dress I had chosen for her wedding, she threw her arms around me and sobbed.

"Brylee, I don't know how I can ever thank you for all you have done. The dress is perfect and so is everything else. I know how difficult this has been, but I will never try to take your mother's place. I just want to be your friend."

"We are friends," I told her. "I know how much you love my father."

She was standing in front of the freestanding oval mirror in the master bedroom, turning right and then left in the dress I had purchased as she studied her reflection.

"I feel just like a bride! Tomorrow's going to be perfect, isn't it?" she asked me.

"It will be the most beautiful wedding ever. I'm going to take lots of pictures, and have planned a sort of honeymoon night for you. I hope that wasn't being too presumptuous."

"You'll never overstep your bounds, Brylee. You're family, and you never have to prove yourself to anyone, not even my brother."

"Jake's just concerned about you and Trevor."

"I've known him since the day he was born, and I love him dearly, but even I know he can be mean when he wants to. Things would have been much different if Wendy had lived."

"Who's Wendy?" It was the first time I had ever heard her name.

"His almost wife. She came from a rich family in Sydney, but she was killed during a boating accident just a few days before the wedding. He's never gotten over it. I know you won't believe this, but he used to be the happiest, kindest man in the world."

"I'm sorry," I said as the light of understanding dawned. "No wonder he reacted the way he did when I asked if he wanted to help plan a celebration. It must have reminded him of a very difficult time."

"It was hard on him, but he'll come around someday. We just have to be patient. I'm afraid he thinks that love is a sentimental emotion that brings nothing but pain. He uses that to keep from getting hurt again. I know he admires you."

"Really!" I said in mock disbelief. "He acts like he detests me."

"He doesn't detest you. If he did, he would ignore your presence more often. He shoots barbs at you because he's forgotten how to act when attracted to someone for the right reasons."

"He's not attracted to me, I can assure you of that," I countered, thinking about the ungentlemanly way he had treated me all afternoon. "But he is definitely attracted to every girl in Edna."

"That's only because they pose no threat. He uses them because they let him, and then he forgets about them until the next time. It's different with you. He wants to let you in, but he can't because he cares."

"If that's true, he has an awfully strange way of showing it."

"He's a man! Do you think it has always been easy to love your father? That year after your mother's death was horrid. He blamed me for what had happened and completely ignored Trevor. That was the most horrific time of my life. I needed his support because I was dealing with my own pain and guilt, but he simply wasn't able to be there for me. If I had kept my distance, your parents might still be married, and you never would have run away."

"What happened to my mother was an accident. And I ran away because I was young and foolish and believed something that wasn't true."

"But your father and I should have handled things differently."

"He explained everything and I get it, so let's not talk about it anymore. We have a beautiful wedding tomorrow, and I was wondering if I could take Trevor to Edna after the festivities? We could see a movie and then get a hotel room for the night. I would love to get to know him better. There hasn't been much time for that since I got here."

"Trevor will be thrilled," she said, looking at the flowers I had purchased for her to hold during the ceremony and the ones to put in her hair. They would be kept in the outdoor icehouse that was used when the power grid failed. Jake had picked up several blocks of ice before we left Edna.

"I think he's felt a little left out today, but knowing he can spend time alone with his big sister will help," LeAnn was saying when my mind drifted back to the present. "We decided not to tell him about the seriousness of Jack's condition until absolutely necessary. We don't want him associating our wedding with his father's death. He needs some good things to remember."

"How was father today?" I asked her.

"Getting weaker. He told me he thinks it's time for Hospice to come more often."

I bit my bottom lip to keep from crying again. "It's not fair that we don't have more time with him. He's still a young man."

"Too young to be taken from us," she agreed. "But that is only one of the reasons why what you are doing for us is so special. You've had to accept so much since you came home."

I knew what she was getting at—the awkwardness of planning my father's wedding to the woman he had cheated on my mother with—but that was all in the past. We had tomorrow to deal with, and I was determined to make it a day of joy to be remembered with gladness.

"We're almost family," I told her. "I know you would have planned things differently if there had been time."

"I would have planned it just the way you did, Brylee. Jack and I do not have a lot of close friends. It's kind of hard getting to know other people when you work seven days a week just to make ends meet, but I haven't missed one moment of town life since moving out here three years ago. I have been with the man I love. Not many women have that chance. I hope I'm not jinxing anything by wanting to get married. In light of the divorce rate, it almost seems like I might be ruining a good thing, but I really want to be his wife."

It almost seemed like she was pretending his illness was only fleeting, but who was I to break that illusion? Reality would come crashing down soon enough for all of us.

I went to the den to see my father after my visit with LeAnn. I wanted to return the small amount of money remaining after my purchases for the wedding.

"You don't have to give that back to me," he said, as I handed him a small stack of bills.

"But it's not mine," I told him. "I found some great deals, and things didn't cost as much as I anticipated."

"You worked miracles, Brylee." He said, leaning back in his desk chair. His face was drawn, and I could tell that he was in a great deal of pain.

"I just did what I always do—look for bargains. I can't believe how many people in Edna care about you."

"I've lived here all my life and have made a few good friends. I'm just guilty of not spending much time with them. There was always so much bloody work to be done, and of course, I always thought there would be more time for friends once I was old enough to retire. Not that I ever seriously considered doing it."

"I can't see you ever slowing down."

I realised too late just how insensitive my words had been, but he didn't say anything about it.

"I never expected my life to end like this, although I should have known it could happen. It's the most common cause of death in the outback, but I always figured I could beat any odds. So I kept on smoking and working for things that really do not matter in the end."

"You were providing for your family."

"That's what I always told myself, but I would give back every plug nickel I ever made if it meant getting to know my own daughter."

"I understood how busy you were. This ranch couldn't run by itself even with Asum and Keida's help. I always thought they would be here forever."

Asum and Keida, both aborigines by birth, had been with our family for as long as I could remember. Keida had been the one to teach me about growing into a woman and where to find all the leaves and berries necessary to make every poultice ever needed. Asum had called me "Little Missie" and had taught me how to skip rocks in streams, where to find the best honey and how to get it without being stung. I missed their familiar faces and earthly wisdom. Together, they had taught me about the Rainbow Serpent and how it had created the earth and controlled everything that happened on it.

"So did I," he replied. "But one day, not long after your mother was gone, I came back to the house and found both of them gone. I guess they got the wanderlust and went back to their tribe in the outback. I've missed them a lot."

"I used to listen to mother and Keida talk about all kinds of things when they thought I wasn't paying attention."

"That doesn't surprise me. You were always a curious child, so bright and intuitive."

"Like Trevor?"

"You're cut from the same piece of cloth, at least partially. I have tried not to make the same mistakes with LeAnn and Trevor that I did with you and your mother. If I had chosen a different course, things would never have escalated like they did."

"We don't have to rehash that now," I told him. "I no longer have ill feelings towards anyone."

His eyebrow raised most subtly. "Does that include Jake? I've watched you around him. He pushes you because he likes you, and you stand up to him because you have something different in mind for your life. That's exactly what your mother did with her father. She told him she was going to marry me, and look what it cost her. I am not one for giving advice, but I certainly hope that inborn pride doesn't lead you into making the same mistake she did. Lashing out in anger, doing something to spite someone else, or accepting something simply because it seems attractive at the time, doesn't make for a happy life. You need to be equally yoked to the person you're with."

"I am," I said. "Ben is everything I ever wanted."

"Can you talk to him about everything? Can you work and fight and play together? Do you think about him from morning until night? Does he make your blood boil with passion?"

I was beginning to feel uncomfortable. My father had never talked to me like this before, but he had more to say.

"I was never around to give you any direction, so I guess I am trying to make up for it now. I want you to be deliriously happy. I want you to know what it's like to love with your entire heart, and maybe even do foolish things. I married your mother because I wanted to protect and take care of her. She had never been with a man before me. And yes, I did love her, but we weren't right for each other. I needed someone who could experience all of life with me. She had never been out of her father's house until I brought her here, and everything about the outback terrified her."

"It's not like that with me," I reminded him as I moved over to the sofa and sat down. "I've been on my own for a long time."

"But I still sense such an innocence in you."

"Maybe that's because I choose to be this way. I have been through some very tough things, and there were times when I didn't know if I could go on, but what I believe gives me incredible strength. I don't need all that passion and excitement. I am perfectly happy with the simple life."

"Perhaps you are different from your mother in that respect, but you are also part of me."

I couldn't continue with this conversation. It was making me think too much. I was going to marry Ben. That was the end of the discussion. I didn't need a man in my life like Jake. He could have his barflies and ticket agents. Maybe one of them would be his next Wendy.

"Could we talk about something else?" I asked. "Did you and Trevor have a good day? He really enjoys playing checkers."

My father leaned back and took in a huge drag of oxygen. "We had a great day, but he is going to need you when his world falls apart. He knows I have cancer. He just doesn't know that this time I will lose the battle."

"We can't dwell on that," I said. "Trevor is really excited about the flower he's going to wear. I bought both of you new shirts. I hope you don't mind."

He suddenly got up and crossed the short distance to the sofa and sat down beside me. It was difficult for him to move in his weakened state, and I wanted to help him with the small oxygen tank he carried, but I didn't want to make him feel any less manly than he already did.

"I think that was a marvelous idea. I haven't bought a new shirt in ages."

I willed myself not to cry as I snuggled into the crook of his arm. He rested his hand lightly on my leg. It felt no heavier than one of the colorful birds in the tree outside the den window.

"I decided you couldn't look like a derelict tomorrow. You're going to be married to the woman you love. Just capture every moment and hold it in your heart."

"That's what I'm trying to do," he said, kissing my cheek. "I don't deserve having you for a daughter. You're bright, beautiful, forgiving and caring. You're exactly the kind of woman I hoped you would become. I'm glad you will be staying on for a bit after I'm gone. LeAnn and Trevor are both going to need your strength."

"I think you underestimate both of them," I told him. "They're just as strong as I am, maybe even stronger, especially LeAnn. She didn't run away when things got tough. She stuck by the people she loved."

"LeAnn is older than you are. That gives her a different perspective. Promise me that you will forgive yourself for being human, and please think about what I've said. We all make mistakes, but we don't have to let them determine our future. Now . . . ." He took my hand and pressed it to his lips. "If you'll leave me alone, I have a few things to do before tomorrow."

"Then I will see you in the morning," I said, rising to my feet before bending down to kiss his cheek. Tears were tickling my throat again, but he needed me to be strong, and I did not want to disappoint him ever again.

Chapter 14

I slept fitfully that night. I wasn't sure if it was anticipation of the coming day or over-stimulation from trying to prepare for it. The only thing I knew was that my life was changing again, and it wasn't just because LeAnn and Trevor would become part of my family in a few hours. I was changing inside, and that scared me.

Not that I was backing away from the goals I had set for myself. I still wanted everything I had when I left California, but I was becoming more than confused about a present that had collided so completely with a past I had thought was completely over for me. The longer I remained in Australia, the more I realized that I missed it, and I didn't know why.

Morning was almost a relief because it meant I would be too busy with wedding preparations to think. The phone downstairs rang at six am. I pulled on a light pink robe and rushed down the stairs, hoping I could get to it before it disturbed LeAnn and my father if they were still sleeping. But I needn't have worried. I could smell coffee brewing when I got to the bottom of the stairs. LeAnn must not have been able to sleep either. But it wasn't LeAnn in the kitchen with the phone to her ear; it was Jake. I tried to retreat without being seen, but he called out to me just as the kitchen door swung shut.

"Don't run away. Nora wants to talk to you."

I turned around and tightened the robe around my neck before taking the phone he offered.

"Hi, Aunt Nora," I said, without looking at him. "Did you come up with something LeAnn could borrow for today?"

"I certainly did. How about a bracelet from my teenage years? It's pure silver and very dainty. I've had it in my jewelry box for years. It's a little too fancy for herding cattle and sheep, but it should do the trick. What do you think?"

"It sounds perfect, I just hope everything else I have been working on turns out half as well. I've never planned a wedding before."

"Well, not to worry, love," she said. "I have a roast in the crock pot with potatoes, carrots and onions. That should take care of dinner. Were you able to get everything you needed in town?"

"I think so," I replied. "Everyone was so kind. I had forgotten how friendly Aussies were. Will the twins be coming today?"

"Afraid not! They're still in Sydney, but I am glad you will be staying on for a while. You cousins need to get to know each other again."

"Yes, we do," I admitted. "It's been far too long. Maybe we can plan a sort of family reunion in the next couple of weeks."

"We can do that, but let's not worry about the now. Jack said the ceremony was at four. Ned and I will be there by two, unless you need us earlier. This wedding has been a long time coming. Maybe it will give your Uncle Ned a push in that direction. Not that our life together hasn't been great, but I kinda like the idea of a wedding ring."

"Then I will see what I can do to nudge him in that direction. We women have to stick together. See you when you get here."

Jake was standing in front of the sink, drinking a cup of strong, black coffee. "So what are you women plotting now, other than catching some unsuspecting bloke unaware? I figured you had made every plan you possibly could yesterday."

I twisted my lips until what I wanted to say was nothing but a memory. "We were just finalizing details. Are LeAnn and Father awake yet?"

"I haven't heard a sound from that direction. Of course, they were up late. I think it must have been about four when their bedroom light went out. They are probably resting up for the big day."

"Don't you ever sleep?" I asked. He always seemed to know exactly what was going on at the ranch—day or night— and that intrigued me perhaps a little more than it should have. He was like some feudal lord of the manor. I just hoped he wasn't spying on me.

"Sleep is for old people and infants," he replied. "As long as there is plenty of strong, hot coffee, I'm good to go."

"But that's not healthy. Your body needs time to rest. It can only do that when you're sleeping."

"Don't tell me you are worried about my sleeping and eating habits? You're sounding more like a wife every day. Do you irritate your boyfriend the way you do me?"

He glared at me, and I glared right back.

"I don't have to! He takes good care of himself. He wants to live a long, happy and healthy life."

"And you think I don't?"

"I would never presume to know what you think," I said, turning my back on him and heading towards the door that opened into the entry and the stairs leading to the second floor of the house. I was going back to bed even if I couldn't sleep.

"Just a minute," he said, putting a restraining hand on my shoulder. "I didn't mean to start a fight. I really do admire you. It takes a special person to accept the things you have. LeAnn and Trevor are lucky to have you in their lives."

"Is that another attempt at a compliment?" I asked, remembering the failed one from the day before. "Or am I still just a pain-in-your-neck with ulterior motives?"

"I wouldn't say that, exactly."

"Then what would you say? You have to know by now that I am only here because I love my father and my new family. I promise you that I will stay no longer than is absolutely necessary. I have the most wonderful man in the world waiting for me back in California."

"I'm not asking you to leave, and it is none of my business what you do once you're gone. I just hope you won't make any more promises to my sister and Trevor that you have no intention of keeping. Lee seems to like having you around."

I threw my hands in the air and looked directly at him. "Can't we stop the sparing for just a few hours? I can't deal with anything except the wedding today."

I was pretty sure he had something more disparaging to say, but I was saved by the sound of someone walking in the front hallway.

"I thought I smelled coffee," LeAnn said as she pushed open the door and walked into the kitchen. "I heard rather loud voices. You aren't arguing again, are you?"

We looked at each other and pretended to smile.

"We were just saying what a perfect day it is for a wedding, not a cloud in the sky," I responded, putting my arms around her and kissing her cheek. "So happy wedding day. Why don't you let me fix a tray for you and Father? He's awake, isn't he?"

I felt a moment of nausea. Some day soon, I would ask that question and not get the answer I wanted.

"Yes, but he's being a lazybones this morning. I told him to stay in bed because by tomorrow he will be a husband, and I will have a list of honey-dos for him a mile long."

She smiled, but I knew what she was trying to do. She wanted this day to be as normal and special as possible, not one spent wondering how many more days they would spend as husband and wife. If she could pull off that charade, I could certainly play along with her for as long as she felt it was necessary.

"I'm sure he will be thrilled to hear that," I said. "Now crawl back in bed, and I will have breakfast for both of you in a few minutes. Would fruit and toast be okay? I could fix something more filling if you'd rather?"

"No, toast, fruit and coffee will be fine. I seem to have wedding day butterflies having a field dance in my stomach. Jack and I have been together for a long time, but it still feels like the beginning of a brand new life. Am I being overly silly and sentimental?"

"Not at all," I told her, wishing I had the power to make her dream of happiness last just a little longer. "You're getting married today. It should be one of the happiest days of your life."

"And it will be," she said as tears filled her eyes. I was afraid she was going to cry, but once again, she surprised me with her strength and courage. "I have all that I need to be happy right here in this house. Thank you for being so kind, Brylee."

The smile I gave her faded from my face as I watched her leave. It was an impossible situation, but she was living through it with grace. I just hoped I could be as strong as she was when the final hours of my father's life came.

I wished Jake had left the kitchen when his sister did. I'd felt his cold, condemning eyes on me the entire we had been talking, and did not have it in me to be pleasant to him until I'd had a nice hot and healing shower. But instead of leaving, he got two mugs out of the cupboard.

"Don't you think it's a little naïve to behave like this is a normal wedding day?" he asked me as he filled them with coffee from the machine on the counter.

"Maybe, but it's what LeAnn wants. She knows they don't have much time left together as clearly as the rest of us do."

"I can understand her pretending because she's not ready to accept the inevitable, but why aren't you angrier with this God you claim to have accepted? He's taking your father away, and death is the end of everything. You cannot go back and change it."

His voice was filled with more than cunning curiosity. It was almost as if he was challenging me to defend what I now believed, but I wasn't going to let an argument over religious beliefs upset the joy that needed to be felt on this particular wedding day.

"I have no reason to be angry with God? He's not killing my father! I'm sad, but I have faith that I will see him again, just like I will see my mother. This life is not all there is."

He looked at me with amused amazement as he put two pieces of bread in the toaster. I was getting fruit out of the refrigerator and putting it in bowls that could be put with the rest of the food on the large tray I had found in the pantry.

"Only the young and foolish who have yet to experience much of life can be that easily influenced with religious platitudes," he said. "Life is simply a game to be won or lost. When it's over, it's gone, no matter how many Gods you claim to believe in."

His words stung, not because he was trying to prove a point, but because he had no idea how much Heavenly

Father loved him. I knew that feeling well. It was how I had felt until I was introduced to the doctrine of eternal life and salvation.

"I'm sorry you feel that way, but I still believe our lives here are part of a much bigger plan. If life wasn't meant to go on forever, why do we have families we love?"

"Because it's evolution in action! Do you think the first cavemen were wrapped up in the idea of loving families? They were just trying to survive, and it was easier to do that as a group. A man or a woman, alone, stood little chance against the elements and wild animals."

"That's your interpretation," I responded. "I happen to believe we have an Eternal Father who has a plan for everyone and wants us to be happy."

He snorted his disapproval. "Religion is for weaklings who can't deal with the realities of life, but then I suppose there are a few people I wouldn't mind seeing again."

I wondered if he was thinking about Wendy. He must have loved her very much. Otherwise he would not have turned into such a cynical, hard, untrusting man. But I knew that when the time was right, God could touch even the hardest heart because he had touched mine and given me something to believe in again.

All the food was on the tray and ready to be taken to my father and LeAnn, but preparing breakfast together without bloodshed wasn't the only thing that had happened during that early hour in the kitchen. Jake and I had made it through our first real conversation. It might not have been the most pleasant, but it had occurred without shouting or bloodshed. Maybe there was hope for us becoming a family after all.

My plans for getting an extra hour of sleep, or at least attempting sleep since I could never stop my mind from rehashing past events or worrying about the future, were interrupted by a soft knock on my door and a child's voice.

"Are you awake, Brylee?"

I wanted to pretend I was still sleeping, but this was an exciting day for my little brother, and I couldn't spoil it for him just because I had so many adult things to consider.

"Come on in," I said, rolling onto my back.

The door nearly flew open, and in less than a moment, my little brother was on the bed with me. He was still wearing pajamas, and his hair hadn't been combed. He had the same little cowlick in the back that I did. I wondered why I hadn't noticed it before. Maybe I had been too caught up in other things to really notice how much he resembled our family, especially our father, with his long legs, toothy smile and light brown hair.

"I'm so excited," he breathlessly said, starting to bounce up and down with excitement. His eyes were as big as the saucers I had served our father and LeAnn their coffee on, and the smile on his face was contagious.

"Slow down," I told him. "We don't want to wake the rest of the household." It was a small lie, but I knew if I told him that LeAnn and our father were awake, he would run downstairs and interrupt what I hoped would be a leisurely breakfast for the almost newlyweds.

I was worried about both of them, but mostly about our father. He kept saying he was fine, but I could see the pain and fear in his eyes when he didn't know I was watching him. I hoped today would not be too much. He wanted this wedding, but on a much smaller scale than what I had planned. Perhaps I had crossed the line by building up LeAnn's hopes for an intimate evening when he might not have the strength for it. But it was too late to undo what had already been set in motion.

"I have a surprise for you, Trevor," I told him as he settled down next to me and put his head on my shoulder.

He was so sweet and open to love. How could I be making plans to return to Ben when I had spent so little time getting to know him yet?

"What is it?" he asked. "I've already seen the new shirt and flower."

His sincerity made me smile. "No, Trevor, I have something else in mind, and I hope you will want to do it."

"What is it?' he asked me again, sitting up so he could get a better look at my face. His eyes were the same light blue as mine. Something we had both inherited from our father.

"Well," I began. "I thought we might drive into Edna tonight after the wedding and maybe catch a movie and stay overnight in a hotel."

He looked at me quizzically for a moment. "But what about father and mum? I've never slept away from home before."

"I have already talked to them. They think it's a great idea for us to spend some brother-sister time together."

"But couldn't they come with us? We've never been to a movie together."

My heart went out to him. He had been raised the same way I had, closed off from everyone and everything not directly related to the ranch.

"Don't you want to spend the night in Edna with me?" I asked. This was not the reaction I had anticipated, but I certainly understood where he was coming from. I had been terrified at the thought of being sent away to boarding school because I had never spent a night away from the ranch before then, either.

"Sure, I do," he reluctantly admitted. "I just worry about leaving father. He's really sick. People think I don't notice, but I do."

"Yes, he is sick," I told him. I had the same fear about leaving that he did. "But just because he's sick, it doesn't mean that he can't have a real wedding and a little time alone with his new wife."

"They're alone together every night after I go to bed," he countered. "I haven't slept with them since I was little."

I was failing miserably at being a big sister. My little brother obviously didn't trust me, but then why should he? I had dropped into his life so unexpectedly, and there hadn't been enough time to prove that he could count on me yet.

"Well, this is different," I tried again. "Haven't you ever watched a show about people getting married and going on a honeymoon?"

"All that hugging and kissing is yucky."

"It might seem like that now, but someday it won't. Adults rather enjoy it."

"Even father and mum?"

"Yes, even them, especially since they are going to be married today. It will be a new beginning."

"I guess I could go," he said with a sigh. "Can we get a hotel with a pool? I like to swim."

"Then we will find one with a pool," I promised, brushing his tussled hair with my hand. "And we will have lots of fun together."

That seemed to satisfy him because he jumped down from my bed and headed towards the door.

"I'm going to see my animals now since I won't be here in the morning. I don't want them to forget me."

"That's not going to happen," I assured him as he ran happily from the room. I could hear his footsteps on the stairs. He wasn't even taking the time to get dressed. I hoped LeAnn would not be upset that I hadn't called him back to change. But today was an exception to most every rule, so I settled back on my pillow to think. It was going to be a hard day.

LeAnn was dusting the furniture in the living room when I went downstairs an hour later. I had showered, applied some makeup and fixed my hair. I wanted to be ready in case there wasn't any personal time later on.

"You shouldn't be doing that," I told her. "It's your wedding day. Why don't you spend the morning with your future husband? I will take care of anything else that needs to be done."

She looked at me with a wide smile and sparkling brown eyes. "I can't sit still," she said. "I'm so excited! I never thought I would marry your father. I feel like a princess in a fairy tale."

"Well, you are," I assured her as tears danced in front of my eyes. "And you are going to marry your Prince Charming in a few hours."

"But we won't live happily ever after, will we?" Her shoulders sagged as she picked up the can of furniture polish. "I guess it's a little late to ask for a miracle."

"We're given miracles every day," I told her as I took the polish and cleaning rag from her hands. "Maybe your love story was just backwards."

"Backwards! I'm afraid I don't understand."

"You told me that you and Father had some wonderful years together living your dream life. It might have come before the wedding, but you were still blessed to have it."

"I guess, but it went by so fast. And despite what I have been taught, I still want to believe that marriage is just the beginning of forever."

I wished she believed the same things I did, but I couldn't talk to her about eternal marriage when she was about to enter into a covenant that might only last a few days. She could only hope they would be together again. Some day—when the time was right—I would explain how she could have what she really wanted. Right now, I just need to be supportive.

"It would be nice if life came with certain guarantees, but we only have today, and it's going to be everything you ever dreamed of," I told her. "You're going to marry the man you love, and then we will all be one family. There is so much love here. Just try to concentrate on that."

"I'm trying to," she said, pushing a strand of blonde hair behind her ear and letting a heartfelt sigh escape from between parted lips. "I do pretty good as long as I keep busy. It's stopping to decide what I am going to do next that gives me trouble."

"Work is a blessing, but don't let it steal away any more moments that you could be spending with father. Just think about him and how happy you have made each other."

She put her arms around me and kissed my cheek. "Thank you, Brylee. Your mother and father raised a pretty amazing daughter. I hope you and Ben can share the same kind of love your father and I have. We knew we were soul mates the moment we met. We completed each other, and only wanted to be better people when we were together. I guess it doesn't get much better than that."

"I don't believe it does," I told her, returning her hug while wondering why Ben had not answered my last email. I hoped everything was okay with us. I had forgotten to call him when I was in Edna getting wedding things, but I would try again once the activities of the day were behind me, and I had Trevor tucked safely in bed at a hotel.

LeAnn went back to the master bedroom, and I finished dusting the living room, entry hall and dining room. They were the only rooms we used on the main level of the house, other than the kitchen, and LeAnn kept that room spotless. I hadn't seen as much as a dirty dish in the sink since I arrived.

While I worked, I thought about the house I had been raised in. It had been constructed in the 1940s, and without money to keep up with the necessary repairs, it was hopelessly outdated. The pipes creaked, the seals on the windows let the moisture in and the stucco walls that did not have peeling wallpaper on them needed paint. But it was still home, from the scuffed wood floors to the coal and wood stove to the worn upholstered furniture. The only modern conveniences were showers in the bathrooms, a satellite dish and a microwave oven.

Still, it was hard for me to comprehend that cell phones could not be used when satellites could transmit television signals to the ranch. But I suppose there weren't any towers close enough since few people lived in our part of the outback, and corporations were in business to make money, not accommodate the needs of a few small ranchers. Perhaps even that would change, given time. But that thought reminded me that I still needed to ask my father how to handle the vultures who were constantly trying to get their hands on our ranch.

What we had might not to up-to-date, but the same blood that ran in my veins had built it and that couldn't be lost. In many ways, it was as if time had stood still on the ranch. And it wasn't such a bad way to live, it was just lonely at times. The only people I remember seeing when I was growing up were Uncle Ned and his family, the aborigines we employed to help with the sheep shearing and housework and an occasional salesman that rarely got past the front door.

It was the kind of life I imagined my ancestor, who had been released from the penal system after serving his sentence, must have preferred. And maybe it was the only kind of life I would have known if I had not been sent away to boarding school, or if my mother had not died. But I couldn't get caught up in thoughts like that now; I had to make this day special for all the people who were counting on me.

Still, my mind refused to quit wandering. Poor Trevor, I thought as I put the mop and pail away after cleaning the wooden floors that would be seen. No wonder he was scared to spend the night alone in town with me. Other than the few years he had lived in Edna as a baby and small child, he had spent his life on the ranch with three adults and an occasional visit from Uncle Ned and Aunt Nora—and the twins if they happened to be available. During the time I remained in Australia, I would expose him to everything I could. He needed to learn that there was safety beyond the confines of Hawkins' property.

I was ironing the white shirts I had purchased when he came back into the house. He was still wearing his pajamas, and they had soiled knees where he had been kneeling in the pens with the animals that had been his only real friends.

"How is everyone doing this morning?" I asked, making a mental note to get his pajamas into the washing machine before his mother found out he had been wearing them in the barn.

"They're fine," he said, giving me a look of real concern. "I told them I would be back in the morning to take care of them. We won't be staying late tomorrow, will we?"

"No," I responded. "We'll come home as soon as we've had breakfast if you want to."

He was biting at very grimy fingernails. "That's good because I don't want Newton getting scared. Tabby and the others will be okay, but he hasn't been here very long. Uncle Jake said he would take care of them, but what if he forgets?"

"They won't get scared, and your uncle will make sure they have everything they need," I assured him, knowing that no matter how Jake treated me, he would never do anything to disappoint Trevor. "We'll only be gone for a few hours. They won't even have time to miss you. Now, why don't you jump in the shower? We're going to have an early lunch, and then you can help me arrange chairs and get the living room ready for a wedding. It's going to be a very exciting day."

"Okay, but can I stop in to see mum and father before I do? They have to be awake by now. It's the middle of the day."

"And you are still in your pajamas, young man. Don't you think you ought to get cleaned up a bit before you do? I'm not sure your mother would like the fact that I let you take care of your animals before getting dressed for the day."

That seemed to prod him in the right direction.

"I don't have to get dressed for the wedding yet, do I?"

"No. Just put on something clean, but make sure you knock on the bedroom door before going in."

I didn't want him barging in on them if our father wasn't doing well. LeAnn hadn't left their room for nearly two hours.

By the time I had washed the stemware and had the plates and silverware for the wedding dinner lined up on the kitchen counter, Trevor was back in the kitchen. His head was wet, and he was wearing a clean pair of shorts and a t-shirt.

"They're coming," he said, practically jumping up and down while he watched me put plates on the table so we could have a sandwich and some cottage cheese for lunch.

"Who is?" I quizzed him. "Uncle Ned and Aunt Nora aren't supposed to be here for a few more hours. She needed that long for the roast to simmer."

"I'm not talking about them! Mum and Father are having lunch with us. He's doing ever so much better today. Maybe he's getting well."

I let out a sigh of relief. Our father was okay, at least for the moment, but he wasn't going to get better as Trevor hoped.

"That's wonderful," I told him, hoping that in the excitement of the day he would not notice that I was purposely avoiding the subject of our father's health. "Why don't you run out back and pick three ripe tomatoes so we can have them for lunch?"

He didn't protest but ran happily outside to do as I had asked. There wasn't much of a garden in the plot behind the house, not like there had been when I was a child, but there were tomatoes, onions and carrots—varieties hardy enough to withstand the almost intolerable temperatures of the outback in the summer.

The screen door slammed shut a second time. "That was quick," I called out, without looking up. I was taking some ham and cheese out of the refrigerator to be sliced for sandwiches. "Those tomatoes must have run right into your hands."

But it wasn't Trevor. It was Jake.

"Let me help you with those," he said, advancing towards me.

I'm sure my face registered surprise at his unexpected offer, but I decided not to say anything except, "thank you."

He put the meat and cheese on the cutting board and reached into a drawer for a knife. I momentarily bristled as I remembered the skill he had demonstrated with a knife the day he delivered Newton. Jake was strong, and I believed he could be dangerous if provoked, but I needn't have worried right then. He just brushed the hair from his face and began slicing the meat.

"I took the bike out along the west range this morning," he said. "Ned said he saw a pack of dingoes out that way a day or two ago."

"Is everything okay?"

"Seems to be, but you never know about wild animals. They could be back tonight. You rarely see them during the day. It's too hot for hunting unless they are really hungry."

"How hot is it?" I asked without thinking. It was the outback. It was hot all the time. Why should I expect today to be any different?

"Must be over a hundred already," he replied, stacking meat on the plate I got out of the cupboard for him. "But it could make it to 115 degrees by the time this wedding takes place. It's way too hot, even for this time of year, and that worries me."

I was just about to ask him why when Trevor returned from the garden and Father and LeAnn entered the kitchen. The smile on her face could have lit up the darkest room. Father was holding her hand, and he didn't have the oxygen tank with him. Maybe Trevor and LeAnn would get their miracle.

"Are you doing okay, father?" I whispered.

"More than okay," he assured me. "In fact, I'm great! This is our wedding day."

He squeezed LeAnn's hand and pulled out a chair for her to sit on. Then he sat down next to her in his chair at the head of the table.

I looked over at Jake, hoping he would show an emotion other than the harsh, judgmental resentment he always seemed to express around me, but he just went back to cutting a brick of hard cheddar cheese. I washed the tomatoes Trevor had brought in and put them next to the cutting board so Jake could slice them too.

Trevor obediently washed his hands without being asked and joined his parents at the table. I felt a prick of jealousy. Could I have been a part of that family unit if I had not run away from home? I could only imagine how I might have reacted learning the truth right after my mother's death, but I suspected that my anger might have been twice as intense.

"Have you seen the flowers we get to wear on our shirts, Father?" Trevor asked as they waited for the meal to be served. "They're pretty, but I thought flowers were just for girls."

"Not on a special day like this," our father told him, taking Trevor's hand in his free one. It was the picture of the perfect family that should be allowed more time together. I must have been watching them intently because I didn't notice that Jake was trying to give me the platter of meat and cheese until he cleared his throat.

"Put this on the table while I slice the tomatoes," he said. "We don't want the juice soaking into everything."

I wanted to say something cryptic because he was ordering me around again, but our feud would have to wait. We had promised LeAnn to be civil, and even if it killed me to keep from making a comeback when Jake tried to annoy me, I would not engage. Death wouldn't wait just because we wanted it to.

After setting the platter down, I took my place at the table. I couldn't help but wonder if my mother was watching the proceedings from heaven. And if she was, how did it make her feel? She certainly had a better perspective than I did, but the whole situation was just so bizarre. I felt oddly disconnected from everything, regardless of the fact that I had willingly planned the entire event.

It was a happy meal. Father told us about growing up on the ranch.

"There were always animals to take care of, wells to be dug, and crops to be brought in. We grew more back then than we do now, but it was easier because we had the aborigines to help out. Your grandfather had a couple of dozen or more helping him outside, and there were always several in the house to do the cooking and cleaning. The only problem was keeping them. They weren't much interested in a paycheck and when they got the wanderlust, they just took off. We never knew how many would be there when the sun came up."

"Why don't we have them to help us now?" Trevor asked.

"Well, son," he said. "They are hard to find. Those who haven't joined all the white-folk in towns are living far back in the brush and do not want to be found. They enjoy the simple life, like digging for grubs or skinning kangaroos to eat."

I noticed Trevor's eyes widen.

"You have to understand, son," he continued. "Aborigines roamed this entire country centuries before the white man ever came. They lived off the land, but they respected it and would never kill anything unless they needed it to survive."

"What about snakes and spiders and all the icky stuff?"

Father laughed. "They had more to fear from neighboring tribes and the elements than they did the animals and insects, but if someone got bitten and died, they held this wonderful ceremony with chanting and dancing and moaning. It was a glorious sight watching all those men moving around in their loincloths with their spears gleaming in the firelight."

"I wish I could see it," Trevor sighed.

"Maybe you will someday, son. They have festivals in town sometimes. I should have taken you to one."

"Why don't you tell them about the curse of the flatfeet, love?" LeAnn encouraged him.

He smiled and patted her hand.

"Your great-grandfather wanted to be a soldier more than anything in the world. He wanted to carry a gun and see faraway places, but he didn't have arches in either of his feet, and a soldier could not do his job if his feet always hurt like hell. So instead of fighting, he had to stay here on the ranch and help his father, but he couldn't get the idea of being a soldier out of his mind. He built a target range behind the barn and spent hours shooting cans to see how far they would go into the air. One day, he wasn't paying attention and shot your great-great-grandmother's milk cow. It was the only one she had, and he knew he would be whipped within an inch of his life when she found out, so he ran away into the brush."

Trevor's eyes were gleaming with delight. "Then what did he do?"

"He had a great time for about a week hunting his own food and sleeping in trees at night. But he didn't plan on stepping into a pool of quicksand, and his flat feet acted just like suction cups pulling him further and further into the mud. None of us would be here today if an old aborigine hadn't found him in time. The mud was clear up to his chin, but this old native threw him a vine and with the help of other tribe members, they pulled him to safety. But he lost his favorite gun and never got over it."

"Does that mean I'm going to have flat feet?" Trevor asked, as a look of concern deepened on his face.

"It's something you're born with, and you definitely do not have them. It seems to skip a generation, and since I have them, it's your sons you will have to worry about."

"That's okay," he said. "I'll rub their feet."

That made everyone laugh, even Jake. It was a nice, deep sound that seemed to come from some place deep inside him, but Trevor wasn't concerned about our reactions. He just wanted to hear more stories.

"Well," our father continued. "I already told you that he didn't like being stuck here on the ranch, and he didn't like dealing with two little ankle-biters like your Uncle Ned and me while our father was off taking care of things in the outback. He was an ornery, old bloke by then. He called us hellcats. Said we were more trouble than we were worth, and I suppose he was right."

"What did you do?" Trevor asked.

"For starters, your Uncle Ned and me managed to set the barn on fire when we smoked our first cigarettes. Would have burned the whole damned thing to the ground if he hadn't been watching us. Fire is nothing to play with out here."

"Did you get into lots of other trouble for smoking?" Trevor's eyes were sparkling. It was easy to tell that these stories were as interesting to him as they were to me. I wondered why our father had never told me anything about his childhood. I knew so little about him, only the brief memories I had of him as he busied himself around the ranch and came in for meals at noon and in the evening, if he felt so inclined.

"The worst!" father continued. "First, we got the raiser strap across our backsides for stealing cigarettes."

"That's the big belt on the wall in the den, isn't it?"

"It sure is, son! I don't know which was worse, hearing him smack it together or actually having it hit our flesh."

"You still smoked, father. Why?"

"Because I was a kid who lived in the outback and everyone I knew smoked—your grandparents, all the hired hands, even the aborigines. It was just what you did, sort of like a rite of passage."

"But that's what made you sick."

"Yes, it is!" our father admitted, leaning back in his chair and coughing while he tried to get another deep breath of air. LeAnn left the table.

"It was a foolish thing to do, even though I never thought it could lead to this." He looked intently at Trevor. "Be like you sister, son, and leave tobacco alone. Then you will never have to worry about getting what I have."

Trevor slid off his chair and our father tried to pick him up, but he was just too weak. It was an agonizing sight.

LeAnn came from the other room carrying the smaller oxygen tank he used during the day because it was easier to handle and less heavy than the one that stood by his bed. He didn't protest as she put the small buds in his nose and set the oxygen to flow.

"I thought I could do it," he told her, and I knew he was close to tears. "I wanted to make it through this day like a real man. I didn't want you marrying an invalid."

She kissed his pale lips. "I'm marrying the man I love, and I could not be happier."

I had to look away to keep from crying. The scene before me was just so tragic, yet tender beyond belief.

Father got shakily to his feet with LeAnn's help. "Thanks for the lovely lunch, Brylee. I just wish I hadn't spoiled it."

"You didn't spoil anything," I told him, wanting to rush around to the end of the table and hold him in my arms, too, but there wasn't any room for me. Trevor was holding his hand and LeAnn had her arm around his waist as she helped him to his feet and he was led from the room.

I put my elbows on the table and rested my chin on my thumbs. Our father wasn't going to get well. He was just putting on a brave front for his family. But the saddest part for me was knowing I really wasn't a part of that family. I might share some of my father's blood, but I had lost my place by running away.

I felt a hand on my shoulder, firm and warm, but I didn't look up.

"Your father loves you, Brylee, but you're stronger than Trevor and LeAnn," Jake said. "They need him more than you do right now."

Why did everyone keep saying that? My father had told me how strong I was last night in his den when I had returned the rest of his money, and now Jake was saying the same thing. But I wasn't strong. I had simply built a wall around my heart after my mother's death so I wouldn't be hurt again. Ben's love had broken through it. Maybe all this torment was payback for not telling him that I had been sexually assaulted, but I never wanted to feel that vulnerable again, not even with him.

I wanted to say something to Jake, anything that would make him understand just how much I needed my father. I needed to hear his stories so I could tell them to my own children someday. I needed to know that he had truly forgiven me for running away so I could quit feeling guilty over being an emotionally-driven child. I needed him to hold me in his arms and tell me that everything was going to be okay so I would never be afraid of things I did not understand again. But none of that was going to happen—not now, not ever.

A moment later, Jake removed his hand from my shoulder and was gone. I had missed another opportunity to let someone new into my life. But maybe it really didn't matter. He was only being kind because of the situation. The next time we spoke, he would likely treat me abominably.

Uncle Ned and Aunt Nora arrived promptly at two in their red pick-up truck that was only used for visiting. He kept it in his garage. It was a big boy's toy, and Aunt Nora indulged him, even though the dual-cab Ford had little practical use in the outback. It was too big and too costly to run.

I had never seen Aunt Nora in a dress before, not even at my mother's funeral, but today she looked almost beautiful. Her auburn hair was curled, not in its usual ponytail, and she was actually wearing makeup. Her dress was deep purple with classic lines. I wondered if Molly had helped her pick it out. She usually wore open-collared shirts and kakis just like the men. She was smiling broadly, as if she harbored some secret other than joy over the surprise wedding.

"Hold the door for me," she said as she stepped up on the veranda with a large crock-pot in her hands. "The meat's done, but we'll just let it simmer until dinner. That way, there will be no doubt about it melting in your mouth."

"I can't thank you enough for fixing the meal," I told her, walking in front of her and opening more doors so she would not be slowed down.

"Did you get a lettuce salad made?" she asked as she set the heavy pot down on the kitchen counter and plugged it in. "Those kids have waited a long time to say their 'I do's. I kinda envy them. Not that a piece of paper makes any difference when you love someone, but a girl can dream."

"I did," I replied, looking at her through eyes that had gained more perspective and understanding since I had been home. She was a good woman, hardworking and kind. I hoped that someday soon Uncle Ned would give her that piece of paper that she so obviously wanted.

"You clean up very well," she told me, opening the refrigerator to make sure everything she had requested was ready.

I looked down at my white jumper with the heavy lace edging in the tiered ruffles of the skirt and hoped she wouldn't think I was trying to outshine the bride. My dark hair was curled and hanging down my back. "Thank you, Aunt Nora," I replied. "I only brought one dress since this was supposed to be a short visit."

"And now you've reconsidered," she looked at me with a raised eyebrow that made me wonder if it was a statement or a question. I couldn't tell, regardless of the fact that I was looking directly into her bright green eyes.

"I'm staying for as long as I am needed."

"Good answer, but I think folks around here would like to see you back home for good. Your family has missed you."

"And I've missed all of you," I replied, before nibbling on the inside of my lower lip. The idea of family had always meant a lot to me, even if I'd had no conception of what it really was while growing up. That was changing now, and I wasn't sure I could ever give it up.

"Oh, my," she suddenly sighed, stepping back from the fridge door. "The champagne isn't chilling. Didn't you get it from the cellar, Brylee? It's takes hours for it to properly cool."

"I forgot," I replied, feeling my first real letdown of the day. "Do you know which one Father wants? I'll get it straightaway."

"Don't fret," Aunt Nora said. "You've had more than enough to think about. I'll send Ned down. He knows exactly what Jack wants. We can put it in the freezer for a few minutes first. That should get the process started."

I felt just awful for my oversight, but in a way, it was understandable since I no longer drank alcoholic beverages. Still, I should have been able to remember that no Hawkins' family celebration was complete without something to get everyone a little tipsy.

"I really am sorry about the champagne, but I think I have everything else ready. I put extra chairs in the living room and one bouquet of flowers on the piano and the other one on the hearth. I have all the china and silver set out for after the wedding. But could you take a look around to make sure I haven't forgotten anything else?"

"I will take a gander, but I'm sure everything will be perfect," she replied, patting my arm. "You've turned into a lovely, sensitive young woman. Your mother would be very proud of the way you are dealing with things. I know it's been rough ever since you got home."

She scurried off to inspect what I had done, and I put my hands on the counter by the sink and looked out the window at the clear cerulean sky. There were so many things around the house that reminded me of my mother, but I hadn't given much thought to any of them until now.

The baby grand piano in the living room was hers. She loved playing all the songs of her childhood, from the ones her parents had cherished to the more upbeat ones of the sixties and seventies. She had taught me to play a few simple tunes, but I wasn't the best pupil. My fingers were clumsy on the keyboard, and natural rhythm was not one of my inherited gifts. I wondered if I could play anything now.

Oh, how I missed her. My eyes clouded with tears, but I pushed them back and tried to center on the present. The china and silver I had set out for the occasion had been given to her by a great aunt who hadn't lived long after her marriage to my father, but who had not disowned her either. She always told me that those heirlooms would be mine one day, along with the piano, but now I wondered. Those things belonged to the house LeAnn had been living in for three years. I couldn't take the piano with me, but the china and silver might be manageable if I ever found the right time to ask about them.

Suddenly, I felt like I couldn't breathe. I loved my father and wanted him to be happy, but I loved my mother too. She was the one who had raised me, taught me basically everything I knew until I was sent to boarding school. Her hands had touched everything in this house, except the new sofa in the den. LeAnn was now mistress of all my mother had ever cherished. She had even been sleeping in her bed, and now she was marrying her husband.

I no longer felt charitable and kind. I only felt pain and loss. In a few weeks, both of my parents would be gone, and after I had taken care of my obligations, I would be going home to Ben and leaving everything from my childhood behind.

But how could I make a new life with him and enjoy the happiness that marriage promised when I no longer had any familiar roots, and people I barely knew would have everything I had ever held dear—my home and all its furnishings, the ranch, even the burial plot where my mother had already been laid to rest? How could I not speak up and declare my desire to have a portion of what had belonged to me as a child?

I did have a birthright. Jake had seen right through me on that. He knew my heart's true desires better than I did, and I hated him for it. But why should I want them to have everything? I had a right to more than memories. Nonetheless, I had walked away once and now everything belonged to people I barely knew. I was going to have to accept that eventually, if I ever wanted to find lasting peace.

But even that wasn't my greatest concern at the moment. I couldn't stop myself from wondering how Jake fit into the picture. He was filling the role of a hired hand right now, but what would happen when my father was gone? Would he move into the house with LeAnn and Trevor? Would he sit at my father's desk, drink his whiskey and smoke his cigars? Would he ride his horses and sell his cattle and sheep? Would he sell the ranch to strangers? And would he laugh because he had gotten rid of me by being cruel?

I put my hands on the top of my head and pressed down, hoping that negative thoughts would not destroy what little time I had left with my father. But how would I survive when he was no longer there to administer what was rightfully his? And just how far would Jake go to force me off the land I had once called home? Maybe I had read too many novels and seen too many police dramas, but I was the outsider here and had very few people in my corner.

It was two-thirty, and I had promised to help LeAnn get dressed for her wedding. It was ridiculous to think of her as being part of the monstrous plot I was envisioning in my head. She had been nothing but kind, and she wasn't faking her love for my father or for Trevor.

But try as I might, I could not be sure about her brother. He was mysterious and made it a point to know everything that was going on at the ranch. The only thing I could not figure out was why he hadn't accepted my father's proposition to learn the financial aspects of running the ranch. It would have put him in the perfect place for a complete takeover once my father was gone.

Oh, how I needed Ben with me today. I needed to see the light in his sparkling eyes and run my hands through his sun-bleached hair. I needed to hold his hand and hang on for dear life. He was my link with the reality I had come to cherish and my hope for the brightest of futures. But thinking about him now would only make today harder. I had a wedding to run, so I wiped the tears away with the backs of my hands and pushed myself away from the sink. Trevor came running into the kitchen wearing the new white shirt I had gotten for him and a pair of dark slacks that were an inch too short.

"How do I look?" he asked in an excited tone. "Uncle Ned brought these pants for me to wear so I would look nice today. They belonged to NJ when he was little."

"You look very handsome," I told him as I walked over to straighten the tie he was wearing. It hung nearly to his waist, even though he was tall for a boy of seven, but I recognized it immediately. I had given it to my father for Christmas when I was about his age. Mother had taken me shopping in Edna. It was one of the few times we had gone there together. Most of the things we needed were ordered from the catalogues we received in the mail. Father took care of the other shopping when he went into town on business.

The blue and green silk felt cool between my fingertips. I had never understood why I purchased it since Father never wore a tie, but my mother had not objected.

"Can I put my flower on now?" he asked. "I want to see how it looks."

"It's a little early if you don't want to risk getting it crumpled for the wedding."

He looked so disappointed that I immediately came up with a counterplan. "Why don't we hold it up for you in front of the hall mirror, and you can pin it on permanently when father and your Uncle Jake do theirs. That way, you can be part of what they are doing to get ready for the wedding. Would that work?"

His brow knit for a moment. "I guess so. I really do need to help father. He's awfully tired, even though he says he's okay."

"You're just what he needs today, Trevor," I said with a smile that was hard to maintain. "Father's lucky to have you for a son."

He scampered away towards the den where the men were sequestered, quite forgetting about seeing how his flower would look when pinned to his shirt.

"I'm an irrational fool," I told myself as I walked up the stairs to my room and knelt on the floor by the bed. I was tired, confused and more than a little emotional. How could I not see that having Trevor and LeAnn in my life was a blessing, even if it spoiled my idea of the perfect family reunion in heaven? That was something Heavenly Father would take care of when the time was right. My job was to accept life as it came. That wasn't easy, but I was learning to roll with some of the bunches that kept landing on me.

Jake was just being a bounce, a real bully who liked to push people around. From what I had seen of my father's records, the ranch hadn't been doing that great for years. Too many fires, floods and the ever-present heat had taken away any profits more often than they had left anything in the coffer to work with.

I closed my eyes and asked God to calm my troubled spirit—to help me see LeAnn and Jake the way he did. They had to be good people or my father would never have allowed them into his life. I was just hurt and angry because there was nothing I could control right now. Instead of being alone after my father was gone. I should be grateful that I had a little brother, and would soon have a stepmother who said she only wanted to be my friend.

And my father had not forgotten me. He had taught me to oversee the finances of his own private empire, and he would not have done that if he thought there would be any trouble. He wanted me to be part of my new family. He had even said something about changing his will.

Chapter 15

I washed my face and reapplied makeup. My eyes might be a little red, but people would only think that natural since most people cried at weddings. Then I headed down the stairs and was surprised to discover that my father's lawyer, Buck Henry, had already arrived. I hadn't heard another vehicle approach the house, but I could hear a loud, unfamiliar voice coming from the den and knew we would have to hurry so LeAnn wouldn't be late to her own wedding. I just hoped my father was conserving his strength. He had already been up longer than he should have been.

When the door to the master bedroom opened, I saw LeAnn sitting on a stool in front of the old-fashioned dresser that had belonged to my father's great-grandparents. The glass was milky, but otherwise it had been beautifully preserved. It was just another piece of furniture I had envisioned as being mine one day. Only two things about the room had changed since my mother's death. A picture of my parents on their wedding day had been removed from the wall, and there was a new covering on the bed.

"It's very lovely," Aunt Nora was saying when I closed the door behind me. "I can't believe Brylee was able to find it in Edna. This season's styles are horrible! I ought to know. I've looked at plenty of clothes with Molly. That girl is a born shopper. Just give me some jeans and I'm good to go."

Aunt Nora didn't really expect a comment; she just loved to talk. I had always wondered how she and Uncle Ned had ever gotten together. He was the strong, silent type, and she was a born conversationalist. Maybe it really was true that opposites attract.

Ben and I certainly had little in common when it came to personality. He was confident, outgoing and had dozens of friends. I was more reserved—even sulky at times—and rarely let anyone in. Maybe that was why I felt so alone right now, even in a house filled with family.

"It looks like you will be the one having the next wedding, Brylee," Aunt Nora said, breaking into my bittersweet thoughts. "I was hoping your young man could be here today. We would all like to meet him, and I know your father will want to make sure he's good enough for you before giving you his blessing."

I looked down at the floor as another wave of sadness washed over me. I might be the next one getting married, but my father would never live long enough to see that day.

"I'm so sorry," Aunt Nora continued, putting her hand on my arm. "Me and my big mouth. Ned always says I yabber too much."

"We can't pretend there isn't a huge pink elephant of reality in the room," LeAnn interjected, trying in her own way to comfort both of us. "I'm sure Brylee's young man loves her very much, whether or not any of us get to meet him before their wedding."

I just smiled. How could I tell them that my wedding would be held in one of God's holy temples—a place none of them could enter without a great deal of personal change? It would be just one more thing proving Jake was right. I no longer had any real connection to life in the outback or with my own family. I had moved on to something few of them would ever understand.

"Let's not worry about that now," I replied. "Ben and I haven't even set a date. So it's a little early to be making any plans."

LeAnn looked lovely when she slipped into her wedding dress. I curled her hair with the curling iron I had brought with me so it hung down her back like a flowing cascade of golden satin. The flowers we added to it were the perfect finishing touch. She had already slid the blue garter up past her knee, where my father wouldn't see it until later. She was wearing the silver locket I had gotten for her in Edna and a small silver brooch with diamonds that had belonged to my great-grandmother.

I felt another small tug of envy. The brooch was something else I had thought would be mine one day. Not that I would ever wear it. Brooches were no longer in style, but my father had given it to LeAnn as the something old I had talked to him about. She had pinned it onto the bodice at the exact point where the neckline formed a "v", and it looked like it was meant to go there.

She would wear it with love and pride long after my father was gone. I would simply have put it into a jewelry box, looked at it occasionally and promised to pass it on to my own daughter when I had one.

Aunt Nora was loaning her the delicate bracelet she had described to me over the phone.

"Now, don't look so startled," she said as she fastened it around LeAnn's slender wrist. "I know that bracelet seems out of place coming from me, but I do have a few nice things I wore as a girl. It belonged to my grandmother and will belong to Molly when she decides to get hitched."

"It's very beautiful," I told her as LeAnn lifted her arm until the gold caught the sunlight and began to shimmer. "And you look radiant, but I haven't taken any pictures and need at least one before you stand in front of the judge. It's for a project I am working on."

I ran from the room and up the stairs to where my cell phone lay on top of the dresser I was using. It had been plugged into an outlet the night before, so the battery was full. I would keep it in my pocket so no photo opportunities would be missed. Not that I was a photographer by any means, but I knew the kinds of pictures I wanted taken of Ben and me when we got married. If I could replicate some of those, LeAnn's scrapbook would be amazing.

By the time I had taken several shots of LeAnn in her wedding dress, Trevor was knocking on the door to say that Father was ready for us. I gave my soon-to-be stepmother a hug and told her to give me five minutes before making her entrance. I wanted to make sure everything was ready before she walked down the short aisle I had created for her between dining room chairs.

Buck Henry was standing in front of the fireplace, looking all-important with his chest puffed out and a leather-bound black book in his hands. He was rocking somewhat impatiently back and forth on the heels of his feet. Father stood in front of him with the small oxygen tank draped over his left shoulder. This was the first time I had seen him since lunch. He looked tired but very handsome in his white shirt and dark pants. He was even wearing the tie I had impulsively picked out when purchasing his shirt. It was the same color as LeAnn's dress. I took a picture of him talking to his friend just moments before Trevor moved to his side and took his hand.

All his boyish enthusiasm was gone. He seemed to know this was a solemn occasion. But more importantly, he was giving our father strength. It was another of those all-too-frequent moments I'd had lately when the pain of having been replaced was almost too much to endure.

"You're doing a good thing today."

The voice caught me off guard, and I turned to see Jake looking at me. But it wasn't the Jake I had seen before. This man was dressed in a white shirt and dark pants like the rest of the wedding party. He was freshly shaved and his dark, nearly shoulder-length hair was pulled back in what looked like a piece of twine. He had clipped his nails and shined his shoes. He actually looked good because he didn't have that stern, foreboding look in his eyes—the look that told me he didn't trust me any more than I trusted him. I wondered if he was thinking about Wendy.

"Well, it would not have been possible if you hadn't allowed me to accompany you to Edna yesterday. I'm not sure I thanked you."

"You did, but that's not what I am talking about," he said, staring at me strangely. "The flowers are great, and I know LeAnn will look lovely in the dress you picked out. But it's what you are doing right now that really matters. You're making this day special for them. It can't be easy watching your father marry someone else."

"I love my father," I told him. "And your sister and my father love each other very much. Why shouldn't I be happy for them?"

"Because this wedding means LeAnn and Trevor will have legal rights they didn't have before. That has to hurt when all this could have been yours."

I wished he wasn't looking at me so intently with his steel gray eyes that seemed to bore into my very soul. If I lied to him, he would know it, and our brief interlude of civility would be over.

"You are correct," I told him. "This isn't easy, but it doesn't mean it isn't right. LeAnn has seen my father through everything these past few years, and I am grateful she has been there for him."

I clutched my cell phone even tighter as he leaned his lanky frame against the doorframe and kept studying me with his dark, brooding eyes. Was it possible that any woman could ever truly understand him?

He seemed to be enjoying my discomfort. "But gratitude doesn't stop the pain of losing your childhood home to someone else," he said.

"None of that matters any longer. I will soon have a new home with my husband."

"Perhaps, but you are still human, and humans get angry before getting even. You aren't planning a sneak attack for after the wedding, are you?"

His question angered me. Why did he have to ruin everything by being so mean? No wonder he wasn't married. No sane woman could tolerate his arrogance.

"If you will excuse me," I said. "I would like to get a few more pictures before the wedding starts, and I want to see if Uncle Ned will take a few of them during the ceremony. LeAnn has asked me to stand with her. I'm sure my father has asked the same thing of you."

"Good on ya," he said. "I guess I will just slip into the background where I won't be noticed until the ceremony begins. I'm not much for weddings. They are too bloody confining for a man."

I turned my head as he walked away. Confining them might be cruel to a man who could never be happy with just one woman. I would be eternally grateful that Ben was the marrying kind and that I was the girl he wanted to spend eternity with.

I snapped a few pictures of the wedding cake, the flowers, and the men as they talked about ranching even on a wedding day, and then I caught up with Uncle Ned as he looked down at his watch and nearly ran out of the living room.

"Can't talk now," he said in his deep, penetrating voice as he rushed past me, brushing my arm with his hand. "The kids are here."

"But I thought they couldn't come," I said, following him into the hallway.

Uncle Ned didn't look much like my father. He was tall and thick through the shoulders. But the real difference between them was in their faces. Uncle Ned had deep laugh lines around his eyes and mouth. I couldn't remember my father ever smiling much. He wasn't stern, and he rarely raised his voice, but he had never seemed really happy, not like he did with LeAnn. It made me wonder, yet again, if his marriage to my mother had ever brought him any joy.

Aunt Nora must have been waiting right inside of the bedroom door for my signal to send LeAnn into the living room because she stuck her head into the hallway at the sound of commotion.

"What's the holdup?" she asked. "We have a bride in here who wants to get married."

"It's Uncle Ned! He said the twins were here."

It took less than a second for her to throw open the door. "Hold on, LeAnn," she hollered over her shoulder. "NJ and Molly are here."

She hurried after me, all the time muttering her complaints about Uncle Ned being the most mulish bloke on the planet because he liked surprises and she hated them, and how worried she now was that there would not be enough food for the wedding supper and her own home wasn't ready for a proper homecoming for her children.

"There you are," Uncle Ned shouted out as he ran down the front steps of the veranda to greet his progeny as they climbed out of a silver Dodge Charger. "I was beginning to think you would miss the whole shindig."

He put his hands on his son's shoulders and gave him an affectionate man-hug.

NJ was nearly as tall and broad as his father, but he had his mother's complexion and coloring. His sandy-colored hair was trimmed short, and his eyes with their almost invisible eyelashes danced just like Aunt Nora's did.

"Hi, pops," NJ told him. "I brought more champagne. Wouldn't want to run out on such a special occasion. It's in the back seat in a cooler. It was the last six bottles of the good stuff on the shelf at the liquor store. Ernie got it for me, so you don't have to worry about me being arrested again."

"That's my boy," Uncle Ned told him. "I was afraid you might have decided to try using that fake ID again. I was serious when I told you if you got into trouble again, you would be on your own. No more baling you out."

"I haven't forgotten, old man," he said.

"Let him alone, Ned," Aunt Nora told him as she gave NJ a hug and a sound kiss that he returned without hesitation. "Your father should have told me you were coming. I don't have anything prepared at the house."

I felt a jab of pain as I stood on the veranda and watched their reunion. This was how families were meant to be, but I hadn't given mine a single thought when packing my suitcase after my mother's funeral. But distance and a new life could not replace everything. My family might be a little rough around the edges, but I wanted to be part of it. My life with Ben was merely a bandage until I was willing to expose all the old wounds and let the real healing begin.

"What about me?" a beautiful redhead retorted as she walked around the front of the car.

"And how is my ever glamorous and precocious daughter?" Uncle Ned said, wrapping her securely in his strong arms. She seemed to melt right into him.

"In need of a swift kick in the hindie," NJ playfully said. "She was supposed to help with the driving, but slept all the way like the drogo she is."

She peeked through her father's arms and scowled at her brother. "It's not my fault you stayed up half the night with those loser mates of yours. And if you want to talk about who is being a drogo, who is getting the better grades at the university?"

Aunt Nora slapped her hands together with a crack that startled even the birds in the trees. "All this bickering can wait until we get home. It's hot as Hades out here, and in case you have forgotten, we have a wedding to attend."

Uncle Ned just laughed and put an arm around each of his children's shoulders. "It's so nice having you here. I had almost forgotten how bloody peaceful it is at the ranch with just your mum and me. Now try and be pleasant. Your Uncle Jack isn't doing too well."

Apparently, my cousins had not changed much since I'd last seen them. NJ was still skirting trouble, and Molly was still into looking both fashionable and beguiling. It made me wonder how two such practical and hardworking people could have produced such materialistic offspring.

I was still standing on the veranda when NJ ran lightly up the steps, picked me up in his arms and whirled me around in the air. "This can't be cousin Brylee," he said when we had stopped moving. "You have become a bloody knockout, filling out in all the right places."

"And you're still a horrible tease," I replied as I tried to steady myself. My head was lightly rolling. I had not been twirled in the air for years.

"Guilty as charged," he said with a smile that showed his braces had done wonders for his teeth because his overbite was completely gone. "But it is good to see you again, cuz. If I had known what a looker you turned out to be, I would have come home sooner and brought a bunch of my mates with me."

"Stop it," a sullen voice said. "Brylee doesn't want to meet any of your obnoxious mates. Daddy said she is engaged to some bloke in the States."

"Hi, Molly," I said, looking at the ravishing beauty in front of me. Her hair was a deep copper, and her skin milky white and smooth. She carried herself with both grace and confidence.

"It's good to see you again," she said, giving me a quick hug and a light kiss on each cheek. "You look just like your mother, except for the color of your hair."

I wondered how she could remember what my mother looked like so easily. There were days when I had to close my eyes and really concentrate to form her image in my mind without looking at her picture first. We had spent so little time together the last four years of her life. I could feel the anger creeping back. If I hadn't been sent away to boarding school so many things in my life might be different . . . .

"Snap out of it," I told myself as I opened the screen door so Molly could get out of the scorching heat. She was wearing a flowered sundress with spaghetti straps, a fitted waist and a very short skirt. Her sandals were four-inch wedges. No wonder she appeared to be nearly as tall as her brother.

I held the screen door until Uncle Ned had gone into the house with the cooler, and then followed, letting the screen door slam shut behind us. I was more careful with the wooden door that had been bleached by the sun.

So here we were! All the family I knew about in the same house together. It hadn't been like that since the day of my mother's funeral and wake.

I stood in the doorway leading to the living room with my hands clenched tightly in front of me, and an unsightly crease between my eyebrows as I surveyed the mixture of people I had left behind and the new ones who had come to the ranch during my absence. I could no longer think about that sunlit room with any degree of pleasure, even though I had decorated it carefully for the wedding. It was the place where I had seen my mother's closed coffin the moment I walked through the door after hours alone on a bus, crying with disbelief and uncertainty.

I had not understood the depth of that pain until now, and I would feel it again when my father was gone.

"Brylee," my father's voice floated to me through a very upsetting haze. He was motioning from the front of the living room. "I would like you to meet my very good friend, Buck Henry. He will be performing the ceremony today."

I walked the short distance to the hearth and politely extended my hand to the man who was standing with my father. "Nice to meet you," I said.

Buck Henry's eyeglasses were sitting too far down on the bridge of his hawk-like nose, and when he smiled, I could see yellow-stained teeth—a condition many old Aussies had from too little brushing and flossing and too much coffee, tobacco and alcohol.

"Jack's told me a lot about you over the years, but he really didn't do you justice. You are a fine-looking young woman."

I felt a flame of color rush to my cheeks. Compliments still made me uncomfortable, although Ben was working with me on that.

"Thank you, sir," I replied. "It was very kind of you to come clear out here for a wedding on such a hot day."

"Wouldn't have missed it, child," he said as he twisted his shoulders. "I'm just sorry the misses couldn't come, but she was feeling rather poorly and the drive would have been a little too much for her."

"Understandable," father replied. "I'm just glad you made it."

Buck Henry was still looking at me, and a little too intently. "Your father and I have been mates for over forty years. We both started ranching about the same time. My oldies were some of the original convicts sent here from England, just like yours were."

My father coughed, and I looked over at him. We needed to get this wedding over so he could sit down and rest. But he just took a long drag of oxygen and adjusted the strap on his shoulder so the small tank wasn't so noticeable.

"What my mate here isn't telling you," he said with a wane smile that I knew cost him a great effort to make. "Is that he found a little gold mine on his property and has become a wealthy bloke, unlike the rest of us who are still hoping we can keep our herds alive until we get them to market. You should see his house in Edna. It's almost as big as St. Andrews Cathedral."

"Really," I said, hoping my tone adequately expressed some interest. He could live in a virtual palace for all I cared. The only thing that concerned me right now was making sure my father survived the wedding.

"Your father is right about the house," he said. "I've done well financially, but the wife and I never had any children. I would give up almost everything I have amassed over the years to have a family like your father does. What man doesn't want a son to carry on the family name, and a daughter who is as pretty as a picture?"

I knew he was trying to be kind, but his words stung.

"What man doesn't want a son to carry on the family name?" That's what he had said, and I knew it was true. My father loved and cherished my little half-brother. Even a stranger could tell by watching them interact.

"Are you ready to begin?" I asked my father, hoping he would not see the jealousy in my eyes because I wasn't his son, the apple of his eye. "If so, I think your bride-to-be is very anxious to become your wife."

He took my hand and squeezed it. "I'm as ready as I will ever be."

But the pain he was so obviously trying to hide told me to hurry. He couldn't remain on his feet much longer, and he would find it intolerable to be sitting down during the ceremony.

"I'll have Molly pin on your boutonnieres while I see to the bride."

She wasn't in the living room with the rest of us, but I knew where to find her.

I knocked softly on the door to the master bedroom, and Molly opened it for me. She was rubbing the back of her neck, and I wondered if she was still stiff and tired after the long drive from Sydney.

"Would you mind getting the boutonnieres for father and the others and seeing that they get pinned on right?" I asked her. "They're in the fridge in the kitchen."

"Sure," she said, shrugging her pretty shoulders. "There's nothing I can do in here anyway. Jake gets one, doesn't he? I would love to get my hands on him even for just a moment."

"Molly," her mother reprimanded in the tone she used whenever she wasn't pleased by something her daughter said. "Can't you think of anything besides all the bloody attractive blokes in the world?"

"I can, but it's not nearly as much fun as fantasizing," she replied with a shake of her head.

She walked somewhat jauntily out the door, leaving me to wonder if I was the only woman in Australia who did not find Jake Johnson captivating. Even Aunt Nora admitted to having a certain fondness for him. As far as I was concerned, the other women were welcome to him. He might be rather good-looking in a rugged sort of way, but he had a cruel streak that really frightened me.

But instead of dwelling on all the things about that irritated me, I turned my attention to the bride. LeAnn looked lovely. Her blue eyes were bright and clear as they rested on me. "How's your father doing? I told him not to push it, but you know how stubborn he can be."

"Father's fine," I lied. LeAnn didn't need that worry as she stood in front of Buck Henry to take her vows. "But I think he's anxious to get married, and there have been a few minor, but wonderful delays. He sent me to see if you were ready."

She took a deep breath and let the air out slowly. "Then let's do this. I simply do not understand why I am so nervous. Jack and I have been together nearly fifteen years."

I didn't want to think about the amount of time and all the intimacies they had shared while my mother was still alive. I was trying hard to put all that pain and anger behind me, especially today. So I reached for the cell phone that was in my pocket.

"Could you give this to Uncle Ned?" I asked Aunt Nora. "He said he would snap a few pictures during the ceremony."

"Then you don't want Ned taking them," she responded. "He. will just cut people's appendages off. I'll take lots of nice ones for you if you will just show me how this thing works. All this digital stuff is a little too fancy for me."

"It works just like a film camera," I assured her. "If it shuts off, just enter the numbers 2147 and look for the little camera icon. Everything else is self-explanatory."

"For you maybe, but I'm old school. Nonetheless, I will give it my best for you love," she replied, looking at my phone with a mixture of confusion and hope. Aunt Nora was a good woman—a real rock people could always count on— but like my father and uncle, she really had not taken to all the new technology that made life so much simpler for the rest of us.

Molly opened the door and stuck her head in. "The flowers are pinned on, and everyone is waiting. I brought your bouquet, Aunt LeAnn, and I assume this wrist corsage is for you, Brylee."

"Thank you," I said, glancing at the small flower arrangement in her hand. I hadn't even looked inside the box containing the boutonnières. The florist must have included it as another kind gesture. I would have to call and express my thanks.

"Is there anything else I can do?' she asked.

"You could turn on the CD player that is sitting on the piano. I couldn't find the Wedding March, but I am hoping the music selected will fit the occasion."

I suddenly felt even more nervous than LeAnn. What if something went horribly wrong? The best plans could always go wrong, especially when the people involved were a strange mixture of family like ours.

"I can do that," Molly said, chewing down on the gum she had in her mouth. "You really ought to see Jake, Mum. He's quite the handsomest bloke I have ever seen in his white shirt and tight pants."

"Molly," Aunt Nora scolded again, peering over her shoulder at LeAnn. "We've had this discussion before. Jake is too old and experienced for you."

"A girl can dream, can't she? It's not like I am going to seduce him. I just like looking at him." She put the flowers in my hand and left the room, closing the door soundly behind her.

Aunt Nora turned to face LeAnn. Her face was almost the same color as her hair. "I am so sorry. I don't know what gets into that girl sometimes. I think she deliberately tries to say things she knows will shock me."

"She's young," LeAnn said with a smile. "And Jake is a good-looking bloke, even if he is my baby brother. Besides, he knows Molly is barely legal. And even if he didn't, she would find herself with a lot of competition from the women in Edna if she ever tried to get more than his passing attention."

I didn't like all this talk about Jake. The man I knew hardly deserved it, but I seemed to be in the minority when it came to that.

When I gave LeAnn her long-stemmed daisies and baby's breath to carry, she put her arm around my shoulders and kissed my cheek. I was glad Aunt Nora had followed her daughter out of the room. Intimate moments were hard for me.

"I can't thank you enough for all you have done," she said as tears filled her eyes. She dabbed at them with her index finger. "You have been such a dear since you got here, and you've had so much to deal with: a new brother, your father's live-in lover, my difficult brother, your father's cancer, and now this wedding. I don't know how you have managed to survive all of it."

"Your constant kindness has made it easier," I told her. "I know you and my father love each other very much. There isn't anything in life more important than that."

She smiled her thanks. "You really are a God-send, Brylee, and I am very grateful that in a few minutes we will be a real family through marriage. It's what your father and I have always wanted."

I thought about what she had said as I left the room and walked down the short aisle I had created to stand on the right side of Buck Henry. Was there really more to this marriage than just giving LeAnn and Trevor my father's last name legally? It was a new idea, and one I would mull over once this day was over.

A few moments later, I heard the bedroom door open and close. LeAnn was coming. The music was playing softly in the background. Uncle Ned, Aunt Nora and their children rose to their feet. They were the only people in the audience with the exception of Trevor, who was sitting on a chair as close to where the wedding was taking place as possible. Jake was standing next to my father.

I watched my father's face as LeAnn moved gracefully towards him—the skirt of her dress rippling at her ankles. I could see the love he had for her in his eyes, and it filled me with both joy and pain. I had never seen him look at my mother that way. No one deserved to be with someone they did not, or could not, love with all they had to give. I was so glad I had Ben. When he looked at me, I felt radiantly alive and very beautiful.

Once LeAnn reached my father's side, he took her hand. It was a simple gesture, but it grabbed at my heart. These two people who loved each other so much would soon be parted, and it didn't have to be that way. If they had the blessings of the gospel like I did, they could have forever and not just a few weeks to celebrate their life together.

I felt Jake's eyes resting on me as Buck Henry began the short ceremony that would unite my father and LeAnn for the rest of their mortal lives. It would also make Trevor a legitimate heir to the ranch—both a gift and a liability passed from one generation of Hawkins to the next. Trevor would be the eighth generation from our paternal ancestor who had gained his freedom and homesteaded the very ground on which we stood.

There was so much family history to unravel, and I had no idea where to start. Uncle Ned and his family were the only living relatives I had now—at least the only ones I knew about. Would I ever find my mother's people and would they be receptive to my presence if I did?

I tried to still my thoughts and concentrate on the vows my father and LeAnn were making. After all, it was their wedding day, and they deserved a few moments of happiness before the realities of life descended on them again.

Jake was still watching me. I didn't need to glance in his direction to know that. It was both unnerving and rude, but I suspected that was what he intended—to needle me on the most important day of his sister's life.

He was physically appealing, as Molly had said, tall, dark-eyed, broad-shouldered and muscular. I was glad his white shirt had long sleeves that completely covered his tattoos. I just wished he had removed his earrings, but they kept me grounded in who he really was—a man who could unleash anger without provocation or remorse. And I definitely wasn't naïve enough to believe that anything would change once LeAnn and my father became husband and wife.

I heard LeAnn say, "I do."

The ceremony was over, and my wandering thoughts had forced me to miss most of it.

"Now, if we can have the rings," Buck Henry said.

That was Trevor's cue to take the ring to our father so he could place it on LeAnn's finger. I could see a single row of diamonds on a silver band—simple, yet striking and solid. The ring was just as unpretentious as LeAnn, but what surprised me was the fact that two rings had been attached to the small, blue satin pillow. When had LeAnn picked out the silver band with three small diamonds in it for my father? That must have been one of the person errands Jake had run yesterday—one he had not felt I deserved to know about.

I looked down at my left hand. The ring Ben had given me was a single-carat diamond on a gold band. I had been so thrilled when I first saw it sparkle in the candlelight. He had taken me on a midnight picnic to his favorite cove on the beach. We had listened to the waves crash against the rocks and looked deep into each other's eyes as we lay on the blanket with the candle illuminating the area just around us. That's when he said he was in love with me. Then he pulled out a small, black velvet box and told me to open it.

"I know this might seem a little sudden, Bry," he said. "But we were told when we left our mission to find a worthy young woman, get married, and raise a family. And that's what I want to do with you, if you will have me."

His proposal caught me off guard, but it had only taken a moment to tell him "yes". He was the most incredible man I had ever met, and I had hardly dared dream that he would ever want to marry me. I had loved him from the moment our eyes met. It had just taken him a little longer to arrive at the same conclusion.

I watched LeAnn and my father exchange rings. Then he took the oxygen plugs out of his nose and handed them, along with the oxygen tank, to Jake. When he kissed LeAnn, my tears broke loose like a hole in the Hoover Dam.

And then everyone in the room was clapping, and the new couple turned to face their family. Trevor grabbed both of them, clinging tightly as if he never wanted to let go.

"We're a real family now, aren't we?" he asked. "This means we will always be together."

I saw tears in my father's eyes. "It sure does, son," he said. "We're family, and no one can separate us now."

How I wished that was true. I watched Jake take my father's hand and shake it. He was so tanned and strong, and my father so pale and weak.

"Thanks for making an honest woman of my sister, Jack. I know how much this means to both of you."

Then he stepped back and looked at me with what appeared to be a challenge in his eyes that simply asked, "So what are you going to do now that they are married?"

I looked away from him and reached out to give LeAnn a hug and a kiss.

"Congratulations," I told her. "I am very happy for both of you."

My father extended both of his arms, and I walked right into them and put my head on his shoulder. His embrace wasn't the strong one I had known as a child, but it was tender and filled with love.

"I love you, Brylee," he whispered. "I wish I had known what it meant to be a real father when you were little. You deserved to be part of a family where your parents expressed their love to each other and to you."

"I knew you loved me," I whimpered, hoping my mascara would not run and stain his new shirt. "And I didn't give you much of a chance, always siding with mother."

"And I always pushed you away because I was afraid of being hurt. LeAnn changed that for me, and I know she can help you, too. You are going to need each other when I'm . . . . " He started to cough and choke.

I pulled away and covered my mouth with my hand to keep from crying out while Jake handed the oxygen tank back to him and made sure the buds that made it easier for him to breathe were properly inserted.

"Guess it's time for an old bloke like me to get back to my new reality," he said, letting Jake put the strap to the oxygen tank back over his shoulder.

"It's okay, love," LeAnn told him, moving quickly to his side. "You have made me the happiest woman in the world."

She took his hand and led him towards the sofa. He didn't even protest. It was almost as if he had become the child who obediently followed the one person he knew he was completely safe with. How I wished it could have been me he trusted as much as he did his new bride.

Silence descended on the room as those who were present reconnected with the loss we would all be facing when Jack Hawkins was no longer with us. Uncle Ned was the first to recover.

"Well, old man," he said, leaning down to give my father a hug and a brotherly slap on the back—even though I noticed that it was far more gentle than in the past. "You sure know how to throw a fine shindig. It's got me thinking that if an old dog like you can tie the knot, maybe it's time for me to re-evaluate a few things in my own life."

I heard Aunt Nora take a deep breath while folding her arms defiantly across her chest. "Now don't you go making any fancy plans without talking to me first, Ned Hawkins. I might have a few ideas of my own."

"You always were an opinionated woman." He walked over to her and kissed her cheek. "Life certainly has not been dull with you these past twenty-some odd years."

"And don't you ever forget it," she brushed past him and went over to congratulate LeAnn and my father.

I looked at the two couples that were so obviously devoted to each other, with or without having taken part in a ceremony that bound them together by law. How would Ben and I feel about each other when we had been together as long as they had? Our romance was still so new, and there was so much we did not know about each other.

"I think we should drink a toast to the new couple," NJ said as he carried a tray with champagne-filled glasses into the room. "I even fixed one for the little squirt here." He nodded towards Trevor. "I don't think a little sip of the bubbly will kill him."

Trevor straightened his shoulders. It was easy to see how happy he was to be included in what was going on, rather than being treated like a child.

I was the one who felt a moment of panic! How could I drink champagne when I was planning on going to the temple with Ben in a few months? But if I didn't make a toast with the others, it would only offend the people I loved.

I looked around as everyone else in the room took a glass in their hands. Now was another moment of truth as to whether or not I was totally committed to the new way I had chosen to live. "Oh, Father in Heaven," I silently prayed as my chest began to heave. "Please help me! I don't know what to do."

The hot sweat of fear and indecision was washing over me when I heard a voice.

"I think Brylee and Trevor should have soda instead," Jake said, coming to my aid so uncharacteristically that I was forced to look at him. Molly's hand was resting on his arm, and she looked rather pleased with herself. "Trevor hasn't had much to eat, and Brylee will be driving into Edna later."

He didn't need to continue. The implication about having another accident was abundantly clear and no one dared object.

"I think that's a marvelous idea," Aunt Nora said, and I wondered if she remembered what I had told her about not drinking the night after my arrival and was testing me to see if I really meant it. "I'll just hurry right along to the kitchen and get it."

"Brylee can do that," Jake told her. "And while she's gone, I will claim Trevor's glass for myself. A confirmed bachelor like me might need two drinks to make it through the toast I have ready for Jack and LeAnn."

I didn't wait for anything else to be said, I simply made my way to the kitchen, opened a can of Sprite and poured it into two glasses. I had no idea why Jake had stood up for me, but now was not the time to question his generosity.

Trevor didn't seem to be upset when I handed him a glass of soda and put my arm around his shoulders. He just smiled up at me and leaned his small body closer to mine. Maybe it helped that I was drinking the same thing he was.

"Now that we are all ready," Jake said, lifting his glass in the air. "I just want to say that Jack Hawkins is the best bloody mate I have ever known, and I am mighty glad he fell in love with my sister. She is the best among women. She had to be raising me after our parents were killed. I was a hellion back then, and I'm afraid I am not much better now. But I intend to do right by my family, regardless of what it takes. To Jack and LeAnn—two of the finest people I have ever known. May you always remember the joy of this day, surrounded by people who love you? You make marriage an enviable state."

"Here, here," was echoed around the room, and the first toast was over.

I looked down at the glass in my hand after taking a quick swallow. He had clearly defined the terms of what our future relationship would be if I stepped out of line. It was cruel and hurtful, but I doubted anyone else in the room noticed. He was very careful about vocalizing his more obvious barbs in private.

Uncle Ned spoke next. It was only a matter of time before I was expected to say something congratulatory. I listened as more toasts were given and the glasses refilled, and then it was my turn.

"I have never made a toast before, and have only known LeAnn for a few weeks," I heard myself say. "But during that time, I have seen how utterly devoted she is to my father and my little brother. I have felt her quiet strength and patience, and watched her care lovingly for those around her. I can see why my father fell in love with her." Tears were stinging my nose, but there were a few more things I needed to say.

"I came back to a lot of changes that sort of rocked my world again, but how could I not be thrilled to have a little brother who has welcomed me into his world with complete acceptance. And I can only hope that when Ben and I are married, we can love each other the way Father and LeAnn do. Thank you for welcoming me into your family. I feel very blessed to be a part of this special day. May God bless both of you for your goodness! I love you."

It wasn't a traditional toast, but I wanted everyone to know how I felt about the couple sitting on the sofa in the living room, where I had spent so much time with my mother. Life really wasn't about possessions like the piano or the brooch my father had given LeAnn. It was about people, and I was very lucky to be surrounded by my rediscovered family.

Buck Henry excused himself after the last toast was made and all the documents had been signed, saying that his wife was expecting him home early enough for a late supper.

Uncle Ned walked him outside, and the rest of us adjourned to the dining room for a meal of our own.

Aunt Nora had prepared an incredible dinner, even if it wasn't fancy, and the rolls Mrs. Mahoney had sent were fresh and flaky. At its conclusion, the wedding cake was placed on the far end of the table next to where my father and LeAnn were sitting. Regardless of the fact that my father looked incredibly tired, he rose from his chair and put his hand over LeAnn's as she ran the knife into the center layer of the cake.

In the traditional way, they fed each other the first bite. There were smiles and laughter and more pictures were taken. Then the top layer was removed so it could be frozen, and more champagne was served with the cake. Trevor and I opened our second can of Sprite.

"Don't look so sad. It isn't the end of the world," a deep voice said from over my shoulder as I picked at the wedding cake on the plate in front of me without tasting it.

"I'm not sad," I said, looking up into Jake's darkly tanned face.

"You could have fooled me," he whispered. "You haven't eaten a single bite. It's not too bad, even if there is too much frosting."

I wasn't ready to play more games, but apparently that wasn't what he intended. He walked immediately past me and sat down at the table by Molly, who looked up at him adoringly. They were soon lost in conversation. I didn't bother eavesdropping. I just felt sorry for my young cousin because Jake had been able to reel her in. Molly was young and beautiful and must have had plenty of other more suitable guys after her, but like the girls I had met in Edna, something about him had her mesmerized.

I had never understood the attraction to bad boys. They might offer excitement, but they were dangerous and could break a girl's heart. I liked men like Ben. They were solid and stable, and I never had to guess where I stood. The life I had chosen would be pleasant and peaceful. I needed that. All the discord and changes of the past few days had thrown me into another tailspin.

"Well, this has been quite a day for celebration," Uncle Ned said as he rose from the table. "But I propose that we all scatter so the bride and groom can have some privacy."

"A great idea!" Aunt Nora stood up beside him. "Come on, girls," she said, including me with her own daughter who did not look like she wanted to leave Jake's side. "Let's get these plates rinsed so they can be put in the dishwasher. God must have been looking kindly on women when that was invented."

Aunt Nora always moved rapidly, and this occasion was no exception. Her side of the table was cleared before Molly and I were on our feet.

"I'll start loading things in the car," Uncle Ned said, falling into step behind her. "What would you ever do without me?"

"Hush up, you old goat," she affectionately chided, pulling at the beginnings of his new goatee. "You are the one who should be glad I'm around. Who else would keep all your smelly socks mended?"

I knew they were only teasing as they always did, but I hoped my father and LeAnn hadn't heard. They didn't need to be reminded that their hours of wedded bliss were numbered.

But I needn't have worried. LeAnn and my father were in a world of their own. She was sitting as close to him as possible and had her arm around his shoulders. They were whispering animatedly to each other. Trevor had disappeared and so had Jake.

The plates, glasses and utensils were soon rinsed and on their way to the dishwasher. I was helping Aunt Nora, but Molly just stood leaning against the counter with her arms crossed in front of her.

"Listen, cuz," she said as I inserted the last of the dessert plates into the dishwasher. "I'm sorry for being a brat. I don't know what happens to me when I get around Jake. He is just one of those blokes who can drive a girl crazy."

"No worries," I told her, wondering if Aunt Nora had told her to apologize for her rather childish behavior.

"I shouldn't take my frustration out on you just because you have found someone wonderful to marry. I was acting like a real mongrel—one of those despicable girls no one likes to be around because all they do is flirt—but the blokes I meet are just so predictable. It's infuriating."

"It took me a long time to meet Ben, and it didn't happen until I had quit looking. I know that sounds lame, but it's true. You will find the guy who is right for you when you least expect it."

She frowned. "I hope so, but I'm not ready for a serious relationship yet. I just want to be young and have fun. There is plenty of time to be saddled down to one bloke. Will we get to meet your Ben before the wedding?"

"There are a few logistics to work out," I replied. "We just got engaged and so much has happened since I got here."

Why was I being so non-committal? Was it simply because I was dealing with too much other stuff that needed to be settled before I could realistically think about building a life of my own, or did I truly believe Ben would not understand why my family acted the way they did? They were good people, even if they did not live their lives the way I had chosen to live mine.

"I really am sorry about Uncle Jack," Molly said, obviously noticing my hesitation about saying anything more about my own life. "He's a good bloke and doesn't deserve to die when he has so much to look forward to."

"Thank you," I told her, biting down on my bottom lip to keep it from trembling. My cousin had never been known for her tact. "It's hard to accept that he won't be around much longer."

"Well, our parents have been stupid and so has NJ."

I looked around to see if Aunt Nora was there, but she had already left the room.

"What do you mean?" I asked, wondering how she could go from sympathy to condemnation so quickly.

"That stupid smoking! I know it's all the rage, but I hate it. Why can't they just quit like I did? It's killing Uncle Jack, but do my brother or parents seem to care? Don't get me wrong, they feel awful about what is happening to Uncle Jack, but they still light up whenever they feel like it. I tell them how I feel, but they are just the most stubborn bunch of Aussies in the world."

Her confession surprised me, even though it shouldn't have. People everywhere were recognizing the dangers of smoking. But for the first time since coming home, I had found someone in my own family who felt the same way I did about the nasty habit.

"My father was still smoking when I got here just a few days ago," I told her. "He said there was little reason to quit when it was killing him anyway."

"I know!" she exclaimed, flinging her hand in the air. "It's so dumb, and my entire family is doing the same thing. Why can't they believe they could end up the same way? I gave up those awful weeds more than a year ago."

I didn't want to talk about this right now, but the look of total anguish on her face, and the tears in her eyes made me reconsider. Her family still had a chance. My father had lost his. I handed her a clean dishtowel.

"I have learned something about personal agency this past year, Molly. You can not force people into doing anything against their will."

"Even when it is for their own good?"

"Especially then. Learning how to make wise choices is one of the reasons we are in this world, and change has to come from within. I don't have any of the answers, but I do know that I can not judge how anyone else lives his or her life. All I can do is love them."

She looked at me as if I had lost my mind. "I don't know how you can say that after everything that is happened. I am so angry right now I could spit."

"Is there something else that is bothering you?" I asked.

"Stuff is always happening, but how can you be so calm in the face of all of this?"

"I guess it's because I found God."

"So have I," she said. "I go to Mass every week like a good Catholic girl, but I still get angry, and sometimes I just want to pound the whole lot of them."

I was just about to tell her that revenge was never the answer when NJ walked into the kitchen and told her to move her arse if she didn't want to walk home.

I followed my cousins outside to their car. Uncle Ned and Aunt Nora had already left.

"It was good to see both of you," I told them as they stood leaning against the car. "I hope you will stop by the house again before heading back to Sydney. I would like more time for us to get reacquainted now that we are all adults."

"Sounds like a plan," NJ said, "But I'm still going to see if I can talk you into coming to Sydney for a few days while you are still here. You might be engaged to some bloke in America, but you can still party with your cousins for a night or two."

I smiled at him. "Thanks for the invite, but I won't be going anywhere for a while. I promised Father I would be here for LeAnn and Trevor for as long as they need me."

"Good on ya," he said, sliding in behind the wheel of his fancy car. "But what about that guy you are supposed to be marrying? Men have needs, and he won't wait around forever."

"I think we will be all right," I told him as he closed the car door, but his statement made me wonder just how long Ben would wait for me. He really wanted to get married and start a family.

Chapter 16

Trevor was waiting inside the front door with his backpack slung over his shoulders when I returned to the house.

"I'm already," he told me. "Mum packed my bag for me."

"I can see that," I told him, running my hand over his light brown hair that looked almost blonde like his mother's when he was standing outside in the sun. "It will only take me a few minutes to change my clothes and throw a few things in my overnight bag. Then we will be on our way."

"Do I have time to say goodbye to my animals?"

"I thought you did that when you fed them before the wedding."

"I did, but I have never left them overnight before. I don't want them to get scared."

"Then do it," I told him with a smile. His concern for his animals only reassured me of his own fear at leaving the safety of the ranch, even for just one night. It would be a new experience for both of us. I had never spent the night alone with a child, and I was a little scared, too.

After telling our father and LeAnn goodnight, we put his backpack and my small suitcase on the back seat of the jeep I had rented. It was going to cost a fortune by the time I returned it, but I had called the rental company to extend my contract. They had been helpful, especially after I explained the situation.

We had only driven about 20 feet down the hard-packed dirt driveway when Jake came running out of the bunkhouse, motioning for me to stop. He had changed from his white shirt and black pants into the open-neck shirt and khaki cargo shorts he almost always wore. I stopped the car and pushed the button so the window would slide down. Would I ever get used to driving on the left-hand side of the road again? It seemed so awkward after all the time I had spent in America.

"What's up?" I asked him, annoyed that he had intruded on my time with Trevor.

"Listen, I don't want to get in your face, but I want you to be careful tonight."

"I will," I assured him with a quizzical look. "I know how to drive."

"I'm sure you do, but there is something I need to talk to you about. Can you just get out for a minute? This is private." He looked over at Trevor, who was sitting very still just looking at us.

I opened the car door and stepped into the warm night air. It never cooled down here like it did in Los Angeles.

"So what is it that you cannot say in front of Trevor?" I asked, flaying my hands into the air.

But instead of answering me outright, he took a firm grasp on my arm and pulled me to the far end of the jeep, where Trevor couldn't see us unless he took his seatbelt off and turned around. I wanted to shake myself free, but he didn't give me the chance.

"I'm not trying to be mysterious," he said, slowly releasing me. "But I would feel a hell of a lot better if you would let me fly you into Edna. I don't like the idea of you and Trevor being on the road after dark."

It wasn't my favorite activity either, but it could not be helped, and I certainly wasn't going to let him think I was incapable of taking care of myself and my little brother. Besides, his plane only had two seats, and Trevor would hate the idea of sitting on my lap or riding in the cargo hold all the way to Edna.

"We will be fine," I told him with a sense of bravado I didn't really feel now that he had made such a big deal of us traveling alone at night. "I have been driving the Los Angeles freeways and am perfectly capable of handling a country road in the outback.

"I'm not worried about you meeting other cars on the road," he said, giving me an annoyed look. "It's the exact opposite. What if you have car trouble or hit something in the dark?"

"Then I guess we would stay put until someone came to help. I do have roadside assistance with my rental agreement. I even have a blanket and water in the jeep, and I always carry granola bars in my purse."

"You think you have it all figured out, don't you?" he said as his jaw clenched. "You are not in America anymore. You are in the Outback, where bad and unexpected things happen all the time. People have even been known to disappear."

"Aren't you being a little paranoid for such a macho man?"

He glared at me, and I realised I wasn't helping myself.

"Maybe you should be a little more fearful about things you don't really understand," he replied. "But if you won't listen to reason, at least take this with you for protection."

He held out a small object wrapped in a man's handkerchief. I didn't need to ask what it was.

"No!" I said, taking a step backwards and putting my hands in front of my face as if for protection. "I am not going to carry a gun. I've never even held one before."

"But what if something happened and you needed to protect yourself and Trevor?"

"Oh, my gosh!" I shook my head in disbelief. "You are a male chauvinist. You think women can't take care of themselves."

His look of concern turned to near hostility. "If you want to get yourself killed, that's fine by me, but you are taking my nephew away from the ranch, and I will not tolerate anything bad happening to him."

I could only shake my head. "I can't believe what you are saying, Jake. Trevor is my little brother. I would protect him with my life."

"Well, you better," he said. "Because if anything happens to him, your life will not be worth living. And that is a promise I will keep. He is all my sister has."

"And he is the only brother I have. How could you possibly think I would let anything happen to him?"

"Because you're not God! He gives and takes whenever it pleases him."

"You have that wrong," I retorted with an equal amount of disdain. "He is loving and kind, but he has given us agency to think and act for ourselves."

"Are you telling me it is your father's own fault that he is dying? Just how insensitive are you?"

"I love my father and would do anything in this world to help him, but some things just cannot be changed. I hope you won't make the same mistake he did."

I turned around and retraced my steps to the jeep. I was shaking uncontrollably. This was one confrontation I had not expected. Jake was simply the most insufferable man I had ever met.

"What did Uncle Jake want?" Trevor asked once we were on our way down the long, dusty driveway.

I looked in the rearview mirror. He was still standing in the middle of the road where I had left him. Score one for me!

"He just wanted to make sure we had everything we needed."

"That was an awful long talk just to say that. He looked angry."

"Oh, I don't think he was angry," I lied. "He was just concerned. After all, this is your first excursion away from the ranch."

When I looked over at him, I wished I hadn't said that. He looked so little and scared, but he was being brave, and I loved him even more for that.

"We are going to have a wonderful time. I brought my phone so we could take lots of pictures. Don't you think our father and your mother would like that?"

"I guess so," he said. "Do you think they are worried about me? I don't want something to happen to father when I'm gone."

I turned to him and tried to smile. "Father will be fine. He has your mother and your Uncle Jake to take care of him."

I wished I could believe what I had told him, but only God knew how much longer our father had. I could only pray that he would not be called home while we were gone. If that happened, Trevor would never forgive or trust me again.

"Hey, Trevor," I said, trying to break the dark mood that had settled between us. "Did father ever tell you the story about how the first English settlers got here?"

"He said our great, great—I don't remember how many greats—grandfather came here on a convict ship. I forgot what he did that was so bad."

"He stole some bread to feed his family. I don't think that was a very good reason to punish him and send him away, do you?"

"No! He was just trying to take care of the people he loved. Father said he would do the same thing if Mum and I were starving."

I smiled into the darkness. "I am sure he would. He loves his family very much."

"Then why does he have to die?"

I had anticipated this topic coming up while we were away, but had not planned on it happening before we even got off Hawkins' land.

"We talked about this a little while ago, didn't we?"

He fidgeted in his seat and picked at the seat belt that was wrapped around him. "Yes, but I still don't get it."

"There are lots of things in life we don't understand, like how the world was made or how the stars stay in the sky?"

"No, but we could if we were smart enough."

"That is right," I told him. "And someday we will understand everything. Just as we will understand why father can't stay with us as long as we want him to."

I could hear him sniffing lightly in the darkness, and it nearly broke my heart. He was too young to have his whole world shattered. I would try to lift his spirits.

"But we have been given something very special I didn't even know about when my mother died."

"What's that?' he asked, rubbing at his eyes with his small fists.

"Each other! Don't you think it is pretty amazing that I have a brother and you have a sister? Our Heavenly Father helped us find each other so we could become friends."

He leaned back in his seat and sighed. "I am glad I have a sister, but I don't understand why nobody will talk to me about father. He's getting sicker every day."

I felt a sudden burst of anger towards both LeAnn and our father. If they wanted to keep playing the pretending game, that was their choice, but they needed to consider Trevor's feelings. He was a child, and no one was trying to help prepare him for the inevitable. It wasn't fair, but I could not talk specifics to him. I had promised to leave the major explanations to his parents when they were ready.

"How about I tell you a story?" I asked as he stared out the window, looking both dejected and miserable. I hadn't meant for this to be a bad experience. I had just wanted us to have some time together and give Father and LeAnn a chance to be alone, quite likely for the last time.

"I suppose," he said.

"Father used to tell me about the 'Big Dry' that lasted from 1937 to 1947, when the country withered and the strong winds whipped up the parched soil in the outback and carried it to cities hundreds of miles away. It blinded all the people driving on the roads and clogged up all the machinery. And if that wasn't enough to raise havoc with all the ranchers and town people, on Ash Wednesday, strong winds drove forest fires along 450 miles of the coast from Adelaide to Melbourne. In some places the fire caused a vacuum where fireballs were sucked up at speeds of more than 100 miles per hour. The skies were filled with what looked like the explosion of giant fireworks—very awesome to look at, but very destructive. After two days, seven little towns had been wiped out, 2000 homes destroyed, and more than seventy people had lost their lives."

"I wish I could have seen it," he said, turning to face me with what appeared to be nothing short of rapt interest.

"Not me," I said. "It was awful and lasted for two years."

"Did it hurt Father at the ranch?"

"Our father wasn't born yet, but the ranch was far enough away from the coast that the house we still live in wasn't in danger, but it did force all the ranchers, including our grandfather, into selling all but their best sheep at rock-bottom prices—like five dollars an animal because there wasn't anything for them to eat. Father also said that grandfather was lucky because some of the ranchers in New South Wales were forced to sell theirs at fifty cents a head."

"That's not very much money, is it?"

"Not when you consider how much it costs to raise them."

Suddenly, he became pensive. "I never want to sell Newton," he lamented.

I reached over my hand and ruffled his short hair. "You don't have to worry about that. Father would never allow it."

"But what about when he isn't here anymore?"

My heart sank with a new kind of sorrow. How could I ever help my little brother understand what I was incapable of understanding myself?

"Your mother, Uncle Jake, and I will be there to make sure it doesn't happen. Our ranch will stay in the family, and you will get to run it someday just like you've planned. I promise you that."

It was a fool's promise, but one I would die trying to keep. Trevor didn't need any more disappointments. I looked over at him again, but he had closed his eyes. Maybe it was better that way.

I thought about our father as I drove along the little-used highway leading into Edna. He had never lived away from the outback, but surely he'd had dreams when young. Had those come to a screeching halt when he found out I was on the way? He was too honorable a man to turn his back on us, but he certainly had not been prepared to provide for a family. He had been forced to move in with my grandparents since he could not afford a place of his own for my mother and me.

Their marriage had been doomed from the start. I didn't know how they had managed at all. Ranching might be some people's idea of a perfect life, but it was fraught with hard work, poverty, constant stress and even danger. Complete livelihoods could be lost with one act of nature, like the Big Dry. My family had never recovered from that. It didn't sound like much of a life to me.

Still, I had to admit that the Australian Outback had some of the most beautiful scenery in the world with its clear, deep water holes and vast, patterned landscapes under a cerulean sky. I had seen most of that in books since we had never traveled far when I was young. But I knew it provided a refuge from the crowds and political strife of the cities and was a source of spiritual renewal for those who were suffering overexposure to the complexities of modern-day living.

As a child, I had felt nothing but sadness for the aborigines who had been stripped of their birthright and forced to the edges of a white civilization that did not appreciate what they had cherished for centuries. I had loved listening to the stories Asum and Keida told in their broken English about wichety grub being a delicacy and how they speared kangaroos, possums, snakes, fish and large lizards so their families could eat. They also knew where whales would be stranded, so they could collect their blubber.

The women of the tribes collected seeds, yams, roots, honey, fruits and berries, but spent most of their time and energy looking for water they carried back to their tribes in a cooloma, or curved dish hollowed from a knot of wood. It was also used to dig for grubs and termites and pound the seeds they found into a sticky powder to make bread. They relied on their instincts, memories and navigation skills to find the water holes and soaks—marshy areas where insects and small animals loved to hide.

I had thought of it as a fascinating life where men could hurl the woomera, or throwing stick, more than 150 feet, and where they slept in the open air or in shelters made from local vegetation. When the weather turned cold, they would keep warm by lighting fires with friction sticks or curling up with each other or with semi-domesticated dogs, cousins of the wild dingo, who followed them everywhere.

They owed their loyalty to their tribe. Children were often betrothed at birth, and many girls were given to men much older than themselves. Although the male members of the village had only one wife at a time, both the men and the women had a number of potential partners who provided them with an accepted channel for premarital or extramarital liaisons.

But what still fascinated me most was their belief in what they called the Dreamtime—the period when supernatural spirit beings moved over the earth to give it life and form. They thought of it as a parallel reality because they believed humans were the descendants of mythical ancestors and were irrevocably linked to them and the land they created. Every feature of the earth, every rock and water hole, contained the spirit of his or her ancestor.

I hated what civilization had done to their culture. Those who had not left the coast or found jobs with ranchers in the outback had been rounded up and forced onto missions or reservations much like the American Indians. They were considered non-people, never counted in the census, allowed to vote or even own property of their own. They had to receive official permission before they could take a job, and then their wages were paid to the Protector of Aboriginals, usually a policeman.

While things were better for them now, most of them still preferred living in the outback rather than dealing with the unfair practices of the white people who had stolen their land. I wondered if Asum and Keida had just wandered off like everyone thought, or if something else might have happened to them. I missed them because they had been such a huge part of my past.

I looked over at my little brother, who had fallen asleep. I could hear his soft breathing but didn't want to wake him since he had been up since dawn. But I was getting almost too sleepy to drive, so I turned on the CD I had been listening to on my way out to the ranch. Had it only been a little over three weeks since I had returned? In many ways, it seemed like I had never left, and Ben was just a dream from another lifetime. Maybe Asum and Keida had been right about Dreamtime all along.

When we got to the hotel Father had told me about, I discovered that he had already made a reservation and paid the bill. The uniformed girl at the front desk asked me if I needed any help with our luggage. I looked down at Trevor who was standing beside me, his eyes heavy with sleep, but his hands secure on the straps that held his backpack in place.

"We'll be fine," I told her, taking the key she offered. Our room was on the main floor, just a few yards from the indoor swimming pool that smelled of chlorine and light sweat. Trevor was so tired he didn't even ask if we could see how the water felt.

Our room was plainly furnished—two queen-size beds, a dresser with a mirror, a nightstand, and a small table with two padded chairs. The bedspreads had geometric designs in gold, musty green and brown.

"Which bed would you like?" I asked Trevor, but he had already thrown his backpack on the floor and was sprawled out on the bed closest to the door. I didn't have the heart to disturb him, so I just removed his sandals and let him sleep.

It was plenty warm in the room, even with the AC going. He would not need a cover until early morning.

I sat down on the other bed and sighed. I was tired of being strong and forgiving. I wanted to be with Ben so he could take some of my burdens away. Without thought as to what I was going to say when I heard his voice, I took my cell phone from my purse and went into the small bathroom and closed the door. There were three rings before Ben answered.

"I was beginning to wonder if you had dropped off the face of the earth," he said in a breathy tone that made it sound like he had been running. "I haven't talked to you in almost ten days."

"Didn't you get my email explaining what was going on?"

His pause let me know he was trying to decide what should be said. "I'm sorry, Bry. I know I should have replied, but I was nursing a bruised ego. I can't tell you how much I was looking forward to picking you up at the airport. I even planned a welcome home party."

"I'm sorry to have missed that," I said. "You know I would have been on that plane if I could."

"I get the fact that you need to be with your father, but that doesn't stop me from wishing you were here."

"I will be home as soon as I can. I promise."

"I don't suppose you have an idea when that might be?"

My head moved back and forth in the dark. "The doctor gave him six weeks, but one of those is already gone."

"So it really could be another month or two before I see you again."

I wanted to tell him that he could come where I was, but something held me back. When I didn't say anything, he took up his side of the conversation again.

"It wouldn't be so bad if we could talk more often. Certainly, your father has a landline you could use."

"He doesn't have long-distance coverage. I thought I explained that in my email."

"You did. But it sounded a little far-fetched. Are you telling me that certain of life's greatest necessities still haven't reached your home in the Outback? But even if that is true, you could have called me collect."

"Doing that never crossed my mind, Ben," I admitted, suddenly feeling so tired I could barely keep my eyes open. "So much has happened the past few days."

"Maybe I am just being insensitive, but I want my future wife here with me. I've been worried about you. We all have. It's not like you are just visiting family across state lines. I put everyone's names, whom I knew, on the prayer list at the temple. How is your father doing, other than awful? I have known people who died from cancer, and it's a terrible way to go."

"Not good! The doctor put him on hospice, so he is home where we can take care of him. He didn't want to die in the hospital."

"Can't blame him for that," Ben said. "But I feel like a jerk for talking you into going without me."

"There's nothing you could do."

"I could hold you in my arms and give you all the love I have in my heart."

I choked back a sob of loneliness and fear, quite different from the tears of frustration and grief that had become such a part of my life.

"I know why you didn't feel you could come and you were right about my father and me needing time alone. Despite the fact that he is dying, w have been able to connect on a personal level, and I wouldn't trade that for anything."

"Then I am happy for both of you. I just wish you didn't sound so sad. But I do have one piece of good news. I got the job at Herricks and have been here for three days. That means when you get home, we can start making wedding plans in earnest because at least one of us will be employed. We can even start looking for a place of our own."

"I would love that," I told him as another wave of sorrow washed over me. "And I am absolutely thrilled about your new job. I wish I could be there to help you celebrate. I know how much you wanted it."

"We will do that when you get back, but I can't talk much longer. I am on my lunch break, and it wouldn't look good if I was late getting back to my desk, my first week here."

"I understand. I just needed to hear your voice."

"But if you are calling me on your cell phone, it means you're not at the ranch. What's going on? It must be the middle of the night there."

"My father and LeAnn got married today, so I brought Trevor to town so they could have a little time alone."

"Wow," he said. "Things have been moving fast. How do you feel about it?"

"Surprisingly good. They love each other, and she has been amazing with him."

"Well, I am glad they finally made everything legal. You sounded upset about their relationship when we last talked."

"They don't see life the way you and I do. No one here does."

"But I know you have been setting a good example. That has to make you feel good."

"It does! I just wish they understood death the way we do. It would make what everyone is going through so much easier."

"It sounds like there is a lot of missionary work to be done in your part of the outback."

"When the time is right," I replied.

"It was my experience in the mission field that people are the most receptive to the gospel when they are facing the loss of someone they love. It is comforting to know they can be with them again."

"I agree, but I am still the wayward child come home. My father isn't happy about my leaving the Catholic faith, and I am having trouble trying to convince some people that I am not here to claim a birthright."

"I don't understand. I thought you said LeAnn and your father have been very kind and understanding."

"They have been as long as we don't talk too much about religion, but LeAnn has a brother who is not as forgiving or understanding. He thinks I am the devil incarnate when it comes to his sister and my step-brother."

"I don't like the idea of you being anywhere around him. He sounds like a dangerous man."

"I think he could be. He wanted me to carry a gun with me tonight."

I heard his intake of air. "You didn't do it, I hope."

"Never!" I exclaimed. "I have no idea how to use a gun, and know I could never hurt anyone or anything—even if I had to."

"Now you are scaring me, Bry. I know your father is dying, but you need to get out of there and come home. I don't want anything to happen to you."

"It won't," I assured him. "But father has been teaching me the financial end of running a ranch and needs my help until we can find someone trustworthy to take over."

The pain in my chest suddenly exploded, and I felt like I might throw up. It had not been my intention to let the man I loved know of my plans for staying in Australia indefinitely this way. But it was too late to take any of my words back.

The confusion and pain in his voice were unmistakable. "What are you saying, Bry? I thought you would be coming home once the funeral was over. I know you can't give me a time and date for that, but you make it sound like you could be there forever.   What about us and our plans to get married?"

"Our plans haven't changed," I assured him. "And I will not be here one moment longer than necessary, but I couldn't very well refuse my father's one dying wish. You would not do that with yours?"

"Point taken, but I don't have to like it," he said. "I want you back in my arms where you belong."

"And that is exactly where I want to be, too," I said as tears trickled down my cheeks and landed on my pink shirt, making oblong, wet spots. "But I don't have many choices right now. I love my father and want to spend as much time as possible with him."

"And I am making that harder by not understanding?"

"I love that you want me to come home, but I can't just walk away and not look back like I did before."

"I would never ask that of you, but I do wish I could be there to help you through all of this."

"Me too, but I will be fine. And it does help knowing that you have got a job you love. I promise to find one for myself as soon as I get back. I really wasn't that fond of living your parents' basement, kind as they were to offer it to us."

Ben laughed. "So you think we are better than Brian and Chelsea? They saved a lot of money the year they lived with my folks."

Chelsea was Ben's oldest sister. She and Brian had been married for three years and were expecting their first child.

"It worked perfectly for them, but I really would like a place of our own. I want to take care of you and show you just how completely my heart belongs to you."

"Stop that, or you will have me in tears," he said. "Despite my many weaknesses. I am a sensitive kind of guy."

I bite the end of my thumb until it hurt. "That is one of the reasons I love you so much, Ben, but even I know that California surfers don't cry."

"We've been known to do it at weddings, births and funerals." He suddenly stopped speaking and all the animation left his voice. "I'm sorry, Brylee. I didn't mean to say that."

"You don't have to watch what you say around me, Ben. Death is as much a part of living as birth is. Besides, it just means I can get my parents sealed sooner."

"What about his new bride?"

"I am leaving that in God's hands," I replied, since I had no idea how his marriage to LeAnn might complicate that. "I know his life with my mother wasn't all it could have been, but someday they will both be perfected. That leaves endless possibilities."

"Always my practical one. Gosh, I miss you, but I have to go. I don't want to get fired before cashing my first paycheck. You will be careful, won't you? And send me an email when you get back to the ranch. I promise to answer as soon as I get it, and I will definitely quit behaving like a jerk."

"You're not behaving like a jerk. I have laid a lot on you, but it is not by choice."

I felt bad saying that because everything I did was by choice, even if I didn't like it. I could walk away from my father any time I wanted to, but my choice right now was to be with my family instead of going home to Ben.

"Gotta go, honey," he said. "Don't forget to write, and don't forget that I love you."

"I love you more," I said as the phone went dead on his end.

I washed my face, put on a knee-length nightshirt and climbed into bed. Ben loved me, and he understood why I couldn't come back until I had finished the work I'd promised to do for my father.

The last thing I remembered as I drifted off to sleep was the way Ben looked when he was riding his surfboard, his hair wet with ocean water and a smile lighting up his face. I was so lucky to have found him. I would write every day because I couldn't afford to take our relationship for granted. It was truly one of the great miracles of my life, and how he would love surfing in the ocean off the tip of Australia. We would have to come back often once we were man and wife.

Chapter 17

The sun was just beginning to peak through the part in the drapes when I first tried to open my eyes the next morning. I felt stiff all over. That was a good sign that at least I had slept and not moved around all night like I usually did. But once my eyes became accustomed to the darkness in the room, I saw that Trevor was dressed and sitting cross-legged on his bed with the TV remote in his hand.

When I moved underneath the sheet, he looked over at me. "I didn't mean to wake you up," he said. "I was trying to be quiet."

I stretched the full length of the bed. "You didn't wake me, Trevor. It was time to get up. Are you hungry?"

"A little," he admitted.

"There are a couple of granola bars in my purse. Why don't you eat them while I jump in the shower? Or we could go for a quick swim first."

"No," he said. "I need to get home to my animals. They will wonder what has happened to me. But I did have a good time. Thanks for bringing me."

"But we haven't done anything yet. Just a quick swim wouldn't take long, and I did bring something special for us to play with in the pool."

"What is it?" he asked, dropping the remote onto the bed.

"Well," I said. "It is in my bag. It might take a little work to get it so we can use it, but I think between the two of us we could make it happen."

His curiosity was piqued, and I decided to make the most of it. I wanted him to have at least one pleasant memory from our first trip to town.

It took longer than I had anticipated to fill the floating mattress with air, but that didn't matter because we were both laughing at how little progress each breath of air made. I took several pictures just because it felt so good to see him smiling for a change.

The sun had yet to come up when we changed into our suits, but the pool was open so we splashed and giggled as we took turns sliding on and off the air mattress. I taught him how to retrieve objects from the bottom of the pool just like Ben had taught me, and for nearly an hour, we were able to forget what was waiting for us at home.

By the time several other families joined us, he was tired and ready to get out. I put him the shower first, and then turned on some cartoons for him to watch while I took my turn getting all the chlorine off.

But I realized something as the first cool drops of water hit my shoulders. (It was a mistake to take a hot shower during the summer because cool water helped lower the body's core temperature and lessened the chance of heat stroke.) Concentrating on Trevor's needs had helped me forget my own problems, if only for an hour or so. I had to find some way of helping him through the agony of losing our father when the time came. LeAnn would have enough sorrow of her own to deal with.

When we stopped at the front desk to return our room key, the young man working there asked if I was Brylee Hawkins. When I nodded, he extended a folded piece of paper with my name on it. The very gesture made me feel physically ill.

"What does it say?" Trevor asked, trying to stand on his tiptoes so he could see what was written, but I deliberately shielded it with my free hand. The note simply said, "Call home before you leave."

Every nerve in my body tingled. Jake wouldn't be asking me to call him without a very good reason.

"Who's it from?" Trevor asked, tugging on my arm since I had yet to answer his first question.

"Your Uncle Jake wants us to call before we head home," I said, trying to keep the fear I felt inside from showing. "He probably wants us to pick up something so he won't have to fly into town later today."

I hoped Trevor believed me because I couldn't look at him. He would immediately know I was keeping something from him.

Jake answered the phone after the second ring. He must have been waiting in the kitchen for my return call.

"What's up?" I asked, looking at Trevor with what I hoped was a reassuring smile.

"Have you been watching the news?"

"No," I replied, heaving a sigh of relief. At least this wasn't about my father. "We just left our room, and Trevor was watching cartoons. Is there something important we should know about?"

"The weather service has put out an advisory for rain. I haven't seen any dark clouds out this way yet, but it will take you a couple of hours to get back, and you know how fast these storms come up."

"Thanks for the warning! We were just going to grab something to eat, and then we will gas up and be on our way. We should be there around noon. How are the newlyweds doing?"

"Your father is fine, at least as far as I know," he said, immediately calming my fears. "They haven't left the bedroom yet this morning."

"That's good," I said. Trevor was frowning at me, but I gave him another smile. "We'll see you when we get there."

I hung up my end of the conversation and told Trevor about the storm warning.

"What about father and mum?" he asked.

"Still sleeping, but they should be up by the time we get there. Now, how about some breakfast? I've heard that kids really like Maccas or McDonald's, as we call it in the States."

He didn't object to my suggestion, so we pulled in at the Golden Arches a few minutes later.

"What can I have?" he asked as we walked inside. Dozens of people were lined up in front of the counter, and the kids who worked out front were busy shouting orders to the ones who worked in the back.

"Anything you like," I told him. "This is our little mini-vacation."

I looked down at him and smiled. He was such a cute little guy and had the best manners ever. LeAnn and my father had raised him well. I hoped I would be half as lucky with my own children. Now, he just needed to learn that the world away from the ranch was a safe and okay place to be.

When we had placed our order, Trevor reached into his pocket and took out a twenty-dollar bill.

"Father gave me this money in case I needed it, so I can pay for breakfast," he said.

His generosity brought fresh tears to my eyes. None of the kids I knew in L.A. would offer to pay for anything if they thought they might be able to buy something they really wanted.

"Put your money away, little brother. This is my treat. Buy something you really like or put it in the bank so you will have money to help pay for college."

"Is college really expensive?"

"It sure is, but worth every penny! Everyone needs to have something they can do when they grow up."

"But father said the ranch would be mine someday. I don't need to go to college for that."

I couldn't fault his logic, but it brought back fresh wounds. Would I ever get over the fact that our father was leaving everything to my little brother? But I couldn't blame him for wanting to make sure the ranch stayed in the family. He hadn't known if I would ever come back.

When we got to the ranch house a couple of hours later, Jake was sitting on the veranda smoking a cigarette and drinking a can of beer. I wondered if he always drank this early in the day. If he did, he could add a rotting liver to his already damaged lungs.

I handed Trevor his backpack, and he ran up the stairs and into the house without saying anything more than a brief hello to his uncle. I knew how anxious he was to make sure his parents were okay. I felt the same way about seeing our father.

"I haven't seen any clouds," I told Jake as I stopped at the top of the stairs before stepping onto the veranda with him.

"It looks like it might have been a false alarm, but our luck won't hold out forever. Something is going to happen. It always does."

He blew a puff of smoke in my direction.

I wriggled my nose and turned away.

"Look, I know you don't approve of smoking, but you cannot condemn other people just because they don't feel the same way."

"I'm not condemning anyone," I told him as I continued on my way. "It's your life. You can do with it anything you like."

Over the next few days, we settled into a new routine. Since I had learned as much as I could about the ranch's finances and had transferred all the records into an Excel spreadsheet file on the computer, it meant there wasn't much left to do, except visit when my father and I were alone. It was hard at first because we had not shared that much as father and daughter when I was little, but after a few uncomfortable hours, he took a photo album off the shelf in his den, and we began looking at pictures together.

Maybe it was just the situation we were in, but the photos helped us talk about our feelings—all the hurt, the missed opportunities, the misunderstandings, but mostly about the love we shared for each other. Sometimes, I just curled up next to him and listened while he talked about our ancestors and why the ranch was so important to him. And always at night, I knelt by the side of my bed and thanked God for bringing me home and allowing me to get to know my father before he was gone.

It was during those days of solace that I started to understand how important the family you were born into really was. I had not been born to my parents by chance. We had known each other before we came to earth, and I believed that we had made promises to each other. They would give me life, and I would make sure their temple work was done so we could be a forever family someday.

We did not discuss religion. It didn't seem important because I knew he would accept the truth, just as my mother had done once he was on the other side of the veil. But what I didn't fully understand was my responsibility to the new family I had been given. By all rights, I should be less than eager to accept them, but if I couldn't forgive and forget what had happened, I would be the one on the outside when the final judgment came.

During one of our afternoon visits, when he was feeling a little stronger, he asked me about my life in L.A. I didn't want to burden him with things that would only be upsetting, like my being sexually assaulted—rape was much too hard to say—living in a women's shelter, or planning to get married in one of God's holy temples. So I told him about some of the more neutral experiences I'd had. I told him that while I was waiting for a green card that would allow me to go to school there, I had worked as a waitress at *The Outback*, a rather expensive place to eat that claimed to know how Aussies cooked. Their screaming onions weren't bad, but it sure wasn't the home cooking I was used to. Keida had been a true master in the kitchen.

The owner of the establishment liked the idea that I had been born and raised in Australia and that my accent was thick, regardless of how much I tried to make it less noticeable. He said it brought more authenticity to his restaurant, and he seemed to be right because we were booked solid every night I worked. I soon found that I was gathering my own group of regulars, and I was getting pretty good tips, too. My boss appreciated having me around and made sure I had a full meal each night. There was usually enough left over for a light lunch the next day.

I told him how I had lived for a short in a small, two-bedroom apartment with two of the waitresses from work who were hoping to make it big in Hollywood. I had no ambitions for a career in the movie or television industry, so I was no threat and our rooming arrangement worked. They shared the larger of the two bedrooms, and I took the smaller one in the back whose only window overlooked the alley. Sometimes in the middle of the night, I heard people rummaging through the garbage cans. It made me sad knowing there were homeless people in my neighborhood, and it didn't matter that most of them were prostitutes and junkies. They were human beings, and I tried to help out by giving them money for coffee or a hamburger whenever I could.

He loved hearing about my experiences as a university student and told me more than once how he wished he had been there to see me graduate. Technically, I hadn't even graduated from boarding school, the equivalent of high school in the United States, since I had run away from home before taking final exams. But due to a few glitches in the system and the fact that I had secured a scholarship as a foreign student, no one really hassled me about it.

I told him about meeting Becky and Ben without going into any details about the principles of the gospel or my conversion and baptism. He seemed satisfied knowing that Ben loved me and his family accepted me. His only regret was knowing he would likely never meet his future son-in-law, but he did write Ben a letter and made me promise to give it to him before we were married. When I asked him what it said, he only told me that he had a few words of fatherly advice for the man who had promised to love and take care of his only daughter for the rest of her life. I tucked the letter away in the bottom of one of my dresser drawers. I knew Ben would read it to me when the time came.

I didn't go into how difficult life had been for me personally. When I left home, I took my IPOD, laptop computer and enough clothes to fill two suitcases. I had two thousand dollars in the bank, and used that for a plane ticket, food and other necessities the first few weeks I was in Los Angeles. After that, I lived in a women's shelter and took what work I could get until I became familiar enough with the area and my own ability to survive to start really moving forward, but none of that seemed relevant now that I was home, and he was so close to death.

On a less cumbersome note, I emailed Ben every night, and he answered by the time I was ready to write again. We never said anything earth-shattering because we had both settled into our own routines. He went to work and then spent his evenings with his family or friends. On Saturday, he went surfing, and on Sunday, he attended his church meetings and ministered to his assigned families and anyone else who might need it. He had been called as the first counselor in the Young Men's presidency, so he spent Wednesday evenings doing scouting things like earning merit badges, camping and community service projects.

My life was very static when compared to his. I rarely left the house, and even my conversations with my father were becoming strained. There was only so much to talk about during the times he felt well enough to do so, and watching him wither away was awful.

I was more than a little relieved when LeAnn decided that she was the one who needed to be home now that I understood the financial aspects of the ranch. My father agreed. It was fine to know things in theory, but my education would not be complete until I became as comfortable checking on the sheep and cattle and anticipating disasters as I was balancing the books.

Father still joined us at the table for most meals, but I noticed that each day his appetite decreased, and I could almost watch the pounds slip from his slim frame. I knew the cancer was eating him from the inside out, and no matter how often I prayed for strength, I always felt a little less able to deal with life when each new day began.

It wouldn't be long until his heart just quit beating. What was I going to do then? Could I really stay here with people I barely knew and do what my father had asked? Ben was waiting for me at home. He was my rock, my hope and my future. With him, I felt safe. Here, I still felt like I would never truly belong.

I missed church for the third time on Sunday. I had thought about driving into Edna the night before, but in light of the short amount of time we had left as a family, I felt God would understand. I would make up for my absence as soon as I could.

Jake was sitting across the table from me at breakfast, and his deep voice and the sound of my name being spoken brought me out of my sorry reveries in a hurry.

"I really do think it's time for Brylee to venture a little farther away from the house. These rides she and Trevor take are fine as far as they go, but we will be gathering the sheep for shearing at the end of the week, and I really need an extra hand driving them to Ned's."

"I can do that," Trevor said. "I ride real good, and I am old enough to help out."

"You do indeed, son," our father replied. "But Jake needs someone who sits just a little higher in the saddle than you do right now. Give yourself a few years, and there won't be anything you cannot do."

Trevor's look of joy dissipated. He had been raised riding horses and taking care of animals, but more than anything else, he loved our father and never wanted to disappoint him. I knew how he felt. I just wished I knew even a fraction of what he did, but I had been coddled and kept in the house. What I knew about ranching would barely fill a seamstress's thimble.

"I'll go," LeAnn said. "It shouldn't take more than a day or two."

"Thanks, love," our father told her. "But Jake is right. Brylee needs practical experience in running a ranch. It won't seem real to her otherwise."

I wish people would quit talking about me as if I weren't there. Besides, how hard could it be to drive a few head of sheep to Uncle Ned's? I might have been away from the outback for over five years, but I could stay on a horse. I had been riding almost every night since I came home.

"I can do it," I said. "When did you want to leave? I can be changed and have a horse saddled in half an hour."

Jake laughed, and I threw him an agitated look. Why did he always have to be so unpleasant, even when I was trying to be uncomplaining and accommodating?

"What's so funny?" I asked.

"In case you haven't noticed, it is a new century, Miss Hawkins. We won't be using horses."

I knit my brow in confusion. He made everything about the life we were living complicated, even when it didn't have to be.

"Don't get defensive, love," father said. "What Jake is trying to say is that horses aren't used much anymore except for pleasure and checking on the herds closest to the house. We use the plane as much as possible, but when we round up the herds, we use motorbikes."

"You have got to be kidding," I lamented.

At least LeAnn had the courtesy not to laugh. Even Trevor was snickering.

My father was the first to recover, but that was only because he was so weak. "We're not talking about big Harleys. These are simple off-road dirt bikes. They can go almost any place a horse can, and they are ten times faster getting the job done."

"Maybe we shouldn't push her, love," LeAnn told him as she rested her hand on his forearm.

"Nonsense," father assured her. "They are just like riding a regular bike, only she won't have to pedal. All she needs is a little practice. Jake can have her riding like a pro in a couple of days, and Trevor can follow along with one of the four-wheelers while she learns."

"Look," Jake said, never taking his eyes from my face. "If Brylee doesn't think she will be able to remain on a bike, I will fly into Edna and see who is hanging around the pubs. There are plenty of drifters who would welcome a few days' work."

One part of me wanted to tell him to go ahead and get anyone he could to help him. The other part of me didn't want to disappoint my father, so I continued with my lame attempt at bravado.

"When do I start learning?" I asked Jake, returning his amused look with a determined one of my own. "I suppose I had better find some jeans to wear. I brought hiking boots with me. I hope they will be okay."

Jake took a final sip of coffee and slid his chair away from the table. He didn't look happy now that I had accepted his challenge, but I didn't care. I was doing this for my father.

I left the kitchen as soon as possible, but just as I put one foot on the bottom stair leading to the second floor and on up to the attic so I could find the clothing I had left behind five years earlier, LeAnn called my name.

"Listen, Brylee," she said, coming into the hall behind me. "You really don't have to do this if you don't want to. Jake is just trying to bait you. He likes to see how far he can push people. It's not an endearing quality, but you can rest assured that he respects you or he would not have gone along with your father with this. He hates liabilities of any sort."

"I guess I should be flattered that he doesn't consider me a liability," I replied with a shake of my head. If this was the way he treated women he respected . . . . Well, I didn't want to think about the alternative. Being one of Jake's conquests did nothing but leave a very unsavory taste in my mouth.

"I will be fine," I told her. "I am usually a quick learner and will take it slow until I get the hang of it."

"But learning to ride on flat ground is entirely different than riding in the outback," she cautioned. "I totaled a bike right after I moved out here and broke my arm. Your father and my brother both think I am too klutzy to help with any roundup, but they have the good sense not to mention it when I am around."

"I'm sorry! How did it happen?"

"I wanted to prove to your father that I was invaluable, so I got careless. Instead of riding over a bunch of branches on the trail from an angle he suggested was best for a beginner, I thought I could jump it like he did. I rode into it head-on, but I wasn't experienced enough to handle the jolt. I let go of the bike's handle and ended up in a ravine. I am not saying the same thing could happen to you. I'm just cautioning you to listen to Jake and even Trevor. You don't have to prove yourself to anyone."

"I won't," I promised.

But she wouldn't let me go without one final word of warning.

"Don't let Jake get to you, and make him do the hard stuff. You are only there to help. He is the one responsible for making sure everything goes okay, and he doesn't like people getting in his way."

"I will take it slow and easy and keep my distance."

"You're good for Jake," she said, surprising me with her candor. "He always thinks women are just there for his pleasure. He needs to be put in his place once in a while. In some ways, I wish you were not engaged to someone else. You are the kind of woman he needs—strong, dependable and not afraid to speak your mind. But I really should not be talking like this when you have already made up your mind. I have an old long-sleeved shirt of your father's that you can wear. It's going to be hot and dusty, and I would hate for you to ruin something good."

"That would be great," I said, thankful that all the talk about Jake was over. He was the last man on earth I would become involved with, even if I hadn't met Ben.

"Wait here for a minute, and I will get it for you."

She hurried off to the master bedroom, and I stood on the stairs, my hand resting on the railing while I wondered if I really was strong enough to stand up for myself when push came to shove. There were moments when I had—like the night I had taken Trevor to Edna, but that seemed like child's play when compared to what I might be facing now. If it weren't for my father, I would never even consider learning how to ride a motorcycle, let alone go on a roundup with Jake.

"Here it is," LeAnn said, handing me a tan, long-sleeved shirt with plaid patches on the elbows. "It's not much to look at, but it is better than ruining something you would like to wear again."

I took the shirt and thanked her for her thoughtfulness. Then I went up to my room to get ready for my newest ordeal. Learning how to ride a motorcycle was not something I should be doing on the Sabbath, but I prayed that God would forgive me for not keeping his day holy. I was learning to ride for my family, and they didn't understand that Sunday was not just another day of the week.

I was back in the kitchen in less than five minutes. I had braided my hair and my sunglasses were in my hand. Father was still sitting at the table.

"Where is everyone?" I asked him.

"They've gone with Jake to get the motorbikes gassed up and ready to go."

I sat down beside him and rested my head on his shoulder. I suddenly felt like a child again—a child who needed her father's love and approval.

"What's all this about?" he asked, bringing his left arm across his body and patting my arm. "You know you don't have to do this if you would rather not."

"But I do," I told him. "I just needed to be close to you for a moment." Tears, which by now had become my constant companion, were filling my eyes again. I sniffed them back.

My father's voice was husky with his own emotions when he spoke. "This is not an easy time for any of us, but I really appreciate all you are willing to do for the common good. I have tried to be strong for LeAnn and Trevor, but I'm scared. I am scared of dying because I don't know if it is the end of everything, and I'm scared to leave my family. I want to watch both of my children grow up, get married and have babies. I want to sit on the veranda swing with LeAnn and watch our grandchildren play. I want to ride over this beautiful land again and feel the wind on my face."

Suddenly, he put his face in his hands and started to cry, great gulps of sadness that came from deep within.

It was my turn to comfort him, but I didn't know how. I could only put my arms around his neck and hug him as tightly as I dared.

"I want those things too, Father," I told him. "I want you to meet Ben, and I want you to give me away when I get married. I want you to turn to when I need help or advice or just want to share something happy or funny. I have asked God why this is happening so many times, and I haven't received an answer, but I do know one thing for certain."

"What's that?" he asked. "I could use some certainty besides my own death right now."

"I know we will live again after this earth life is over. Just as I know that we will be a family again if it's what we really want."

"I don't know how you can be sure of things like that," he said as he struggled to regain his composure. It was the first time I had ever seen him cry. He hadn't shed a tear at my mother's funeral. "I have never thought much about the religious aspects of life until now. I always thought I would live to old age like my father and then it wouldn't really matter, but this cancer thing isn't going away. It almost makes me wish I had paid more attention to what the Catholic priests over the years have been trying to tell me."

"It's not too late."

"It is for me! I could have Father Frederick come out to hear my last confession, but that doesn't seem quite right. The worth of a man's soul, and his place in the afterlife—if there is one—should not be measured by death-bed repentance."

"I believe that too, Father. We are a sum total of everything we have done, every thought we've had, but I know God loves you. We will all have a chance to make things right—either in this life or the next."

"I hope that's true," he said, covering my hand with his own. "I'm glad you have found a religion that has given you peace."

"It could do the same for you."

"Maybe, but I can't worry about that now. My body is getting weaker every day. I don't have much time left."

"Don't say that! You could have months, even years."

"That's not going to happen, Brylee, and you know it. It is all I can do to get dressed each morning. A person knows when the end is near. I'm upping the morphine every day, and it is getting less effective. I don't tell LeAnn because she is having a hard enough time, but the Hospice nurses don't sugarcoat anything for me when we are alone."

I knew it was useless to argue when he was right. Cancer was merciless. It was destroyed from within. "Have you talked to Trevor yet?"

"No, and I don't think I'm going to. He is so scared right now that he will hardly leave my side, except to go riding with you. What would he do if he knew I only had a few days or even weeks left? And honestly, that is all the time I have. I don't want him spending our last few days together worrying about when the end will come. I think it is kinder for everyone just to let nature take its course. When my time is up, I know that you, LeAnn and Jake will make sure Trevor understands."

"I'm not sure understanding will happen. At least not right away, but I will be here for as long as I am needed."

"I wish I didn't have to ask that of you, love. I know you must miss that young bloke you are going to marry."

"I do miss Ben, but he understands that this is where I need to be right now." I paused before continuing. "No, father, this is where I want to be right now. I just wish I had not run away."

"Listen," he said. "We have discussed that matter until there is nothing left to say. We can't change the past. If I had been honest from the beginning, things might have been different, too, but maybe they happened the way they were meant to. I only know that I am glad my beautiful daughter made it home in time for me to get to know her. Maybe that God of yours did have a hand in that."

I could have spent the entire day sitting next to him and feeling his heart beat along with mine, but that wasn't an option that would last for long. LeAnn was soon in the kitchen looking for me.

"Jake thought you might have changed your mind about learning to ride a motorbike," she said when she saw me at the table, resting my head on my father's shoulder. "And I am sorry for interrupting, but he is ready and so is Trevor. I have some bottles of ice in the freezer for you to take. You shouldn't be away from the house without water."

She opened the freezing compartment of the fridge and handed me three large soda bottles that were frost-covered and brittle. "These should last until you come in for lunch. They will melt into water in thirty minutes as hot as it is. And you don't have to worry about your father, I will make sure he's okay."

"I know that," I replied as I rose to my feet and kissed his sallow cheek. It would be so easy to fall apart after the poignant exchange we had just had, but I couldn't do that to my father. He wanted LeAnn to believe that he was handling things. I just needed to feel grateful that he now trusted me enough to share part of what was in his heart. "I will see both of you in a couple of hours."

"Just don't take any chances," father said. "And never forget how much I love you."

There had only been a handful of times in my entire life when my father had said that to me, making his declaration even sweeter. "I love you too," I said before walking outside into the sun.

I wished I'd had the foresight to look for a hat. It was going to be another scorcher, and every part of my body that wasn't covered with clothing would get burned. Trevor was already sitting on the smallest of the four-wheelers, waiting for me.

"This is going to be so much fun," he said when I handed him a bottle of ice that was already starting to melt. "Uncle Jake said we could ride out to the south range once you get used to the motorbike. I just wish I was bigger so I could ride one with you. I want to so badly."

"I would trade we are riding in a heartbeat," I whispered. "I know you would do better on it than I ever will."

He laughed as I looked at the medium-sized motorbikes that had been parked side by side just outside the shed door. They didn't look large enough to support me, and I almost wished they were Harley's. Ben would be more than astonished when I told him what I had done. He hated motorcycles and swore he would never ride or own one. Deaths from carelessly riding them were reported on the news every week. I certainly hoped I would not become another statistic.

Jake came out of the shed holding two helmets.

"Here, sport, put this on," he said as he tossed the smaller one in Trevor's direction. I wasn't surprised that my little brother caught it. He was used to doing things that were very foreign to me.

"This one is for you."

He shoved a black helmet with a chin guard into my hands.

"Where's yours?" I asked.

"I'm not wearing one."

"But I thought that was a safety precaution everyone should take."

I looked over at my little brother, who was fastening the helmet's strap underneath his chin without protest.

Jake snorted his disapproval. "Laws were only made to be broken. I figured you would call for a celebration if I fell off and broke my bloody neck. Then you wouldn't be subjected to any more of these forced outings."

"What you do with your life makes no difference to me," I told him, glad that the motor on the four-wheeler was now running so Trevor couldn't hear. I would never be intentionally rude to Jake in front of him. "I'm just grateful you are willing to sacrifice some of your valuable time to teach me how to ride. I'm sure there are other things you would rather be doing."

"Jack's the boss. I do what he tells me. By the way, nice shirt."

I looked down at my father's tan, patched shirt. It was several inches too big across the shoulders, and I'd had to roll the sleeves up, but for some reason, it gave me courage. And like Jake, I was only doing this because my father had asked me to.

"Thanks," I told him. "I think it brings out the colour of my eyes."

He smiled. I knew he didn't want to, but the corners of his mouth had definitely turned upwards.

"You are definitely your father's daughter. Stubborn as hell and even witty when you want to be."

His almost compliment struck a tender cord in my heart. I loved my father dearly, in spite of having run away from him.

The motorbike Jake expected me to ride was no taller than my bicycle back in Los Angeles, but it had a motor, and that was what scared me. I would much rather be sitting on something with four wheels like my little brother if it was going to move on its own.

"Alright," Jake said. "It's time for you to get on and give it a try."

My heart was in my throat, and my palms were moist, but I walked over to the nearest motorbike, put one leg over the seat and sat down. This wasn't going to be a pretty sight. I was uncoordinated, and I was scared—a real recipe for disaster. Besides, I wasn't even sure how to turn the darned thing on.

"Don't sit there like a statue," Jake said, as he stood a few feet away with his hands on his hips, shaking his head at me. "You've got to get to know your ride; become one with it, or you'll end up in a heap by the side of the road."

"At least that wouldn't disappoint you," I retorted.

I shouldn't have pushed him so far, but he had been the one to start it, and it was easier returning tit for tat than letting him browbeat me all the time.

"Look," he said, pulling me off the bike with one hand and nearly knocking it over. "This isn't going to work if you won't take it seriously. When you are riding on the ranch, anything can happen. You don't know the terrain, and there won't be anyone around to hold your hand. If you get hurt out there, you might not be found for days. I don't want some scaredy-cat girl making things harder for me. Go back to the house! You're useless."

He stomped off towards the bunkhouse, leaving me standing there with a black helmet on my head that made me look like some biker dude's chick, and feeling like I had just been kicked in the stomach. If I'd had any doubt about what Jake thought of me before, it was erased now. He hated me. He had made that abundantly clear.

"It's okay," a soft voice said, and I felt Trevor's hand slip into mine. "Uncle Jake sounds mean sometimes, but it is only because he doesn't want you to get hurt. Mum did that when she was learning to ride."

Tears were stinging my eyes, and my lips were quivering, but I wouldn't let Trevor see just how upset I really was. He wanted to believe that his uncle cared, but that wasn't the way it worked with us. His contempt for me was no longer even slightly laughable.

"I'm afraid you might be wrong there, little brother," I told him. "Your Uncle Jake doesn't like me and only thinks I ill get in his way."

"But you won't! I'll teach you how to ride."

"That's very sweet of you, Trevor, but how can you do that when you are not big enough to ride a motorbike by yourself?"

"Because I have been on one with father lots of times. I know what the gears are for and how you have to lean into a turn just enough so you won't tip over."

"I don't know. Maybe your Uncle Jake is right. Maybe he should find someone in town to help him round up the sheep, but you are very sweet for offering to help."

"Come on," he coaxed. "I can do it! It really is simple. I'll show you." He ran over to his four-wheeler and climbed on.

I found myself smiling. How wonderful it would be to have the confidence of a child again.

"What are you waiting for?" he impatiently asked while I was trying to make up my mind. "Just get on behind me, and I'll do the rest."

Wondering what was wrong with my head, I took a deep breath, walked over to where he was and sat down on the leather seat behind him. No one would get hurt unless he went too fast. Centrifugal force alone would see to that.

"You can put your arms around me so you won't be scared," he said.

With a smile, I did as he instructed. I must be suffering from some kind of malady to put my life in the hands of the seven-year-old little brother I had known for less than a month, but it was better than returning to the house in defeat. At least this way, we could say we'd had some fun.

But I needn't have worried about my safety or his. Trevor knew exactly what he was doing. His hands were small, but he worked the gears on the four-wheeler like it was something he did every day. In a few seconds, we were flying down the dirt driveway. I watched the dry vegetation pass by and suddenly felt very much alive. It was getting hot, but the breeze stirred up by our movement was pleasant and slightly cool. When we got to the main road, Trevor slowed down and leaned to the right. I followed his lead and soon we were heading back towards the ranch house.

"You're good, little brother," I told him when we came to a stop in a small cloud of dust. "You ride like a pro."

"You can too," he said, climbing off the four-wheeler with a look of immense satisfaction. "Now, it's your turn."

I took a deep breath and slid forward on the black, shiny seat.

"Just remember that the left hand is the brake, and the right hand is the gas."

"Okay," I said, knowing that I could not disappoint Trevor. He believed in me, even if I didn't believe in myself. In the next moment, he was on the four-wheeler with his arms wrapped around my waist and his head resting against my back. It was a warm, comfortable feeling—one I had never felt before. And then we were on our way back down the driveway, but this time I was the one determining just how fast we would go.

"It's almost fun!" I thought as the dust erupted behind us, and I saw the trees pass by in fairly rapid succession. It wasn't the least bit like riding a bike. There was power beneath me, and I wouldn't tip over if I hit a rock or a twig. It was almost more freeing than riding Rupert. When we got to the end of the driveway, I slowed down and tried to lean into the turn like Trevor had shown me. My turn was rather slow and jerky, but on our way back to the house, I wanted to shout for joy. Trevor's kindness and encouragement had shown me that it was okay to believe in myself even when others didn't.

"I knew you could do it," Trevor said when we got back.

"Only because you are an excellent teacher, but I am afraid riding a motorbike isn't going to be as easy when I only have two wheels underneath me instead of four."

"But you said you ride a normal bike."

"I do! All the time."

"Have you ever crashed on it?"

"Plenty of times," I said. "Who hasn't?"

"And even if you got hurt, you got back up again, didn't you?"

"Yes, but I don't think this is quite the same thing."

"Sure it is," he insisted. "If you feel like you are going to tip over, all you have to do is put your feet on the ground."

I was amazed at his intuitiveness and his level of confidence, and his ability for one so young. But he didn't have nearly as far to fall as I did, and he wasn't scared. That was because our father had been interested enough to spend a great deal of time with him, teaching him everything he needed to know to be a rancher.

"You make a good case, little brother, and I guess my health insurance from the university is still good, for a couple more months anyway."

I had made arrangements to pay the premium until Ben and I were married. That would be happening soon if I hadn't come home and if I hadn't found out that my father was dying.

I swung my right leg over the seat of the motorcycle and then planted my feet on the ground. It felt awkward, but I sat there while Trevor showed me how to start the motor and where all the gears were. It wasn't much different than driving a car when it came to mechanics, but it certainly wasn't as safe without even a seatbelt for protection.

"I'll go along with you on the four-wheeler," Trevor volunteered. "Just to keep you company."

I wasn't sure that having him ride along with me would help if I crashed, except that he could go for help. I would be mortified, of course, but how could I just ride away when he had already taught me so much?

"Okay, then," I said. "Let's give this a try."

I started my motor and so did Trevor. After a couple of false starts that left me eating his dust, I managed to get the bike into first gear and began my slow ride. Fortunately, it didn't take long to discover that going too slow was just as dangerous as going too fast. When I hit a small wash in the road, I nearly tipped over, but my feet automatically went to the ground just as Trevor had said they would, and it saved me from a nasty fall.

After that small incident, I knew I would be okay, so I took another deep breath, gave the bike more gas, and soon I was the one leaving a trail of dust. When I got to the end of the dirt driveway, which was nearly five miles long, Trevor was waiting for me. This was certainly his element, and I knew in my heart that this land belonged to him, not me, whether I learned to ride a motorbike or not.

I pulled up beside him and let the engine idle.

He was literally beaming. "See, isn't this fun? I knew you could do it."

"Not without your help," I told him.

And when I really thought about it, I knew that was true. I hated getting dirty and sweaty, and learning how to ride a motorbike on the Sabbath was the last thing I wanted to do. But as I looked down at him, even getting hurt would have been worth it just to see the smile on his face. He had been sad and afraid far too long.

"Do you want to go for a ride down the highway?" he asked, breaking into my thoughts.

I looked at him and smiled. He was so little, but he had the heart of a lion.

"I think you need a driver's license for that, little brother."

I loved calling him that. It made me feel more connected to him and more protective, too.

He frowned and looked down at his dusty shoes. "Then let's take the long way back to the house."

"What's the long way?" I asked. "I'm not ready for a bumpy trail yet."

"We will just be riding through the big field behind the barn. It's not hard. Father lets me do it all the time."

I hoped he wasn't exaggerating. I'd had enough adventure for one day and wanted nothing more than to take a long, cool bath, but I needed to become more adventurous like him.

"Then lead on, and I will follow," I told him.

He smiled and put his four-wheeler in gear. It definitely wasn't a smooth ride. There were shallow gullies left by past torrents of rain, and it was impossible to see the ground beneath all the dried grass and shrubs, but I kept my eyes focused on the terrain and managed to make it back to the barn.

When we got there, I sat on my bike while removing my helmet and trying to wipe some of the dust from my face. That was when I realized I hadn't thought about what was happening with our father the entire time we were riding. Perhaps that was why Father had suggested I go with Jake. I wasn't the help he needed, but I would be too focused on the job to worry about him.

Once the noise from the engines went silent, I heard clapping. Not the excited clapping one hears when a favorite team scores a point, but the slow, methodical clapping of someone who wanted to make a point. I looked around to see Jake leaning against a post in front of the bunkhouse with a cigarette dangling between his lips.

"Impressive," he said, walking over to join us. "I didn't think you had it in you."

"It just took the right teacher," I responded, wishing I had the courage to tell him exactly what I thought about him, but I needed my father to believe that I could handle anything, and that included a man as miserable as Jake Johnson.

"You may feel pretty smug about riding around here, but it's nothing like what you will experience in the outback where we are going."

Score another one for me! He had just committed to taking me with him.

I climbed off the bike and brushed at the dust that covered all my clothes, but my victory was short-lived.

"If you are really serious about helping out around here," he continued. "You will get back on that bike and go for a real ride with me."

"Maybe I have had enough riding for one day," I said without looking at him.

"Then you will be totally useless on a trail drive. Rounding up sheep isn't some picnic where you lie around on a blanket and daydream. It's hard work, and we don't quit until all of them are at Ned's."

"I get that," I snapped back, forgetting that my little brother could hear us bickering. There was just something about the way Jake talked to me that made me want to scream. But instead of apologizing to Trevor like I should have done, or going into the house where I really belonged, I found myself climbing back on the motorbike and replacing the helmet.

Jake crushed his cigarette out in the dirt, climbed on his own bike and took off without waiting for me. It was just another way of showing his contempt. Without considering all the ramifications, I waved goodbye to Trevor and followed him. I had no idea where he was leading me, but I didn't want more regrets. If that meant enduring Jake's presence when I would rather be bitten by a snake, so be it.

So I said a silent prayer as I set out on another adventure I wasn't prepared for. Since our motorcycles were dirt bikes, they didn't have the speed of the Harleys I had seen in Los Angeles, whose leather-clad riders kept up with the traffic that was usually moving at 90 miles per hour, despite the posted speed limit. Our bikes also had wider wheels and the seats were closer to the ground. And if I got into trouble, I knew exactly what to do. Besides, while Jake might be mean and nasty, I had no doubt that he knew what he was doing, and I could learn from him if I really wanted to.

We left the safety of the flat ground where the ranch house and outbuildings had been constructed and were soon riding up a hill and further into the brush. Everything was dry and dusty, and I could feel the dirt particles clinging to the fine hairs in my nostrils, making it more difficult to breathe.

Shades of brown were the colour of the outback when there hadn't been enough rain. I wondered if that was why the aborigines liked wearing brightly coloured clothing so much. It set them apart from their surroundings, adding life to an otherwise dreary landscape. All the trees we traveled through looked identical to me, regardless of the fact that there were over 500 species of eucalyptus trees alone. It was known as the "Aussie" tree, and the ranch was covered with them. They weren't full and leafy like the Palm trees and other varieties found in California, but they were stately, and their branches always seemed to be reaching towards the sun whose rays helped give them life while scorching everything else.

But the shrubs of the outback were different than the sparsely spaced, gray-brown trees. They were dense and thick and filled with living organisms, people seldom saw, from lizards and snakes to crawling insects and flying pests that were everywhere, especially when it was dry. As I rode along, I passed Salt Brush and Whitewood and Wilga bushes. Their spiny branches seemed determined to rip apart the denim jeans I was wearing, and I knew I would have several large gashes on my arms and legs when I got home.

But even as hot and miserable as it was to ride in the heat of the Australian sun and eat the dirt Jake's bike was stirring up in front of me, I was glad to be out in nature again. Beetles, wasps, or ants might bite me, but I might also see a few Corellas—beautiful, white birds with gray-tipped wings who left their roosts at dawn to soar into the air where the light made their feathers look almost translucent.

And if I was really lucky, I might see a Bird of Paradise or an Eastern Banjo frog, if there was enough water. Or some of my other favorites like red kangaroos, Koala bears, tiny foxes or even a wild pig or two. But I didn't want to see any wild dogs. They frightened me with their snarling and teeth sharp as razors. I had seen what they could do to sheep and that was enough for me.

I lost track of the number of hills we climbed as we rode along and had no idea how far away from the ranch we had gone. It was easy to get lost in the Outback where one clump of something looked just like every other, and where no definitive landmarks could be used for direction—unless viewed in relation to something that was familiar. I just hoped part of Jake's tactic for getting rid of me didn't include losing me in some remote area where I would never be found. I had so much to live for once I made it back to Ben. I just had to survive my time here and adjust to the idea of no longer having my father around.

A short time later, I saw Jake's bike slow and then stop at the base of a huge gray-green tree that stood a short distance away from the crest of another hill. He stepped off and began looking around while I caught up with him. When I got there, he was drinking water from a canteen.

"I don't suppose you brought any water with you. If you are going to survive out here, you have to be prepared."

"Guilty as charged," I responded in my own defense. "I had the water bottle LeAnn gave me when I first came outside, but I hadn't planned on going for a ride with you."

"When you leave the ranch, there are four things you always need to carry with you: water, jerky, a solar blanket, and a gun. Those are necessities if you ever get stranded."

He offered me the canteen, and I gratefully took it. Now, if he would just hand me a tissue so I could blow some of the dust from my nostrils, I might feel a little more like a person than an object of contempt. Unfortunately, that would be asking a little too much from him.

"Thank you," I told him when I handed the canteen back.

He took it and then opened a small package of jerky. He put a piece of it between his teeth and ripped a chunk of it away before starting to chew.

"Have some," he said, thrusting the package towards me. "You must be hungry. You didn't eat anything for breakfast."

I hadn't noticed before, but my stomach was empty, so I took a small piece of the dried meat and handed the rest of it back to him. I didn't like jerky! It was too strong, too tough, and the residue it left was far from pleasant. But I still put a small piece of it in my mouth and tried to adjust my taste buds to the flavor as Jake moved to the edge of the hill and looked down.

"The sheep like to hide in the brush on that next hill," he said as I walked over to join him. "As you can see, it's pretty far from civilization, but I guess they like it that way. Sheep are some of the dumbest creatures on earth, but if you can get the lead one headed in the right direction the rest of them usually follow. But heaven help you if they get spooked. They will run helter-skelter, and it might take you days to find them again."

"So how do you keep that from happening?" I asked, taking a second look at the next ridge. It looked just like all the others we had ridden over. If he was trying to wear me down, he was doing a good job of it. All I wanted was a good meal, a refreshing bath and my bed—not necessarily in that order.

"You are quiet and you are careful," he said without looking at me. "And it always helps to know where to find them."

"Do you know where they are, other than just somewhere over the next hill?"

"I have a pretty good idea. There is a sinkhole beyond the ridge. It was almost dry when I rode out there last week. That's one of the reasons Ned and I decided to get the sheep shearers here early. We could lose half the herd in a week if this drought continues. We have been talking about shipping most of them into Edna to be sold after the shearing's done.

But I would appreciate you keeping that to yourself for now. Your father doesn't need any more worries than he already has."

"But he owns this land! He has a right to know what's going on."

"And I will tell him as much as I think he should know. But the bottom line is that we either sell them now and get a better price, or we wait until everyone else is selling theirs and basically give them away."

"Are things really that bad?" I asked. From the records I had entered into the computer, it was hard to tell exactly what financial shape the ranch would be in at the end of the current fiscal year.

"You're a smart girl. At least that is what your father keeps telling me. Do you really think animals can survive without water?"

"No, but can't you keep them closer to the ranch and feed and water them there?"

He shook his head and gave me a look that could have started a fire. "We are not talking about a few head of sheep, Brylee. Where could we keep close to 5000 head closer to the house? They can forage just fine out here because they will eat what cattle won't, as long as there's enough water. I don't want to be digging mass pits for them. Do you?"

"No," I said.

"Then you had better start thinking and acting like a rancher. Your father expects you to help the rest of us keep this enterprise going, and you can't do that unless you get over being daddy's little girl who sits in the house and expects everyone else to make all of the tough decisions."

I hated that he was right. I had studied the ranch's financial records, but while we were not destitute yet because the ranch was paid for, Father had borrowed against it several times. If we couldn't repay those loans, we could lose everything.

When thought about in those terms, loving something that was doomed to failure seemed futile. The elements were always working against the ranchers, so why did men like my father, Uncle Ned and even Jake work so hard to keep things going? It was easy for me to see why Buck Henry and all the others had sold out to investors who had the resources to make it through a few bad years.

"I love this land," Jake was saying when my mind reverted back to the present. "It might not seem like much to some men, but it means freedom. It means we don't have to answer to anyone. We make it or break it on our own."

He kicked at a tiger snake that had come out from the brush beside us. I took a step backwards, even though I knew it was harmless. I hated snakes. I also hated scorpions, spiders and lizards, but one had to take the bad along with the good in the outback. The members of my family accepted that. I wasn't so sure I ever could.

Chapter 18

I thought a lot about the good and bad aspects of fighting a seemingly endless battle against nature as I practiced riding the motorbike the next day. I could understand the obsession with freedom to do as you liked, but there was more to life than struggling. And I was so tired of being hot, dirty and sweaty. It wasn't so bad in the house, but I no longer felt like I could spend an inordinate amount of time there. My father was spending more time in bed, and LeAnn was always with him. Trevor was allowed to be with them if he was quiet, but he was mostly encouraged to spend time with Jake, me, or with his animals.

It pained me to see how fast our father was slipping away. He grew tired just walking from his bedroom to the kitchen table for meals he barely touched.

If LeAnn was as concerned about his condition as I was, she never let on. She treated him with the utmost love, respect and dignity. She took his arm and walked with him as slowly as he needed to go, and she was patient and tender when he needed to rest while they were talking. She reminded me of Mother Teresa ministering among the poor and needy in remote areas of the world. She made no demands and never asked for anything. She wasn't given to hysteria or fits of uncontrolled crying. She showed my father in everything she said and did that he was the center of her universe, and she loved him totally and without reservations.

I was grateful for her willingness to be there to take care of him so patiently. I still cried too much and too often and felt sorry for myself because I had lost five years I would never get back. But what hurt most was knowing that my father loved LeAnn more than he had ever loved my mother, and that my little brother was the light of his life.

One night after Trevor was asleep, my father, LeAnn and Jake sat at the kitchen table drinking coffee. It was late, and I was exhausted, so I rose to my feet to excuse myself.

"I know you're tired, but we would like to discuss something with you before you head up to bed," my father said. "It's kind of important, and we do not want Trevor to overhear."

"What is it?" I asked.

"Trevor's birthday is on Wednesday, and we would like to have a special celebration for him since this might be the last one. I wish yours was sooner."

"Don't worry about me," I told him. "I have had lots of great birthdays over the years."

But for the life of me, I couldn't remember any of them. A therapist I had seen a few times after arriving in the United States told me I was suffering from Post-Traumatic Stress Syndrome. I had thought that a rather odd diagnosis to explain my severe depression until she explained that the disorder didn't just happen to soldiers who had seen battle. It could happen to anyone who had lived through a traumatic event, and the way my mother died certainly qualified.

"Your father and I were thinking about getting him a puppy," LeAnn said, as I forced my thoughts back to the conversation. The habit of allowing my mind to drift when others were talking was becoming an annoying habit, even to me. "He loves animals so much, and heis going to need a special friend."

"That's a great idea," Jake said. "I will fly into Edna in the morning and check the pound. What kind of a dog were you thinking about?"

"Something that won't get too big," LeAnn replied. "I know it will end up being a house dog, and I don't want it ruining anything."

"You don't have to worry about that, love," my father told her. "There isn't anything in this house of much value, other than the people who live here."

She leaned over and kissed his cheek. "I know you are right, but I'm sure there are a few things that have sentimental value to Brylee."

"Nothing a dog could possibly hurt," I said, wondering how anyone could think about material possessions in light of the great loss we were all about to experience. "You need to get Trevor a dog that is right for him. Size shouldn't be a huge consideration."

"You might not feel that way when it chews holes in your favorite shoes or knocks over some vase you have an attachment to," Jake interjected with an infuriating smile.

He was on the verge of violating the terms of our agreement to be civil to each other when we were around LeAnn and my father, but I chose not to engage in a verbal battle over something so trivial.

"What could I get him?" I asked. "I really don't know what little boys his age like to do except for riding horses and four-wheelers, and he already has those."

"Maybe you should go into town with Jake tomorrow," LeAnn suggested. "That way, you could go to a toy store and look around. We will also need wrapping paper, balloons and anything else you can think of to make the day more festive."

I wanted to tell her that going on another outing with Jake wasn't a good idea. We had almost come to blows when we had gone into Edna before the wedding, but I couldn't do that to my father. I had seen the light of expectancy and love in his eyes when he talked about Trevor's birthday. Residual issues with my own childhood, even coupled with the animosity Jake and I were trying to keep hidden, were not reason enough to take that away.

"What time do you want to leave, Jake?" I asked without looking in his direction.

"Just like that? I thought you would put up more of a fuss since our last trip to town wasn't so pleasant."

From the corner of my eye, I saw LeAnn give him a fiery glance. It should have made me feel vindicated, but it didn't. "That's in the past. All I want to think about now is how we can make Trevor's birthday the most spectacular one ever."

"Then meet me by the plane at 8:30 in the morning. I don't want to fight any crowds."

"I'll be there," I told him before putting my arms around my father's neck and kissing his cheek. "I love you, father. Sleep well and don't worry about anything. We will make sure Trevor has the best birthday ever."

I went to the small airstrip behind the barn ten minutes early the next morning so Jake would have nothing to be irritated with me about. I had done a lot of thinking the night before and had come up with a spectacular idea that I had called Uncle Ned and discussed with him the moment I jumped out of bed. I wanted us to go on a family picnic as part of Trevor's birthday celebration. LeAnn and I could prepare the food, and Uncle Ned had agreed to make sure a horse and buggy would be available so Father could go with us. He was much too weak to ride a horse, and it would give him another chance to see more of the land he loved.

So it really didn't matter that the conversation on the short flight was minimal. In fact, it was far preferable to arguing or feeling like I had to defend myself. All that mattered was creating memories that might help as we endured the dark days ahead.

When we arrived in Edna, Jake immediately went to the ticket counter to talk to Janet. He had already told me to meet him back at the airport by noon, so I walked right out into the sun and made my way to the open-air marketplace that was several blocks away.

Oh, how I wished things could be different for Trevor. He was quiet by nature, but his blue eyes were always darting from one thing to another, and I was certain that little escaped him—except for what went on behind closed doors, and the fact that our father was dying and there would be no remission this time.

The toy store was crowded with children pulling things off the shelves while their mothers told them to behave, or they would leave empty-handed. One of the boys looked about Trevor's age, so I asked the woman who appeared to be with him what he liked to play with.

"Gosh," she said. "You don't look old enough to have an eight-year-old son."

"It's for my little brother's birthday, and I want to give him something extra special."

"Come over here, Ryan," she said as the boy, engrossed in looking at Transformers turned his head towards her.

"But I want to play. You said I could get a toy today."

"And you can, but this nice lady would like to find something for her little brother's birthday. What would you suggest?"

He looked at me curiously. "I don't know. What does he like to do?"

"He likes to ride horses and four-wheelers. Other than that, I really don't know, except that his parents are getting him a new puppy."

"That would be cool," he said. "I have a dog named Jack."

My heart began to race. This was the first time I had heard my father's name when it wasn't referring to him, and it made me want to scream out in pain. But I couldn't do that in a public place around strangers. They would think I needed to be committed, and they would be at least partially right. I had never felt more sad, alone and discouraged than I did right now.

"That's a good name," I told him. "I hope you take very good care of him."

"He tries," the woman replied as the boy went back to investigating what was on the shelves. "But I think he is more into playing ball and video games than spending time with his dog."

"Thank you for your time," I told her. I had to get away from them before I started to cry. Their life seemed so normal, and ours was anything but that.

After walking around the store in confusion for thirty minutes, I decided to get Trevor a skateboard. I had seen lots of kids his age riding them in L.A. I wouldn't be the best teacher, but at least I could stand up on one, and it would give us another opportunity to spend time together. I got elbow and knee pads to go along with it. Then I asked the clerk where I could find party supplies. He directed me to a store at the other end of the street.

Jake was waiting for me at the airport with a dog carrier and several bags of dog food. There were a few smaller packages sitting on the floor in front of the ticket desk. Janet was holding a reddish-brown, squirming puppy in her arms.

"Guess I beat you this time," he said, looking at the skateboard I was holding underneath my arm, and the other parcels I was carrying. "I'm not so sure my sister is going to let him ride on one of those. It's a little dangerous for a child, don't you think?"

"He rides horses and four-wheelers by himself," I countered. "This is far less dangerous than they are."

He didn't bother to react but turned his attention back to the girl holding the puppy.

"Guess we had better be on our way, Janet," he said.

"But you will be back soon, won't you. Bubba's has a new band. I've heard they are really good."

"Can't make any promises for the next few weeks, love," he responded. "The shearers are coming in a few days, and we have to get the sheep corralled at Ned's."

"Understood," she said, handing the puppy back to him. "But I miss you. We used to spend a lot of time together."

"And we will again, but things are rather hectic right now."

"You mean with Jack's condition?"

I felt my world reeling for a second time that morning. I knew people cared, but they had their own lives and would forget about what was happening in ours the minute we left.

"That's part of it, but I am also a working bloke, in case you have forgotten," Jake replied with one of his smiles that seemed to make every woman, but me, melt. "I don't have a nine-to-five job like people in town."

"I know you have other responsibilities, and I don't mean to complain, but a girl does like a pleasant diversion now and again. Is there anything I can do to help?"

He shook his head. "Not at the moment, but if I think of something, I will give you a call."

I suddenly felt sorry for Janet. She obviously cared about him, just as Beth at the diner did, and Jake could easily break both of their hearts. I was so glad I had Ben. He was easy to read and never played games. Why hadn't I taken time to call him while I was in town? It was too late for that now.

Jake squatted down to put the puppy in the kennel, and the little dog began to whimper and shake.

"Good-bye, Baby," Janet said, leaning as far over the counter as she could. "Be a good little girl for Trevor."

The puppy was trying to get away from Jake, and I could hardly blame her for that. Apparently, she had more sense than most of the other females in town.

"Let me hold her on the ride back. She's scared," I said.

"Women!" he retorted, but he put the puppy in my open arms anyway. "I will throw this other stuff in the back of the plane, but you had better keep track of her. There isn't time to get another one."

I knew he was just trying to make me feel like an incompetent outsider again, and wondered if the puppy sensed his hostility because she settled down in my arms and closed her eyes. I didn't know what breed she was, but she had long ears, soft hair and the saddest eyes I had ever seen. Trevor was going to fall in love with her.

The flight back to the ranch was uneventful. Jake didn't try any fancy maneuvers like he had done the day after I came back when he took me to check on the cattle. In fact, I wasn't entirely sure he was even aware of my presence. Something was definitely on his mind, but I wasn't about to comment on it. I much preferred the silence because it gave me time to think. I didn't want to miss some important detail about Trevor's birthday, like forgetting to chill the champagne at my father's and LeAnn's wedding.

Uncle Ned had promised to bring the horse and buggy to the house just before dusk the next evening while I was taking Trevor for a ride. The horse would be put in a section of the barn where my little brother never went, and the buggy would be put next to Jake's plane. He would never know they were there unless he went looking. My job, which seemed almost impossible now, was to keep him occupied for the next 36 hours so none of his surprises would be ruined.

My biggest fear was being able to keep him away from the bunkhouse where Jake lived. That was where the puppy would be kept, and he liked going there almost as much as he did taking care of his animals. It was hard for me to understand how a man who treated me so abominably could be so kind to a child, but from what my father had said, Jake had been with Trevor on and off practically since the moment he was born. When I thought about it in that light, it didn't seem so strange that he would be overprotective with both his sister and his nephew. They were his family, and he knew next to nothing about me.

LeAnn was absolutely delighted with the new puppy when she went to the bunkhouse to see it and found a huge green Christmas bow to put on the top of the kennel. I wondered how Jake would fare with the little animal since she didn't seem to like him but decided it was best not to ask any questions or make any suggestions. He could handle whatever arose on his own.

Besides, I didn't want Trevor overhearing a conversation that might ruin his birthday surprises. Everyone involved seemed to feel the same way. LeAnn was going to bake and decorate the cake while we were out riding and hide it in the pantry, and Father was going to try his hand at wrapping a few presents. I wished he could be there for my next birthday, but that wasn't even a possibility. Mine was nearly six months away.

I got up before it was light the next morning so I could take the motorbike out before anyone else was up. I was nervous about riding it on the weekend when Jake and I would be rounding up the sheep for shearing, but I was even more nervous about him watching my practice rides. I felt clumsy and childish in his presence because his dark, intimidating eyes watched everything I did. I knew I would not be able to ride like a pro, but I was hoping to make enough progress that he wouldn't have to rescue me from anything.

After dressing quickly, I said my morning prayer with an added emphasis for my safety, and headed quietly down the stairs and into the kitchen. The sun wouldn't begin its ascent until I was a fair distance away from the ranch house. I knew LeAnn would keep an eye on Trevor until I returned. Despite my father's impending death, she was trying to keep things as normal as possible for Trevor, and he still did his school lessons right after breakfast in the morning.

I grabbed a couple of water bottles from the fridge and a granola bar from the cupboard before heading out the back door. I didn't need to worry about a gun or a solar blanket. I did not intend to be gone very long or go that far away.

I understood that leaving the house in the dark by myself wasn't the smartest move, but I left a note on the kitchen table saying I would be back by nine, so no one needed to worry. I had taken my helmet into the house the night before, so I wouldn't have to turn on a light in the shed to look for it. Jake always kept gas in the bikes in case of an emergency, so all I had to do was guide it far enough away from the bunkhouse that the sound of the motor turning over wouldn't awaken him.

The warm outside air made the hair on the back of the neck stand erect after spending the night in an air-conditioned house. How I longed for the ocean breeze in Los Angeles, where the temperature was always mild, but that luxury didn't exist in the outback. Without rain, the earth would just get drier and all but the hardiest plants and animals would die. It seemed a pointless existence for everything, but death and the process of dying was as much a part of God's plan as giving birth and living was. I dried my eyes before placing the unsightly helmet on my head.

My plan was executed with precision, and by the time I made it to the end of the dirt road that joined the house to the highway, I knew that I needed time alone to clear my head even more than I needed to practice riding. Far too much had happened since coming home, and I had barely begun coming to terms with any of it.

So, I headed into the brush the way Jake had taken me the first time I had ridden with him, and followed the trail our bikes had made. I would have no trouble finding my way back to the house. This was the last time I was going to rehash the past on a conscious level, but I needed to go over everything one more time so I could release the constant pain in hopes of finding a modicum of joy at some point in the future.

My reminiscence began by wondering why I had never spent any time enjoying what the outback had to offer before this trip home. I understood that my mother thought it inappropriate for the young lady of the house to get dirty and run free, but I had still come home for holidays and summer break when I was well past the age of childhood. Why hadn't I spent any time with my father then doing the things he loved?

Children need time with both of their parents. I had learned that watching Becky and Ben interact with theirs. They shared more than just family bonding. They were best friends. If I'd had that kind of relationship with my father, perhaps I would never have left Australia. Perhaps I would have seen his pain and felt compassion enough to help him through the awful guilt and turmoil he felt at my mother's death. But I had never known what my father was feeling until recently.

Riding through the tall, dry grass and dirt bowls, I thought about how anger was the only emotion that had driven me from my home and country, but I now knew that divine intervention had played a part in that flight as well. If I had stayed in Australia, I would never have met Ben, and would have no knowledge of the Plan of Salvation or of my Heavenly Father's great love for me. Maybe it hadn't been such a bad trade-off, except that I had never gotten to know my own father and now it was too late to learn much more than I already did about him.

I stopped on the crest of a small hill and looked out over the khaki green and brown vista. There were a few long-horned cattle at the base of the hill trying to find refuge from the emerging sun underneath a lone, tall tree. It was incredibly sad! If we didn't get rain soon, the cattle would have to be rounded up and sold just like the sheep. I could see the shape of their ribs underneath their hides. I wondered how many more calves had been born and how many more mature animals had died because there wasn't enough feed and water.

Balancing myself on the motorbike, I removed my helmet and then pulled a bottle of water and the granola bar from one of the side packs. The water was warm, but still supplied the liquid necessary for my own survival. I had spotted a herd of sheep about 20 miles from the ranch on Rustler's Ridge. It looked like all the other ridges on the ranch to me, but Jake had pointed out a rock on its south surface that almost looked like the face of a stern cowboy. Why had I never bothered to ask my father anything about the ranch I had grown up on? He must have a million stories to tell. I wondered how many of them Trevor had heard.

I decided to make my way back to the house by taking what looked like a much shorter route. I was feeling a small amount of bravado, and it would be nice to tell my father that I was learning how to take care of myself without needing constant supervision. But my one moment of boldness turned out to be far less satisfying than anticipated. It was impossible to see the ground, and I jolted along at a far slower pace than anticipated. The tires fell into washes and bumped over rocks and branches that were impossible to see, even though I was staring directly at the ground in front of me. I would have turned around after the first mile or so, but I could see the top of the barn whenever I came to another ridge, so I knew I was headed in the right direction.

Nonetheless, it was nearly ten when I rode back to the shed. Jake was waiting for me, his hands resting dangerously on his hips.

"What the hell is the matter with you?" he shouted. "Do you have a death wish or are you just plain stupid?"

I shoved the bike's kickstand into the hard, dry earth. "I don't know what you are so mad about? I thought you would be happy I was out practicing. Heaven forbid I slow you down come Friday."

"You will slow me down anyway. Less than a week of experience riding a motorbike isn't going to prepare you for some of the country we will be riding through. My only hope is you won't get your bloody neck broken on my watch. It would destroy your father."

"Then why have me go with you at all? You've had plenty of time to find someone else."

"What I do is none of your business."

I stood my ground facing him, my own eyes flashing. "It is my business if it concerns me or the ranch. I made a promise to my father, and I am going to keep it."

When he didn't respond in the amount of time I thought was appropriate for a comeback, I turned my back on him and started to walk away. There were tears of anger and frustration in my eyes, but I had to keep them from falling. I would never let him know how much his words could still hurt me.

"Listen, Brylee," he said, falling into step beside me. "I guess I deserved that, but leaving the ranch by yourself isn't a good idea. Even Trevor knows better. What if something had happened?"

"Well, it didn't," I told him. My knees were shaking, but my fury would keep me from crying. "All you have done since I got here is tell me how stupid and useless I am. I may not be able to ride a motorcycle without getting killed where you will be taking me, and I may not know much about sheep or cattle, period, but I did spend four years at UCLA learning how to run a business."

He just stood there looking amused, so I continued my tirade. "If you would spend even a fraction of the time trying to work with me as you spend putting me down, we might actually accomplish something. As I see it, our differences should be our strengths. I want to help rebuild this ranch. I want it to be a place where future generations of Hawkins can enjoy its beauty and make a living too."

He leaned back against a beam on the front porch and folded his arms across his chest. "You can make all the pretty speeches you want, but we both know what is going to happen the minute your father passes, and you have spent an appropriate amount of time mourning and doing what he asked. You will be right back on that plane, and the rest of us will be left here to carry on without you."

"You don't know that," I countered.

Ben was being very understanding right now, but he wouldn't wait forever. He wanted a wife and a family, and if I wanted to be that wife and give him that family, I had to go home as soon as I could. Besides, as fast as technology was changing, I could manage the ranch's finances from Los Angeles as effectively and efficiently as I could sitting in my father's den. That should make Jake deliriously happy. Once everything was satisfactorily settled, he would never have to see me again.

Fortunately, my ride with Trevor that evening was much more enjoyable than my morning ride and confrontation with Jake. I simply could not understand why he was always so angry with me. I tried to stay out of his way and not do anything that might agitate him, but for some reason, he simply could not let his original impression of me go. That seemed childishly unfair since I had been here for over a month and had never once complained within his hearing distance. In fact, I could not recall complaining at all, and I was the one making the greatest concessions.

I could have told my father that I simply wasn't interested in staying in Australia. He would have been hurt, but he would have understood. Yet, I had surrendered my own happiness for the common good. I was risking everything by staying here and trying to keep what still seemed like an unreasonable request. My father had to know how much I loved Ben and wanted to marry him.

Nevertheless, I was old enough to make my own decisions. I was staying because I wanted to. What that said about my relationship with Ben or what would happen when we saw each other again was anyone's guess.

Still, it wasn't easy knowing that someone would be glad when I was gone. Maybe Jake would even be glad when my father was gone. That would leave Trevor, LeAnn and him to run the ranch, and they could do with it whatever they wanted. Maybe they would even sell it and pocket the money. I knew LeAnn didn't want that now, but grief could do funny things, and sometimes all people wanted was to get away so they could forget.

"Brylee," Trevor's voice brought me back to reality. He was tugging on my arm and there was a look of scared excitement in his eyes. We were sitting on a log watching the sun make its descent towards the west.

"Look at that snake. Isn't it big?"

I glanced in the direction he was. An enormous snake with cold, black eyes and a darting tongue was inching its way towards us, its head poised for action. I had seen snakes before, but nothing the size or colouring of this one. Panic gripped me when I realised it was an Eastern Brown, one of Australia's most poisonous. I should have been paying closer attention instead of letting my mind wander. There wasn't time to get away from it now, and Trevor was closer to it than I was.

The continent had over 140 species of land snakes. Around a hundred of them were venomous, but only twelve were likely to inflict a wound that could kill. The most poisonous was the Tarpan, but the Eastern Brown came in second. I had seen pictures of it holding its neck high when agitated and looking like an upright "S". It was usually fast-moving, and while it did not use humans as targets for food, it would not hesitate to strike if it felt threatened.

"Dear Father, help us," I pleaded as panic turned into terror. I watched helplessly as its forked tongue flicked in and out of its mouth. Snakes use their tongues for smell. Reason told me that it was more intent on getting to the water than investigating us since snakes in general were shy and inoffensive, but if it felt threatened . . . .

Trevor and I were sitting directly between it and the small trickle of water that had once been a stream cascading through the south side of the ranch.

"Sit really still, Trevor," I whispered.

He did as I asked, never questioning my authority. Obedience was a beautiful thing.

I watched as the snake continued to slither in our direction. I hoped it would not sense my fear because I had never been so terrified, not so much for myself as for Trevor —the little brother I had promised everyone I would protect. Each second seemed like an hour. We were both wearing heavy, leather boots, so our feet were protected, but if the snake shot its venom upwards where our skin wasn't protected, we would never get to help in time.

The snake continued its slow, swerving advance. I glanced sideways at Trevor. He was sitting still as a statue, his eyes fixed on the predator as it started to pass in front of us. The beating of my heart was like a time bomb ready to explode the moment it had to.

No wonder Satan was often described as a serpent. Its cold, black eyes and sleek skin provided a sharp contrast to the dusty underbrush. Sin was like that. It was compelling like a snake's eyes, enticing like its smooth movements, and it definitely caused an adrenaline rush. Otherwise, people would not be drawn so easily to it.

It came within an inch of Trevor's boot, but it didn't seem to notice that it wasn't a rock, possibly because it was so dust-covered. I watched in a state a suspended animation as its body with its telltale markings moved slowly away.

Once its head disappeared into the brush, I motioned for Trevor to get silently to his feet. Luckily, our horses were tied to a tree in the direction from which the snake had come, and once it made it into the water, we should be safe enough to make a quiet retreat.

"Was that a poisonous snake?" Trevor asked as we climbed on our horses and began the journey home. He appeared far less shaken than I was, but then he was used to being in the outback and had likely seen far more snakes than I had, even dangerous ones.

Still, I carefully considered how much I should say. I wasn't entirely sure the snake was an Eastern Brown because they could be almost any shade from tan to brown and even have faint, black bands, but instinct had warned me not to take any chances.

"I'm not positive, but it is always best to be cautious," I told him. "It's too late to reconsider after one has been bitten."

"I hate snakes," Trevor said.

"So do I! That's why I always like to keep my distance. It is too hard to tell a good one from a bad one."

"That's what father always says. Do you think we should tell him about it?"

"I don't think we need to worry him since neither of us was hurt, and we are not entirely sure what kind of snake it was."

"It looked like an Eastern Brown," he said, surprising me with both his candor and his knowledge. "Father and I saw one just like it when we were out riding once."

"What did you do?" I asked.

"We just sat still until it left. Father said that nothing in the outback was going to hurt us, unless we did something to provoke it."

"Sound advice," I replied, grateful that was exactly what we had done. "Did he say anything else?"

"Not really! Only that snakes have a much right to be here as we do."

We continued our ride without saying anything more. I might have dismissed the snake's presence to make Trevor feel better, but if we had ridden near a nest of baby snakes, it would be best to avoid the area for a while. Young Eastern Brown's were more aggressive and less patient than the adults.

LeAnn opened the screen door leading into the front hallway once we had given our horses a good rubdown, plenty of water and a few oats. I could smell the faint odor of cake, and hoped Trevor wouldn't notice. It wasn't that he didn't know when his birthday was, but he liked surprises.

"Uncle Ned just left," she told us. "He felt bad that he didn't get to see either of you."

For me, it was a signal that things were still going as planned, but Trevor looked disappointed. "He will be back for my birthday tomorrow, won't he?"

LeAnn put her arm fondly around his shoulders. "He and Aunt Nora wouldn't miss it for anything. We will have cake and ice cream when they get here."

"And prezzies?" Trevor's eyes were bright with anticipation. What could be more exciting for a child, except Christmas?

"Naturally, there will be prezzies, and maybe even a surprise or two. Did you and Brylee have a good ride?"

"The best, but we saw an awfully big snake and had to sit really still for the longest time. It almost touched my boot."

I was grateful he hadn't mentioned the probability of it being poisonous, but LeAnn still glanced at me, her eyes wide with interest. "What kind was it?" she asked.

I was standing next to an occasional table with a bouquet of silk flowers sitting on it. "I'm not sure! Just big and ugly, but I didn't want to take any chances."

"That's good," she said, giving me the worried look of a mother whose only child might have been in real danger. "You have to be careful out here. Things are not always what they seem."

"Oh, we were real careful, just like father taught me to be," Trevor said, shaking his head. "Is he still awake? I want to tell him about it."

"He is resting, so don't stay long," she cautioned. "Birthday boys need to get to bed early so they can enjoy all their surprises."

"I'll hurry," Trevor said as he ran through the door leading into the main hallway. "I don't want to miss anything."

LeAnn led me into the kitchen, where she poured a glass of iced tea. "Can I get you something?" she asked.

"I'm good," I told her before sitting down in the chair across the table from her. I was exhausted. It had been a very long day. "Is everything ready for tomorrow?"

"I think so," she said, taking a sip of tea. She looked as tired as I felt. Worrying about Father was beginning to affect her health. She was thinner and more hollow-cheeked than ever.

"The cake is cooling in the pantry. I will ice it before Trevor gets up in the morning."

"What kind did you make?" I asked.

"Chocolate, of course. I used a family recipe that has been handed down for generations. I love birthdays! At least I always have in the past. Tomorrow isn't going to be easy for any of us, but the prezzies are wrapped and waiting in the bunkhouse, and the horse and buggy are safely tucked away in the barn."

"You have been busy," I said. "All I did was take Trevor for a ride."

"You underestimate what your presence here has done for all of us, especially your father, Brylee. He feels so much better knowing that finances are in order. I never had a head for business."

"I'm sure you would have managed just fine without me."

"You haven't seen me try to balance the checkbook," she responded with a tired smile. "We are very grateful to you. We knew that when his cancer came back, there would be no reprieve, but you have made even that easier."

"I don't know how you can say that."

"You will understand when you are a parent. Not knowing where you were or what was happening to you affected your father greatly. Now that he knows there is someone special in your life to take care of you after he's gone, a tremendous weight has been lifted."

I fingered the red and white-checkered tablecloth. It was clean but very nearly threadbare in places. "I'm sorry I made life so hard for him and for you. He told me what happened the year after I was gone."

"I was afraid they would have to put me in a nut house," she responded. "It wasn't easy raising a child basically alone.

Your father and I weren't together as often as you might think. That year when he basically confined himself to this house and his whiskey bottle was the worst thing I have ever gone through, and that includes losing my own parents and raising my kid brother. If Jake hadn't come back when he did, I don't know what would have happened to Trevor and me. I know the two of you have your differences, but I am glad you have been able to put them aside, just a little anyway. Your father needs all of us right now."

"You don't have to worry about us as long as there aren't any sharp knives around."

It was my attempt at humor, but it failed miserably. Maybe I wasn't looking hard enough for Jake's redeeming qualities because LeAnn made it sound like he had some.

The door between the kitchen and the main hallway opened. "I'm ready for bed," Trevor announced. "I can't wait for tomorrow."

"I can," LeAnn responded. "In a few hours, my baby boy will be eight."

Trevor let out the most exasperated sigh ever. "I'm not a baby, mum."

"Maybe not in years," she told him. "But you will always be my baby. That's just the way things are. I'll walk up with you and turn out the light."

"Okay, he said. "But I need to kiss Brylee goodnight."

I opened my arms to him. He felt so warm and full of life. How different my life would have been without him.

"I will see you in the morning," I said, kissing his cheek.

He returned my kiss and gave me another hug. " I am ever so glad you are here. I never, ever want you to leave."

I wanted to reassure him, but how could I? It was like I had two separate lives, and no matter which one I chose, I would be giving up something important. It was a decision I didn't want to make.

After LeAnn had taken Trevor up to bed, I went to say goodnight to my father. I would not stay long, but knew sleep would be impossible unless I had seen his face. "How are you feeling tonight?" I asked.

He struggled to sit upright but simply could not do it. "A little more tired than usual, it would appear."

I leaned down and kissed his cheek, wondering just how many more nights I would be able to do that.

"Trevor told me about the snake you saw," he almost whispered. "You have got to be careful. The news says they are extra bad this year—not enough water for anything. That makes even the lost timid creatures more aggressive than usual."

"I will," I assured him. "I haven't forgotten how dangerous the outback can be."

"Good on ya, although I almost wish I had not insisted you go with Jake this weekend. But I want you to learn to love this land and what it represents as much as I do."

"I do love this land. It was where I was born and where I grew up."

"But not where you intend to spend your life?"

"I want to be here, Father, and I want to be with Ben. No matter which I choose a part of me will be lost."

He sighed wearily. "I wish I could make things easier for you, but I am beginning to think there isn't much about life that is easy. I can't imagine what it will be like not being here with you and LeAnn and Trevor. You are my whole bloody life!"

I sniffed back unwanted tears. "You're our life too."

"It almost makes me wish I believed in a heaven like you and LeAnn do, but I have lived my life rugged and hard. There has never been much room for God until these past few weeks. I have been watching you, Brylee. You have a quiet strength I've never seen in anyone before. If your new religion has given you that, then it can't be all bad."

A soft ray of hope filled my soul. "It really is quite wonderful! I know where I came from, why I am here, and where I will be going when I leave this life." I couldn't say death. It seemed to permeate everything around me. "Of course, where we ultimately end up takes a little more effort, but I know I will be with the ones I love again, and that definitely includes you and mother."

"Do you think she will ever forgive me for what I did to both of you? I never got to tell her I was sorry."

"She's already forgiven you and will welcome you with open arms when you get to heaven."

He gripped the hand I offered him as tightly as he was able to.

"She was a good woman, but she should have married someone who could give her the kind of life she deserved."

"She loved you, father! She told me."

"Did she now!" He sounded surprised. "I know she loved me when we were young and foolish, but life was hard out here, and after you were born, she pulled away."

"She didn't understand what drove you so hard and knew she could never be the kind of wife you needed, but she never stopped loving you."

"I took her away from the wealth she had always known, and the kind of life she had been prepared for."

"Mother told me stories about her childhood, and the governess who raised her. She said her parents never had time for her. They were always busy with charity functions, parties and making more money. I think she was very lonely. She said you were the most handsome, exciting and dangerous man she had ever met, but most important, you made her feel like she belonged."

"That's only because I scoffed at the wealthy and made fun of the rich, bloody blokes that came to court her. But I truly thought I could make her happy, and I did love her. She was the most beautiful girl I had ever seen with her soft skin and delicate features. I never realised until it was too late that the way children are raised has a great deal to do with how happy they will be as adults. Your mother would have found more fulfillment with one of the "yuppie" blokes her father picked out for her."

"But then you never would have had me!"

His smile seemed sad and took away some of the pain. We'd had this discussion before, but some things needed to be repeated.

"Your presence has been one of the greatest joys of my life. I just wish I had known how to be a father when you were growing up. I made every mistake possible."

"We all made mistakes. I certainly could have been a much better daughter, but I believe there will be plenty of time in the next life to sort things out."

"I hope you're right," he said. "I worry so much about leaving, but it's been better having my entire family together."

I wanted to tell him that I'd stay on the ranch with LeAnn and Trevor, but he'd know I was only saying it to make him feel better.

His next words startled me. "Can I give you one piece of fatherly advice?"

I knit my brows in confusion. "You can say anything you want."

"Then this is what I want you to remember after I'm gone. Love isn't always enough to make a marriage work. You need to consider how you were raised and the role you want your own family to have in your life. Once your mother and I were married, she never saw her family again. She claimed it didn't matter, but any fool could see that a part of her was always missing."

"She never blamed you."

"Perhaps not outwardly, but I know what it cost her never to be included in anything that happened in their lives.

She never saw any of her sibling married or met any of their children. She didn't even know if they had any. Holidays were spent at the ranch, and no one ever called to see how she was doing. I never gave any of that much thought until both of you were gone, and by then it was too late. Just don't make the same mistake with Ben. Make room for both sides of your family, or there will always be a part of you missing."

I wiped at the tears that were clouding my vision. I didn't want to cry again tonight.

"This land is your heritage, Brylee. I want you to consider very carefully what it would mean if you walked away again. I'm sure Jake and LeAnn and Trevor could keep the ranch running, but this is where your own family has lived for decades and where most of them are buried. It's a part of who you are, whether or not you want to accept it, and I never want you and Ben to end up where your mother and I did."

His words haunted me, and I felt more conflicted than ever as I lay in bed that night and tried to sleep. Was he trying to guilt me into staying by intimating that he didn't really trust LeAnn and Jake to run things until Trevor was old enough to do it himself? Or was he simply telling me that if I left home again, I would someday regret it even more than leaving the first time?

I did love this land! I loved my father and had grown to love Trevor and LeAnn, but I loved Ben, too. I wanted to spend the rest of my life here and all of eternity with him. I had been so certain that was what God had in mind for me until I came home. Now my new faith and my new testimony were being challenged, as was the ideal life of peace and happiness I had planned on living with Ben. But what if God expected me to put on hold, or even sacrifice, my life with him so I could be a missionary to my own family? It was something I couldn't discuss with the man I loved. He would think I was falling out of love with him.

To be continued . . . .

Enjoy this excerpt from

Lost

Indecision's Flame - Book 2

I don't remember falling asleep, but I must have because Trevor's knock on my door the next morning brought me upright bed. I knew I'd been thinking about birthdays when I'd crawled underneath my covers, but for the life of me, I couldn't remember a single one of my own, except for the last one I'd spent with Becky and Ben. There had been cake with candles and presents, lots of them.

Becky had given me a new sweater, a muted yellow, my favorite color. She said it wasn't cashmere but it sure felt like it. Ben's parents had given me several church books and his grandmother a set of dishtowels she had embroidered. In fact, all of his siblings had given me a little something to remember the day by, but his gift had been the one to move me to tears. It was my own set of scriptures with my name engraved on the soft, blue leather, and a forever message written inside the front cover. I read it every night before going to bed.

It still bothered me that I couldn't remember much about my childhood. The therapist I had seen once or twice after being a victim of sexual assault had told me it was perfectly natural for someone who had been through traumatic experiences like I had to have lapses in memory, and that when my body and mind had recovered sufficiently I would be able to recall most of what I thought I'd lost.

But I wasn't sure that was true. It had been over three years and nothing had happened yet. I was still having trouble processing most of my past and learning how to express what was really on my mind. Still, I had noticed one area of rather surprising growth the past few weeks. I was learning how to accept other people, forgive their sins and weaknesses, and I wasn't running away from anything. I was confronting my father's upcoming death, trying to be there for everyone who needed me, and I was even learning how to bite my tongue when it came to my dealings with Jake.

"Hey, Brylee," Trevor called out, interrupting my musings. "Can I come in? I have been up for ages, but didn't want to wake mum and father."

I blinked a few times allowing the world to come into focus. Exhaustion was my new state of being after days spent in turmoil and fear. In ways, falling asleep as I had last night without feeling compelled to dwell on unanswered questions had been a huge relief. I much preferred thinking happy thoughts about the life I wanted with Ben, but most of those had fled since coming home. It had been nearly two months since we had seen each other. That was longer than we had been engaged before I left.

There was no denial in my thoughts as I sat there in the growing light. I knew I was risking the life and eternity I so desperately wanted by staying here in the land of my birth just waiting for my father to die, but how could I have chosen otherwise? I kept recalling what he said the night before about the importance of including both sides of the family when a couple decides to get married.

Ben would never meet anyone from my past unless I invited him to come. My family might not be anything like his, but they had given me undeniable characteristics and traits, and I needed to get to know as much about them as I possibly could. That was the only way the disillusionment and loneliness my father had described in my mother could be averted. But as much as I wanted Ben to meet my father, LeAnn and Trevor, I never wanted him to meet Jake.

He was the most offensive man I had ever met, but I understood why my father had kept him around. Besides being part of the family, he was doing work Jack Hawkins was no longer able to do. For that reason, I was trying not to hate him, even though he was not at all like the man I was going to marry. I had been more than blessed to meet a man as handsome, kind and loving as Ben.

"Of course you can," I said, realizing that I had to stop my destructive thoughts before they ruined Trevor's birthday.

The next instant, the door flew open, and he raced across the room.

"I can't wait to open my prezzies," he said, as his feet left the bed and came down with a thud that lifted my own legs in the air.

"Slow down," I told him as I pressed the fleshy part of my hand into my forehead. I could feel the beginnings of a headache. If I didn't take something soon it could turn into a migraine, and I would have to spend the rest of the day in bed with the blinds drawn.

"You aren't sick, are you?" he asked as his feet hit the bed once again, and he sank to his knees.

"Just a little headache," I assured him with a smile. "What time is it anyway?"

He looked at the travel alarm clock on the nightstand by the bed. "It's almost seven."

No wonder he was so anxious for the day to begin. People got up before dawn in the outback. It was the only time of day that was even remotely pleasant in the summer. Once the sun came up, the temperature climbed to over 105 degrees by mid-morning. My body was still having trouble adjusting to the change in climate, and breaking a sweat before I even made it out of bed was far from pleasant.

But the coming of this new day, which should bring so much happy anticipation since it was my little brother's birthday, would just bring more uncertainty and increased worries about how much time our father really had left.

"Have you been downstairs to make sure your mother isn't up?" I asked.

"Five times!" he admitted. "Uncle Jake was drinking coffee in the kitchen when I went down last. He told me not to bother them and then took me to help with his chores. I had already taken care of my animals, so when I came back to the house and they still weren't up, I decided to check on you."

I opened my arms to him. "Come here, little brother."

He slid across the light comforter until he was in my arms.

"Happy eighth birthday." I kissed the top of his head. "We have some wonderful surprises for you today."

"What are they?" he asked, pulling himself out of my embrace so he could see my face. It took so little to please him, and I wished I didn't feel like such a grouch.

About the Author

JS Ririe is the pen name for Jan Hill. She spent her youth in the country where she learned to appreciate solitude, making her own fun, and reading romance novels from some of the masters like the Bronte sisters, Louisa May Alcott, Victoria Holt and Phyllis Whitney. She penned her first novel as a teenager but never pursued what is now her greatest passion until becoming the lead witness in a federal case brought against the school district where she taught broadcasting and journalism. Writing Brylee's story as she waited two years to testify helped her through a terrifying time. She lives in Utah and has two children and two living grandchildren who help bring meaning and joy to her life.

A Note From Jan

Thank you so much for reading this novel. I'd love to stay in touch with you. Please consider joining my MAILING LIST so I can send you periodic newsletters about upcoming book releases, special offers and more. The link to sign up for my mailing list is: http://eepurl.com/dCPYVf . I promise that I will not spam you, will not sell your email information and will treat it with care.

One last favor: Your rating/review of this book helps me to keep writing. I would really appreciate it if you could leave a review. It shouldn't take more than a minute or two. You can reach the page directly at http://amzn.to/2BXNSdv

Thank you again,
JS Ririe

www.JanHillBooks.com
For contacting the author: JSRirie@JanHillBooks.com